THE
ENCHANTED
HACIENDA

J.C. CERVANTES

THE ENCHANTED HACIENDA

PARK
ROW
BOOKS

PARK
ROW™
BOOKS™

Recycling programs
for this product may
not exist in your area.

ISBN-13: 978-0-7783-3405-7

The Enchanted Hacienda

This edition published by arrangement with Harlequin Books S.A.

Park Row Books
22 Adelaide St. West, 41st Floor
Toronto, Ontario M5H 4E3, Canada
ParkRowBooks.com
BookClubbish.com

Printed in U.S.A.

For Joe

Thank you for the unforgettable line.
And if you happen to read this, I love you.

THE
ENCHANTED
HACIENDA

1

Life doesn't always turn out the way you expect it to.

Of course, you don't begin to realize this until it's too late and you're sitting in your boss's office being canned from a dream job.

"That's it?" I say, blinking in astonishment against the afternoon light spilling in through the impressive floor-to-ceiling windows. "I'm just fired?"

"Not fired," Stan says gently as he steals a glance at his watch. "Let go."

I really hate semantics. Ironic for a book editor, I know. *Ex* book editor. And yeah, it's at a small indie publisher, but damn if I don't love it.

My eyes fall on the dreadfully limp orange lily on the windowsill behind him. Scientific name, *Lilium*, a flower with multiple meanings from *beauty* and *birth* to *magnificence* and *majesty*. But in this color, it can only mean *dislike, hatred, revenge.*

I want to laugh, wondering if Stan knows he's got a dying

bloom of revenge looking over his shoulder. Of course, I say nothing. I rarely tell people I spent my childhood summers on a lush and magical flower farm in Mexico, and I *never* mention that my family's land grows enchanted blooms with the power to cast spells. First, people would question my grip on reality. Second, it's a four-generation well-kept secret.

Stan's gaze follows mine. "Yeah, I know I need to throw it out."

"Lilies are used to break love spells or fend off spirits," I say matter-of-factly. "Sometimes they're used to keep visitors away."

Stan turns back to me; an inquisitive expression passes over his pale face. "Did you study horticulture or something?"

"Or something," I say, managing a ghost of a smile. I'm about to tell him it's bad energy to keep a dying bloom around, but why bother?

"You're such a great team member," he goes on like he's reading from a script. "But this is about seniority." Then, as if he wants to wash his hands of the blood, "A decision from the top...out of my control really."

I quickly do the mental calculations. I'm the only newbie unless you count that Kenny kid in publicity with the fancy-ass pens, who wears his pants an inch too short because he likes to show off his designer socks.

I pull my pride up off the floor, swallow, lift my chin and say, "Okay, so how does this work?" I've never been fired before unless you count that one time at KFC when I was a freshman in high school. "Do I get two weeks or..."

Stan fills in the *or* part of my question with, "I'm afraid not, Harlow. You need to clean out your desk today." In my boss's defense, he looks stricken, like he isn't in the biz of firing starry-eyed twenty-seven-year-olds from their dream editing jobs. "But you can wait until the end of the day if you like, or..." He clears his throat twice. "Most everyone is out of the office at a book-seller meeting, so now might be...easier."

I feel a cramp in my heart. Is that even possible?

"But what about my books?" I just acquired my first adult speculative novel. I imagine the beautiful heart-thundering manuscript sitting in my inbox, catching fire. A small voice rises inside of me. *See? This is what you get for wanting too much.*

"We'll be reassigning your *book*." He emphasizes the singular noun like an insult.

Reassign? That can only mean one thing: Charlotte *with* seniority and cold blood flowing through her reptile veins is going to get it, but she'll never *get it*. She'll never understand the magic sprinkled between each word, floating off each page.

A prickly heat rises up my chest, spreads across my neck. I can practically feel the red splotches popping up all over. I suddenly wish I had worn that cashmere turtleneck I just bought instead of this silk blouse.

"And I'm happy to write you a letter of recommendation. A glowing one," Stan says like he just wants me to get out of his office so he can be done with the deed and go about his day of giving away my lifeblood to a lizard.

I drag myself to my cubicle and "clean out my desk." It doesn't take long. I leave a light footprint and only have a few personal items: a photo of me and my two sisters, Lily and Camilla, from our trip to the Swiss Alps last year, a *Go Fast Don't Die* jacket from the back of my chair, and a vanilla candle my boyfriend, Chad, gave me that I hate the smell of so much I never burn it. Unfortunately, my only bag is a clutch that won't fit all the contents of my professional life, so I snag a freebie canvas book bag from the back room and stuff my belongings inside. I catch the elevator, ride thirteen floors down, speed-walk through the lobby, and then have my breakdown the second the September sun hits my face.

The tears come; the blubbering isn't too far behind. A few people stare at me with wide eyes, probably tourists. I collapse onto a bench and take deep breaths, trying to pep talk myself out of this one. *It's okay. I'll find another job. It'll be better with more opportunities.*

My shoulders slump with each affirmation.

Who am I kidding? This was the job I had waited for, had risen at sunrise to get to the office early because I was so excited to be a part of this team.

Blubbering semi under control, I find my phone and dial Chad to tell him the news, to tell him to make me that tomato soup he's so good at, the one he always accompanies with little grilled cheese strips for dunking.

"Hey, baby," he says.

As soon as I hear his voice, the terror of putting into words what happened hits me like a grenade and I freeze.

"Harlow?"

"Can you..." I don't know where to begin. I'm suddenly shaking and struggling to get words past the lump that's taken up residence in my throat.

"What's wrong?" he says, sounding alarmed. That's Chad. He smells *problems* like a police dog sniffs out cocaine. I can already see how this is going to go. He's going to begin with the surface "issue" of me getting fired and what that means for my career. Then he'll go to the next layer and realize that a girlfriend with no job means reduced social status for him. He'll never get to the deepest layer though. The shame and utter sadness I feel. So why was he my first call? Because I'm a lifetime subscriber to the *Get It Over With* channel. I just have to get the words out and then everything will feel better.

"Nothing... I just..." I take a long deep breath, and what comes out next sounds as broken as I feel. "Cannedcutbacksnoseniority."

"Hang on," Chad says, and I can hear him talking to someone in the background but it's muffled like he has his hand over the phone. He's probably clearing his paralegal or some other attorney out of his office so he can comfort me in privacy.

I hear someone phony laughing, and then, "Okay, I'm back. Are you sure they fired you?"

"Chad," I say, wholly insulted as I begin walking to the subway. "I am absolutely sure."

"I told you...publishing isn't predictable."

"Seriously?" Anger rises hot as I try to jerk my sunglasses free from my blouse's neckline but they get tangled in a gold chain, and before I know it, I've pulled too hard and they fall to the ground. A lens pops out. "Shit!"

"Don't be mad, I just mean that... I want you to be happy. Secure."

Meaning an active member of society, worthy of a boyfriend who's partner at Coryell, Stray, and Ball.

I retrieve my busted Guccis, and weave between a throng of schoolgirls in private school blazers and plaid skirts.

"Can you make me your tomato soup tonight?" I ask, hating how pathetic I sound, and probably look.

"Babe," he says, like I've just asked him to slay his firstborn child. "Tonight is my big promotion dinner celebration. With the partners. Remember?"

All I hear are curt sentences, each carrying the weight of a single message: *How could you forget?*

I press my fingers to the bridge of my nose and squeeze. "Right... I...don't think I can go." I swallow hard, cursing the sun for being so damn bright. Doesn't it know my life is putrefying on the sidewalk right now?

I am so not in the mood to hang out with the tightly wound, Rolex-sporting, inflated egos that Chad calls partners. I'd rather get salmonella.

"Harlow!" Chad practically hisses. "I need you there. We talked about this."

I'm being selfish. I know I am. This is a big deal for him, and

I can't let my getting fired ruin that. And it doesn't matter that I'm a heap of humiliation, and that I have to say goodbye to a book I fell in love with that Charlotte will edit to unreadable oblivion, and I'll have to see it on bookshelves with her name in the acknowledgments and...

I stop the one-way train of pity party consciousness barreling through my head and do a mental reset. "My eyes are insanely puffy," I say, reaching for witty, but coming up woefully short.

To Chad's credit, he tries to match my tone. "You have a bathroom filled with eye creams."

I manage a minuscule smile, so small a stranger might mistake it for a grimace.

Chad lowers his voice. "Come on, Harlow. It's just for a few hours. A short reception then dinner. You don't even have to stay for dessert."

Except dessert is my favorite food group.

I nod. "Okay. You're right. Sorry..."

"Meet me at five thirty? I'll text the address."

"It's not black-tie, is it?" I would for sure remember that detail, given dress codes should be illegal in all fifty states.

"No, but elegant." Code for the *understated* version of me. As in no leather, no smoky eyes, and NO heels that make me taller than Chad.

Check. Check. Check.

After we hang up, I wonder what I just apologized for. I wonder why Chad never said *he* was sorry that I just lost a job I loved.

By the time I get off the subway in the East Village, I've adopted a new resolve. A plan to pull myself together, at least for tonight. First step? I stop at a flower stand a few blocks from our apartment building. There isn't much of a selection. To the average Joe, the stand is a plethora of vibrant colors, rows and rows of roses, carnations, hydrangeas, daisies, lilies, a few sad little peonies. But none of those send the exact right message that I'm looking for.

I pick out a trio of lovely sunflowers, bring a bloom to my nose and breathe in its clean earthy scent. I feel a sharp tug in my chest, a sort of homesickness I always feel when life throws me a curveball. After I pay for the bouquet, I head home, realizing that Chad doesn't know the symbolism of the Helianthus, the sunflower: *devotion, opportunity, ambition, happiness,* and *good luck* but I'm sure he'll appreciate the gesture.

If my mom or Tía had grown these in the enchanted soil of our family's land, it might have taken months and would've required very specific conditions using very specific threads of magic. The real family power, though, is in how they combine blooms, or how they concoct elixirs, using petals, leaves, and stems to create prosperity, love, health, hope, protection, or even to cause separation, doubt, fear, and misery. It's all so complicated and beautiful and alchemical, and the magic happened to skip me entirely. Unlike my two sisters and pair of primas and every other ancestress before me. And also, unlike my sisters and cousins, I wasn't named for a flower.

My mom told us the story countless times when we were growing up: the Aztec goddess Mayahuel whispered the given names of each child in the family. So while my sisters are all named after beautiful blooms, I was given the very regrettable name that translates to *heap of stones.*

As I enter the small but bright postwar subdivided townhome with inlaid oak floors and oversize windows, my phone rings. It's my younger sister Lily. She knows something is wrong. It's both a curse and a blessing that the women in my family are so tightly woven together, connected by some unexplainable thread of energy that makes it really hard to have a private life. And right now, I don't want to talk, to explain, or relive. Not when I have to de-puff my eyes and paint on a smile big enough to carry me through tonight's painful, self-congratulatory *my dick is bigger than yours* conversations. A minute later, she sends a text.

What's wrong?

I consider ignoring it, but then realize if I do, she'll call my only real friend in the city, Laini, who bartends at a chic hotel downtown and is therefore free at this time of day to go on a wild escapade to locate me and confirm that I am alive and well, that indeed nada is wrong. So I reply, I busted my sunglasses.

And

And what?

I'm a dr. I can help.

Lil isn't a shrink. She's actually in her last year of OB-GYN residency in San Diego, but she's an absolute fixer. If anyone has a problem, she thinks she can make it better. Need a vacation? She'll book the whole thing for you. Mention you're out of soap, she'll ship decadent designer bars next day air. Tell her you've had a shit day? She'll send a bartender friend over with two bottles of Macallan Rare Cask.

They teach you to fix shades in med school?

That's like first year. Right before suturing hands—you know, same thing. Basically small instruments, precision items.

I can feel her smiling on the other side of that text, which only makes me smile too. Lmao ok. Mtg soon text you later.

I hate lying to her, but I can't bring myself to initiate the Estrada Drama that I know is going to explode in my face once I tell her that I was "let go." She'll send me a plane ticket to come to San Diego so she can "fix" my life, which will likely include self-help books, time with her friends who have it "so much worse" than I do, and the ninety-minute *life is too short* harangue on why I should be *writing* books not editing them. Except how can I write anything if I have absolutely no idea where to start? If I can't even find my own voice?

Her next message calls me out. You always text me during meetings. What's wrong?

Nothing! Tired.

Is it Bad Chad?

I laugh in spite of myself. My sisters have never really warmed to Chad even though he's a smart, well-employed, charming guy. So what that he likes to work...a lot, or that he doesn't dance or watch comedies or like to travel outside of the country and has never been to our family farm in Mexico?

We've only been together nine-ish months, so it's not like I'm ready to take him home anyway. Plus Hacienda Estrada is a surefire way to get someone to break up with you because once an outsider meets the family, gets our vibe, witnesses our bond, tastes our crazy, they run for the hills. And you better believe that my entire family (sans me) has employed the tactic successfully for the unrequited partner that can't let go. Of course, it can have the opposite effect on the Keepers. Take Camilla for example. When she brought home the gallant Amir, she left with a rock on her finger, tied for life to the greatest guy in the universe who would burn down the world, himself included, for my sister. Deep down, I know the farm would never make Chad a Keeper.

I answer Lil's question with one of my own.

Shouldn't you be delivering babies or staring at a vagina?

She sends me a red heart. I send her my signature skull. With a sigh, I tug off my heeled sandals. And as I make my way to the kitchen, I step out of my leather pencil skirt, slip off my silk blouse, lacy bra, and overpriced underwear so I can wrap myself in the feeling of glorious uninhibition. It's the only time I can fully untangle all the threads that bind my speed-racer mind. My nude habit used to drive Chad out of his mind with lust. We always ended up twisted in the sheets, his needs met, me unsatisfied. Those were the good old days, which lasted approximately two months three days and sixteen hours. And then we became that couple who are scrolling on their phones over dinners in nice restaurants.

I place the sunflowers in a tall green vase, fill it with water, trying to remember their other symbolic meaning I can't quite put my finger on as I set them on the entry table beneath a gilded mirror.

Black streaks of mascara are etched into my reddened cheeks; my ombre-dark hair spills out of the low knotted bun I so precisely created this morning. And my eyes are so tragically swollen, I look like I've gone a couple of rounds with a heavyweight boxer. It's definitely going to take a few cosmetic miracles to pull myself into the decent *understated* shape.

"You're not going to feel sorry for yourself," I tell my reflection, forcing a stiff upper lip. "You're going to pull your shit together, pull out the ice globes, pour a glass of merlot, put on a dress, and have the goddamn time of your life."

As much as my voice is filled with conviction, my reflection isn't buying it. Neither is my heart.

With a groan, I drop my gaze to the invitation on the table. It's a crisp white linen card with a pink sweet pea tucked inside. It arrived yesterday from my mom, a formal request for my presence at the family's annual Ceremony of Flowers happening two days from now. I was surprised when I received it because it's four months early, which is bizarre since everything about the Estrada family magic is about precise timing. We have always planted the seeds and whispered the moonlit blessings at the same time every single year, not a moment sooner or later. And as much as I've pestered, neither my mom nor Tía will tell anyone what's up. I thought the sweet pea was a clue; the flower symbolizes adventure and travel, but maybe it's Mom's way of telling us all to have a safe journey to the farm?

For half a second, I consider getting a head start on packing, but I'm too tired, and in desperate need of that glass of merlot and a rose-oil infused bath if I have any chance of transforming tragic me into a quasi-happy me for Chad.

Tomorrow I'll start packing and trying to get on with the rest of my life. But tonight? Tonight is Chad's night. He's worked hard for this promotion. And I'm not going to let him down.

A stream of dusty sunlight dances on the yellow petals of the sunflower. And that's when I remember the other meaning of the Helianthus: *false appearances* and *unhappy love*.

Well. Shit.

2

I plunge myself beneath the rose-oil infused bathwater. Warm, lovely, calm…and best of all silent.

If only lungs weren't a thing and I could stay submerged.

From beneath the water, I think I hear a knock on the front door. *Oh God, please be UPS with my suede boots.* For half a second, I worry that Lil hopped a supersonic jet to come "fix" me. I run a quick pro/con list of what I need more right now.

Definitely the boots.

But less than twenty seconds later Laini walks into my bathroom, and I scream like she's the second coming of Jason.

"You didn't answer the door," she says casually from the threshold. "And you know how I feel about being ignored."

"You scared the shit out of me. How did you…"

"Followed Mr. UPS and used the extra key you loaned me," she says with a sly grin.

"I could have freaked, hit my head, died on contact," I growl.

"And you'd be banned from my funeral because my family would never forgive you for murdering me."

Laini sighs, tucks a golden lock of hair behind her ear. She's model stunning as in five foot ten, glossy long hair, flawless skin that defies even the tiniest pores, and a smile that brings humans to their knees. A good reason why she gave up her finance job to bartend—more C-notes in tips. We met when we were ten on my family farm. Her mom came for a healing heartbreak bouquet, and they stayed a month. Every summer after that, Laini and her mom showed up for the "peace and beauty" of it all. Truth be told, Laini was another reason moving to the city came so naturally. I knew I would have someone nearby who understood my home.

"Well, if you died then I would eulogize the shit out of you," she says. "But I guess today ain't your time. Now, are you going to get the hell out of that disgusting water or..."

"It's rose infused."

"Whatever helps you sleep at night."

I clear my throat and manage, "How about a little privacy?"

She tosses me a towel and makes no effort to offer me *any* privacy. Typical Laini. I wrap myself in the towel and step out of the tub and into my black fuzzy slippers.

"So what's up? Let's have a drink and you can tell me what's new."

I throw on a silk robe and follow her to the kitchen where she pulls bottles from her oversize bag and begins to mix a concoction of gin, sugar, champagne, and some red syrupy stuff.

"It's called *Revenge Is Better than Sex*."

"Catchy."

She shakes the concoction with cracked ice in a cocktail shaker, pours, and pushes the glass across the counter toward me.

"Chad texted," she says.

Because he didn't want to have to be the one to have to comfort me, I think as I take the first sip, settling onto a bar stool. The concoction is sweet, bitter, subtle.

"This is amazing," I say, trying to pretend we aren't going to have this conversation right now.

"I'm really sorry," she says with a pout only she could get away with. "I know how much you loved that job, but you're too good for them and maybe this is the universe's way of telling you to write your own book instead."

"Yeah, well, the universe should lose my number," I tell her, wishing I sounded tougher than I feel.

"Harlow."

I meet her gaze. "And you should open your own bar, create a mixologist guide, and call it a day."

Laini's expression is unreadable. Something between glare and smirk. Or is she about to sneeze? It's hard to tell.

"Touché," she says. "I guess your trip home is good timing, then?"

I nod. Sadly, it's perfect timing.

Laini raises her glass with a sigh. "To shitty moments that we spin gold from."

Just as I'm about to cheers to that, I come up short. My glass hovers. "Gold like what? And please don't give me some cliché BS about a better job."

With a deadpan glare, Laini says, "I am NEVER cliché." She has me there. "Look," she goes on, "bad things happen all the time and sometimes they lead to brilliant changes like…" She gives a light shrug. Her eyes twinkle as a smile spreads across her mouth. "Meeting a tall dark and mysterious stranger in a totally unexpected but perfectly timed way."

"You meet those all the time."

She frowns. "I meant you."

"I have Chad."

"Right, Chad's…great but, Low, it's not like he's you know…

he's not—" she lowers her voice to a whisper as if we aren't the only two souls in my kitchen "—the one."

The words land with force. I know she's right, but I wasn't looking for *the one* when we met. I was looking for a companion, someone to watch old movies with, to go to karaoke night with. I've been leaning on the fact that he's nice, responsible, has a real job, a nice apartment. He's safe and that's felt like enough.

Wanting to change the subject, I clink my glass with hers. "To shitty moments."

"And to tall dark mysterious strangers."

I roll my eyes and laugh despite the day I've had and the evening I'm about to have.

A moment later, Laini says gently, "What can I do?"

"Help me pick an appropriate dress for Chad's celebration tonight?"

This earns me a frustrated grunt. "It's so effed up that I have to work and you can't go out with me instead and drown your sorrows in a Guerlain facial at the Waldorf."

"Duty calls," I say, not sure my words nail the humor I intended.

Laini shakes her head. "Patriarchal BS. And if you must go, then you are *not* going to wear an *appropriate* dress. I mean honestly, Low, what the fuck does that even mean, 'appropriate'?"

"Laini, I have to."

"Says who?"

I take another sip, wishing I could down the whole revenge concoction but no way can I show up at the dinner tipsy. "Society?" I say. "Clubs of professionally educated paper pushers?"

She offers a devilish grin that makes my pulse pound with worry.

"So basically guys named Chad." She throws her head back, laughing at her own humor.

I roll my eyes.

"Fine," she says. "I'll let you go. But only in a dress that screams, 'Fuck the patriarchy.'"

By the time I get to the restaurant (twenty minutes late) and make my way to the private rooftop, I'm a bundle of nerves. I know it's going to be a miserable night of soul-sucking fakery, made worse because I wore a sensible black sheath dress Chad would approve of. I know he'd approve of it because he bought it for me saying it would balance my wardrobe that had too much "color." I was so close to listening to Laini and putting on the bloodred, one-shoulder dress that screams *vixen*, but in the end, I just couldn't do it. Tonight is about Chad. To make myself feel like less of a sellout and glam as hell, I put on a pair of fabulous stilettos, personal pieces of armor to help me through tonight.

As soon as I step off the elevator, the cool night air sends a chill down my spine. The softly lit rooftop is inviting with thick green vines growing along distressed brick walls. Even from twenty feet away, I can tell that the white blooms in the greenery aren't real. If my mom were here, she'd gasp and give her speech on the horrors of fake florals.

Each linen draped table has a lit votive candle and a single daffodil. Whoever made that selection clearly doesn't know that white daffodils can mean new beginnings but that a single bloom actually symbolizes bad luck. *Ugh! Shut up, brain.*

When I see the mingling crowd, I'm filled with relief that the reception is still going on. I had this catastrophic image of me walking into a moment of toasts and that people would gaze at me with disdain, everyone all thinking the same thing: *Who does she think she is?*

The gathering is made up of around fifty people, all wearing dark *understated* suits that definitely cost more than my monthly publishing salary. Servers circulate effortlessly with silver trays hoisted over their right shoulders, and pleasant expressions plastered onto their faces.

"Harlow." I spin to find Ted, the Coryell part of the firm. The first name on the letterhead also means the oldest, *on your way out* partner. Ted's balding badly, and gravity has not been kind to his eighty-year-old double chin. He places a hand on the small of my back and I startle, annoyed as hell that he thinks he can touch me just because it's what the "boys from his generation do."

I pull away as he says, "You are a true beauty," and adjusts his hearing aid.

And then I see Chad. He doesn't look impressed by my *true beauty.* He's by my side a second later, taking in the appropriate dress with a smile until his gaze lands on my strappy stilettos, and I'm not sure if he wants to burn the shoes or kill me for wearing them. The heel is only three inches but it's enough to put me at Chad's height of "six feet tall." Why do I feel the sudden need to defend myself, *I'm not taller than you!*

"Do you want something to drink?" he asks, his whisper light on my bare arm.

"A dry martini?" I say softly, trying to not feel itchy with dread.

Chad flags down a waiter and orders, "A club soda."

I flash angry eyes at him, which he must read because he whispers in my ear, "You smell like you've already had a drink. And you're late."

I want so badly to tell him he's wrong, that I only had a sip and that I should be commended for my amazing discipline and levelheadedness, but he's got that gleam in his eye that tells me he's already sold himself on some narrative about my intentions.

Ted is lifting his glass to us, beaming like Chad is his prodigal son. "We are so pleased our Chad here is finally joining us at the grown-ups table and leaving that bullpen."

I nod and smile as the waiter hands me my fizzy water. If this weren't a big night for Chad, I would have marched to the bar and demanded a double martini. Fuming, I lift my glass. "To Chad."

He gives an appreciative nod followed by a tiny grunt I'm sure only I can hear. A few other lawyers from the firm slip into our little circle, giving me polite nods and smiles that I return, and each one feels like a tiny piece of my soul being sucked from my body. God, I hate these kinds of parties. The kind where your primary job is to impress as many people as possible, talking up your game, embellishing your title, status, life—spinning so many lies you're not even sure what's true anymore. Of course, no one is ever really listening. They're already onto the next drink, next convo, next embellishment of their own.

"And you?" Ted asks me. "How is that job of yours?"

"Editing, right?" a tall woman wearing a double strand of pearls asks. What's her name? Esther? Elaine?

I nod, refusing to play their game.

"Working on any interesting books?" someone else asks.

Chad's gaze on me is so intense I think I might combust.

"Always interesting," I say, wishing we could just change the subject.

"Well," Chad says, wrapping his arm snugly around my waist. "She's in between jobs at the moment. You know how publishing can be. So many ups and downs."

This earns me sympathetic nods and kind murmurs, and my heart is pounding so hard I think it's going to leap out of my chest and jump off the nearest ledge. I bite back making a scene, repeating the mantra, *This is Chad's night. This is Chad's night.*

"I tell her all the time to take a few months off," Chad goes on. The bold-faced lie is too much and my skin starts to heat up; the splotches are rising to the surface ready to turn redder than Laini's cocktail. "Maybe look at another field," he goes on. "Something more…"

Don't say it. Don't say it.

"…lucrative."

Wow, he really hates these shoes.

"I do hear editors don't make that much," someone says nonchalantly. "Total robbery if you ask me."

"It's really not about the money," I insist, finding the most subtle, nonhumiliating tone I can. "It's a passion industry and the feeling that you're helping someone tell their story—"

"Babe," Chad cuts in with a snort that sounds like it's on its way to a derisive laugh, "passion alone doesn't put food on the table."

Nods all around that make me feel sick. I grip my glass tighter, imagining my *nice safe* boyfriend dangling over the edge of the Empire State building, my stiletto heel hovering above his hand.

"He's right," Ted says. "In my day, it was about sacrifice, being of service."

Of service? I want to shout. *Like lining your pockets with more green than you'll ever need in a lifetime?*

Just then, I see myself from a distance. Standing at Chad's side, nodding and smiling and being grossly underestimated and picked apart and not allowed to be some bolder version of myself. A voice rises inside of me, a whisper that vibrates through me, *this isn't your life. There is a better, truer way.*

Chad throws out his winning smile. He's ready to change the subject; I am not. "But shouldn't we all find the beauty in life?" I say, still clinging to that whisper. "Can't we be of service *and* do work we love?"

"Her family grows flowers," Chad says with a condescending tone and expression I hate. As if his response is a reason for my inherent need for passion and beauty.

"Ohh," Ted says, "how delightful. You come from gardeners."

My blood is boiling. "Our farm is over fifty acres." *And is fucking magic, you pompous ass.* Where's some hemlock when you need it?

Chad leans closer, still clutching my waist with one hand like he's afraid I'll bolt if he isn't pinning me in place. I wiggle free of his touch.

"They ship all over the world. It's a pretty impressive operation," he says, like maybe he's realized he's pushed me too far. Except he wouldn't know about my family's business. He's never stepped foot on the farm. "And Harlow is amazing," he adds, a clear attempt at backpedaling. "She can identify any flower anywhere and tell you its meaning."

"Really?" Esther/Elaine says. "What about those?" She points to the single daffodils.

Bad luck is on the tip of my tongue, and I have never wanted to spit out words more, but I tamp down my hurt ego and say, "Daffodils mean new beginnings."

A few surprised chuckles, energetic nods, and raised eyebrows make me feel like I'm on display, a token of entertainment. I excuse myself to head to the restroom where I lean against the wall in a fully enclosed stall that feels more like a powder room. I need air. But the air in here smells like a horrid imitation of peonies and I feel sick. I should fake sick. Pretend I have food poisoning.

I wash my hands, thinking maybe I'm overreacting. I mean I did wear heels that make Chad look short, and I *was* late. Is this a moment of self-sabotage? Or is this me standing up for myself?

I head back to the reception with a new determination to begin again. I grab a martini from the tray of a passing waiter and come up behind Chad when I hear my name in a stranger's mouth and then Chad's words through a laughing breath, "You know how dramatic Latinas can be."

I freeze. Mortified, feeling naked and raw. And entirely enraged.

Chad must see the gazes drifting over his shoulder because he turns slowly.

My eyes flick to his. If I had seen regret there, if I had seen an apology, I might have held it together. *Maybe.* But my arm is already moving swiftly and the martini is already on his face and the gasps have begun and I'm grabbing my clutch, and running to the stairs because the elevator will take too long and I need to get the hell out of here.

My feet pound the stairs to the rhythm of *out. Out. Out.*

A few shock-filled minutes later, I step onto the busy street where it's begun to rain.

And then I run.

3

By the time I get home, my chest is heaving, my heart is thundering and the anger is blazing so hot I could burn it all down.

The apartment. This *life*. The absolute falsehood of it all.

My mind reels as I try to process what I've just done, the knowledge that there is no coming back from this for me and Chad, and maybe that's okay? Maybe my subconscious picked these heels knowing that our breakup was always inevitable.

The truth is, I moved in with Chad "temporarily" after a friend of a friend's room-share went south and because Laini's place is so tight a small child barely fits in the bathroom. But one week turned into two and two weeks turned into four months and four months turned into…this.

I think about texting Laini, but then I remember she's working tonight and the last thing I need to do is get her riled up. If she knew the hellscape I just endured, she'd likely put a hit out on Chad. Okay, maybe not a *real* hit, more of a hypothetical revenge plot.

My phone starts to vibrate the second I walk through the door. It's my mom; she knows something's wrong. Of course she does. Thanks to my amplified emotions, she can tell I'm upset. And the more intense the feelings, the stronger we can all sense that something is up. The same way we all knew the moment Camilla fell in love with Amir, even before she admitted it to herself. Like I said, it's a blessing and a curse.

Pretty soon a steady stream of texts is coming in from Lily, and Camilla, and then my younger cousins Dahlia and Lantana join in. The text shit show looks something like this:

Lil: What the hell is up with you, Bean.

Cam: I can feel the Real Housewives vibes from Ca. Talk to me!

Lantana: You're giving me a headache and making me itchy.

Dahlia: Please tell me you're okay. I'm worried. Call me.

Wow—am I really that much of an emotional storm right now? I mean, it's not like that time I was skiing in New Mexico and got stuck on the top of a mountain and didn't have a cell phone. I was so scared, I thought I was going to perish on that mountain before my family sent the search and rescue crew.
Fear.
That's by far the most powerful emotion. Is that what I'm feeling underneath all this indignation and rage? Fear of judgment? Of being alone? Of failing yet again? Or is it something else?

I know my mom won't stop calling, so I answer her third call with, "I really can't talk right now but everything is okay and—"

She cuts me off with, "Obviously not true. What happened?"

It's seven fifteen on a Thursday, and I've lost my dream job, and an

unworthy boyfriend, and the apartment that comes with him, and worst
of all, maybe even myself along the way.

I lean against the wall in the entry, staring at the *false appear-*
ances and *unhappy love* sunflowers. "I threw a drink," I admit,
pausing, waiting for her to fill in the holes so I won't have to.
Maybe she needs another clue. "In Chad's face." Still no response. "At his promotion reception?"

"Mmm." Which still doesn't count as a response but it also
tells me she's thinking, weighing, considering. Instantly, I feel
like a child wanting to collapse into my mother's waiting arms,
wanting to say, "Make it all okay."

"And now I'm moving out."

"Okay."

"And I don't have time to talk, but I've already changed my
flight to a red-eye in a few hours from now and…"

"Corazón?"

Just hearing my mom's soft gentle voice makes me want to
burst into tears. "Yeah?" I say, wishing I didn't sound so weak,
so juvenile. Here's the thing about my mother, Jazmín, a name
that carries the power of healing, love, and peace. She never
judges, never chastises, has never used the words, *I told you so.*
She is never surprised or shocked. She is the oasis in the desert
of this life for me and my sisters, the ship that keeps us safe in
the storms even when we are the storm.

"It's all going to be okay," she says. Her forever optimistic
truth for every one of life's occasions. "Remember Mayahuel's
song."

When all has been destroyed, the goddess shall rise.

Right. The goddess who granted my family their magic. A
lot of kids learn fairy tales, fables, or stories from the Bible, but
in my family? The very first tale you learn and commit to heart
is the tale of a young and very beautiful goddess named Mayahuel whose jealous grandmother hid her in the farthest corner

of the universe, wanting nothing more than to conceal the goddess's beauty and power.

I can practically hear my mother's singsong voice recounting the tale.

Lost in her dark and lonely despair, Mayahuel dreamed of love, of freedom, of tearing down the walls of her secluded prison.

I blow out a long breath, thinking I know exactly how she felt.

A minute later, I'm in what used to be my closet and quickly change into a comfy sweat suit before trying to decide what to pack, but all I can think is how many damn shoes I have. Where did they all come from?

I quickly pack a suitcase, not slowing down enough to even smooth, fold, or roll the garments like a decent human being would. Chad will have to ship the rest, or maybe Laini can. But to where? The farm? No, I don't plan on staying. Staying feels like defeat.

But if I'm not staying, then where am I going? Back here? Doubtful. I don't even want to be in the same city as Chad. But this is where editors live so I have to come back. I press a hand to my forehead.

A sudden ache sweeps through me—not for Chad exactly, but for the lie I've been living. The lie *I* crafted. All because I so badly want to be as independent and successful and remarkable as everyone in my family. Somehow, I thought moving to the most competitive city in the world and getting a job in one of the most competitive industries in the world would say, independent, successful, remarkable.

I mean, if I can't have the Estrada family magic, I still want to feel like there's significance to my work, my life. Except, that's not how things turned out. And now I'm worried I am and always will be *un*remarkable.

I realize I have to park all this self-misery for now. I have a plane to catch.

Lugging my suitcase down the steps, I stop in the apartment's foyer, tie the belt of my trench and take a quick look in the entry mirror. I tug my beanie lower, wishing I could just hide my entire face and body underneath it. I want a reset button, a do-over, a chance to make different choices. "I want to find the better and truer way," I whisper.

In that single breath something happens.

The sweet pea I had set in the same vase as the sunflowers turns toward me, a barely there motion that I must have imagined. Or not. I blink. Stare at the arrangement wide-eyed, waiting for the bud to shift again. It doesn't.

Maybe I brushed against them? Or breathed too hard? Or maybe I'm officially hallucinating. I roll my eyes at my reflection in the mirror.

Operating on pure instinct (or maybe because Bad Chad doesn't deserve them), I remove the trio of sunflowers, stuff them under my arm, and walk out of the town house that was never mine.

By the time I'm off the plane and through customs, it's 1:00 a.m. and I'm surprised when I see my younger cousin Dahlia sitting in the corner of the waiting area with her face planted in a romance book, and there's a travel mug hovering near her mouth like she's far too busy to take a sip. I walk right up to her, watching as she turns the pages faster than any human could conceivably read.

Then, as if she can sense my approach, she lowers the book and leaps to her feet, pulling me in for a long deep hug that I sorely need right now.

I spent the last two thousand miles steeped in self-misery, and now? Seeing my cousin, I'm ready to leave it all behind me.

I glance at the book. "How is it?"

"Meh? Sex scenes could be way hotter."

"Because you've had so much?"

"Harlow," she says, giving me her stern professorial voice. "I am a grad student studying human love and intimacy. I know about hot sex."

Dahlia is in grad school at Stanford, studying psychology. She's already had two papers published, has worked under premier professors on the cutting edge of relationship psychology, and is now starting her own podcast with some other kid wonder named Archibald the Third. Really. That's his name.

I give her another squeeze, realizing how much I've missed her even though it's only been a month since we were all together. She smells like freesia and clean sheets that have dried in the sun.

"I wasn't expecting you," I say, happy she's here. She's a few inches shorter than I am, and naturally beautiful like her namesake, which means dignity. "Mom said everyone wasn't coming until Saturday."

Her hazel/gray/brown eyes twinkle with mischief. They're the moodiest eyes in the family, always changing color depending on her temperament. Right now, I read her hazel eyes as eager. "I'm curious as shit, so I came to the farm early to see if I can get the two osas—" (as my mom and Tía Rosa are affectionately known) "—to spill the beans about the early timing."

I chuckle that her curiosity of what the osas are up to has surpassed mine.

"And did they spill the beans?" I ask as we make our way through the silent as a graveyard airport. "Because no way is it for the Ceremony of Flowers. It's too early!"

She rolls her eyes. "Pssh…if they had, you would be the first to know. Well, after Lil because you know…she's my favorite."

"Right. Because she's going to deliver your babies someday?" We all know that Dahlia's favorites change like the wind depending on who she thinks she's going to need most.

"I probably won't even have children," she says with a dramatic wave of her hand, "but Lil *does* call in prescriptions when I need them. And she's seeing a new hottie surgeon. So I get to live vicariously through her *Grey's Anatomy* life."

"Ohhhh. So she's your drug pusher *and* source of entertainment these days," I tease.

"What more could a woman ask for?" she says with a wry smile that makes her dash of freckles more prominent.

I laugh and pawn my suitcase off on her, which she takes happily.

I smile at Dahlia, wondering if her gift for healing has influenced me. Only hours ago, I was the most miserable person on the planet, but now Dahlia has mysteriously made me feel lighter, less burdened.

Everyone in my family has a unique gift where the flowers are concerned. Well, everyone but me. The magic is not only in the land but in our sangre and according to my mom, the Estrada women haven't seen a healer in a generation. Dahlia's magic does have its limitations though. She can't heal lethal wounds or terminal illnesses. But she can help heal a broken heart, or a shattered soul. When she was seven, the healing flowers spoke to her and ever since then she's had a unique intimacy with them, knowing exactly which bloom or combination would work for whatever brokenness needs curing.

"Hey, I'm sorry you got pickup duty," I tell her since the airport is an hour's drive from the farm.

"Are you joking?" she says brightly, sweeping a shiny black bang out of her eyes. "I volunteered."

Remembering her text, my spirit sinks and memories of the last day flood back into my exhausted mind. "Were you really that worried?" I ask.

"Your mom told me all about it. Damn. That was a ballsy breakup. And soooo cinematic. You might be my favorite cousin after all."

"I'd rather *not* be cinematic." God, did I really throw a drink in Chad's face? In front of everyone at his firm? I tell myself he absolutely deserved it. But now, with hours and distance between us, I wonder if I overreacted. Couldn't I have just walked away?

But in the end, it wouldn't have changed my decision to leave. That, I am absolutely sure of.

"Harlow," Dahlia says with a calm encouraging expression. "Everyone wants cinematic. They just don't have the courage to do it. It's in the research, you know. Just like everyone wants to find true love, or some version of it."

"You're a hopeless romantic."

"Which is why my *Always Amor* podcast is going to be a smash hit."

"Agreed. But maybe you should fall in love first to make it… more believable?" I snap my fingers. "Hey, I know—maybe you could date Archibald." I act like it's the idea of the century, as if no one else has ever mentioned it before. It is so obvious she's into him.

Dahlia pulls up short and throws me an evil glare. "Bean, he's my TA. Definitely would be a breach of conduct. It's safe to say I will not be birthing his children anytime soon."

"Okayyyyy whatever you say." But I see a small smile curving her mouth, and I'm already grinning because it feels so good to be with family, to be chatting about nothing in particular, taking up the mental space reserved for self-loathing with the absolute warm ball of healing magic that is Dahlia.

"And he's my business partner," she goes on. "I mean he doesn't know it yet, but I am definitely going to get him to be. So he is not *boyfriend* material. Did I ever tell you that he has an annoying allergy to book binding…like how? He can't even go to the library or a bookstore. Are you hearing me? A *bookstore*! And he slurps his pasta." She's getting very worked up over her *not quite business partner.* "Plus he has about as much passion as a fruit fly."

"Uh—male fruit flies are the Casanovas of the insect world," I say so matter-of-factly I surprise even myself. "They dance, and sing with their wing vibrations."

This earns me a dubious look. "And you know this because?"

Research for a book. That I never wrote. Correction: that I never begin.

"You're blushing," I say, ignoring her question because this is much more interesting than my nonwriting life.

With a glower, she tells me, "You are officially not my favorite anymore. Unless…"

Playing along, I laugh lightly. "Lay it on me."

"You tell me every single detail about Bad Chad," she practically purrs. "You should for sure be a guest on my podcast. People would eat it up."

I place a hand over my heart and smile. "Oh my gosh. Me?" She's nodding vigorously. "And my failed love life?" My fake smile melts into a frown. "Absolutely not."

Warm, sweet smelling air rushes me as the sliding doors whoosh open. The black sky stretches on and on like a sheet of velvet. I'm home.

We climb into the Mercedes sedan and make the hour trek home. I offer to drive, but Dahlia insists as long as I keep her awake with every detail of my crappy day. I decide to indulge my cousin with all the horrid little details of the "dinner," leaving out the early part of my day when I got fired. I'm not ready to talk about it, and if I'm lucky everyone will just assume I quit. That might be worse though, since I've never stuck with anything or any romantic partner in my life. Not graduate programs, a short stint as a literary agent's assistant, and an even shorter one at an indie bookstore. I can see my headstone epitaph now: *Harlow Estrada: short stinter.*

It's 2:00 a.m. by the time we get to the hacienda, a sweeping gated colonial estate tucked into a lush country hillside. A nearly full moon rises high above the tree-lined road that leads to the two-hundred-year-old house, a place that feels like it's always been here.

Every stone, every beam, every edge and corner.

Legend has it that the soil called to my great-great-grandmother when she came through this land on her way to somewhere else. But *somewhere else* wasn't in her future because the Aztec goddess of agave, Mayahuel, appeared to her and told her that if my great-great-grandmother used the land according to her instructions, the goddess would grant our family's female descendants an unimaginable magic. My grandmother agreed and the rest is history. Except that somehow, I was left out of the goddess equation.

An instant relief fills me as Dahlia cruises closer to the house. "It feels so good to be home," I tell her as the sheer emotional exhaustion of the day finally catches up to me.

"I know the magic is in our blood and in the land," she says softly, "but I swear, sometimes I think it's in these walls too."

With my suitcase in one hand and the sunflowers in the other, I open the impressive wood-carved doors with the hand-painted tile next to them: Casa de Las Flores y Luz.

The house is quiet, still. It smells of roasted ancho peppers, old leather, and fragrant blooms that instantly soothe me.

Even in the darkness I know that there are bouquets of fresh flowers everywhere: an abundance of lilacs, snapdragons, honeysuckle, and orange blossoms, each a sharp contrast to the stone walls, soaring metal windows, and rustic hand-hewn timbers. Our house excels at unpretentious elegance, a blurring of the lines where all the main rooms open onto terraces, where the outdoors and indoors meet on the threshold of a shared and rare beauty.

When my grandmother died ten years ago, my mom and Aunt Rosa moved here, to fulfill the promise made to Mayahuel, that an Estrada woman descendant would always be present on this land.

My parents divorced when I was eight; I think the magic and the folklore and all of it was just too much for my dad. But my parents have stayed friends; sometimes I think that was the better match, and now he's remarried and teaches biology at UCLA.

Dahlia and I make our way through the welcoming stone arch and head down the dimly lit colonnade toward the wooden staircase. An old grandfather clock ticks in the library.

We turn a corner and...

"Ahh!" I shriek.

Spooked, Dahlia climbs up my back, choking me with her death grip. I'm trying to claw her off me, but she's morphed into human Velcro.

My mom, in a silk white robe, looking more ghostly than human, is descending the stairway, shushing me while simultaneously rushing toward me with her arms extended.

I manage to shrug off Dahlia as my mom smothers me with besos y abrazos as if I didn't just see her last month, or that I don't FaceTime her every single day.

Dahlia mutters something about her book and worthless nightmares and heads to her room. "And no one better wake me before noon."

When the smothering is done, I say to my mom, "You didn't have to wait up."

"We didn't," Aunt Rosa says, trailing down the stairs in her linen pajamas. She's the younger of the two. Her hair is stylishly short, dyed a brilliant red, unlike the raven black it was the last time I saw her. My mother on the other hand, has tiny streaks of gray at the temples of her dark hair, but her skin is flawless, youthful, radiant. She's probably using that wildflower elixir she tried to pawn off on me last time I was home. Although, the enchantments of our flowers have limits where the Estrada women are concerned. We can't use the magic with the intention of our own benefit. For example, we can't make someone fall in love with us, or manipulate someone's mind, or land a job, or change our futures, unfortunately.

My aunt takes the sunflowers from me. "Ay, pobrecitos. All wilted."

"Chad didn't deserve them," I say through a yawn. "Hey, I

know this sounds crazy, but I swear I saw the sweet pea you sent lean toward me earlier. Is that even possible?"

A cryptic glance passes between Tía Rosa and my mom, there and gone in an instant.

"What?" I ask, knowing something's up.

"You must be tired," my aunt says. Translation: *you're seeing things.* Except I didn't just imagine the look they shared.

My mom loops her arm in mine and guides me up the steps. "Your room is ready. A sprig of English ivy and daisies on the nightstand for a good night's sleep."

God, it feels so good to have someone take care of me.

"Did you really punch Chad in the face?" Tía asks gleefully as she follows behind us.

I glare at my mom, realizing the entire family must know by now. Then to my aunt, I say, "No, I threw a drink in his face."

"Then he deserved it," she says confidently, and I love her for it.

We stop in the hallway upstairs. The aged limestone wall is lined with oil paintings of all our women ancestors, surrounded by their namesake blooms, and looking more regal than I could ever feel. I imagine my own painting hanging there someday; I'll be wearing something timeless and tasteful, but it still won't live up to the others because I'll be surrounded by piles of stones.

"Are you going to tell us why you invited everyone early this year?" I ask, thinking Dahlia isn't exactly known for her sleuthing skills. Not that she isn't fantastic at digging; she just sucks big-time at being covert and usually gives herself up before she's even begun. "Because no way is it for the Ceremony of Flowers."

"You'll know in thirty-six hours," Mom says, giving me a gentle nudge into my room.

"Just tell me no one is dying."

She sighs like I've personally affronted her. "You think I would send such a beautiful invitation for bad news?"

Tía Rosa and I look at her, smile, and simultaneously say, "Absolutely," knowing full well she has a flare for the dramatic.

After a quick shower, I fall into my velvet-lined bed. Curling the pillow closer, I feel something underneath. I click on the table lamp to take a look. My mom has planted a sprig of holly under my pillow, symbolic for enchantment, good cheer, and good luck among other things. I need them all, I think.

Then, as I fall back on my pillow and close my weary eyes, I remember that my mother sometimes uses holly for the power of *dream magic*. Two minutes later...

I'm climbing a steep mountain, searching for something I can't name. I hear laughter echoing in the distance. My laughter. And then my own voice hums with a frequency of...magic, "It's time."

My mind conjures the question before I can speak the words, for what?

And then a woman's voice I don't recognize tells me, "It's time for the beginning."

4

⁓⊰⊱⁓

I wake to a series of texts from Chad.

Mostly one-liners that don't do anything to help resolve our situation. Seeing Chad in this new *eyes-wide-open* light makes him so incredibly easy to decode. Maybe it was always this easy. Maybe now I'm just seeing *him* for who he is.

Seriously, Harlow? Code: *how could you do this to me?*

You totally misread everything. Code: *I won't apologize because I did nothing wrong.*

You made an ass out of yourself. It was a joke. Code: *You humiliated me.*

Where are you? Code: *When are you coming back?*

Couldn't face me? Code: *I deserve an apology.*

Snuck off in the middle of the night. Nice. Code: *I'm pissed you got the last word.*

I feel no regret as I stare at his words on the screen that go from angry to desperate to angry again. A part of me wishes I could ignore his messages, this thing that's already in the past.

But I know deep down this relationship, whatever it was, deserves full closure. I decide to send him a voice memo so he can't read between the lines of my text and infer all sorts of emotions and meanings that aren't there.

I hit the record button and after a deep breath, I say, "Hey... last night was miserable on all levels and I really don't want to rehash it. We were never good together, and we both know it... so let's call it a day. You can tell people whatever you want but it's over between us." I send it, wondering if there is anything left to say. If we, he, *this* is only worth a single paragraph. I send another recorded message: "Laini will come get my stuff."

I wonder if I should tell him to be well or have a nice life. All the words I come up with seem melodramatic and cheap. How do you say goodbye to someone with dignity and kindness when you're already on the other side of the door?

"I will always wish you success in life." Oh God, I sound like a dollar greeting card. Delete. "Best of luck with everything." Hell no. Delete. "I hope you find happiness." Good enough.

And I mean it. The message is authentic. Just because Chad wasn't for me, doesn't mean he won't be for someone else.

Next, I call Laini because there are a million missed calls from her, which tells me that Chad called her. He probably thought I had gone to her apartment.

She answers with, "So you finally left him."

"I did."

"God, my breakup drink worked better than I thought."

I laugh. "Is that what it was?"

"Oh, for sure. You think your family is the only one with magical talents. Who needs roses when you've got whiskey?" I hear a whirring; she's probably juicing. A second later, the whirring stops, and she says, "You okay?"

Actually, I feel good, like a weight has been lifted off of me. "Better than okay. Like *how*, Laini? Why did no one tell me?" *How did I not see it until now?*

"We did."

"Oh." Right. But to be fair it's a lot easier to have 20/20 vision when you're outside of the Matrix.

"Should I ask the hard question?"

She wants to know if/when I'm coming back. "I'm not sure what I'm going to do," I tell her. "Maybe it's time for a fresh start." I twist the sprig of holly between my fingers, remembering the dream, and wondering what the woman meant by, *It's time for the beginning.*

My brain sticks on a single word: *the.*

As in one.

Maybe the dream lady meant a new beginning is inevitable because of the end with Chad. But then wouldn't she have said, *a* beginning? Here's the thing that drives me crazy about dream magic: it's always so subjective and abstract, requiring you to put the pieces together yourself.

"Well," Laini says, "I want to be a shitty friend and force you to come back here so I don't have to go through the grief of living without you, but the semidecent human in me knows that you'll make the right decision for you." She pauses then goes in for the kill. "And now you can write that book!"

My pulse picks up speed, double-timing its normal rate of calm in favor of near panic. Here's what people don't understand. You don't just sit down and write a book. I mean, I guess some people do, but I need to plan, outline, develop character arcs, come up with a plot. I've tried to sit down and freestyle write, just to see where it takes me, but I always land in a corner of webs I've spun from chaos because I have absolutely no idea where the story is going. Or what I even want to say. But here's what I do know—I want to write something magical, something that reflects the enchantment people don't even realize is growing beneath their feet. But magic is so big and wild and unpredictable, where would I even begin?

And then there's the small voice that whispers to me in the

middle of the night, *Are you really the right person to write about magic?* And I can't even argue with the logic of it, because I don't possess *any* magic. Is my proximity to it enough?

"Mmm-hmm." I walk to the window and look out across the gray mist blanketing the farm. The abundance is all-encompassing. For as far as my eyes can see, waist-high foliage and blooms take up every inch of space, adding rich hues of pink and orange and green to the morning's light. "I don't know what I'm going to do."

"Well...as long as you do *something*. I think that's the most important thing. Keep trying and you'll figure the rest out as it comes."

I've never been good with *as it comes*. I prefer a safe climb. Planned, curated, predictable steps. Slow and steady wins the race and all that.

"Yeah. I guess," I say. "Hey, can you do me a favor?"

"Name it."

"Can you get my stuff for me?"

"For sure, but..." She hesitates. "Do you want me to send it to the farm?"

I don't want anything sent here; it feels too final. Like I've made a decision I haven't yet. And it's unfair to ask her to store my wardrobe in her microscopic apartment. Damn, if I wouldn't miss some of those pieces that my minuscule salary could never afford, but my indulgent mother's allowance could. Even so, I'm not about to spend all my cash on storage in the city.

"Give me a few days to think about it?" I say.

"You got it. Just make sure I'm the first to know what you decide. I mean, after your sisters, and probably cousins. God, I really am like tenth in line, aren't I?"

I offer a playful laugh. "You can be my number one non-blood sis."

"Yeah, whatever that means," she grunts. "I love you and I am proud of you. I'll spend my lonesome time creating a drink just for you so that when I see you again, we can toast to new beginnings. Maybe I could come down for a visit. I really do miss the farm."

"My mom would love that," I tell her. "She always says you're her favorite daughter."

This makes Laini bubble with laughter. But it's true. My mom adores Laini; she's always had a soft spot for her since Laini's mom was pretty broken up over a series of failed relationships and left my best friend to fend for herself. Or at least until the flower magic put her back together again.

After we hang up, I realize that I'm suddenly starving and my head is filled with static, and all I want is a deliciously dark brew from Pasaporte, hands down the best coffee spot in town.

When I peer into my suitcase, I'm not sure if I should laugh or wilt. Okay, so the contents tell me where my head was last night. I've got two pairs of flannel pajamas, one pair of knee-high boots, a cashmere scarf, two pairs of jeans, a graphic tee, and one NYC sweatshirt. Nothing that's weather appropriate for the year-round temperate Mexican weather.

Thankfully, I have a closet full of clothes here, but they're all pretty old because I hate throwing anything out. I'm one of those *but I might wear it again* people. And see? I was right. I rifle through the racks, each section like a well of memories for my different fashion phases: there's my Courtney Love phase, my athleisure-wear phase, and of course, my sundress phase. I select a white sundress and my perfectly worn in, never going out of style tan ankle boots.

And since I can't find a nude strapless bra because past me didn't think about the value of undergarments, I go braless. I can generally get away with the no bra thing except that this damn dress has these itty-bitty buttons running up the chest that are in danger of popping. Who in the hell designed this? A man with tiny fingers, I decide as I manage the last button and slip out of the house before anyone can stop me.

The air is unexpectedly crisp as I head out to the barn to grab my cruiser bike. A few minutes later, I'm flying along the ditch bank beneath the shade of ancient oak trees, high above the wide-open fields of vibrant blooms that feel like a dream-world belonging just to me.

This is a place of no seasons. It's a temperate climate, but even if it weren't, our blooms thrive regardless of external conditions. Here you can find summer blooms like the pink-orange heads of dahlias beside small white petals of apple blossoms growing next to autumn flowering perennials like asters and Chinese lanterns. The magic makes for an easy production schedule. And regardless of what the year's orders require us to grow, each Estrada has her own garden filled with the flowers after which she is named. Since I don't have a floral name, my mom planted something different for me.

"Your garden is so unique," she told me when I was only six years old. I can still so clearly remember pressing my small hands into the cool, dark soil.

"Why?" I asked her, wishing with all my might that I had been named Rose or Azalea or any other flower with meaning.

"Because this one is unexpected," she told me. "Each bloom a surprise."

Her reasoning made me feel special. I grew to love the suspense, the waiting to see which blooms would appear and disappear according to the phase of the moon.

My mom always tells me and my sisters that wherever there are flowers, there is the feeling of home. It's true, but nothing, and I mean nothing in the world, trumps the feeling of *this* place: captivating, comforting, enchanting. I can feel the magic rising, vibrating, pulsing with life all around me, enveloping me in its love.

Before I get to the end of the crop, I send a silent thank-you to the goddess Mayahuel as always and make a mental note to visit my garden after I caffeinate. I wonder what I'll find: Oleander for caution? Hawthorn for hope? Rue for regret? Or maybe Iris for faith.

Soon I'm pedaling down a long dirt road surrounded by the sweeping scenery of vineyards and undulating green scrubby hills. The countryside is alive with vegetation like palm trees, jacarandas, mesquite, and ocotillos. Horses and sheep graze in golden fields. Dogs bark in the distance. Birds swoop overhead. And for that single untouchable moment, all feels right with the world.

Fifteen minutes later, I'm bumping along the cobblestone streets of our picturesque town, breezing past colorful homes, shops, galleries, boticas, and souvenir emporiums. I smile, comforted by the familiar beauty that is El Viento, a place where the sun sets slower and the moon rises faster and the stars shine brighter.

I'm inside Pasaporte not two seconds before I hear, "Harlow!"

I spin to see Roberto, the owner, fifty-something, on his third marriage to someone half his age; he also happens to be my godfather.

He picks me up and whirls me around, forcing a laugh to erupt out of me.

"¿Qué estás haciendo aquí?" I squeal.

"Amor, I own the place," he says, switching to English.

I smack his chest playfully. "I thought you'd be at one of your other bougie restaurants in Mexico City or…"

"Needed un poco change of pace," he tells me. "Your booth is open. ¿Qué quieres beber?"

"Surprise me," I tell him as he heads to the bar where a couple of new baristas are staring, likely wondering who I am and making all sort of assumptions, but today is the first day of a new beginning and nothing, absolutely *nothing* is going to sour my mood.

I take the two steps to the small back area and find my favorite booth tucked in the corner where the day's light doesn't reach. I love the café's dark rich leathers, tan colored walls, and stacks of journals that can be found in every nook and cranny. This was Roberto's very first business venture; he named it Pasaporte to remind himself of his dream to travel the world. Over the years he found himself in conversations with travelers that passed through here, so he began bringing in journals to give visitors a place to record their adventures. Before he knew it the place was filled with stories from all around the globe. We call those people vagamundos, *those who wander the earth.*

The journal idea caught fire and pretty soon there were *love* journals, *funny* journals, *mystery* journals, *life's big questions* journals. You name it, there's a journal for it. But what I love most are the stories that are recorded in the pages, better than any book I'll ever read and a gold mine for story ideas.

I slip into the booth nearly knocking over the jar of pens as I pick up the green leather-bound journal with gold embossed letters: *First Impressions.* I don't know why but a strange feeling of triumph spreads through me; or is it giddiness, or maybe the feeling of freedom? Or possibility?

Staring at the journal, I wonder if today is the day I find the spark, that magic flicker of an idea for a story that begs to be written, that haunts my days and nights, that won't let me go. An old receipt slips out of the book. Five words scrawled sloppily across the section where the tip amount should go: *What do you really want?*

The answer rises inside of me: *I want to be inspired.*

A server brings me a large mug of coffee that smells like a nutty dark chocolate.

With a contented sigh, I sit back, open the journal, and just as I'm about to read, two things happen at once.

A cool swish of air.

And someone snagging the journal out of my hands. I'm too stunned to process that a guy in aviators and a wrinkled T-shirt has just slid into my booth and is now hiding behind the pages of the journal. Correction, wrinkled T-shirt with a small hole near the shoulder seam.

"Excuse you!" I say, indignant.

He says nothing.

"Hey!" I practically kick him under the table.

Still hiding behind the journal, he says in a low voice, "Do you see a blonde girl, short, wearing a pink sweater anywhere near me or in the general vicinity?"

I glance around, but there are no windows in this area and I can only see the edge of the bar, so it's not exactly a great lookout perch. And no way am I about to get up and check the café for this guy. I don't really give a rat's ass about why he's hiding from pink sweater girl. "That's my book," I insist.

"Please," he says, his tone even, but polite, "just help me out here."

With a grunt, I tell him, "No, I don't see anyone like that. Can I have my book back now?"

Slowly, he lowers the journal, so I get a better look at the intruder. He's maybe thirtyish with jet-black hair, cut short, but definitely leaning toward curly if he let it grow another inch. His shades are in danger of slipping down his nose but not enough that I can see his eyes, and the Rude Rogue looks like he hasn't shaved in days. As a matter of fact, between the wrinkled shirt and the almost beard, he looks like he just rolled in from a desert island. I'd absolutely put him in the category of ex-athlete who thinks *sloppy* is a fashion trend, except that his hair is too precisely cut, and nails are too precisely trimmed, and glasses too precisely clean. The guy is a walking contradiction.

His lenses are so dark I can't tell if he's looking at me or the book, so I clear my throat and gesture to the journal.

He points to it. "This is yours? Does it have your name in it?"

He's joking. Surely he has got to be kidding.

I cross my arms and lean back casually. "As a matter of fact, it does," I lie because no way am I letting this guy ruin my mood or inkling of inspiration I was just feeling.

He starts to flip through the pages. "Oh, wow...this stuff is really good," he muses. "Are you Tiffany who says her first impression of Jack was hate at first sight?"

My blood is boiling. "Yep."

"Nice to meet you, Tiff." He doesn't extend the customary hand. "I'm Benjamin."

Are we really going to do this? Introduce ourselves and make small talk, when all I want to do is read in peace and drink my coffee and not have to socialize with a stranger.

"Okay, Benjamin." I grind out every syllable like it's a dagger. "Can you leave now?"

"Why are you frowning like that?" he asks, pushing his shades back up so I still can't see his eyes. I bet they're green, maybe hazel. Like a murky swamp where there's no sun.

"Why are you wearing shades inside?" I ask, refusing to give him an inch.

He taps his long fingers on the table to the beat of the jazzy café music. "I'm hiding."

"Yeah, I got that, but why?"

"First tell me why you're frowning."

"I'm not."

"Kinda still are."

I inhale sharply, release slowly. "How about this? How about you leave now so I can enjoy my coffee in peace? And then you don't have to worry about my face."

"Not until I know the coast is clear," he says, ducking low. "She's like a police dog. She'll sniff me out, so if you don't mind, I'm just going to hang out for a few minutes? I'll be quiet and here..." He pushes the journal across the table. "All yours."

Actually, I do mind, but I'm more curious than enraged now, so I ask, "What did you do to her?"

Expressionless, he asks, "Why do you assume I did anything?"

"You have a very punchable face."

"And you can tell that in under the two minutes we've been sitting here?"

"Face is immediately obvious. Plus I'm a great judge of people."

He leans closer and I pick up the faint scent of sandalwood. "I'm going to bet that's another lie, *Tiffany*."

I take a slow sip of my coffee never taking my eyes off of him. I decide to prove my point and start with the easy stuff. "You're American."

"Did the accent give me away?" There's a slight quiver at one corner of his mouth, and I think he might actually smile but he doesn't.

"Your name is Benjamin," I go on, guessing that he hates the formality of that designation as I add, "but people you like call you Ben."

"Mmm. Profound." He tilts his head with clear condescension.

And given that he's bold enough to slip into a stranger's booth and ask for favors tells me that, "You're someone who thinks quickly on his feet and knows what he wants." *And your amazingly good looks have taken you far, but not far enough to make up for your lack of manners.*

I pause, knowing I'm on the right track by his silence and the fact that I have always been freakishly observant. Maybe it's the *almost* writer in me, mining the details of people, places, events, thinking that maybe someday that information will be put to good use. "And you happen to look like the victim of a crime because it's been a long night and no one knows you here so appearances don't matter, especially not when you're running away from your girlfriend, which also tells me you're in the business of something ego driven or something that requires you to be on all the time so you absolutely welcome anonymity."

His jaw tenses and I taste victory. "Wow," he breathes. He

lets out a low whistle, but his face is still devoid of all human expression. How does he hold it blank for so long?

Okay, here it comes. My congratulations on being so perceptive. Any moment now. He's going to eat crow. Right this…

He looks down. Removes his shades, then ever so slowly, he looks up.

His wretched, unshaven, excruciatingly handsome face breaks into a smile.

Damn.

5

His eyes are not green.

Nor are they hazel. They are dark pools of chocolate with swirls of amber. But it's not their color, or their warmth that just stopped my heart; it's their depth and unique shape, the way they soften right at the edge, like he has a persistent expression of compassion and concern that even the false smile he's beaming at me can't reduce. The two don't match. And yet…

Okay, now I wish he would put the aviators back on. Ironically, I felt much safer when I couldn't see his eyes looking at me. My skin feels prickly, red splotches are lurking. What the hell is my problem? This is Laini's fault. She cursed me with her talk of *meeting a tall dark and mysterious stranger in a totally unexpected way* and now look. Maybe there is some magic in her drinks.

Benjamin speaks first, keeping his eyes squarely planted on my face while he rolls a coin over his knuckles. Where did that come from? "You may be observant," he says with a whisper of a smile, "but you're wrong."

"Doubtful."

"I'm in the business of sleep and she's not my girlfriend."

I sip my coffee, studying him, trying not to look entirely unnerved. Sleep? Did he just say sleep? Maybe he's an anesthesiologist, or he sells mattresses? Neither one of those feel right though. He's probably a serial killer who puts people to sleep permanently.

I was still trying to figure out what I got wrong when he says, "And she's a journalist."

Alarm bells are ringing in my ears. I do another once-over, trying to match his face to a mental catalog of famous men. He's definitely not famous. I can't help it. I bite. "Why is a journalist chasing you?"

A young server I haven't seen before comes up and asks him if he'd like anything.

"He's not staying," I say.

"I'll have what she's having," Benjamin tells the girl who clearly thinks I'm not here or that my wishes are trash. How did this man take my sacred quiet space and turn it into a swirl of chaos and hormones so quickly?

Ignoring the journalist question, he sets down the coin on the table, leans back in the booth, stretches his long arms over the top of the seat, studying me with those damn eyes. He's made up of angles: straight, taut, lean, muscular angles.

I glance down at the silver, noticing it isn't a peso or an American currency, but something that looks old, maybe even antique.

Following my gaze, he offers, "It's from a pirate ship."

"Do you always carry pirate money around?"

There's that forced smile again. "It's my lucky coin."

"You believe in luck?"

"You don't?"

Dammit. He's got me. On one hand, he seems like the kind of person who makes his own luck, but those eyes—they tell a different story. One of hope and belief in things bigger than himself. Before I can stop myself, I offer a self-assured shrug and say, "Sometimes."

There's a flash of surprise that sweeps across his face. It gives me the confidence to add, "But you also make your own luck."

A smile plays on his mouth, curving up like I'm going to get the real deal, but then he goes serious and says in a low voice, "My turn."

"Excuse me?"

"Your name's not Tiffany," he begins.

"You've already guessed that." I throw him a haughty smirk.

He ignores me, rubbing his chin, studying me. "You're American. But you're not here on vacation. Something tells me you come here a lot. You have family here." He nods like he knows he's right, but I don't want him to be right! Not if I got him wrong.

"And you drink your coffee dark because you like to seem deep and strong and mysterious."

Or maybe I just like it bitter, I want to say, but instead, I point to my cup. "Wow. Excellent guess."

"You like to read the journals because you're curious, maybe even voyeuristic." His eyes narrow and still manage to look gentle. "Other people's lives fascinate you. Your own life is boring." He shakes his head. "No, that's not right. Safe, predictable, but you don't want it to be."

Heat flares across my chest. Why do I feel like I've just been insulted? My life is not boring! Just a little bit on hold. And maybe it was safe a couple of days ago, but not anymore. I feel like I've leapt off of a cliff and there's no net to catch me.

"Are you done?" I manage, but my heart is already sinking and my head is already exploding because I hate how right he is. Am I that much of an open book?

He looks at me, really looks at me like he can see something no one else can. And the way he's studying me is making me nervous and itchy and altogether breathless.

With a grin, he says, "I could go on."

"Please don't."

He throws up his hands in defeat. "Can I at least say one more thing on the subject?"

"No."

But he's already talking over me. "I've known a lot of people, most are obvious, ordinary, but every once in a while, I meet someone...who defies all that."

The heat in my chest is now an inferno. But no way am I falling for some bogus pickup line that he probably uses all the time with annoying success. And yet, deep in that murky guarded place inside of me, I like that he thinks I'm not ordinary or obvious.

"And you?" I ask. "What camp are you in?"

He shrugs and I feel like I've touched a nerve, but no way can this man think he's ordinary or obvious or anything other than a giant ball of mystery.

"Well," I say, feeling my mojo coming back. If there is ever a time to be daring, it's now, with a man I'll never see again. "I disagree with you. I think that most people are interesting, fascinating even, if you just give them the chance to tell you their real story."

"Real." There isn't a question there, and yet there is an invitation to tell him more.

"Yeah, I mean most people hide who they are from the world because... I don't know, maybe they think that whoever they are isn't attractive enough, smart enough, good enough. But if you give them the chance, they usually surprise you."

His eyes brighten, grow even more curious like I've just lit a match inside of them. "Ah—so if everyone has a scintillating story, what's yours?"

I hesitate, watch as his eyebrows draw together, and I wish I could get into his head, that I could see his thoughts, the words he isn't saying. "That's not how you get someone's story," I tell him. "You have to start with the right question."

"Oh yeah? Like what?"

"Like, what's the one thing that sets your soul on fire?"

He's struck silent and I feel a wave of triumph. He'll never answer the question; he'll never reveal that part of himself to a total stranger, and then... "Dirt."

I bark out a laugh, thinking he's messing with me, but his expression is thoughtful, pensive even. "More specifically, wide-open expansive land with no end in sight, with nothing on it except possibilities."

Now it's my turn to be struck silent.

"And you?" he says.

It's a dare, to tell him if I'm worthy of his earlier assessment, the girl who defies obvious and ordinary. My stomach does a flip as the truth spills from my lips, "Words."

"Explain."

"Just that. I like to read them, write them, analyze them, rearrange them..." My voice trails off unexpectedly. Maybe this was too much soul truth, but he's leaning forward like he wants to know more. He studies me with those dark eyes, and I think I'm going to melt into the booth. I've known him all of twenty minutes and yet he already knows what makes me tick. How did that happen?

"Is that why you come here?" he asks. "To read these journals? Or—" he hesitates, rubs his hand across his chin thoughtfully "—do you write in them?"

I gather myself, shrug. "Both."

His gaze drops to the First Impressions journal. He slides it to his side of the table, brushing his bare arm against mine. His touch feels like a thousand jolts of energy exploded in that microscopic speck of skin. My pulse kicks up a notch as I imagine what it would be like to touch more of him. Or to have him touch more of me.

My cheeks go hot as he studies me; his eyes giving up nothing that might tell me he felt it too. He picks up a pen and begins to write, obscuring my view of the page with his arm. He's making a show of it, like he's trying to get me to ask but I refuse. It's too expected, too ordinary. But damn, what I wouldn't give to see his words.

The server delivers his drink with a very pleasant smile, which Benjamin doesn't seem to notice because he's still writing. Finally, he closes the book, takes a gulp of his coffee, glances over his shoulder, and stands, keeping the book in his grasp. "Well..." he says, drawing it out, waiting for me to fill in the blank. I have no idea why, but I want him to know my real name.

"It's Harlow."

His eyes twinkle like I've just surprised him. "Well, Harlow, thanks for saving me."

"So you're not going to tell me why some journalist is chasing you?"

"It's a boring story, and something tells me that you aren't into those." He drops a few pesos on the table for his coffee. Then begins to walk away.

"Wait!" I holler, wishing I didn't sound so juvenile. "Your lucky coin."

Turning back, his dark gaze meets mine, holds it there a beat before he says, "I think you need it more than I do."

And then he's gone.

6

I roll the coin, still warm from his touch, between my fingers. It's imprinted with some kind of symbol but so worn I can't make anything out.

"I don't need your luck," I whisper.

But apparently, I do because I spend the next thirty minutes searching for the First Impressions journal Ben scribbled in only to find out that there are four of the exact same book and two are being used by patrons and the other two reveal absolutely nothing because I have no idea what I'm looking for. I doubt that the Rude Rogue bothered signing his name or dating the entry.

When I ask my godfather why he has so many journals, he only laughs and tells me, "Because there are limitless first impressions in this world."

And now I'll never know Ben's first impression of me, which shouldn't matter in the big scheme of things, but I'm suddenly deeply curious what he wrote. Probably something like: *this girl needs more than coffee and a lot more than luck.* But how delicious would it be if he had written something like, *her mere touch sent my heart soaring.*

God, I'm pathetic. Have I officially slipped into the vacant space where plenty of writers spend their time, inserting themselves into tales much bigger than their reality?

I hang out at the café for a bit longer, engrossed in the Broken Hearts journal. If there is ever a story spark to find, it's always in a broken heart. The pages are filled from top to bottom with one-liners, words stacked upon words in neat square paragraphs as if there is anything neat about having your heart wrecked. Shouldn't this be a messy diatribe about the fragilities of being human? Sometimes, when it's dark and I'm halfway to sleep, I wish I knew what this felt like, to love someone so deeply, so enormously, that they have the power to break you, even just a little.

I read about "anonymous" who got left at the altar. Benicio who lost his faithful dog to cancer. Mason who found out Sarah was cheating on him with his brother. Theresa who merely wrote, *everything seems worse when it's dark out.* I close the book and feel an immediate and all too familiar pang in my chest that always leads to *what-if.*

What if I could feel the depths of the human heart like all these tragic journalers? The idea grows as I clutch the book to my chest. *I would finally have something to write about.*

The realization is painful and immediate. No one has ever created art without a crack in their center. Without shedding blood.

Placing the book of heartbreak back on a bookshelf, I exit the café. I leave the bike parked and head out on foot, wandering aimlessly through town, lifting my face to the sun, which has decided to make an appearance, its golden rays warming my skin. I text my mom to let her know where I am and that I won't be home anytime soon. If anyone will understand, she will. It's one of the things we uniquely share, this absolute need for solitude. Something I gave up when I moved to the city. I thought I could carve out a space somewhere in a library or a bookstore, but the excessive energy of New York was always right there, pulsing beneath the concrete, reminding me I didn't belong no matter how hard I tried.

I spend the day near the park in the plaza; it's the center of town surrounded by shops and restaurants and a large cathedral with a pink facade and Gothic spires that stretch toward the cumulous clouds.

It's one of my favorite places in town to people watch, to imagine the lives of the strangers passing by. Where do they lay their heads at night? Who do they love? What's their deepest fear, wish, regret? And every blonde I see, I wonder if she's *the one* who followed Ben. Or maybe it was a ruse? But why would he lie? She's probably his ex, I think sardonically.

After a while, I find my way to the center of the park, a pocket of space surrounded by a lush rose garden and shaded with sprawling trees that are beckoning me to sit and stay awhile. I climb into one of the hammocks stretched beneath the shade and lean back.

As I close my eyes, Ben's words echo through me: *Other people's lives fascinate you. Your own life is boring… Safe…*

I shake off my irritation at the truth of his words. Not about my life is boring per se, but I always lean into security and protection. I seek shelter, not because there's a storm but because I'm always waiting for one.

The thought ignites something in me, and I feel myself wanting, longing to be the girl he saw—the one who defies the ordinary.

I think about the goddess Mayahuel; she's always reminded me of beginnings, of what might or could be. I think about the way she was locked in a prison of her grandmother's making, how she was destroyed and still she rose. My mother's voice infiltrates my memory as I close my eyes and let the tale wash over me.

When Ehecatl, the serpent god of the wind, heard her siren song, he followed the music straight to the goddess and they fell in love instantly. So great was their need to be together, the god wrapped a breeze around them, forging their very souls as the two floated across the sky, lost in their passion. Mayahuel's grandmother was enraged. She wanted revenge but she knew that it would be futile to try and destroy a love this deep, so she plotted to kill the lovers.

When Ehecatl learned of the evil plot, he quickly swept Mayahuel to Earth where they held each other. The goddess knew what was coming and no ounce of the god's power could change it. But she was willing to break, to die if it meant becoming her true self. At the same moment they were transformed into a beautiful agave plant.

Soon the old woman found them. She cursed the power of love, and shredded the plant with a machete, not realizing that Ehecatl had escaped. She took the pieces of her destruction and made a meal for her demons who hungrily consumed it. But such love isn't so easily destroyed.

Unbeknownst to the bitter woman, a tiny green spire was left on the desert floor, a spark of hope for the grief-stricken Ehecatl who planted it in the richest soil. Night and day he shed tears at the site until the plant blossomed into a mesmerizing agave, awakening Mayahuel.

From that moment on, the goddess promised to be a symbol of beauty and love, to ensure that her magic lived on forever. She kept that promise when many years later, she came upon a traveler with a pure heart and asked her if she would carry the goddess's legacy. If the traveler agreed, Mayahuel would bless all the young woman's female descendants with the power to grow mystical flowers, to create enchantments, and to forever protect love, passion, and beauty. She told the woman there would be a cost though.

The woman asked, what kind of cost?

That is for each soul to discover. And even then, the woman agreed.

To seal their agreement, Mayahuel sang the traveler a song, one that would guide her in her darkest hours: When all has been destroyed, the goddess shall rise.

I throw an arm over my face and think about the burdens carried in my family, trying to discern each cost for the promise my ancestor made. Lovers lost. Dreams dissolved. Lives given. I've often wondered if I've somehow been spared. If I won't be asked to pay a price since I don't carry the magic or a blessed name.

"I want to find the better and truer way," I whisper.

Then, in the span of a blink, a breath, a heartbeat, five words come to me.

The land knew her first.

I bolt upright, feeling a shift inside of me, telling me that something extraordinary just happened. And as I repeat the line aloud, I feel a sense of adoration for the words, a sense that they belong to me, that they're a gift from somewhere else.

By the time I head back to the farm, it's dusk. I've already eaten at the panadería, and picked up some of the pineapple pan dulce my mom loves before passing Encanto, our family's flower shop with its ochre facade, wrought-iron-covered windows and weathered teal door that harkens back a couple of hundred years. The store is marked by a cobblestone walkway festooned with baskets filled with sunny sprays and fresh blooms.

A place that is steeped in memories and immutable magic.

To the general passersby, it looks like a lovely vintage florist. But to the locals and a select few, this is the spot where you place and pick up your order of magic. After you sign the nondisclosure agreement, that is—a modern addition. We operate using a whisper network, whispers carried on the wind of our town, El Viento, named for the goddess who is responsible for its creation.

Mom always says that those who are meant to find us, do. That we're a fate-driven business; the goddess still plays a role in our family, guiding the whispers with a gentle hand, and ensuring they reach the right hearts.

Still, there is always the risk that someone will learn about the mysticism and our practices. Of course, the farm is protected by a powerful spell, but every once in a while there is a crack in the facade. Over the years my family has run off a few unwelcome characters who have threatened exposure, or tried to steal a bloom or two, and every time they've failed in their efforts. And then there are the nonbelievers who just want to check things out, to test the rumors, to *see* if maybe, just maybe, there really is magic in the world. They're the easiest to deter because deep down they may want to believe but their walls are too high to ever *really* believe.

Most orders for magic are submitted a year in advance (and only if my mom and Tía agree to accept them) because it can take that long to grow the right flowers in the right soil, to nurture just the right level of enchantment and mysticism, to develop the perfect spell.

When I was little, it was the destiny of it all that felt so romantic, so within reach and out of bounds at the same time. Every year I would stare at the logbook dreamily, the client names and their ailments, as I imagined what blooms would be chosen, from which garden, using what brand of magic. Would it require Dahlia's healing magic? Or maybe Mom's dream magic? Some people merely want a yes or a no, and often dreams can carry such messages. Although, our family magic always comes with a warning. *You might get more than you asked for.*

And then there's Camilla's ghost magic. She has the ability to connect someone with a deceased loved one momentarily, although it doesn't always work because, as she likes to say, the afterlife is riddled with mystery that even magic can't unlock. That's when Lil's brand of memory magic is sometimes employed; it's for those who want to relive a moment as if it were happening in real time, or sometimes when the pain is too great and letting go isn't enough, she helps people to forget.

But it's Tía's and my prima Lantana's magic that has always captivated me the most. They are the only ones the flowers speak to regularly, using a language only they understand. When

Mom isn't sure about a recipe or bouquet, she enlists her sister or niece to improve the odds of success.

Of course each form of my family's unique magic comes down to the delivery. Dahlia uses tinctures and brews because the power of her magic must be ingested. Whereas Mom can use her dream magic with a simple spell and a petal under a pillow. Lil's memory magic requires inhaling a spelled concoction. But it's Cam's delivery system that is by far the most complicated. In order for her to conjure a ghost, she has to not only enchant the right flowers, but then bury them at the exact right time, sometimes carving a name into the stem of the blooms.

All of this magic comes to a head at the annual Celebration of Flowers, when each Estrada woman asks for the goddess's blessing for her garden, when their own hands and hearts enchant the soil, urging the plants to grow and bloom. It's a tradition that ensures a piece of their magic is always present even if they aren't. And as beautiful and beguiling as it is, it's always a reminder of what I don't possess. And while I participate, I know deep down my presence doesn't influence the magic.

As I'm passing the angel fountain at the edge of town, repeating my new chant, *the land knew her first*, I glance down a long road and see him. Ben's walking briskly with his back to me. He's changed into a white long-sleeved T-shirt and jeans, and he's wearing a baseball cap. *Still in hiding.*

I shouldn't. Really. But against my better judgment I do. I follow him, sticking close to the colorful walls and weathered gates, tucked into the shadows of the day's last light.

Ben walks fast, like he knows where he's going. A block later, he steps into the bookshop. I'm only forty feet or so away from the store, so I can't see what he's doing, what books he's looking at. I don't know what gets into me, but this time I don't wait. I slip across the road and inch right up to the window, peering around the corner, hoping, praying he doesn't see me.

The shop is empty, making it easier for me to see toward

the back where Ben is standing with the clerk, pointing to the antiquarian case. I know because I've stood there before, staring, pining, wishing. Not for the books, but to be important enough to leave a mark so big your work has to be guarded by a golden lock.

What are you buying? I wonder. Someone nearby lays on their horn, startling me out of my stupor. When I turn back, Ben is standing in the window, staring at me.

I jump back, practically yelp. God, this is so humiliating.

Instinctively, I turn, ready to rush away but not before he raises a single finger that asks me to wait. No way. I'm not letting him prolong this embarrassing moment any longer.

But I do, and less than a minute later he's standing in front of me with a paper sack in hand. His very dark, very thick eyebrows almost waggle. And his shirt hugs him in all the right places. "You're following me," he says, his voice on the verge of amusement sending me to the verge of mortification.

Familiar heat rushes to my cheeks. "Hardly," I manage. "I... I saw you and thought I should give this back to you." I hold up the coin, silently praising myself for thinking so quickly.

"That's a gift. For you."

My cheeks grow hotter. "I don't even know you."

"And yet you're following me."

"I just said..."

"Keep it," he says. His voice is deep, even, controlled. Still, I hear a spark of humor.

I clutch the coin in my now sweaty palm. "You like old books?" I ask, gesturing to the bag, desperately wanting to change the subject, willing to trade breath right now for a peek inside.

His gaze follows mine. "It's a gift."

This guy's a regular Santa Claus. I nod, wishing I knew who it was for and why he bought it and what the title is and...and... and. "Why did you ask me to wait?"

Without skipping a beat, he says, "I wanted to ask you for a recommendation."

Oh.

His dark eyes grow nearly black in the waning shadows. "What's the most romantic restaurant in town?"

My heart plunges as I realize that I am insanely attracted to this man who just bought a very expensive gift for someone he wants to take to the most romantic restaurant in town. Perfect. Way to pick 'em, Harlow.

"Uh…that would be Corazón. It's a rooftop restaurant that connects to the cathedral. They have this incredible string quartet and really great lighting and…you probably need a reservation."

His mouth twitches. "I was right." I am so not understanding. He must read my perplexed expression because he says, "You *are* from here."

"Or maybe I just had dinner there last night," I say, annoyed that this guy is getting under my skin.

"That was a lot of detail and enthusiasm for one dinner."

"I notice things, okay?"

"So, you're not from here?"

I hate the idea of giving him the satisfaction of being right. But I'm not from here in the way he thinks. I was born in California. I didn't grow up in this town. Sure, I spent my summers in El Viento visiting my grandmother, and too many holidays to count, and this place has always felt more like home than anywhere else in the world, but it's not because of the time spent here; it's because the land has claimed my past, present, and future.

Ben is staring at me expectantly.

"I call more than one place home," I say. And the moment the words are out of my mouth, I can taste the aftereffects of the lie. I have no other home right now. The idea of it sends an ache through me.

"Oh yeah?" he says, sounding genuinely interested, or maybe his intention is to put me in the hot seat and watch me squirm. "Like where?"

"Where are you from?" I ask, realizing this has been a one-sided conversation for too long.

Ben regards me silently a moment, then says, "I call more than one place home."

I'm surprised that his response doesn't make me bristle, but even more surprised that a genuine laugh rises out of me fast and effervescent.

A sound comes from his throat. A grunt? A halfway laugh? A slant of sunlight spills across half of his face, illuminating his warm eyes, and I have to stop myself from inching closer.

"Thanks for the recommendation," he says. "I'll check Corazón out."

That single three syllable word springs from his mouth effortlessly with a perfect accent, inspiring an even deeper *Benjamin* curiosity in me that feels like it's burning a hole through my center.

And just as he begins to step away from me, the curiosity blazes so hot, I blurt, "So, she found you?"

His dark brows pinch together as he looks at me pointedly.

"The journalist," I say. "She must want more than an interview." Dear Lord, did I really just say that out loud?

He laughs—it's a deep hearty sound.

"You're funny, Harlow."

And then, for the second time today, he turns and walks away.

7

By the time I park my bike in the barn, the sky is dark and the gibbous moon is high, casting an incandescent light over our land.

The entire ride home I can't stop thinking about Ben, about how he's clearly not into me—that he doesn't feel the same attraction I do because if he did, no way would he walk away from me twice without getting my number. And then my traitorous mind conjures images of his angular face, his near smiles, those warm eyes, and that damn antique book.

I need to clear my mind so I head toward my garden. I pass the moon garden, which is near my own. When I was little, the jardín de la luna was my favorite place on the farm—I used to imagine the most fantastical night creatures swooping in to pollinate the flowers, to offer their gifts of magic to Mayahuel. Sometimes I would linger here for the splendor and fragrant air; I wanted to cling to the promise these flowers make: *I will bloom even during dark times.*

I'm surprised to find my mom there when I arrive. She's leaning against a hoe, wiping her forehead with her forearm. A few
outdoor lamps provide dim lighting.

"Hey," I say.

Glancing up, she smiles. "My wayward child returns."

"I just...needed to think."

"About Chad?"

If she only knew how far from the truth her assumption really is. I shake my head. "Oh God, no. That's for sure over. I
just feel..."

I search for the word that she supplies. "Relief?"

"Relief," I echo as a tremulous smile tugs at my mouth. Although, a small part of me is terrified to check my phone, which
has been off most of the day. At least I know he won't call me.
It's too personal, intimate, revealing. And maybe that's why
things never took off for us—neither one of us really ever let
the other in. Could I have fallen for Chad if he had been more
vulnerable? If I had been? No. Not even then. There was never
that *it* factor. And I don't mean attraction, I mean that profound
knowing that is soul deep, intangible, and recognizes something
my mind never could.

Love.

"And did the time alone do you good?" my mom asks.

I nod, and just like that my mind replays the day like a highlight reel. The quiet, the sunlight, the peace. And Ben. I push
his eyes and smile and angles out of my head; no way is that guy
living rent free in my mind.

That's when I notice Mom's been weeding. There is nothing
beautiful growing in my patch of land, a mere eight-by-eight-
foot plot, except for some discarded wormwood. Its silvery leaves
and drooping golden flower heads look sad in the moonlight,
which is appropriate given that their meaning is *bitterness*. Is that
what my mom's been doing, rooting out my frustrations? Trying to clear the garden before I can see what it's become? But

before I can ask, she tells me, "The wormwood dried up the moment you came home. I'm just clearing it for the new crop."

A crop of absolute mystery, I think. But my garden, for better or for worse, does not lie and whatever grows next will reflect what's going on inside of me.

"You look more rested," she says, studying me like she can see things I can't. Knowing my mom, she probably can.

If there were ever a perfect time to tell her I've been fired it's now, but there is something about the moonlight and the way it's illuminating her face, or maybe it's the quiet sanctuary of the moonlit landscape, that makes me hesitate.

I take the hoe from her and drag it across the earth, yanking up a few stubborn roots in the process, wishing I could force a Mexican aster (harmony) or even better, an elderberry (creativity and rebirth) to sprout from the soil.

"Do you want to talk about what prompted...*everything*?" Mom asks. Her voice is soothing, gentle. That single word carries the weight of the last four months.

"Not really."

She steps closer, places her hand on my bare arm. This small gesture brings me instant comfort. I feel a softening deep inside, and the words spill from me before I realize they're out. "I was let go. Cutbacks." I keep my gaze on the dead stems of bitterness lying in a heap in the dark soil. "And I have no idea what to do or...if I should go back... I don't even like New York but all the editing jobs are there and..."

I'm. So. Lost.

Her arms are around me in a second, and I slump into her embrace, fighting the tears, the ache in my chest. "Do you think a flower worries if it's going to bloom?" she asks.

I hold her tighter.

"Harlow, you don't need to know anything right now, and you don't need to *do* anything. Give it time. The answer will come."

When, Mom? When will the answer come?

We break apart, and her tender gaze makes me wonder why I don't come home more often.

"Oh, I forgot." I hand over the sack of sweet breads I picked up at the panadería, which she takes happily but then sets on a nearby stone bench before she meanders over to the far edge of the garden near the Hylocereus tree, a night blooming cactus also known as the Night Queen. She's always been here, the thirty-foot guardian of the moon garden, powerful in her roots, but still requires some form of support. All year long she grows, sprawls herself across a cluster of boulders in a strange octopus-like fashion.

In a few hours, she will flower a white bell-shaped bud, slowly, inch by inch, until the bloom reaches ripeness at midnight. And then, when dawn breaks, the flower will shrivel and die.

Truth be told, she is my favorite plant on the farm, so defiant in her timing, withholding of her beauty.

That night I dream of dead petals falling all around me, until they've consumed me in their darkness. And when I wake the next day, I bolt upright, blinking in disbelief at the clock on my nightstand. How could it be noon? I never sleep this late. Ever. *Why didn't Mom wake me? She knew I wanted to go to the airport to pick up my sisters.*

It's just like her to let me sleep in. Always complaining that my sisters and I don't get enough rest.

I hear voices trailing up the stairs from the kitchen below. I'd know those voices anywhere. Camilla and Lily are here. I throw off the blankets and race down the stairs, rounding the corner in an out-of-control sock-slide that sends me right into Cam's arms.

Lil throws herself into the mix and before I know it, we are a heap of squeals and laughter. I haven't seen my sisters in four months, the longest we've ever gone. When we aren't together, it feels like something is missing, and when we are, everything in life feels more manageable—like my heart can finally rest.

After we break apart, Lil shoves me. "Damn nice of you to wake up."

"I was exhausted," I reply, figuring the last few days are finally catching up to me.

"Maybe Mom drugged you with a sleep flower," Cam jokes. My older sister's dark hair is cut into a shiny bob, which makes her refined jawline look even more refined, if that's possible. She wears the family crown for most stunning bone structure.

My gaze falls to the dozens of flowers strewn across the gray marbled island. "What's all this?" I lift a lilac-colored primrose to my nose and breathe in its sweet scent. "What's this for?" I ask, recalling the meaning of this particular color. Confidence.

Cam and Lil share a silent glance before Cam says to me, "We were creating a bouquet...for you."

"You think I need confidence?" I growl. "I just threw a drink in my ex's face at his own party and moved out of the apartment and left the city and..." God, I'm so unimpressed with myself.

Cam pulls a pitcher of Jamaica tea from the refrigerator and pours everyone a glass while Lil says, "You didn't call me or text me. I need details ASAP."

And where Cam oozes charm, Lil oozes strength, fortitude, a power that makes even men with the most accolades squirm in their seats. For years, her mentors begged her to go into some kind of specialized surgery because she *has the chops*, but in the end, she chose women's health because that's what means the most to her. It's the Estrada way—to follow the path of your dreams, to do the thing that makes your spirit soar. Unless you're me anyway.

"Don't change the subject," I say, feeling off balance as I take in the flowers in the bouquet and determine their meanings quickly. They each equal some iteration of confidence, good fortune, protection, and fulfilled wishes. This is a symbolic bouquet; I know that from looking at it. There is no enchantment to be found here, nothing that would magically grant me confidence, good fortune, protection, or a wish. If it were that simple, I'd use the flowers to make my life easier every single day. But like I said, we can't intentionally use the magic directly for our own gain.

"The bamboo was my idea," Lil chimes in. "Remember when we were kids and we would carve our wishes in the shoots and bury them on the farm?"

"And they never came true," I remind her, sounding like a total grouch. "And I don't want or need protection," I add, but regret the words the second they take flight. Not because they aren't true, but because of the obvious irritation tied to them. My anger isn't at my sisters. It's at myself, for the choices I've made that have brought me to this very moment, to their accurate assessment of me. Hell, even a stranger saw it.

"Okay, let's just forget the bouquet," Cam says, blinking. Her natural-looking false lashes nearly touch her cheeks. "Tell us what happened, jita. Take your time." My older sister carries her charm effortlessly, doling it out at the exact right moments in the exact right amount. Not too much to be overbearing and not too little to be *almost* charismatic. It's one of the reasons she is so good at running her inn. People absolutely adore her.

"We've been calling and calling," Lil says, twirling a bamboo shaft in her hands like a baton. Or a weapon. Her face is bare of any traces of makeup, and her long chocolate hair is tied into a side braid where she's tucked a bit of Queen Anne's lace. The effect is both romantic and beautiful, a softening of her otherwise fierce beauty that has always reminded me of a siren.

Leaning against the counter, I take a sip of tea and say, "I turned off my phone because I don't want to talk to him." Then I spill all the details Cam is so hungry for. When I'm done, I stare at Lil, standing in a beam of warm sunlight. "Is your hair purple?"

She rolls her eyes. "I did it for a baby shower. Don't ask," she warns, holding up a hand. "The hair-color box lied. It is *not* temporary." Her expression tightens as she tips her head farther into the light. "Is it really that bad?"

Cam gives me a *go with it look* so I say, "Not at all. Just a few strands and I bet it's gone in a couple more washes."

Lil's honey brown eyes glitter with mischief. "Well, you sound like a baddie, and I'm proud of you. I wish someone had taken a video for me. Poor little Chadley." She holds up her glass of tea. "Let's reenact it. Throw this in Cam's face."

Cam offers a warning glare. "Do it and I'll curse every purple hair on your head."

Her threat isn't without validity. She once concocted an elixir to curse a bully in fifth grade who punched Lil in the stomach. The kid's eyebrows vanished for a whole day. It was pretty epic until Mom told us that curses might feel good in the moment, but that the aftereffects are karmic and would ultimately bring harm on us. Cam had a stomachache for a week, but through all the howls and pain she cried, "It was worth it."

Wrapping an arm around my shoulder, Cam says, "What our ill-mannered hermanita means is that we're proud of you for standing up for yourself. He's unworthy of you and you're absolutely right, it took confidence. You made the right call, Bean."

A warmth spreads across my chest. "You guys could have told me you *hated* him."

"And ruin all this fun?" Lil says with a smirk. "Even if we had told you, you wouldn't have believed us. You were too far in."

"Far in? It's not like I was in love with him."

Cam shakes her head. "Far into a life you wanted that you thought he was a part of. You had a whole vibe going. The city, the job, his career. I think you convinced yourself that was what you wanted because it seemed like you *should*, but in the end, it just wasn't you and probably never would be. You saved wasting your youth, truly."

God, she's so right.

"A life that went up in spectacular flames," I say, realizing that there's no way I can keep the truth from my sisters. There never is, and as I open my mouth to tell them about being fired, Cam says, "Mom told us already."

While my mom is fiercely loyal, she can't keep her mouth closed where my sisters are concerned. But in fairness, I didn't ask her to keep it a secret. "Welp. Awesome. My life sucks." I fall onto a bar stool and drop my head onto the flower-covered counter.

"It does not," Lil insists, rubbing slow circles across my back. "We will support your unemployed butt for years if that's what it takes. You just have to do my laundry and cook me dinner in return."

"You know I can't cook."

"Okay fine," Lil says. "Just laundry. But seriously...you still have us and let's face it, we're the best part of your life."

"Okay, *best part of my life*, tell me what to do."

"Want me to memory magic you?" Lil asks with a straight face. "We could erase Chad from that pretty little head of yours, pronto."

"Liliana!" Cam chides. "How will she learn about relationships if she erases those memories?"

Lil deadpans, and just like that she's wearing her beautiful siren face. Her thick perfectly groomed eyebrows twitch. "You think Chad was put in her path to learn something? Puhlease! He was a pit stop, a blip in the road to her greater destiny. And besides, men are not the destination."

"Says the woman with a string of men," I say.

"Men I choose to tie onto that string."

"Someday, Lil," Cam puts in, "you're going to meet someone who knocks you on your ass and burns your rule book into ashes."

"That will never happen." Suddenly, Lil's face brightens. "Want to do a divination ceremony? See what's coming around the bend?"

We don't do divination often, mostly because my mom and aunt abhor forecasting one's future. They always say it doesn't leave any room for discovery and that discovery is where true futures are made. Plus divination takes immense energy and it depletes our crops.

"I'd rather not incur Tía's wrath," I say.

Cam nods, twisting a stem between her fingers. "You have to jump, Har."

"From the highest cliff that makes you sick to think about," Lil adds with an enthusiasm I wish I could emulate. "And if it doesn't make you sick, then the cliff isn't high enough."

Great. Another Estrada sister pep talk filled with useless metaphors. I lift my head, ready to say something witty when they say in unison, "Write the book."

I merely nod, thinking about the words, *the land knew her first.* I've been repeating the words all day, turning them over, inspecting each one, knowing somewhere inside of them there is a story. "I'm working on it."

"Swear?" Lil says.

I nod. *Well, I'm going to work on it.* "So how about we address the immediate issue?" I ask.

"Do you mean unpacking all this secrecy about why we're here?" Cam sneers.

"Yeah. Have either of you gotten the truth out of Mom or Tía?"

Lil makes a face. "Those two are iron traps."

"As if I don't have a life," Cam says. "As if I can just leave the inn, hop on a plane, and come here at the snap of their fingers."

"Here we go," Lil growls. "The hardworking Camilla Estrada who is so much busier than everyone. It's not like I'm a doctor saving lives!"

"And *I* have a business to run," Cam argues.

"For rich people!" an incensed Lil shouts.

"Guys!" I say. "Everyone is busy. We get it."

My sisters' luminous faces fall into pouts that might as well be screaming, *except for you.*

Cam steals a glance over her shoulder before she whispers, "We could…you know…make a truth elixir."

Her words stun Lil and me into silence. Only because we know she's serious and it's 100 percent doable. Whenever the women in our family are together, there is a greater energy created, a more powerful magic channeled. Hence why we do the blessing ceremony together. And while I don't have their gift with the flowers, my bloodline still allows me to act as a participant.

"Mom would kill us," I say, chewing on the idea with a seriousness I shouldn't.

Just then Cam's phone buzzes on the counter. She checks the message that just came in. Her mouth twists to the side as her eyes scan the screen. "Shit."

"What?" Lil asks, reading over her shoulder.

"Lantana's flight was canceled," Cam says with a long sigh. "Something about weather."

"How convenient," Lil chimes in.

"So, where's Dahlia?" I ask.

"She went for a quick hike to the cascades," Cam says.

"You think Mom will delay the big reveal until Lana's here?" I ask, curiosity rising. "I mean her and Tía made such a stink about us *all* being here."

Lil offers a villainous smile. "That truth spell is looking better and better."

"No need for spells," Tía announces, waltzing into the kitchen, waving a hand over her head; her fingers graze the dried bunches of lavender hanging from the rough-hewn beams. I swear she has bionic hearing. Mom is right behind her, her gaze landing on each of us with equal force, or disappointment. "You're making this a much bigger deal than it is," she insists.

"Mom," I say, "you asked all of us to fly here early. That's hardly a small deal."

"You're the one making this way bigger than it needs to be," Lil tells Mom. "You could have just called us. You didn't have to create all this cloak-and-dagger stuff."

"That wouldn't have worked," Tía says as she pokes around in the refrigerator. "What we have to tell you absolutely requires you to be here. And forgive me, pero, you wouldn't have come without the mystery."

I hate to admit it, but she's right. We were raised on mystery and secrecy. "Except that Lantana *isn't* here," I say.

"Then she wasn't meant to be," Mom replies with a tiny shrug.

Yes, because our entire lives are ruled by an unseen force that doesn't always play fair.

Lil says, "And you swear it isn't bad news, Mom?"

Even though my little sister wears a thick skin, she's really the most tenderhearted of us all. I think the pressures of med school, of carving up cadavers, and seeing so much death in residency hardened her in a way that is going to take a lot to thaw someday.

"No bad news," Mom assures, her eyes shifting to Tía, a smile playing on her lips.

A few seconds later, I hear the front door open. Dahlia.

The kitchen falls silent. Gazes sweep from one face to the next. Tía is the first to speak. "The time has come. Vamos." She raises her eyebrows at us.

She really should have been onstage.

As we trail the two matriarchs out of the kitchen, Lil whispers to me, "This better be goddamn good."

And for once, I agree with my hermanita.

8

When the Estrada women descend on the farm, there is a tangible energy that is both peaceful and stormy, joyful and overwhelming, soothing and exasperating. It's in the way the light hits, the way the air moves. The flowers sense it too; they seem brighter, taller, fuller, infused with more magic than at any other time.

We're all sitting under a deep portal that beautifully frames the eastern fields. The air is filled with the sweet scent of honeysuckle, and I could close my eyes and doze off except for the fact that Mom just dropped a bomb on us.

"You what?!" Lil cries at my mom and aunt, echoing what I know the rest of us summoned Estradas are feeling.

I exchange confused glances with Dahlia and my sisters before I say, "You brought us all the way down here to tell us you're going on vacation?"

Tía smiles broadly like a game-show host, announcing that I've won a car. "Exactamente."

Mom rolls her eyes. "It's only for ten days."

"But why all the mystery?" Cam asks, wearing a mask of absolute calm, cool and collected I wish I could pull off. "Why not just call us?"

Mom breathes in and out, pressing her hand against her trim waist. "As you know, at least one female descendant must always be here for the magic to work."

Here meaning the twenty square miles of farm and town.

"And you all would have come up with every excuse in the book to not come," Mom adds. She goes on to tell us that she and Rosa have never been on vacation together. I can't even blame them for wanting to get away. This farm is a big responsibility with six employees, production and harvest schedules, loads of orders, and complex systems to manage.

"And we leave tomorrow," Tía announces, snapping her fingers over her head like a flamenco dancer. "Italy, here we come!"

"So, we're your prisoners," Lil says, her voice raised.

"We would totally have helped out without you tricking us," I say.

"If we had just had some notice," Dahlia insists.

"Are you sure about that?" Tía asks, her expression daring us to mine our hearts for the truth which is, Mom's right. We would have found any reason to not come down, to not agree to assume this huge responsibility. Still, we could have worked something out seeing how much this means to them.

"I'm super happy for you guys," Dahlia says, "but uh...you can't really expect us to just drop our lives for ten days."

"We don't," Mom says, turning suddenly serious. "We only expect one of you to."

Cam's mask slips and she barks, "I can't be gone from the inn that long, Mom!"

"I've got rounds and new med students coming in to rotate!" Lil protests.

Dahlia launches to her feet. "I've got a huge project due. I can't just leave school to run a magic flower farm."

I brace myself, knowing where this is going.

"It should be Harlow," Lil blurts, pushing my shoulder a little too aggressively. "Come on, Bean. Serve as tribute."

"Me?"

Dahlia looks at me pensively. "It really should be you."

Cam and Lil are nodding their agreement so hard I think they might strain their traitorous necks. I suddenly feel like I've just been thrown into a massive pyre headfirst. "Seriously?" I groan. "I have to move and make decisions and..." *write a book, start a life.* Annoyance bubbles up in me hot and painful. Everyone assumes that because my life is sort of on hold right now, my time is less valuable and theirs for the taking. My voice rises with each word of my protest, which only starts a storm of Estrada bickering. *And in case no one has noticed, I have zero magic, so no way should I be guardian!*

Tía claps her hands loudly, bringing the arguing to an instant silence. "All this fighting is why we had to unfold our plan like this. The flowers will decide who stays."

"And that," my mother adds, "requires you all to be here."

I can practically see the light bulbs over my sisters' and cousin's heads.

Mom hands us each a white iris petal, known for its faith and virtue. "You will each sleep with this under your pillow tonight. Whoever's petal turns to blue will act as the guardian. And *that* is the final word."

And it is. No one says anything else as we all retreat to our own corners of the hacienda. It wouldn't do any good to huddle in commiseration. Not when the flowers might overhear us. Not when our near futures are in the hands of a magic still deciding.

That night I slip the iris petal beneath my pillow and then for good measure, I set Ben's lucky coin next to it. Falling into bed, I think there is no way the flowers will choose me, the Estrada with no magic, whose bitterness garden was just weeded.

With absolute confidence, I fall into a deep sleep. I dream I'm in a bookshop, a faceless man in a trench coat is standing next to me, handing me an antiquated book of poetry. The moment it's in my hands, unfamiliar white iridescent flowers begin to grow out of the pages. Stems wrap around my hands, and wrists, twine up my arms, reach into my mouth.

I wake up gasping, clawing at my neck as if the flowers have followed me into the real world. After a few calming breaths, I sit up. The morning's light streams into my room. My pillow has been knocked to the floor, and when I turn...there on the white linen is a tiny blue petal.

This has to be a mistake. I stare at it for a long moment, trying to decide if I'm still dreaming. Then I jump up and run to the door, when it flies open. Cam, Lil, and Dahlia fill the threshold with their sympathetic expressions and then the apologies fly with a whole slew of reasons why this could be a good thing for me: *quiet, peace, time to think.*

"All the things most people wish for," Dahlia says cheerfully.

But what they really mean is, *time to write your book.* I suddenly wish I had never told them my heart's desire. But when I shared the truth, I didn't have the gift of foresight to warn me of all the roadblocks. I didn't realize it would be so hard to begin. That the fear of failure would have such sharp teeth.

"I've got no problem being alone," I insist. "I just... I'm the wrong person for the job."

"The flowers say otherwise," Cam offers, tugging me into a hug. I glance over her shoulder at the damn pirate coin now on the nightstand and all I can think is, that thing is definitely *not* lucky.

Mom doesn't even give me the courtesy to act shocked when I tell her. All she says is, "Trust the flowers."

I'm so filled with panic I can barely get a thoughtful sentence out. "Mom, the flowers are mistaken. I'm the last person who should be guardian. What if I kill everything? What if there's an emergency?"

"You know every inch of this farm, jita," she says so calmly it only drives my panic through the roof. "Your tía and I have chosen the right time of year to leave, and there are so few orders to be picked up, which Fernando will take care of."

Fernando is the foreman, the manager, the guy who keeps the day-to-day operations running smoothly so my mom and aunt can focus on the magic. He's been with our family forever, following in the footsteps of his mom and her mom before that. That's the prerequisite for working with the magic—a long and trusted family history. And when his wife died more than a decade ago, my grandmother had a casita built for him on the farm because "walls have memories" and he needed a fresh start.

"The farm will hum along," Mom goes on. "Nothing can go wrong. All you have to do is be here."

Which means everything can go wrong.

"You're going to get deep wrinkles with all that frowning," she says. "Don't worry. We'll go over everything before I leave."

Then I lean into the obvious even though it hurts to say it. "But I don't have the magic."

My mom pauses, considers, offers me a hopeful gaze. "You were born with the same magic in your blood as the rest of us, and just because it never manifested doesn't mean it isn't there."

The Encanto flower shop is a burst of color, exquisite, and untamed with its vintage walls, weathered cabinets chock-full of clay pots and silver vases. Vines and brambles are wrapped dreamily around the antique chandeliers, dotted with rare blooms, which gives an utterly magnificent first impression.

The air carries a blissful fragrant scent both sweet and citrusy. And even if you don't know that magic resides inside these walls, you'd still sense that there's something special here, something that draws you in, and that's what drives so much of our non-magical business selling nonenchanted flowers. We keep on a few *not privy* employees who carry out the normal duties of a regular florist like arranging, fulfilling nonmagical orders, and managing inventory.

"Harlow!" I hear his voice before I see Fernando sweeping around the corner, arms wide-open. I hug his thin frame tightly, happy to see him.

Pushing a pair of crooked wire glasses up his nose, Fernando says, "You are more beautiful than the last time I saw you."

"So you know about the breakup," I tell him, laughing.

He looks to my mom, perplexed. "Breakup?"

Okay, so his compliment wasn't driven by pity. "Never mind," I tell him.

As if he can read my mind, he slips back into teaching mode. "No worries, Chiquita. All is in good hands while your mom is gone. I am only a phone call away."

For the first time I feel a sense of, *maybe this will be okay.* Ten days of quiet and solitude, to think, to process, to discover what comes next.

As if to prove his point, Fernando shows me the refrigerated cabinet where only three magical bouquets and one elixir are left, ready to be picked up. Each with a tag that includes the name of the person who placed the order and directions for how to use the magic.

"But no worries," he tells me. "You won't have to deal with these. I will make sure they make it into the right hands."

"Then why show me?" I ask, genuinely curious.

His thick salt-and-pepper eyebrows pinch together. "For a *just in case* scenario."

The ringing bell of the front door draws his attention away, and he leaves as Mom tucks her arm in mine and says, "See? Easy. All you have to do is be."

Why does that sound so much harder than it is? I'd rather have a list of duties outlined, specific, measurable. I work best in orderly environments when I know what's expected of me.

"Unless there is a *just in case* scenario," I remind her glumly.

"Amor, the flowers chose you for a reason," she says. "You must trust that."

I think about the whisper on my first morning here: *It's time for the beginning.*

When we get home, I check my personal email. Mostly ads, a couple of sorrys from old colleagues, and then there's one from Charlotte. My heart begins thudding in my chest the second I see her name.

Dear Harlow,
I wish I was writing this under better circumstances, but I wanted you to know that *Beneath the Dark* is in good hands. I've already had a call with Sara, and while I'm sure she's disappointed, she's a professional.

My eyes glaze over. Sara's the author of the book I had to leave behind, and although I hadn't begun editing her work, we had such a strong connection during our initial call, discussing how well our visions for the book aligned.

I read the last line of Charlotte's email at least ten times before the tears start.

I also wanted to thank you for acquiring such a lovely book.
I promise I will do right by it.
Wishing you all the best,
Charlotte

Lovely?
Is that all she can say about the depth and wonder and absolute magic that is *Beneath the Dark*?

Just then Dahlia pops her head in. "Want to join me for some honeysuckle orange blossom facials?"

I shake my head, and she must see my woeful expression because she flies into the room and lands on my bed. "What's wrong?"

I show her the email and her entire body slumps. "Oh."

"Yeah, I really wish she had never sent this message. I mean, I'm sure she's trying to be nice."

"No, she's not," Dahlia argues.

"I mean, just let me get over it already. Right?"

"She's like the boyfriend who broke your heart but won't let you forget it because he's always sending you texts," Dahlia says, taking my hand in hers. "Look, she's an ego-driven person who wants you to know she got something you loved, which is likely motivated by her excessive insecurity probably developed in childhood when she never felt good enough."

"Wow, you got all that from a few lines?"

Dahlia smiles as I drop my head onto her shoulder. She runs a gentle hand over my hair. "I promise everything is going to be okay."

"I'd settle for *half* of everything being okay."

Dahlia pulls back so she can look me in the eyes. "Sometimes you have to destroy to build."

"You should forget the PhD and write for Hallmark."

Her mouth fans into a small smile. "Want me to stay with you?"

Yes! Don't leave me alone with the magic!

"No, I need to be able to do this," I tell her. "And like you said, you've got school and…"

"You know all of us would drop anything for you, for each other."

She's right, and I feel so much comfort in this nugget of truth. But I know deep down it's time to *leap off the cliff*, to really figure out what I want, not what everyone wants for me, and definitely not what I think I *should* want.

After Dahlia leaves, I twirl the tiny blue petal between my fingers and before I can process another thought, the petal wilts in the palm of my hand.

9

The next afternoon, everyone runs out of the house like it's on fire. Between the flurry of goodbyes and the hugs and the I love yous, the scene is a blur, except for the lingering emptiness I always feel when the members of my family leave one another.

I've never been alone in the hacienda; it's an odd almost haunting feeling, and as much as I love solitude, this feels like something different. Like the flowers know that they've been left in the care of the nonmagical Estrada, and they don't like it.

Well, it's their own fault, I think bitterly.

Regardless, I have ten days stretching in front of me, and I plan to use them well. I'm going to channel the goddess, remake my life, choose daring and not safe. So, I get to it on Day One. I make a margarita with that aged añejo tequila my mom saves for special occasions before I find a good book in the study, a gothic thriller I've never heard of, and plant myself poolside near a row of pomegranate trees.

Even though the business of the farm is humming along outside these stucco walls, no one will bother me here beneath the banners of jute shade.

Wrapped only in a towel, I sip the decadent elixir until the heat overtakes me, and I shed the wrap in favor of glorious nakedness. I guess life isn't half bad for an unemployed, single, almost thirty-year-old after all. I'm not even beyond the book's first sentence when my phone rings.

"Hey, Laini." I'm so happy to hear from her I could cry.

"Are your ears burning?" she asks.

I curl my feet up under my legs and smile. "Should they be?"

"I was just talking to a friend whose cousin is newly single and he is gorgeous and would be so perfect for you."

"What happened to meeting a dark mysterious stranger under unexpected circumstances?" *Like sliding into my booth at Pasaporte and passing off a very unlucky coin.*

She pauses, then, "We could absolutely set it up to happen exactly like that."

I laugh.

"Whoa. What was that?"

"What?"

"That laugh. It's your mysterious I've got something to hide laugh. Cough it up. What aren't you telling me?"

I take a long swallow of the margarita, tangy, salty, perfect. "I met this guy," is all I get out when Laini begins to shriek like I've just announced my engagement. "It's not what you think," I tell her, filling in the details so she gets a very clear picture of Ben and his confoundingly annoying presence.

"You have to find out what he wrote in that book!"

"I tried," I say with a sigh. "He didn't exactly sign his name. Anyhow, it's a thing of the past and—"

"He got to you."

"Did not."

"You wouldn't still be thinking about him if he hadn't. You're like an iron wall, Har."

"Well, thanks for that image, but I swear you're off base."

A snort. "Does this Ben person have a last name?"

"Didn't catch it. Like I said, he wasn't very forthcoming."

"Strong and silent type."

I imagine Ben's deep-set eyes, and a new layer of heat covers my body.

"Change of subject," I blurt. "How's New York?"

"Incessantly boring without you."

"You're just trying to lure me back."

"Is it working?"

"I have to hang around here for a bit..." And then to send the message, *I can't talk about it,* I add, "Family stuff."

"Mmm...okay." I hear the sound of clinking glasses in the background.

"Are you at work?"

"No, just trying to create that spectacular Harlow drink I promised, or did you already forget?" she asks. "See this is how it starts. First me, then the drink then..."

"You mean the one to toast to new beginnings and living grandé?"

"That's the one!" she says cheerfully. "Hey, I might need some of those edible flowers you guys grow."

"Which ones?"

"The yellow ones with the pink tips and no name?"

"Sure, I can ship some to you."

"And, Harlow?"

"Yeah?"

"Say hi to the flowers for me."

After we hang up, I sink into the book, only for my phone to ring a few minutes later.

This time it's Fernando. He must be calling to check on me, to make sure I haven't accidentally burned the place down.

"Hey, Fernando," I say.

"I'm happy you answered." He sounds on the edge of breathless, which puts me on the edge of anxiety.

"What's up?"

"I wouldn't ask if it wasn't important," he begins. I feel a knot forming in my gut. "But I hurt my arm playing baseball with my grandson."

"Oh my gosh, are you okay?"

"Claro, but I need to visit the doctor tomorrow, take more X-rays, and he can only see me at six o'clock. I was wondering if you could watch the shop just for an hour."

The knot tightens. "What about the other employees?"

"We have a pickup," he says slowly.

Oh. Someone is coming for their magic. *Shit.*

"All you have to do is box the bouquet like I showed you," he says. "I tried to rearrange the time but couldn't get ahold of the customer."

Maybe this could be a good thing, a way to show my family that I can be a part of the magic, our legacy. Surely handing someone their magical package can't be that difficult.

I take a deep breath and tell Fernando, "I'll be there."

It's 6:00 p.m. sharp the next day when the bell rings on the shop's door. Above all else, our patrons of magic are instructed to be hyper-punctual.

I can do this, I tell myself as I head to the front counter. *All I have to do is box the bouquet, seal the magic and voilà.*

As soon as I saw the bouquet, I knew it was for a magical bonding. There are three Inca lilies at the center that denote longevity and a powerful bond with another, one sprig of milkweed for hope in misery, and two fern stems for the secret bond of love.

I can tell it's a powerful blend.

I turn the corner to find a young woman, decked in a wide-brimmed sunhat, hair tucked underneath, meandering through the store, touching odds and ends, humming to herself. She's nervous. I don't blame her. Whenever you bind yourself to someone magically, it's serious business and practically undoable.

"Hello," I say, startling her out of her reverie. "Beverly?"

When she turns, I see that she's close to my age or maybe a couple of years older, but it's impossible to ascertain because she's wearing a pair of huge black sunglasses.

"I'm here for—" she clears her throat "—the bonding bouquet."

"Just a moment." I head to the back, remove the arrangement from the cabinet. I can feel the hum of Lil's memory magic vibrate through me. While I don't perform any magic of my own, I have always been able to feel its presence, especially when it comes from one of my sisters.

I set the flowers in a long white box embossed with the symbol of an agave, to honor Mayahuel. Then, with absolute precision, I burn a small bundle of white sage, letting the smoke seal the magic.

I lift the box and smile. See? Not so hard. Feeling like I've found a groove, I practically strut back to Beverly and hand her the box. "The directions are on the tag inside. Basically, you need to give these to whoever you want to bond with under the light of the full moon."

"That's it?" she says. Her voice is soft, unassuming.

"And make sure they smell the bouquet. It's really important that they breathe it in while you're standing in front of them, touching them in some way. There has to be contact between the two of you."

"Okay," she says, staring at the box like it might detonate.

My family rarely creates bonding bouquets and only under the most unique circumstances for couples who both commit to the magic, because the last thing we would ever do is use magic to trick someone. The last time my mom made one of these arrangements, both parties had consented, hoping to reunite in a deeper way after something had been lost.

"This person must be really important to you," I tell Beverly.

"He is," she says. "And I'm hoping this…helps."

"It will," I say confidently, feeling a tiny thrill to be in the position of Eros. There's a power in uniting two lovers who have lost their way. I'm so intrigued I want to ask her more, but she doesn't seem like she wants to stick around. As a matter of fact, she seems like she's in a big hurry, fidgeting, glancing over her shoulder.

"Good luck," I tell her as she rushes out the door.

For the next hour and a half, I sweep up the back area and get things organized for the next day since Fernando isn't back yet and Rocio, a new employee, is out doing last-minute deliveries.

I'm about to turn off the lights when I see him…again.

Ben is standing in the shop window, studying the display of mixed wildflowers. He's probably here to buy the *book person* a bouquet.

I don't know if it's the way he's standing, so casual yet commanding, one hand dipped halfway into his pocket, or if it's the intensity of his gaze, like he's never seen a wildflower before now, but my pulse starts to pound in my ears.

Quickly, I duck behind a spray of hydrangeas and poppies, peering through the fragrant stems.

I glance down at my overalls, a frumpy choice.

He's walking toward the door where he stops, and stares up at the shop's patina sign, Encanto, like he's asking for permission to enter. No one can resist our storefront, or the lingering effects of being in the shop, the closeness of magic that wraps itself around you. Which right now happens to be supremely inconvenient.

Please don't come in. Please don't come in.

He reaches for the doorknob. And just as he turns it, he stops, digs his phone out of his pocket, answers, frowns, then speed-walks down the road.

I rush to the window and peer out as he hurries away. Why do I always end up staring at his back? I get a sinking feeling, watching him walk away. Out of the corner of my eye a bundle of hawthorns shift. I snap my gaze to them. Now still, their long stems are hanging over the rim of the silver container like they might spill onto the floor any second. I quickly right them, questioning their position only moments ago. They were upright, weren't they?

I'm just about to head back to the hacienda when an elderly woman walks into the shop. She has short white hair, elegantly styled. She's wearing a pair of black capris, a white sweater, and simple diamond studs. She holds herself with grace and dignity, and when she smiles at me, her blue eyes crinkle around the edges.

"Hi there," I say. "How can I help you?"

She straightens, gripping her clutch. "Well, dear, I'm here for something special."

With a smile, I tell her, "Then you've come to the right place. Anything in particular?"

She closes the distance between us until she's standing at the counter, her hands resting there. "I'm Beverly. I'm here for the bonding bouquet," she whispers.

I freeze. The world ceases to exist other than this tiny eight square feet that I occupy with Beverly who has to be mistaken. Were there two bonding arrangements? Nope, I'm sure there was only one.

"Ummm... I think there's been a mistake?" I say, wishing I sounded more confident, less on the verge of total hysteria.

Her eyes widen. Her hands grasp the clutch tighter. "I don't understand. Fernando left me a message to come by."

My blood is pumping, my mind is spinning, and I think I'm

going to be sick. I've given the bonding bouquet to the wrong person. But if that woman earlier wasn't Beverly, who was she?

Sixty seconds later, I learn that this woman ordered the arrangement a year ago for her husband who is suffering from dementia in an effort to bring him back to her along with the memories only the two of them share. "I… I spent summers on the Estrada farm. With my friend, Azalea."

"You knew my grandma?" I ask, feeling sicker by the moment.

"You're Azalea's granddaughter?"

I nod. "Harlow."

At this she bristles like she isn't sure she can trust me since my name is missing the flower designation.

Beverly manages a tight smile I'm sure would look incredibly friendly under normal circumstances. "Your grandmother was a dear friend." The woman is now on the brink of tears, and I want to dig a deep hole and bury myself inside of it. "We've waited a year for this bouquet. Who did you give it to?"

"A woman, young." My mouth is dryer than sandpaper, and my cheeks are so hot I think they might melt right off of my face. "I'm so, so sorry."

Shit! I *knew* the flowers chose wrong when they appointed me guardian.

I have no idea how to fix this, what to do. My mom and aunt are seven hours ahead and won't be awake for hours. "I'll call Fernando," I tell the woman. He'll know what needs to be done. Surely this isn't the first time a mistake like this had been made. Right?

Beverly narrows her gaze like a thought is just occurring to her. "The woman…what did she look like?"

With the phone in my hand, I tell her, "Petite, big hat, sunglasses. To be honest I didn't really get a good look at her."

Oh my God. Someone is going to be bonded without their consent. This is bad. Really, really bad. And worse, this poor woman and her husband are going to be left *un*bonded. I have managed to single-handedly ruin four futures in ten minutes.

With a slow and controlled nod, Beverly purses her lips together and says, "I think I know who stole my flowers."

"What?" My skin is itchy all over, threatening to break into hives any second. "Who?"

"That doesn't matter now," she says in a commanding tone that doesn't fit her elegant demeanor. "We must find her."

"Right. Okay." I'm all in. "But how?"

"She's staying at our hotel, Casa de Sueños. You must make haste."

Why do I feel like I've just been dropped into a Shakespeare tragedy? "Wait!" I blurt, more to myself than to Beverly. "She can't use the bouquet until the moon is out!" I glance out the window to the darkening sky where a faded moon hangs low. The hotel is a mile from here. That's a fifteen-minute run if I'm lucky. I'd ask Beverly to come along so she can identify the perpetrator, but I'm guessing she'd only slow me down.

"I'll fix this," I promise. We both head out, and after I lock the shop, I race down the road before Beverly can say another word.

Running over cobblestone in boots is not recommended. As the moon drifts higher, I pick up my speed, pushing past people without so much as a *sorry*. My lungs won't allow for a single word right now and my legs are burning, and I'm getting a horrific blister on my heel that is forcing me to hobble-run. What the hell is my life? Chasing magical blooms and horrendous mistakes around town?

Dementia? Did Beverly say dementia? And now I know why memory magic was used. Sadly, it won't last. He won't be cured of his dementia by the bouquet, but he will be able hold certain memories that are currently lost to him. That is, if I can get the bouquet back in time.

Half a mile away from the hotel, the darkness looms, the

moon taunts me. I rip off my boots and run in my socks through the streets.

When I get to Casa de Sueños, I'm heaving, sweating, and drowning in my own self-loathing and panic.

Thankfully, I know these grounds and I know the setting for maximum moonlight. Within forty seconds I'm tearing across the lawn, toward the rose garden, all the while searching for that rotten thief. When I cut left through the courtyard, I see her standing at the lookout. No hat. No sunglasses, only long blond hair and a tight green dress with a plunging neckline. The bouquet is in her hands.

Relief floods my senses. She hasn't given it to the man yet, his face I can't make out because he's lost in the shadows. They're talking, I'm accelerating.

She laughs lightly, presses a hand on his chest. Then she's extending the bouquet. He takes it from her, raising the blooms to his face. He turns toward the moonlight.

Ben.

Everything happens so fast I don't remember if I shouted or threw my boots or lunged first, but before I know it, I'm airborne, knocking the flowers out of his hands. The bouquet tumbles to the grass. And somehow, he's gotten tangled up with me. All the air rushes out of me when I land...on top of Ben. It's like diving into concrete.

The girl is screaming, crying, losing her mind to a rage I fear will result in violence and land me in the hospital. He's writhing, I'm wriggling. Our foreheads bang against each other. His hands are around me. No, they're pushing me away.

I manage to catch my breath, tug a twig of fern from my hair, roll off of Ben, and look over, half expecting him to help me up. All I see are his dark eyes, that deep scowl.

And then he launches to his feet and growls, "You again!"

10

⁓⁂⁓

I'm locked in a hot box of dread and terror, bewildered by everything that's happened.

Ben is still glaring at me. At least until the blonde hiccups another sob and just like that she has all his attention.

Who is she? Why would she steal Beverly's bouquet to use it on a man who is clearly enamored enough with her to buy her a gift from an antiquarian bookshop and seek out a romantic restaurant?

"What the hell is going on?" Ben grinds out.

I roll to my knees, collecting the flowers and ferns into some semblance of their original form because no matter what is going on here, I have a mission to help Beverly. To make this right.

The girl doesn't answer. I want so badly to tell him she stole an enchanted bouquet so she could bond him to her, but I'm not about to grant him access to my family's magic. The dawning is instant and alarming: *How did this woman even know about the magic?*

I can feel the heat of Ben's gaze before I see it. "Harlow?" His voice has an edge to it, sharp like a galvanized blade that could slice me in two if I'm not careful.

"You know her?" the woman says indignantly, like she's the affronted party here.

"You lied to me," I tell her, ignoring Ben and cradling the little bouquet tightly against my chest. "These flowers weren't meant for you. You aren't Beverly!"

Ben's hand, the one he was just rubbing across his shadowed chin, is now clenched. His eyes go wide with an understanding, with a knowledge I want to get intimate with.

"My grandmother?" is all he says, and I'm on my feet, my mind in a mad dash to put all the pieces together. If sweet Beverly is Ben's grandmother, then he must know about the magic, right? And if that's true then...

The woman is backing up, scowling at Ben. "I—I just wanted you to..." She swipes at her tears violently. "I wanted you...to..."

The emptiness left in the wake of her words is profound. I can only guess what she is trying to say. I wanted you to love me? Want me?

And for the first time my heart sways toward this woman's corner, and I want to offer her a stem of yarrow for her heartbreak.

I think Ben is going to go on the attack, cut this woman down with his barbed words, but he doesn't. His shoulders nearly soften (nearly) and he says so quietly I have to strain to hear, "You can't fake love." And as painful as those words must be for her to accept, they are delivered with a kindness that surprises me given the circumstances. Ben then adds with an air of finality that would wound even an innocent bystander, "And you can't steal what wasn't meant for you."

The woman's face drains of all color. She stiffens, clears her throat, wipes her nose, and says, "The flowers' magic isn't even real," she cries. "You said so yourself."

"And your actions say otherwise."

Her mouth trembles. She throws her head back, clearly looking for some semblance of control. "Clearly, I was wrong!" She takes a step toward Ben.

I'm too shocked to say another word. Plus I think this is between them; I should give them space, but my body won't move.

"I know what you really wanted here," Ben says.

She shakes her head vehemently. "I was an idiot to think even magic could change you." The woman turns on her heel and walks away.

Ben watches her go, leaving me with a view of his angular back, which is rising and falling with emotionally charged breaths that I swear have increased the temperature several degrees. What's he feeling? Anger? Fear? Sorrow? Regret? I suddenly wish I knew, but I am too filled with relief to worry about it right now.

He turns to me slowly, a half revolution, offering me only a side-glance. "I'll take those now."

I look down at the bouquet in my embrace. "No way. I can't let them out of my sight," I tell him. "I have to deliver these myself."

Just when I think he's going to argue, Ben tips his head, takes a deep breath. "I knew I was right about you."

There is a heavy pause that drinks in all the oxygen between us. But I won't ask, I won't take the bait even though my skin is ablaze, and my brain is replaying the memory of landing on his granite chest, slowing to the moment when our heads turned, when our mouths were inches apart, when I saw a glimmer in his eyes that wasn't surprise but something else.

"You *are* from here," he finally adds. "And…you're an Estrada."

I nod, wondering how much he knows about my family, about his grandmother's childhood summers spent with my grandmother. But first, I have to know the story here. "Who is she?" The woman who would trick you into bonding with her?

"A journalist," he replies, echoing what he told me a couple of days ago. And maybe because he thinks I deserve more or he just wants to get it off his chest, he adds, "We spent some time together. It meant more to her than to me. End of story."

So much more that she came down here with him, stole his grandparents' bonding magic and tried to cast a spell over him? I feel suddenly angry on behalf of this woman who Ben can discard with the flick of his wrist. "Seems like a big leap to go this far for a casual…affair," I say. I don't mean for the words to sound so thick and harsh and judgmental. Or do I?

He turns to fully face me now, and the stature of him makes me want to shrink back, but I don't. I stand there with an armful of magic, waiting for him to fill in the gaps, but he doesn't. Instead, he gestures to the bouquet. "Will it still work?" he asks.

I can still feel the hum of my sisters' powers coursing through the stems, charging the petals. "I think so, but… I thought you didn't believe."

His penetrating eyes never fall from my gaze. His thick brows come together not in a scowl or even a frown, but in a warning. Or is all the tragic excitement of the evening firing up my imagination?

"What I believe doesn't matter," he says, folding his arms over his chest, a defiant gesture that tells me I'm not going to like what *does* matter.

A woman's voice echoes across the lawn. "Harlow!"

I whirl. Beverly is rushing toward me; her arms extended. "You have it! You have it!" she cries.

With exceeding caution, I hand her the bouquet, careful to keep the stems swaddled in the paper, to not touch Beverly in any way. "Don't smell them. At least not right now."

"Will they still work?"

"I think so." *I hope so.*

"You must be there," she insists. "To make sure nothing goes wrong again. To make sure we get it right."

I'm about to argue when I remember Ben standing behind me. I turn to gauge his reaction, but he's gone, his long lean form vanished into the moonlit shadows like he was never here at all. I tell Beverly yes, I will be there. How can I refuse her?

Beverly and William Brandt were bonded at precisely 7:58 p.m. The moon was high, their hands connected, each breathing in the fragrance of the magic as he accepted the bouquet—just as instructed. I knew it the moment it happened. His eyes sparked with flickers of gold, a sure sign that the bonding was complete.

I watched this couple hold each other in the moonlight. His arms around her with a familiarity that made me soar with joy and relief and even wonder.

"Beverly. My Beverly." He said her name like a prayer. A prayer I sensed Mayahuel heard.

Before I left the Brandts, Beverly made me promise to come to brunch at the hotel tomorrow, so she could thank me properly.

"I don't think I deserve a thanks," I said. "I nearly ruined all of this for you."

"No, dear," she says gently. "You saved us."

11

~~❧~~

In the sleepy haze of morning, I half wonder if last night really happened.

But then I see the series of concerned what's up with you texts from my family, and I know they caught wind of yesterday's emotional storm.

I have three missed calls from Dahlia—obviously the appointed emissary this time.

I shoot her a quick text that everything is fine, that I'm just adjusting to being alone on the farm. She seems to buy it, thankfully.

But my body does not.

My rib cage tightens with the fear of what might have been, of nearly failing the Brandts, and the image of such a disaster is enough to make me dizzy.

But nothing bad happened. I fixed it.

After a quick call to Fernando to confirm his X-rays came out okay, I roll out of bed naked and walk to the window. The landscape seems to stretch infinitely; a sea of color greets me as the flowers sway lazily in the gentle breeze as if to say good morning.

I touch my fingers to the glass, savoring this quiet moment, silently thanking the goddess again for blessing the Brandts, and saving my ass.

And then the memory of being held by Ben's eyes, when I was a mere two inches from his lips, drifts across my mind's eye un-invited. A shiver snakes through my body. For a brief breathless second, I actually imagined those lips pressed against my own. Except that I've known men like him. The kind who are cool and calculating and grow thorns inside their hearts.

We spent some time together. It meant more to her than to me. End of story.

Men who discard women like day-old socks.

I huff, then suddenly remember that I do not have an appro-priate outfit for brunch at the House of Dreams Hotel.

At least not here at the hacienda.

In desperation mode, I rummage through my closet six times, each time wondering how scanty that sundress *really* is. Clearly, past me had no problem showing off skin, and present me doesn't either, but I can't. Not today. The five-star hotel maintains a very elegant atmosphere, and the Brandts are so decent and kind, and definitely gave off the vibe of "proper" last night. The last thing I'd want to do is make them uncomfortable.

I raid my sisters' closets and damn if I didn't wish they were pack rats like me. I come up with nothing but old concert and travel T-shirts. I don't even bother tiptoeing into Dahlia's closet. She's a neat freak who doesn't believe in storing anything. In a fit of anxiety, I remember the Christmas closet, the same one where Tía hordes all of her holiday gifts months in advance.

I rush down the hall and across a small courtyard, past the long stone trough-fountain, to her room. I open the built-in wardrobe where I know the goods will be stashed and nearly gasp when

I see the gorgeous cocoa-colored, one-shoulder dress hanging above a stack of shopping bags and wrapped Christmas boxes.

I know just by looking at the design, the smooth lines, the sweeping neckline that this is for Lana. She is going to look stunning in it, I think, inching back, repressing the little devil on my shoulder.

"She'd kill me," I say to myself. "Buuuut this is an emergency." And Lana loves emergencies—she's obsessed with the adrenaline rush, the chaos, the promise of acting out her beloved hero drama. I'm totally sure it's what compelled her to become a lawyer.

Still, I can't just take a dress that wasn't meant for me. So I shoot my cousin a quick text: Hey, can I wear a Christmas gift of yours that I really need right now if I promise to replace it?

It takes her a good ten minutes before she sends the message that I knew she would. I have to know what it is first.

I don't want to ruin the surprise

Is it a good gift? Will I like it?

It's gorgeous

Send me a pic.

Lana

Fine. Wear this surprise gorgeous thing. And don't be silly. You don't have to replace it. Just don't mess it up.

She doesn't ask me to replace it because she knows I'm recently dumped and unemployed. Of course, she does. There are zero secrets in this family. Either way, I'm thrilled for her generosity. I type back, You're my favorite cousin.

Not so fast, Bean. I get an IOU. ♥ ♥ ♥ ♥ ♥

A Lantana IOU is rarely a small thing and always collected, but I'm in no position to argue or negotiate so I text, Deal.

Next, I step into the silk, luxuriating in the way it feels against my skin and then the fact that it fits me like a glove. Blessed be shared genetics. And then I realize that shoes are going to be a problem. I have the biggest feet in the family, and unless I want to wear my ankle boots (which, ouch—I've still got blisters), the not-so-well-thought-out knee-high boots I lugged here from New York, or my gardening shoes, I'm going to have to wear a pair of Mom's boring sandals, toes hanging over and everything.

An hour later, I drive into town, valet park, and hurry into the hotel where I'm already a few minutes late.

The resort is striking with its stone columns, hand-carved furniture, iron candelabra, and rich colorful tapestries. I make my way up to the cozy rooftop restaurant, a beautiful perch with inspiring vistas and unrivaled views of the vibrant town below. Each table is adorned with a different bloom: trumpet vines, bellflowers, and French honeysuckle.

None from the Estrada farm.

Not since Mom had a fallout with the hotel owner over occupancy numbers. The owner had this notion that our flowers would act as a wall of protection against any and all business risks. It didn't matter how many times my mom explained that that isn't how the magic works, that the flowers couldn't guarantee numbers, but the woman refused to listen and pulled the account. According to my godfather, who is the all-knowing town gossip, the hotel's occupancy has since flatlined, never moving above or below a meager 50 percent.

I find the Brandts near the far edge of the rooftop terrace. On the linen-covered table, a silver vase holds a single bluebell. The bloom is not only known to be a truth inducer, but also symbolizes gratitude and just looking at their beaming faces as I make my way over, I know they feel it in abundance.

My heart expands three sizes.

"Harlow!" Beverly says the moment she notices me.

As soon as I take a seat, William sets his hand on top of mine and offers me the kindest smile, one that reaches his blue eyes and emits a warmth that soothes my nerves and makes me instantly glad I said yes to this invitation.

"Isn't it a gorgeous day?" Beverly coos as she gestures to the sun inching across the sky in the distance, washing the town in a creamy-peach light that feels dreamlike.

We all watch the sun with a reverence that seems not only shared but earned, and I feel a heady warmth spread through me that I, Harlow Estrada, had some tiny part to play in this couple's love story. I turn my attention to William, watching him as he takes in the view, and just as he turns back, between one blink and the next, I see it. The flicker of light that sparks across his eyes.

Thank you, Mayahuel. He's still bonded. Of course, he is— that's how the magic works. I guess I worried that I somehow mucked it up.

In the midst of our getting to know each other, I find myself glancing out of the corner of my eye in search of Ben. Shouldn't he be celebrating with his grandparents? It's bad enough he didn't come to the bonding ceremony last night. Maybe he went home. Or maybe he was trying to make things right with the ex. My mind is a storm of maybes and what-ifs when I hear his distinct voice behind me, both gravelly and soothing. "Good morning."

My back is to him so I haven't even laid eyes on him yet, and my face is flushing and my skin is prickling with anticipation.

He comes into my view as he leans in to kiss his grandmother on her cheek. He smells of spices and rain-soaked earth, and it takes everything in me not to tilt closer.

"You're late," Beverly says, tsk-tsking.

"A man should respect time," William says, piling it on but in a playful way.

Ben nods like he's accustomed to his grandparents' jabbing. Then his eyes flick to mine, and with the barest hint of amusement he says, "Good morning, Harlow."

"Hi," I say, as he sits next to me and reaches into his sport coat chest pocket. I hate to admit it, even just to myself, but it's a really (really) good look for him. He removes a small gold-wrapped package and sets it on the table. "I'm late for a good reason," he says with a grimace. "I was fighting with the wrapping paper. This is for the two of you."

And then he looks up. Not at William or Beverly or the divine sun, but at me with the full weight of that Benjamin stare that disarmed me at Pasaporte.

Beverly or maybe William reaches for the package with a sound of delight, but I'm not in that moment. I'm in this other one with Ben.

Those dark deep-set eyes have even more tawny flecks in the sunlight. I know without allowing my gaze to slip beyond his that his jaw is set, his lips are neutral like they're deciding if the moment is worthy of his smile. And all of a sudden, I want to see it, the real one, the one he showed me yesterday when he laughed and his whole face lit up.

His gaze drops to my mouth, my chin, my throat. I gulp the warm air like it's my last breath.

Through a half grin, he says, "I'm glad you're here."

"You look exhausted," Beverly tells him, saving me from having to respond.

He quickly averts his attention. "Didn't sleep much last night."

"Must have been all the hoopla," William puts in.

"So much hoopla," I say, wanting to get into the flow of a conversation that doesn't paint me as the obvious outsider.

"And your quick thinking saved us, Harlow," Beverly says.

Ben cuts his eyes to me; he's nodding, his expression is open and amused, curious. And all I want to do is open that skull of his and peer inside. "You have a habit of saving people, don't you?"

My harrumph comes out as a snort, and I'm mortified that my cool calm facade just blew into smithereens. "Hardly."

"Well, all's well that ends well," William says.

Just then the server brings us family platters of delectable pastries, fresh fruit, and a charcuterie board. "And can you please bring us a round of those grapefruit mimosas?" Beverly asks the man before she turns her attention to Ben's gift. The one that looks like a child wrapped it, and I nearly laugh at the image of him struggling with the paper and tape.

"You didn't have to do this, dear," she says as she opens the package. I find myself leaning forward, itching with curiosity to know what kind of gift giver Ben Brandt is.

It's probably a box of truffles, or a tiny silver frame, or something destined for a garage sale.

It's a tattered book. The spine is close to splitting, the tan cover worn from overuse. Beverly gasps, clutching it so that I can read the title.

Veinte Poemas de Amor y una Canción Desesperada. Twenty Love Poems and a Song of Despair by Pablo Neruda.

Okay, Ben has surprised me...again. But it isn't the surprise that has my skin tingling or my head swimming; it's the fact that Neruda is one of my favorite poets, and this—*this* is one of his most important works. It is not only sensual and romantic but honors the wilderness of Chile in a way that connects the poet's words, his spirit, to the land.

"You remembered," a teary-eyed Beverly says to Ben.

Remember what? I turn a curious eye to Beverly, but it's William who fills in the blanks. "It was my gift to Bev on our first wedding anniversary."

Beverly stares at William lovingly. I know what she's thinking. *He remembers!*

"But it went missing a few years later," William adds.

"And we never found another like it," Beverly puts in.

"It's the same edition," Ben says proudly. "I couldn't believe it when I saw it," he adds while Beverly and William coo over the libro like it's a newborn babe. So *this* is what he bought in the antiquarian bookstore. Okay, so my assumptions were way off and it makes me wonder what else I've gotten wrong about Ben.

When the mimosas arrive, William raises his glass. "A toast to love." His eyes flick to Beverly. "And to destiny."

"To destiny," I murmur just as Ben clinks his glass with mine.

A few moments later, Beverly is entertaining us with stories of her and my abuela Azalea, sneaking off to the river, planting their own brand of magic that never bloomed, making wishes under the stars. "Did you know, Harlow," Beverly says, grinning, "that when I met William it was your grandmother who insisted we check with the flowers to make sure he was worthy."

Ben clears his throat and fiddles with his napkin, a clear signal he's not as comfortable talking about Estrada enchantments as Beverly.

"Oh, Ben," she says lightly, "you are such a fuddy-duddy. Magic is real and the proof is right in front of your eyes." She points to William who clearly remembers his life with Beverly; his recollections this morning are evidence of that. But what does he *not* remember? I wonder. What memories are forever lost?

I feel a pinch of despair thinking that any given moment big or small could be erased from the human heart as if it never happened at all.

Ben arches a single eyebrow and pats his grandmother's hand. "We've been over this, Gram, and we decided last year," he continues, "that I am officially *not* a fuddy-duddy."

Beverly breaks into a fit of giggles then tells me, "At a party last year with friends, Ben won at karaoke."

I smile as I take him in with new eyes. I cannot fathom even in my wildest writerly imagination Benjamin Brandt jamming out on a stage. "Oh my gosh—you have to tell me the song!"

Taking a sip of his mimosa, Ben sets down his glass, making a show of dragging out his answer. Then with stunning confidence he says, "Bee Gees—'Staying Alive.'"

Not obvious. Not ordinary.

I expect him to half smile, to throw me a smirk that lets me know he's kidding, but he keeps his gaze intense and he's waiting to see what my response is going to be. I nearly strain a blood vessel in my neck trying to not laugh, to not give him what he wants: a cynic.

"Great song," I manage, straight-faced. I can't begin to imagine his low gruff voice hitting the high notes of the Bee Gees, but what I wouldn't give to hear it!

Beverly says, "It was so good. Benny has such a good voice." Benny?

At this Ben chuckles, shakes his head. "My grandmother lacks objective judgment when it comes to her grandkids."

William finger-taps the table, frowning like he's trying to figure out his role in all of this, or maybe he's just trying to remember the night Ben took off his fuddy-duddy cloak. I've seen it before. My great-aunt used a similar bonding bouquet for her wife when her memory began to fail. And while the flowers ultimately helped her remember their love, she was still only a shell of herself, a shell who couldn't remember the year sometimes, or who other family members were, or where she was from. There were so many times she possessed the same expression William wears now; one of bewilderment, one of searching for the lost pieces.

No one else seems to notice and I'm not about to ruin this celebration so I don't mention it, but I want to loop him back into the conversation, so I revert to the topic of him and Beverly. "How did my grandmother help you decide William was the one?" I ask.

Beverly sets her fork down and says, "Your grandmother consulted with the Hylocereus tree. She plucked a single flower at midnight and gave it to me, telling me that if it was still open at dawn, William was the one for me."

I smile, thinking about the guardian tree, a vine-like cactus with such rare nocturnal beauty. According to the family history, our farm was created with magic, yes, but also with careful precision. Every crop, every boundary, every vine and tree was meticulously planted according to the goddess's instructions.

"And the flower stayed open," I guess, thinking what an impossible thing that was and feeling filled with a deep pride for my roots.

Nodding, Beverly says, "I still have it pressed between the pages of a book."

William sits back then, looking at me. "What is it like coming from such magic?"

I'm not sure what to say or how to begin, so I simply respond with, "It can be a lot, but it's...pretty amazing."

Ben is silent, allowing his grandparents to have the stage, but I can tell his gears are turning, his judgments are being formed.

"What about you?" I ask. "Where are you all from?" *What's your story?*

"Well," William says, wiping the corners of his mouth with his napkin, "I come from...from..." He freezes.

The moment is like a rush of arctic air and I immediately regret the question.

Ben's eyes soften, and he rushes in to save his grandfather. "A long line of businesspeople," he says.

Beverly takes William's hand lovingly. "His grandad built a small hotel in California that grew into a few dozen."

"Yes," William says, nodding like it's all coming back to him. "That's right. And we now operate all over the world."

Beverly is beaming as she looks at her grandson. "And Ben has been running things out of the California headquarters for the last couple of years since..." She stops herself before admitting William's dementia was the reason. It's a reality that has no place in this celebratory moment.

"Ah, right," I say, glancing at Ben who looks out of sorts. "The business of sleep. Have you always worked with your family?"

"For as long as I can remember." He offers a *I don't really want to talk about this* grimace. And I get the sense that this isn't his dream. To run a series of global hotels. I see no pride or joy in his eyes, only resignation.

So unlike when he told me what sets his soul on fire.

Wide-open expansive land with no end in sight, with nothing on it except possibilities.

The rest of the brunch is small talk but it's engaging, and I become more and more enamored with Beverly and William. Maybe it's Beverly's connection to Azalea or maybe it's our shared experience of magic, or maybe they really are just a charming couple. Their desire to rebond with one another makes me think there actually is a forever kind of love in this world.

"And what do you do?" William asks me.

Shit. How do I answer this without revealing my immediate tortured past? Or without sounding like I'm an unemployed twentysomething still searching for the holy grail of her existence. "I'm a writer," I blurt, stunned as the words fly from my mouth. I've never told anyone that. Only things like, *I want to write.* I've never felt worthy enough to say *I'm a writer.* But wow—it feels good to say.

Beverly looks smitten. "An artist!"

"What do you write?" William asks, his silvery eyebrows rising with interest.

And this is why I should have kept my mouth shut. I should have known such a bold statement would elicit questions like this, questions I'm not sure I can answer.

"Fiction," I say, keeping it general.

Ben smiles, utters, "Words," under his breath, remembering our conversation at Pasaporte. Then, "So, you're a novelist?"

"Trying to be."

Thankfully, at the same moment I'm saved by the bill. Ben takes it and nearly arm-wrestles with his grandmother over who is to pay. "Benny, this is our treat."

William's nodding and reaching, but Ben's already pulling out his credit card. "Please, this is on me."

With a sigh, Beverly says to me, "We cannot thank you enough for everything."

"I'm just so happy it all worked out," I say.

"If you don't mind, Harlow," Beverly says in a quieter voice. "Before we go, I have to ask you a question." I nod my consent as she leans in close like a schoolgirl with a secret. "What is your brand of magic?"

Ben snaps his gaze to me. "You...you have a brand of magic?"

"They all do," Beverly chirps. "It's quite fascinating."

"You didn't mention that," he tells his grandmother with an expression I can't quite read.

"I just did."

Ben swivels to face me, waiting for my answer and my body fills with an overwhelming dread. I don't owe anyone the truth, but I don't want to lie either. Plus I'll never see them again and that bluebell is taunting me with its "truth" buds, magic or not. "I don't have any magic," I say. A heavy shame stomps across my chest. I wish I could say I'm used to the truth by now, but I'm not and I'm not sure I ever will be. Every time I say the words, they seem to grow sharper, crueler, more dangerous.

William says, "But...?"

"It passed over me," I explain, forcing composure. "It's the reason I wasn't named after a flower."

"Oh, Harlow," Beverly says kindly. "I imagine that is challenging but, no matter. You are a force. I could tell when you went running off to save my bouquet." Her eyes flick to Ben whose gaze is still fixed on me. "And if it weren't for you, Harlow, poor Benjamin here would be bonded with that—"

"But I'm not," Ben asserts.

William's nodding. "Better to deal in real facts. Not what-ifs. Those only lead to disappointments and heartache."

Or the truth, I think.

"Well, I hope we'll see you again, Harlow," Beverly says. "Won't you stay in touch?"

"Of course. And you can come visit the hacienda anytime," I tell her as I begin to stand, unsure if this is mine and Ben's exit too.

"No, no," Beverly insists. "You sit. Enjoy the view."

Ben stands when his grandparents leave and just when I think he might follow, he plants himself in a chair across from me, takes a bite of pan dulce and says, "Is it hard?"

"Is what hard?"

"Not being like the rest of your family."

I stiffen, wondering where he's going with this, but I refuse to falter. "We're alike in other ways. In the ways that count."

He nods, stares at me with a question mark. *Like what?*

"And you don't like running the hotels, do you?" I ask, landing the ball back in his court.

He stretches his long legs in front of him and crosses his arms. Like he's settling in for a good story...or interrogation. "Why would you say that?"

"I'm a good read of people."

"Your reads aren't exactly accurate," he says, a corner of his mouth lifting into an almost smile. "I believe at the café you told me, what was it? Oh, right. I was the victim of a crime."

I choke back a laugh. "I said you *looked* like the victim of a crime."

"You also thought the book was for Alicia."

Oh, is that her name? Damn. He has me there.

"And I bet you thought the restaurant was for her too."

Don't fidget. Don't fidget. "It seemed a logical conclusion."

"Except you don't default to logic."

I hate this man.

"Maybe," I say, then to drive my point home I add, "But I grew up in a world you wouldn't understand."

He leans closer and I catch another whiff of rain-soaked earth. *Try me.* "Maybe," he echoes. "But I can't deny that my gramps is different today."

I hold the grin that wants to make an appearance on my face in check. "So how is it that you believe in luck but not magic?"

His gaze falls to my bare shoulder. He holds it there a moment longer than is comfortable. My skin feels like it's erupting in flames while my heart begins to gallop away, and then he meets my eyes again. "Luck can be made."

"So can magic," I say, and immediately regret my choice of words. It can only be made if you already possess it. Suddenly, I want more than anything to make Benjamin Brandt a believer.

"Why didn't you go to their ceremony last night?" I ask, not entirely sure he'll answer the question.

He catches me by surprise when he responds with, "It wasn't about me. Seemed like a private moment."

"Beverly asked me to go," I say as I push my plate away and glance across the town's colorful rooftops. "It was really lovely."

He watches me, squinting as the sun slants across his eyes. "I got all the details. My grandmother loves to spin a story."

"Sounds like my aunt," I say with a breathy chuckle.

Ben's gaze is steady, strong, focused so intently on me that I fear I have jam smeared across my face. "So, I have to know, Harlow."

Oof. That's a terrifying lead in, one that's making it hard to breathe.

"Did you really run across town last night?"

Okay. This I can handle. "I did." I'm unable to hold my smile in check another second. "Barefooted."

He matches my smile. "No."

"Yes."

"Why?"

"Blisters."

Shaking his head in amused disbelief, he glances at his watch. The telltale sign that this conversation is over, but then, "Can I ask about the novel? What it's about?"

Under the table I twist my fingers together. *Well, Ben, it's about nothing because I haven't written it.* "I don't really want to talk about it...until it's done."

"Superstitious?"

"Something like that," I say, wanting to change the topic. "So why didn't you tell me you knew I was an Estrada at the bookstore?" I ask. "And don't tell me you forgot."

Ben's mouth fans into a smile that makes my pulse race. "Why didn't you tell me you're a writer?"

I release an exasperated breath. "I sort of did."

He leans forward, placing his elbows on his knees. "Well, when the book's *done...* I want to read it."

Done. Just the thought of reaching that part of the journey makes my entire body buzz with anticipation and anxiety and hope.

A few moments later, we've made our way downstairs and into the warm sun where I wait for my car. I expect Ben to leave, to tell me goodbye, but he stands there with me like he has nowhere else to be.

I turn to him at a sudden loss for words. What do you say to someone you want to see again, to someone you don't want to say goodbye to, whose story you want to hear, whose dreams you want to know? I feel all of this and more in a single instant, but my words betray me. "Well, good luck with...the hotels and..."

"One more thing." He reaches into his jacket pocket, retrieving what looks like a tiny journal no bigger than his palm. "I went back—I found these on the ground last night. They're from the magic bouquet." He opens the leather notebook. There, pressed between the pages, are five Inca lily petals.

"I didn't know if—" there is a vague and unexpected shyness in his voice "—if you needed them for anything."

How did I miss these? Thankfully, it didn't change the bonding result.

He's already encircling his hand around my wrist and sweeping the petals into my palm.

It's a gentle, kind, and unexpected act. His touch is warm, charged with an energy that draws me closer. Or is it the petals that are vibrating with a magic that isn't Cam's or Lil's or any other kind that I've ever felt?

A tremble works its way through me. I look up, trying to ignore the stab of surprise in my chest when I realize that this small gesture tells me something about Ben: he wants to believe. Maybe.

"Something wrong?" Ben asks. There's a gleam in his eye that wasn't there a moment ago, a look of intensity like he can see right through me.

I shake my head just as the valet pulls my vehicle forward.

Ben steps back. His mouth is barely parted. I stare at his open expression and something comes over me.

"You…you should come see the hacienda too," I stammer, not wanting this moment to end. Not wanting to watch him walk away again. "If you wanted." I sound like a child, and I immediately regret my overzealousness. God, Harlow, pull it together!

There's a moment, a small hesitation. *Say yes.*

He wraps his hand in mine gently. The simmering heat in my belly intensifies and all I can think is, he just got better looking. How is that possible? A rush of excitement burns through me…until Ben says, "I can't."

I'm falling through the concrete, straight into the fires of hell.

Then, like he isn't sure what to do with my hand still in his, he shakes it awkwardly and lets go. "I mean, not right now. I've got a plane to catch."

"Right," I manage. "Sure. Okay. Well…" *Walk away, Harlow. Be the one to walk away.*

"But maybe…" He hasn't even finished his sentence and my pulse is scrambling away at rabbit speed. He hesitates like he isn't sure how to speak the words on the tip of his tongue. "Maybe I'll see you again sometime."

Maybe. Sometime.

I am all too familiar with those words and their potential meanings: *I may or I may not want to see you. I may or I may not really think you're worth it.*

"Or I could call you," he says with a pained tone that makes me wonder how he really feels. In an instant of intolerable lucidity, I remember how thoughtlessly he spoke about Alicia. The last thing I need is to get caught up in another man's drama, regardless of how attracted I am to him. Still, I'm not ready to close the door with any finality, so I say, "Why don't you give me your number?"

His face holds an expression of something between amusement and surprise. I feel suddenly unmoored. And there it is, that winning smile that makes me go weak in the knees. He nods and in less than twenty seconds he's put his number into my phone.

Then in a slow, measured movement Ben leans down. He's coming in for a hug and my body is already meeting him halfway, except we both move in the same direction and I end up bumping my forehead against his nose. We break apart with an embarrassed chuckle.

"Are you okay?" I ask, rubbing my forehead.

"No blood," he says playfully. "Always a good sign. You?"

"No blood," I echo.

"Señorita?" the valet says to me politely, before he tells me he needs to move my car to make room for the others if I'm not going to take it now.

Ben pockets the tiny journal. "Good luck…with the book."

"Same… I mean with—" it's too late to retract the words, to stop myself "—the hotels."

He offers only a tight smile as I cringe, wave another good-bye, and get into my car. And just as I drive away, I take one last look in the rearview mirror at Benjamin Brandt walking in the opposite direction.

12

Under a starry sky, I google Benjamin Brandt.

But it's like searching for a first edition in a city library. Nearly impossible. Sure, there is the occasional interview that reveals a distracted business guy doing the occasional perfunctory interview, and there's an announcement about his new position in some business journals, but other than that, he has a ghost's digital footprint.

The western courtyard of the hacienda is small, enclosed with high stone walls overgrown with climbing roses, gifting whoever is present with their lingering sweet scent. A lower courtyard can be glimpsed through a stone archway, its steps lined with small votive candles set in blue glass.

I tug my long black cardigan tighter around me against the night chill, curl my knees into my chest, and sip my merlot. "He's hiding in plain sight."

I can see it in his carefully chosen headshots, the ones that reveal a fake smile and an expression of forced interest that whispers, *I'd rather be anywhere else.*

I'm torturing myself doing this search. I know this and I do it anyway. I'm probably never going to see him again, and I really shouldn't want to. Ben is the kind of man women lose themselves to, and I can't get lost right now. Not when I can feel a story bubbling beneath the surface. I owe this to myself, to the book, to my future.

After my second glass of wine, I stumble across Alicia—his ex's—Instagram. Okay, maybe stumble is a stretch. I navigated my way through a web of connections to reach her. Only because I'm curious who Ben would "spend time with." Her feed is a highlight reel of a pretty blonde traveling the world, enjoying life, partying with her friends, and otherwise smiling like she means it. There isn't a single mention or image of Ben, which I find odd. Unless, she deleted them or maybe he really was telling the truth about how little time they spent together.

We spent some time together. It meant more to her than to me. End of story.

That could describe my relationship with Chad in three short sentences. He was always talking about a future I knew I wouldn't occupy and, still, I never said a single word to disabuse him of the delusion.

I gaze at the five petals, at their simplicity and softness, wondering why Ben would have decided to save them.

I'm about to abandon my Ben search when my eyes catch a headline and my fingers are already dancing across the touch pad to open it. It's an article about his parents' ugly divorce, before they were both killed in an airplane crash.

Ben was only eight at the time, and his older sister seventeen, according to the article. I feel a stab between my ribs, imagining how painful the entire public tragedy must have been for him and his family. Wondering how this event shaped him, changed him, closed him off. Maybe he's one of those men who is commitment phobic to a fault because he has too much un-processed suffering. Wow—I sound like Dahlia. She'd have a field day with Ben, I'm sure of it. But my instinct tells me there is something else there, just beneath his surface, something silent, unsettled…waiting.

I stare at his contact on my phone's screen. It would only take the press of a button, one touch of my finger to call him. And I want to; I want to hear his voice, to talk to him about that piece of land he mentioned, to see if the undeniable connection between us translates to long-distance too. But I can't.

A warm breeze drifts across the courtyard, wrapping its arms around me before it sails up the rosebushes, dancing between their stems and thorns.

Begin. Begin. Begin.

I know what's being asked of me. I understand what the *it's time for the beginning* dream means now. My book. The story that is swirling around me like dust that I can't manage to grab hold of.

My heart clenches like a closed fist. *I only have a first line*, I want to tell the roses, but I'm too afraid of their thorns so I say nothing.

That night I sleep with the window open; the scents of honeysuckle and lavender drift into my bedroom. Both are messengers of devotion and constancy.

Draped in their loyalty and the hush of the hacienda, I repeat that first line I can't get out of my head:

"The land knew her first. The land knew her first."

And then, as if by magic, the next line comes to me, so full, so complete I grab my journal and write it down before it floats out the window.

Before she took her first breath, before she opened her eyes to this world, the land knew her heart.

★ ★ ★

Call it ridiculous, call it magical thinking, but I wake up with a smile planted on my face, a smile of absolute joy that the next line came to me. But what's even more meaningful is this profound sense that I can do this thing. I can create this story that feels like its burning its way through my chest.

The next two days slip by with the rhythm I have become accustomed to on the farm.

There is an energy here, a hum of movement and breath that is present in every moment of weeding, planting, and harvesting. I so clearly remember my grandmother's worn hands turning the soil that seemed to tremble at her touch. Even when she was diagnosed with cancer and told to rest, she'd wake at dawn and commune with the flowers. Whenever I was visiting during the summer, she'd wake me and tell me that she had a surprise for me and I was always disappointed that it was the sunrise or the birth of a new bud, or a nest filled with baby birds. And now I wish I could relive every single moment with her. To tell her that I now see what she was trying to show me—the ordinary can be miraculous if we allow it.

In life and on the farm, my abuela always told me, *everything is about timing.*

When to plant is just as important as when to harvest or when to pick blooms for the longest show and most potent magic. Some require moonlight, or morning mist, or afternoon sun. Some merely require a breath, a hello, a gentle besito that asks permission before the bloom is plucked.

Measuring time by the life of flowers is a really beautiful way to exist. And somehow in my daily life *out there* I'd forgotten. While it's not easy to go from the bustle of New York to the blissful quiet of La Casa de las Flores y Luz, I'm becoming more accustomed to it, not because I don't love solitude, but because I've never had such an extended version of it and there is a sort of secluded loneliness to the silence that I've never known.

During the day I bike to town, check on the shop, laze about Pasaporte (maybe looking for Ben's First Impressions entry, which I never find), read, swim, and write. The words come, but not the right ones, not the emotionally charged ones I know belong in my story. I'm strangely okay with this. Okay with the fact that I spend more time scratching out the sentences than formulating new ones until the pages in my journal look like a Jackson Pollock painting. It's okay if my process is about starts and stops, a map veering off in multiple directions. It's more than I've ever had before.

Before dinner, I make my usual farm rounds; saying *good-night* and *thank you* to the flowers as I pass, a ritual that is a sacred and tranquil act, made even more so by the setting sun, which has painted the sky a glorious rosey hue. I'm so distracted by its beauty, I almost step on the large silver hoop earring lying in the center of the brick-lined path. An earring that wasn't here last night.

I'm too far off the main road for this to belong to some lost tourist. I dial Fernando.

He answers the phone with, "Hola, Harlow."

"Hi, Fernando. Hey, did you see anyone on the farm today?"

"No. Por que?"

"I found an earring on the north border, and it wasn't here last night."

"Que raro. I was checking out the irrigation near there earlier, but I didn't lose an earring," he says with a chuckle.

I laugh too, but the frown still forms. "How's the arm?"

"I used some of that healing salve your mamá gave me and I'm good as new."

"Glad to hear it. Okay, well, let me know if you see anyone trespassing," I tell him as an uneasy feeling settles in my gut.

"Do you need me to come and check things out?"

"No, it's okay."

"Claro. I'll double-check the lock on the gates tonight, and walk the fence to make sure there are no breaks. No te preo-cupes."

To most, a seemingly innocuous object like an earring would mean nothing, but when you live on a well-protected magical farm, it means everything. My senses are heightened, and I feel tense and on guard as I make my way back to the hacienda.

That's when I notice an unfamiliar white bud growing be-tween the flagstones like an errant weed. A few feet later there is another flower and another like breadcrumbs leading me home. They look a bit similar to elderberry but smaller and more fra-grant. Squatting to get a better look, I pluck the flower from the ground—its scent is subtle with notes of honey and summer rain, and its thin but sturdy green stem is exactly like the one I dreamed of, the one that grew from the pages and wrapped around my hands, climbing up my arms and into my mouth.

Okay, maybe I've spent too much time alone on the farm, I tell myself as I reach for a logical explanation like, *I must have seen these before I dreamed them.*

Pressing my hands into the warm dry soil, I wonder how these beauties sprouted with no water, no care. The loose dirt gets beneath my nails as I turn the soil over and over, in a semi-hypnotic fashion that deepens with each turn. I feel the weight of it for a blink before I let it sift between my fingers.

I eat my dinner by the blue glow of the pool. Thankfully, my mom and aunt have left me nourishment: squash blossom soup, hibiscus flower tacos, lavender flan, and quail with rose petal sauce.

Beneath the pink swirled sky, I send a group text to my sisters with a photo of the hibiscus flower tacos topped with roasted corn, cotija, and avocado slices. Thinking of you.

It takes all of fifteen seconds for their responses.

Lil: that's just cruel.

Cam: I NEED

Then, to drive the dagger even deeper, I text: So good. I should come home more often. I send a selfie of me smiling, corn tortilla poised to enter my mouth.

Cam: Ugh. I'm eating leftover sushi rn.

Lil: what else did you get, Bean?

I quickly tell my sisters the recipes I've been enjoying the last three nights. There's a pause in the flurry of texts, and then...

Lil: oh shit.

Me: what

Then, as if my sisters are all on the same wavelength, Cam texts, hibiscus...lavender...rose?

In a sick and slow awakening, I consider each of the meals prepped in the refrigerator, how they were all made with a bloom of some sort, each symbolizing something similar, something that leads to the same place: unbridled passion. A flowering of the heart. Still, I tell myself that there's nothing to worry about if the food isn't actually enchanted.

I look down at my plate. I've already polished off one taco and was just about to eat the second half of the last one. And that's on top of the last two night's dinners. I feel suddenly queasy, and I'm not sure if it's psychosomatic.

Surely I would have sensed magic if there was any to be found, right? I've always been able to feel the hum of its vibration. Or, have I been so distracted, so lost in my own world that I didn't even notice?

Cam: Is the food enchanted??

Lil: Get drunk. It'll reduce the effects.

Me: Mom and Tía would never dose me with magic and I would have sensed it.

Lil: unless they hid it

No way. That would go against our steadfast belief that magic is a two-way street, not something to conceal.

Cam: How are you feeling? Maybe they accidentally used some enchanted flowers.

No way would they be that careless with magic, I tell myself as I wrestle with the reality in front of me. I'm 100 percent imagining it. See? This is what days of forced isolation does to a person.

My phone begins to ring. It's Cam. When I answer, she loops Lil in and I launch into the conversation with, "Guys, I'm just overreacting, right?"

Lil is in full *I'm a doctor* mode when she says, "How do you feel? Any night sweats? Moments where you don't feel like yourself? Weird dreams?"

"Lil, those are so generic. Glad you went to med school to read me back WebMD," I tell her. "Everyone has weird dreams and moments where they don't feel like themselves." My pulse begins to race. Purely psychosomatic, I reassure myself.

Cam says, "This is different. If magic blooms were used in those recipes, you'd feel the effects for sure."

"But let's be real," Lil puts in. "Lavender is known to create a calm and open mind, roses open the heart, and hibiscus? Well...that's all about creativity."

"Except I don't feel calm," I say, trying to suppress my panic. If I wanted my heart and mind opened, I'd do it myself, I think angrily before reaching another conclusion: Who said they were closed to begin with?

"But none of that could come out unless Mom or Rosa spelled the flowers," Cam says.

My skin is beginning to feel prickly. "I have to go."

"Okay, but stop eating that food," Lil says. "And get drunk. It'll nullify everything."

Cam sighs. "Liliana, that's not true and it's terrible advice."

After we hang up, a sharp anger unfurls inside of me. And just as the dark sky blooms, I send my mom a text: Tell me you didn't do this. The food, the hibiscus and roses and lavender aren't infused with magic. You didn't, right?

For good measure, I gulp down the half glass of wine. I feel fine, perfectly normal if you discount the shiver snaking up my spine. The ache in my chest.

"I need to shake this off," I tell myself as I begin to tug off my sweater so I can throw myself into the pool and drown my suspicions. But I only get one arm free when a sudden force grips me—a spark, a flame, a momentum that surges.

I squeeze my eyes closed. *This isn't happening. It's not happening.*

The energy coursing through me is hot, forceful, wild. An unmistakable pulsing of magic.

Unable to be still another moment, I stand. I try to pace but there isn't enough movement to it, not enough heat. So I run.

Across the courtyard, out the gate, down the stone path, beneath the orange blossoms, past the ancient maguey plant that signifies the very spot my great-great-grandmother met Mayahuel and promised her future and all her descendants' futures to the goddess.

A new fury grips me.

I didn't agree to this life bound by magic but never in possession of it.

I run until my legs burn, until they want to give out, until they've carried me to the edge of my barren garden. For the first time ever, I hate this jardín, hate that it bears my psyche for everyone to see. Hate that unlike the rest of my family, no magic will ever grow in this soil.

If I've ever felt the punishment of my name, it's now. A heap of stones.

I feel an unbearable inexplicable ache inside of me, like I need to vomit the last three nights of magic, but I can't.

All around me, the night closes in. It's in the darkness, and the spiraling bats; it's in the chirping crickets and the swaying branches. It's in the night blooms reaching their stems toward me like helping hands.

Tears prick my eyes.

Tears that have been locked away for so long I'm not sure how long it will take to spend them. I don't like to cry; I don't like to give myself over to untempered emotion, but tonight the hibiscus has twisted its way into my heart.

Dropping to my knees, the tears begin to flow, down my cheeks, my neck, straight into the ground. I dig my hands into the earth, plowing deeper and deeper, chucking heaps of soil to the side. Imagining what it would be like to bury myself in the magic of the soil.

I cry for so many things. The choices I've made, the fear that I allowed to hold me prisoner, the words I can't seem to write, and the magic I'll never possess.

I cry for the woman I want to become. For the woman I might never be.

Begin.

The whisper is so slight, so distant I think it's the wind or my magic-hyped imagination.

I lie across the dirt. It feels like a soft blanket wrapping me in its cool serenity. I pull my knees into my chest and give into the magic, allowing the tears to fall, the emotions to flow freely. I don't know when I'm pulled into a deep sleep, but when I open my eyes, I'm curled into a ball, my face pressed to the earth. The garden is covered in morning mist, so thick I can't see two feet in front of me. The silence enfolds me, and all I can hear is the beating of my own heart.

The world smells like the beginning of summer, like first love and open corazónes and moonlit kisses.

I can feel Mayahuel's presence as I walk through the mist back to the hacienda. It's in the way the flowers stir, in the vibration beneath my skin. It's in the whisper of the morning breeze. And the mysterious white flower that has doubled in size. And I feel a peace that I have never experienced before.

The land knew her first.

There is no rush, only the air in my lungs and the words that will wait for me.

Before she opened her eyes to this world, before she took a breath, the land knew her heart.

Back in my room, I open my journal and write the next line: *It was a lost heart.*

13

‧⁕‧

I'm in the middle of writing about the girl with the lost corazón, inching toward the answer to the question: *Will she ever find it?* when my cell vibrates.

I had turned my phone to Do Not Disturb, but forgot that repeated calls from a chosen few, aka my family, will push the notification.

It's a couple of texts from my mom: I swear to you we did not infuse any magic in those dishes.

P.S. How's the farm? How are you?

Relieved, but confused, I text back: All good. Just nearly ruined a bonding. Had a near breakdown last night and slept in the garden. How's Italy?

Ignoring the question, she knocks out one of her own: Why would you think I infused the flowers?

My mom is impeccable with her word and has never lied to

me before, but if she didn't enchant my meals, then why did I feel all that magic and have such a visceral reaction last night?

I've never experienced anything like it. Which begs the question, why didn't my family descend on me like vultures? My emotions were flaring with the heat of Venus, way too high for them not to have noticed and yet…no one did.

Regardless, I sort of love this new veil of privacy. For once.

I had some dreams, I punch out, thinking right now vague is better.

Three little blinking dots tells me she's typing. Seems like a dissertation since it's taking so long, and I worry it's a million questions I don't want to answer that are going to begin with *what kind of dreams?* and likely end with *what did you feel exactly?*

But the only message I get is, I hope you are enjoying the peace and quiet. Love you.

The next day, I feel so invigorated with story ideas that my pen doesn't lift off the page. I write about Violeta, a young woman who inherits a magical plot of land from an estranged aunt and is furious when she learns that if she wishes to claim it, she must not only live on the farm, but cultivate it as well. It's a hard sell considering she's San Francisco born and bred and doesn't know a black-eyed Susan from a sunflower.

Violeta watched as the morning fog shrouded the city, creating a sense of placelessness, a vacant space between here and there. She found herself longing, but for what she didn't know. A ringing phone pulled her from her reverie. Annoyed by the distraction, she strode across the living room to answer, not knowing that her life was about to change forever.

Just then I hear a sharp scream. I jump up and run out of the courtyard and toward the sound on the other side of the wall. There I see a woman ducking, swatting, and generally freaking out over a couple of bees she has clearly pissed off.

"Stop jumping around," I tell her.

She spins toward me, panic-stricken. I stop in my tracks. Alicia.

My mind is so busy trying to connect the dots that I almost miss the flowers leaning back as if a wind has moved them away from her feet that are stomping around carelessly.

And as the flowers shift, so do the bees, but not before one stings her on the cheek.

Her shriek is enough to make me cringe, but a second later I'm next to her, telling her, "They're gone. Are you okay?"

"It stung me!"

"Well to be fair, the bee thought you were trying to kill it."

She cups a hand over her now reddening face that is five seconds from puffing up. "I was just minding my own business."

"On a private farm?" I can't help it—her unexpected arrival, her blatant trespassing has struck a match inside of me that burns with indignation.

Alicia's fear and annoyance vanishes with a bright but forced smile. "You're right. I am trespassing, but..." She sucks in a sharp breath. "Do you have anything for this?"

I want to send her on her way, walk her back to the main gate and watch her hike down the dusty road toward town, but my heart won't let me. Besides, what if she's a crazy litigious person and decides she wants to sue us for her injuries and then tells some judge I didn't even help her when she asked.

Clearly, I've been listening to Lantana too much.

"You're going to make it worse if you keep scratching at it," I tell her, making a point to lead her back to the house via the north route so she sees as little of the farm as possible.

"This place is really stunning," she says as we enter a shaded patio. I gesture for her to sit on the wooden bench before I go inside and grab a pair of tweezers, some cortisone cream, and the earring I'm now convinced belongs to her. When I return, Alicia's typing something into her phone.

Upon my approach she jerks her head up. Other than her swelling right cheek, she really is classically pretty. Her eyes go wide at the sight of the tweezers. "You're not touching my face with those."

"The stinger has to come out, so either I do it," I tell her, "or I can bring you a mirror and you can do the honors."

She hesitates, smirks, then says, "Just make it quick."

And I do, even though she's squirming like a toddler. Then I hand her the tube of cream. "So you want to tell me why you're here?"

She applies the cream gingerly, wincing like a baby. Jesus—hasn't she ever had a bee sting? "My name is Alicia Jones," she says. "I know you probably think I'm awful—I mean I don't know what Ben told you about me—"

"He didn't need to tell me anything," I say, cutting her off. "You stole a bouquet that didn't belong to you."

"The magical one?"

Heat rushes my chest. "Magical?" I say with a tone that insinuates she's a lunatic.

She stands and offers me that winning smile again. "Look, I'm a journalist and I just want the real story. I mean—your family, this farm, the legend of it all is so compelling and I'd love to do an feature article on your family. Really show the world who you are. People would love it, and it could be really good for business."

She's got to be kidding me. I have to force myself to breathe. "I don't know what you heard or where you heard it..."

"From Beverly."

No way. Beverly would never reveal our family's secret. "Then you're mistaken. And I have some things to do, so if you don't mind."

Alicia's face softens and her blue eyes sparkle even in the shade. It's so clear what Ben saw in her physical appearance, but her vibe, her energy is all wrong.

"Can't I just ask you a few questions?" she asks.

"No."

She stares, and I watch as her expression shifts from curious to frustrated. "Look, I know I probably should have called, but I didn't have your number and I only came here to check things out, to see for myself and…"

I hand her the silver earring. "You must have left this here when you were checking things out yesterday."

Her mouth tightens into a thin line. "If you change your mind…"

"I won't. I'll walk you out."

Alicia sighs, reading my cues for what they are—*you're not welcome here and I don't trust you to leave on your own.*

We make our way around the house and to the main drive that leads to the road in silence. As I open the wrought iron gate, she turns to me and offers a shy smile. "I don't love him."

Him. Ben.

"I just wanted to see if the spell really worked," she adds. "Can't blame me for fact-checking."

"There is no spell—it's a legend as you said. One that sells a lot of flowers," I tell her. "We get journalists like you all the time, and they all leave disappointed."

She hesitates, then says, "Interesting," like the word is a loaded gun.

And as she walks away, I can't help but wonder why I feel like I've just helped her pull the trigger.

For the next week, I'm on guard. Against edible flowers, and uninvited journalists, and mysterious white blooms that seem to be cropping up everywhere, growing so fast I begin to cut them back to clear the walkways.

I've considered sending my mom or sisters a photo of the flower, but I don't want to appear like I can't handle things. I really want to make this work, even if it means flying solo for now.

Which ends up working in my favor because I'm lost in Violeta's story, and when my mind does sneak away to other places like

Alicia: *I don't love him*. And Ben: *It meant more to her than to me. End of story*, I force it back to the page, to a world I *can* control.

As I sip at some deliciously smoky mezcal and continue writing, I realize that the truth depends on who's doing the telling. Or maybe the truth is in what's *not* said, like the threat I clearly sensed when Alicia was here.

When my head hits the pillow that night, all I can think is, gracias a Dios that Mom and Tía are coming home tomorrow.

I can hand over the reins, responsibility, and worry, freeing up more headspace for my book.

I roll over and stare at the bouquet of white flowers I have affectionately named Sueños. A good name I decide because they first came to me in a dream, one I've tried to interpret repeatedly, discarding every meaning until I finally jotted this in my journal: *The blooms are a dream that sprouted from the pages, that attached themselves to me, that grew along my body and went in search of my voice.*

A question in tiny letters lingers beneath the entry: *Will I ever find it?*

14

Mom and Tía come home with armfuls of gifts and stories from their travels the next day.

I'm captivated by all of it, especially the Swedish man named Anders Tía met in the tiny town of Orvieto.

"It's nada," she insists, but her smile tells another story.

Mom laughs. "We'll see." Then turning to me, she asks, "Anything interesting happen around here?"

Define interesting. The near missed bonding, the nosy journalist poking around, the dream flowers sprouting up all over, the words pouring out of me?

"And you're staying on for a bit?" Tía asks with a hopeful lilt in her voice.

Where would I possibly go? I want to tell her. I've given it some thought. Believe me. I could hang with any one of my sisters or cousins, but truth be told, I'm not ready to leave the farm, and more importantly I have a nagging sense that there is something for me here—I'm just not sure what that is yet.

"No plans to leave yet," I say.

Mom offers a knowing smile.

"Did you really think we would infuse magic in your meals?" Tía asks with an air of indignant surprise as she pokes her head into the fridge where the so-called evidence still rests.

I don't bother trying to hide the truth. "Yeah, I did. I had a bizarre reaction to the flowers, got all feverish and... I don't know...sort of clammy."

"Sounds more like food poisoning than magic," my aunt teases, tugging what's left of the lavender flan out of the fridge. After a sniff, she screws up her face. "I am telling you...there is not a single ounce of sorcery in this now rotten dish."

My mom hasn't taken her eyes off of me. She's looking for something, for the truth that my words don't reveal and I can feel my cheeks flush. "We would never trick you like that," she finally says with a seriousness no text could convey.

"It probably *was* some kind of reaction to the food," I say. "I must have left it out too long or something."

Tía tosses the flan into the trash. "See?" she says to Mom. "You worried for nothing. Harlow is fine. Even has some color, thank Dios. Pale is not your look, querida."

My mom nods, but she isn't agreeing with the assessment of the sun-kissed color of my skin. And after Tía leaves, Mom pours us each a glass of cinnamon tea with fresh mint leaves.

I take the lead before she can begin her interrogation. "I don't want to talk about it anymore."

She's going to pry; she's not going to let this go because she never does. She digs and digs until she reaches the answer she's looking for, so I'm bowled over when she simply says, "Okay."

Feeling both empowered and confused, I take a sip of tea and set the thick blue-rimmed glass down when my mom leans against the counter as the sun sets in a magnificent show of gold and pink behind her.

With a resigned sigh, she studies me. "I sense something is different with you, Harlow."

"My tan?" I joke.

She doesn't take the bait. "Something profound, and if you want to talk about anything..."

Is she really coming in the back door? Trying another angle to get me to spill my guts? I feel a tremble moving up my legs. The last thing I want to do is dissect what happened to me that night in the garden. Usually, I can talk to my mom about anything, but this? It feels too private, too deep. Too everything. Plus I'm so embarrassed at how broken I felt, how easily the tears poured out, and even though Mom's right, something profound did happen, I can't bring myself to relive the moment, especially if I can't even explain it to myself. "Thanks," I tell her, "but can we just drop it?"

With a nod, she pushes off the counter, and turns to gaze out the window that opens onto a small courtyard replete with potted olive trees, silvery succulents, and a three-tier fountain with water cascading over its mossy edges.

"What's that?" she asks, and before I can determine what she means she's already making her way through the double doors to the outside. I follow her to the edge of a distressed wood farm table where she's studying a tall vase of the white Sueño flowers. "Where did these come from?" she asks.

"They were springing up everywhere," I tell her. "And they smell really good so I made a few arrangements. What are they?"

"What do you mean, everywhere?" There's a tiny crack in her voice that sets me on edge.

"Like weeds," I tell her, "between stone crevices and in bushes and... I don't know...just everywhere."

"This is canto."

"There's a flower called *song*?" I stare at her dumbfounded. "How come I've never heard of it?"

"Because it only grows on our farm, or at least it used to."

Mom gazes at the arrangement with a sense of wonder that's making me nervous. "Its full name is Canto de Corazón named by your great-grandmother. It stopped growing here at least forty years ago."

"Why did it stop?"

"It just never sprouted again after her death," she says, flicking her gaze to mine. "We thought that it was uniquely connected to her, but clearly that isn't the case."

"What do you mean?"

"I mean that this bloom has reemerged for a purpose. Maybe it has something to do with what it symbolizes."

"Which is what?"

"Cycles. Endings. Rebirth."

Heat floods my cheeks, neck, chest. The flower's symbolism isn't entirely lost on me, and it wouldn't be the first time a bloom has sprung in response to some event in one of our lives. That's how my mom knew she was pregnant for the first time. Salix, a type of willow sprouted right outside her bedroom window overnight, and its meaning? Motherhood.

Rebirth.

Is that the word I've been searching for, the one to describe that strange night in the garden? Except I don't feel reborn. I just feel confused.

"When did you notice it?" she asks.

My nerves are ablaze. "I dreamed about it first." I tell her about the dream in vivid detail, even down to the way the stem felt crawling up my arm and down my throat. And then I offer my interpretation. She nods and blinks in all the right places of my retelling, showing total interest, but I know it's a mask for what she's really thinking. "And then I saw it growing on the farm," I add. "Maybe Tía could see if the flowers will talk to her?"

"They won't."

"How do you know?"

"Because they grew under your watch, which means they're trying to tell *you* something. It has to be the reason you felt the magic. It wasn't in the meals at all, but in the soil beneath you." She averts her gaze to the shimmering petals, then back to me. "Has anything been different for you?" she asks.

"I'm writing," I say, forcing the words past the lump in my throat as I gaze at the rim of my glass. "I mean, the words are coming and..." I glance up at her. "Do you actually think canto bloomed because of me?"

My mom inches closer. "Writing is part of your soul. Clearly whatever creativity or new beginnings you have found here have been felt by the land."

The land knew her first.

I instantly recognize the look on my mom's face: pride, joy, and so much more.

I take a deep breath, filling my lungs with the blooms' sweet, clean scent, wondering where they've been the last forty years. "Then why didn't canto grow in my garden?"

"Magic is a forceful thing when it wants to be, and clearly this bloom wants more than a piece of land."

"You mean it wants more than a piece of me," I say, surprised by my own conviction.

"What makes you say that?"

"The dream...it was so clear, so real—canto wanted inside of me and I think...okay this might sound weird, but I think it helped me find my voice."

A beat of silence passes between us.

"You mean writing?" she says.

"I've never felt inspired like this," I tell her. "It's like I can't get it onto the page fast enough."

Mom smiles, and for a blink I think I see her eyes moisten. "Harlow—this is wonderful!"

"Do you want to read it sometime?" There is no one I would trust with my first words more. "I mean when it's ready?" I feel a sudden tightness under my ribs. Did I really just agree to share my work? Something I've never done before? This one small act makes it all feel so real.

"I'd love to! But first tell me what it's about."

So I do. And as the last word leaves my mouth, my mom's dewy, proud expression clenches into a frown. "Harlow."

"What?"

She hesitates and then, "You cannot write about our family."

I'm so taken aback I nearly gasp. "Mom! I'm not. Didn't you hear me? It's about…"

"A magical farm."

"A piece of land," I correct her. My heart is flailing, looking for a safe place to land. "It's not the same thing. And it's fiction." Why can't she see that?

My mom shakes her head. "Harlow—you know we are the chosen protectors of this magic. You know we've had issues with people nosing around before, and imagine if you write an entire book about it." Her voice is rising. "What do you think will happen?"

"Why do I feel like the bad guy here? Why don't you trust me? Do you think for a second I would ever jeopardize our family? This farm? Jesus, Mom! I'm the one who the flowers picked to be guardian and now canto…" I'm on a roll and can't seem to stop myself before I blurt, "I'm the one who got rid of Alicia!"

"Alicia?"

Shit.

She's going to find out anyway, so I tell Mom everything from the stolen bonding bouquet to the journalist's visit to the farm. It sounds so much worse out loud.

My mom's pacing now, rubbing her forehead vigorously. "Beverly would never reveal the magic."

"Exactly." I chime in, wanting to get back to being on the same side.

Mom throws her gaze to me; her dark eyes are sharp like a hawk's. "Why didn't you tell me?"

"I didn't want to ruin your trip and I handled it."

My mom's expression goes tight and then comes the all-knowing smirk I hate. "You only put off the inevitable," she says. "That journalist will be back—they always are. There is absolutely no way under any circumstances you can write this book. How can you not see that?"

Tears form all too easily, and my chest is filling with a horrible heat that's making it hard to breathe. I have never been the daughter who stands up to our mother. I've never caused enough waves that would require it, but now? I'm ready to create a tsunami if it means saving my book. "For the first time in my life I've found my voice, the story that's worth telling and... the first line—it came to me from Mayahuel herself!"

Her eyes narrow. "And you know this because?"

How can I explain it to her. *I have a feeling? Because I heard it on a headwind?* "I just do."

Mom nods resolutely and as she turns to leave, I say, "Can we please talk about this?"

"Later. I've got to do some damage control."

And just like that Jazmín Estrada has gone from being my mom to being the protectress of this farm and its magic.

And I know which role will win.

15

"Look at these bold colors!" Aunt Rosa cheers as we pluck our way over the rocky earth toward the wooden fence where an embarrassment of riches awaits—beautiful purple hydrangeas consuming the rails.

But unlike the desirable full bloom, Rosa is after a dried flower.

I smell rain in the distance as she floats a hand over a single dried hydrangea. She's asking permission to cut the stem. "Most people make the horrid mistake of drying these out by tossing them in an old box," she says, "or even the trunk of their cars! But the trick is to let them dry on the stem, and to harvest at just the right moment. The timing is much more important than the method."

I marvel at her patience and talent as the bloom shimmers beneath her gentle touch. A yes. "What are you using them for?" I ask.

"A harmony concoction," she says, smiling. Then she offers me a quick wink. "We need that around here."

I cross my arms over my chest and stare at the gray horizon. "She's being unreasonable and you know it."

"*She* is doing what she thinks is right."

I fight the urge to roll my eyes. "And if she's wrong?"

"Aren't we all at some point?" she says, removing a pair of small sheers from her denim apron pocket before cutting the stem at a slant and setting it in a small basket she's brought.

"But this is my life, Tía, and this book…it's no different than growing and harvesting flowers. It means something, and I swear I would never write anything that would put the family in danger."

She presses a finger to her lips, hushing me. Thunder tumbles in the distance as she leans close to one of the rounded blooms now, listening, nodding.

I wait, curious. Finally, I ask, "What did it say?"

Ignoring the question, she says, "This magical land in your book is inherited from an estranged aunt? Why estranged?"

I laugh. "It's not you, if that's what you're wondering." She cuts another stem and adds to her basket lavender, another flower that promises harmony I'm not so sure it can deliver.

"I don't have all the answers yet," I say. "I just know that Violeta is a character worth following and the first line came to me like a whisper on the wind…from Mayahuel."

"The land knew her first."

So my mom told her. It's a strange sensation hearing the words in someone else's mouth.

"Let me talk to my sister," she says.

If anyone can talk my mom down from her ledge, it's Rosa. Her phone vibrates and when she glances down at the screen, a wide smile forms across her mouth. I see the name there with a photo of a white-bearded man in black sunglasses. *Anders.*

"He looks nice," I say.

"Nice? Por favor! El es muy guapo!"

I laugh lightly as she hands me the basket, hikes up her long broom skirt and says, "We better run. Those thunderheads are coming fast."

And we do, like two kids—we race across the farm chased by the storm that isn't going to catch us. At least not today.

A couple of days later, I'm sitting in Pasaporte, nursing my fourth cup of black coffee while absorbing the funny and sometimes sad entries in the Book of Near Misses. Entries that highlight near collisions with a twist of fate; others reveal stories about *the one who got away*. I'm fixated on a particular entry that looks like it was scrawled out in a hurry or under the guidance of a possibly drunk hand. It's titled *The Lost Heart* in which the author begins with, *I should have gotten on the plane*.

I feel a deep ache, a strange grief for a stranger who suffered the loss of love because of a single bad choice. It's silly, really, but I want to tell this person I'm sorry, I want to write a message of comfort even though I know they'll never read it, but what if they could feel its energy?

Just then Roberto slides into the booth, tapping the table like it's a drum. "What's with the chisme?"

I set down my pen and sit back. "What do you mean?"

"That gringa...the blondie."

I freeze. "Alicia?"

"She asks a lot of questions."

"She's been here?"

Roberto runs a hand over his balding head. "Mija, she's interviewing everyone in town about the Estrada family. No one is talking, of course. Didn't your mamá tell you?"

Wave after wave of nausea wash over me. How could my mom keep this from me? "What did you tell Alicia?"

"That she's got it all wrong," he says. "All the magic of this town is right here in my café." He smiles wide and I wish I could share his amusement. "No te preocupes," he says, waving a hand through the air. "She went home. All gone. No más Alicia."

I swallow the ever-growing lump of pain and regret in my throat. "Are you sure?"

"Do you remember Oliveras? Started his own chauffeur company with his brother con nada…"

"Roberto!"

"Sí. Sí. Alicia hired him to take her to the airport." He whistles through his teeth. "Adios, chica!" As he leaves the booth, he pats me on the shoulder. "Don't frown so much. It makes you look old." And then he's gone, and I'm left rubbing the wrinkles I can feel forming on my brow when I hear, "Retinol does a better job."

I look up. "Laini!"

It takes less than two seconds for me to leap up and pull her into a hug. Not an easy task because she is three inches taller than I am and not a "hugger." But in this instance, she throws her arms around me, erupting into laughter. "Did I surprise you?"

As we break apart and each slide back into the booth, I throw her an incredulous look. "Did you not hear my squeal? Why didn't you tell me you were coming? Why are you here? Tell me everything!"

"God, I hate you," she spits. "Your skin…it's so golden."

"Ha! There's a lot of sun around here."

"Or you just have great skin that doesn't burn to a hideous shade of red like yours truly." She tucks a blond hair behind her ear, showing off a pair of amazing sapphire drop earrings. "Anyhow, I'm here for those edible flowers I requested."

I grimace. "Oof—totally forgot. Sorry." I close the Book of Near Misses.

"And also, I was tired of the city," Laini says. "I just needed some sunlight and fresh air, and…" She sighs. "And I wanted to tell you that I moved your stuff out of Chad's, shipped most of it here, but brought you some provisions like those adorable Gucci sandals. How could you not have packed those?"

"I left in a hurry, but thank you. A million thank-yous." Then comes the dreaded question I'm not even sure why I'm asking. "Did you see him?"

"Nope. We coordinated schedules. I used the spare key."

So that's it. There is nothing left of mine in Chad's apartment. Why am I not even a little sad about it? Strangely, I feel conflicted about *not* being sad, like maybe a normal person would be? But then a wave of relief washes over me that he, our life together, is all in my rearview mirror. A tale for the Book of Near Misses. "I'm so glad you came," I tell Laini. "But…how did you know I was here at the cafe?"

"Your mom told me."

"Humph. Did she also furnish you with a dagger to plunge into my chest?"

Laini raises an eyebrow. "What did I miss?"

I unfold the whole sorry tale, and when I'm done, Laini merely sighs and says, "She'll get over it."

"She might not."

"She will because she adores you more than anything, and Low…she's just doing what she thinks is right."

"Tia Rosa said the same thing."

"I always have liked your aunt." Her eyes sparkle with a playfulness that leads right to, "Sooo…where's that First Impressions book?"

I offer up a pathetic pout. "There are four to be exact and don't waste your time. I've searched them all, and like I said, it's not like he signed his name or anything." I don't tell her that I found some possibilities, but none I want to be true.

She's nodding, glancing around for a server. When she flags one down, she orders a double espresso, then turns back to me. "I'm super impressed that you're finally writing your book."

"Which means you have to write your mixology book."

I'm met with an immediate sneer that melts into a smile. "Yeah. Yeah. Yeah. Except that isn't my lifelong dream. Let's focus on one book at a time. Yours. So tell me more. I mean other than Violeta and her inheritance. Like why is her aunt estranged and why does she have to live on the farm?"

"It's kind of hard to explain."

"Harlow."

I take a slow, hopefully discreet, shaky breath. "Yeah. Okay. So you know the gist of it and I'm kind of swinging from the fences here—no outline, just instinct and seeing where the story wants to go. It's still just bits and pieces."

"The world was built on bits and pieces," she says with a twinkle in her eye.

In typical Laini fashion, she knows when to give me space, when to let something go. "I'm so proud of you," she says, beaming. "And when you're rich and famous, and your books get made into movies, I better get a red-carpet invite."

I laugh at the far-flung idea of it. For now, I'm happy just to revel in the story, to imagine actually arriving at *the end* because wouldn't that be incredible? To not only begin, but to finish something? "Deal," I say. "So how long are you staying?"

With a melodramatic sigh, Laini says, "With this sunshine and beauty? How about forever?"

"Yeah, El Viento has that effect on people."

"And you?"

I know she's throwing the same question back at me, but my answer is so much more complicated. I guess I've been okay with the not knowing, with living day by day, not thinking too far into the future. Of letting myself float in the liminal space of the unknown.

"I'm not sure. I think until I finish the book."

"Well, if I were you, I'd never leave," she tosses out like a command. "God, I always forget the farm is so beautiful and this town is so enchanting, and I don't know. It's like it's haunted but in a good way. Haunted with...total charm."

Just then her espresso arrives. That's when Laini nearly jumps out of the booth. "Shit! I totally forgot." She reaches into her bag and tugs out an envelope. "Your mom said to give you this."

My name and the farm address are written in perfect calligraphy across the cream-colored envelope. I turn it over to find embossed initials: *BWB*. For a heart-stopping second, I think it's from Ben until I realize that the initials signify Beverly and William Brandt.

"What is it?" Laini scoots across the circular booth so she's planted right over my shoulder.

I shrug. A thank-you card? I wonder as I open the gold foiled envelope. Inside is an invitation to a renewal of the Brandts' vows and a handwritten note.

Dearest Harlow,
I know it is a great distance, but it would mean the world to us to have you there. After all, it was your quick thinking and de-termination that saved us. I'd feel better knowing your bright and good energy was close by. We need it. And I don't mean to be cryptic, but there is something we need to discuss and I'd rather do so in person. I've purchased a refundable ticket for you in case you decide yes. Please say you'll come.
Love,
Beverly

I reread the words, *I'd feel better knowing your bright and good energy was close by*, and, *there is something we need to discuss and I'd rather do so in person.*

Laini wastes no time hurling questions at me. "Saved? Who are the Brandts?"

Knowing she won't let *this* go, I tell her the entire story, starting with the bonding bouquet and ending with Ben at brunch.

Of course, I leave out the part where his mere gaze sets my skin on fire.

"You saw him again, the guy you met here?" she asks.

"At this very table."

"And you didn't tell me?" She looks wounded.

"Ugh—it's all so complicated."

"Complicated? Seriously? He's a man, Harlow. Not a damn rocket." She grabs the invite.

"Look," I tell her, wishing we could drop this whole thing. "I didn't think there was anything to tell. I mean—"

"This is some serious destiny." She's scanning the invitation.

I nod. "They're really adorable," I say.

"Not the Brandts! You and Ben!"

I don't know what takes longer to process. Laini's words or the impossibility of them. "What the hell are you talking about?"

"You seriously don't see how the universe is working to bring you two together?" she groans. "Pasaporte? The flower shop and bookstore? The bouquet? His grandparents? Christ, Harlow, I thought you were more in tune with these kinds of things."

"Pretty sure that isn't how things work," I insist like I'm some expert on the laws of the universe. "Plus he's..." Charming. Maddening. Beautiful. Unforgettable. "Not for me."

Laini presses her lips together, nods like she's going to agree but I know better. She's only getting started. "And you're so sure of this because?"

"How long do you have?"

"Seriously, Low."

I run a hand through my hair, wondering where the proof of my certainty lies. Knowing it has to be something Laini can understand. "He discarded his ex like she meant nothing and he's so...guarded..."

"The journalist that was nosing around the farm was the same chick who stole the bouquet?"

"The one and only."

Laini looks affronted. "Want me to off her?"

I attempt a chuckle, but it comes out as a loud exhale that isn't enough to loosen the tension in my chest.

"First of all," Laini says, "you don't know the full story behind him and this Alicia person who is clearly shady and tried to manipulate him into loving her. Like what the fuck? Maybe he's a genius because he got out while he could." She quickly shifts to shrewd Laini. "Like you with Chad." I start to refute her comparison when she holds up her hand to silence me. "And second, you're the most guarded person I know, so it's pretty much like calling the kettle black."

She's right. I know she's right. Except, "I'm not guarded."

"So that means you're going to go." There is no inflection in her voice, no question mark begging for a response, but I give her one anyway.

"He might not even be there," I argue.

Laini snorts. "He came all the way here for some flowers and you think he's going to miss a renewal of vows? Please, Harlow. If you actually believed that you wouldn't hesitate."

Just the thought of seeing Ben again makes me feel like I'd be walking into a lightning storm wearing a metal jacket. "Still not going."

"So I'm right."

"Just because I don't have time to go to all the way to Quebec next week for a vow renewal does not mean I'm guarded."

"I mean that I'm right about destiny. And here she is." She points to the envelope. "Signed, sealed and delivered."

It's time to fight fire with fire. I get up and grab a First Impressions journal from a nearby table. "Minus the ones that are dated or signed, there are a few entries in here that could be his," I say. Standing at the edge of the booth with the book open, I read, "'She's beautiful but cold, aloof. No one I'd want to get to know.'" I flip to the next entry. "'I met a girl, right here in

Pasaporte. She's cagey for sure, but had nothing of interest to say. So boring.'"

I look up at Laini, expecting a soothing response but she's frowning like I haven't made my case. I tell her, "There are more."

Laini huffs. "And I'm sure there are glowing ones that you happened to gloss over because they don't fit your narrative of Ben Brandt, who might be more than you think he is and you're too chickenshit to find out."

I stand there, holding that book with all its anonymous entries, and I know Laini is right. I have to go to the Brandts' ceremony. The moment I decide, a guilty thrill courses through me as I imagine his sharp angles, those eyes, that near smile... the man who saved five petals.

"Fine," I say, like I'm making the greatest sacrifice of my life. "I'll go."

Laini erupts into triumphant glee. I half expect her to toss confetti from her purse, but I don't have the heart to tell her that she wasn't the deciding factor. It's the simple fact that I want to honor Beverly's wishes. I genuinely want to celebrate her and William. And I want to find out what Beverly wants to tell me.

This has nothing to do with Ben.

Or maybe it has more to do with him than I want to admit.

Laini takes a sip of her espresso. "So why Quebec?"

Recalling my conversation with Beverly and William, I say, "They met and fell in love there."

"Classic love right there," Laini says. "The kind that died out with all this dating app and social media bullshit."

"And here I thought you were a self-professed romantic," I tease.

"I am romantic," Laini snorts, "just a couple decades too late." She delivers the line with humor, but I can sense the gloom in her truth, which she quickly erases with, "Do you want me to come with you?" Like it's not even a question. "I've always wanted to go to Old Quebec. They call it the mini Paris and you know how much I love Paris."

With a playful smirk, I gesture to the invite. "Doesn't say 'plus one.'"

"Psh. As if I'd ever be traditional or follow a ridiculous social rule."

I laugh. "Then I guess you wouldn't have survived the *classic* love period."

"Is that a no, because I am seriously dying to lay my eyes on this man that has you so hot and bothered."

"First," I say with absolute authority, "I am *not* hot and bothered—" (but I sort of am) "—and second, I *am* somewhat traditional."

As much as I'd love to have Laini as my wingwoman, she'd spend the entire time playing matchmaker. She'd complicate things with me and Ben, and the last thing I want is more complications. What if all I need is a proper goodbye with no maybes?

"So, it's a no," she says with a teasing pout.

"I promise to give you minute by minute updates."

Laini throws her hair back and I catch a whiff of her delicate perfume—white floral and woodsy. "You better." Then turning her attention to the handwritten note, she asks the same question that's circling my mind. "So what's up with the dangling carrot? What do you think Beverly has to tell you?"

"I have no idea."

"Well, I guess you're going to find out. But first things first." She waggles her eyebrows teasingly.

"You're scaring me."

"We need to do some online shopping for the perfect dress."

I drop my head back onto the seat. "Please. Not another *fuck the patriarchy* dress."

"I was thinking more of a *fuck*—"

"Don't say it."

"Then don't think it."

"I wasn't!"

Laini's mouth fans out into a wicked grin. "Fine. We'll call it the *un-for-get-table* dress."

And as she begins to surf the internet on her phone, I feel the tug of that invisible thread tied to my heart. I hear the whisper of canto: *it's not the dress that might be unforgettable.*

16

I'm packing my bags when Mom comes into my room. "It's cold in Canada this time of year."

I hate small talk, especially when its only purpose is to mask what's really going on. "I've got a coat," I tell her.

With a barely there sigh, she sits on the edge of my bed and begins to fold and refold the same sweater. "Harlow, you can't leave with this wall between us."

"I didn't put it there," I say, moving back and forth across the room from dresser to closet to suitcase, dizzy with my self-righteousness and frustration.

"I know you're angry with me," she says. "But I have a re-sponsibility here."

I stop and face her. "So do I. And I would never…"

"I know that. I just…" She takes a breath, hesitates, then, "I have more experience with meddlesome journalists and others who are a threat to this farm, to our legacy."

"Look," I say, sitting next to her, "I've been thinking about it, and I'm sure this book came to me for a reason—it's a story that wants to be told, and you have to understand that it's the first time in my life I feel like magic has touched *me* and…" Why is this so hard? "So I was thinking that what if I let you read the whole book when it's done and then…"

"Really?" she says. "And then what? You're just going to hand over the reins to me? Let me decide if you can publish the book?"

When she puts it like that, I see that the request is unreasonable.

With a shake of her head, she stands and paces to the window where she looks out across the fields. After a moment, she says, "When your grandmother died and Rosa and I came here, I didn't know how much I was giving up." She lets the words settle before turning back to me. "But also how much I was gaining. And I want you to be happy," she says, "to live all of your dreams."

My hope starts a slow descent. "Why do I hear a no coming?"

I'm surprised when she offers, "Can I think about it?"

I know what that means. She wants to use her dream magic to consult the goddess, to search for an answer we haven't found yet. She wants to give me a chance.

I love her for it.

With a nod, I go over and hug her. She smells of fresh soil and dandelions. I fall against the granite rock that she is and always will be.

When we pull apart, she tugs a pair of sandals from my bag. "These are a no. Not suitable or logical or…"

"Mom…"

"Bueno," she says with a sigh. "But when your toes fall off from frostbite, don't be calling me for a remedio."

We laugh and the sound of it fills my spirit.

I've never been to Canada.

And I have this thing about *not* googling the details of a place before I visit. I love that feeling of discovery, the one that leads to total surprise; plus at the end of the day I want to see everything through my own eyes, not some travel blogger's.

But the only surprise I've had so far is a delayed flight that had me on the far side of anxiety until I texted Beverly to let her know I wasn't going to make it in time for the vow part of the ceremony and how sorry and disappointed I was.

In classy Beverly fashion, she called me immediately to tell me, "You just be safe, dear. We will see you at the reception."

After I retrieve my bag, I race through the airport and find an Uber in record time.

The vow ceremony just began a few minutes ago, but if I hustle, I can be at the reception in an hour and a half. Not loads of time to get checked in, take a shower, pull myself together, and make the supposed fifteen-minute drive to Île d'Orléans, the island that sits directly across from the hotel. But I'm a speed beautifier and have definitely gotten ready in a lot less time than that.

I text my mom (family rules) to let her know I arrived, then release a long breath of tension, lean my head back and stare out at the night landscape, which includes a few strip malls, domineering trees, and a very dark sky. I feel a pinch of disappointment. This is *not* a mini Paris, Laini.

A few minutes later, I realize I judged too soon. The moment we drive past the old gates of the city, the entire setting transforms in the blink of an eye; it's as if we've gone through a magical portal and emerged into the past where beauty and simplicity reign.

"This is Old Quebec," the driver tells me proudly, turning down the radio. "We are the oldest city in Canada and," he adds with gusto, "we have the only remaining walled city in North America north of Mexico."

We cruise by elegant gray buildings adorned with brightly colored shutters and window boxes, overflowing with fall leaves, pumpkins, long plumes, shiny ornaments, and the occasional geranium.

"It's beautiful," I say, feeling nothing but delight and surprise.

Next, we turn down a narrow cobblestone street where well-lit cafés and boutiques welcome people bundled in coats and hats. Charm and history seem to ooze from every square inch of this place, and if I wasn't already sitting on a ticking time bomb, I would fly out of the car to soak it all in.

The driver makes a sharp right into an arched tunnel, and a second later we emerge into an enclosed motor court framed by the imposing brick-and-stone walls of the hotel, Château Frontenac.

As I step out of the car, a brisk wind races past, sending a cold shiver through me.

The bellman takes my luggage and escorts me into the breathtaking lobby with its antique furnishings, wood-paneled walls, and glittering chandeliers.

When I get to the front desk, I'm redirected to the thirteenth floor for a private check-in since my room, along with the other wedding guests, is on the "gold" floor. The entire process takes a mere ten minutes, leaving me roughly forty-five minutes to get ready, but I'm so exhausted I indulge in collapsing onto the white cloud of a bed, promising myself only two minutes of peace and quiet.

With a deep breath I close my eyes, curl my legs into my chest.

I drift toward the hazy edges of a dream; it's all sun and sea and the heady scent of Ben. Everything is blurry, but there is no mistaking the outline of a tall figure coming toward me—and even though I can't see the face, the angles give him away. He's reaching toward me, closer and closer, so that I can see his smile, open and irresistible. In the next instant he's standing behind me, his arms wrapped tight around my waist, his head resting against my temple. I can feel his warm breath on my neck as a hand sweeps under my shirt, fingers trace my ribs with the care of a jewel thief.

I press into him, wanting this dream to go to the next step and the next.

Ben raises his other hand, producing a single stalk of fox-glove; tiny bell-like blooms unfurl wider before my eyes as he whispers, "You're late."

I wake with a choking gasp and glance at the nightstand clock: 7:36. I've been asleep for fourteen minutes.

"Shit!" I strip naked and jump into the shower. Three minutes later, I'm toweling off. Seven minutes later, I've blow-dried my hair well enough that I can pull it up into a twist that looks absolutely planned.

I sweep a light rose oil across my face, apply a coat of mascara, a sweep of shimmering gold shadow, and some tinted lip balm, and a touch of eyeliner before I slip on the long ice blue dress that I fell in love with while shopping with Laini. Most of the clothes I brought (thanks to the overnight shipping gods) are new, a truer version of me that feels like a new chapter.

With a cashmere wrap over my shoulders and a clutch under my right arm, I head down to the waiting town car that Beverly arranged to drive me to the island.

"He'll wait for you, dear. No need to rush," she had told me when I sent her my new flight arrival.

Fifteen minutes later, we're crossing the suspension bridge that spans the glossy St. Lawrence River. I'm tempted to roll down my window and take a deep inhale, but I'm not about to arrive looking like a windblown mess.

My mind returns to the dream I had of Ben, sticking on the same point. The foxglove he gave me, also known as witches bells. It symbolizes insincerity, mystery, and deception. And its powers? Magic. Protection. But protection from what? I want to tell myself that it was just a dream, but I know better. Whenever anyone in my family dreams of a specific flower, it's time to sit up and pay attention.

The moment we're across the bridge, I fall in love with the old stone houses with thatched roofs, the rolling fields and orchards that line the winding road. The place evokes a sense of time standing still, a point driven deeper when we turn onto a dimly lit dirt road that gives way to a sprawling farmhouse tucked between a grassy knoll and dozens of tidy rows of grapevines.

"We're here," the driver says in an accent I can't place. His first words to me since the greeting when I stepped into the car.

"It's a vineyard," I say with one part pleasure, the other surprise. Beverly never mentioned the exact type of venue for the ceremony, and I guess I had just assumed a church or a hotel.

I think the driver's going to drop me at the house, but he continues following the winding path. There's a glow up ahead, around the bend, and I'm craning my neck to get a better look as we cruise closer to the source, a tented pavilion. Its warm golden light spills across the edge of the river, flickering across the dark waters.

I sit in the silence of the warm idling car, taking it all in when a knock at my window startles me. The door opens and a young valet with a toothy smile, greets me with, "Bonsoir, mademoiselle."

I'm out of the car and being escorted to the tent's entrance before I can even echo his greeting or register the soulful music or the chatter of a crowd that is so much bigger than I imagined. Beverly had said a "small affair," but clearly we have different definitions of small.

"Bienvenue," the valet tells me before disappearing from my side, leaving me to stand at the edge of this glittering, glorious, Gatsby-esque party alone.

At the far end of the tent is a five-person band with a female crooner who sounds so similar to Norah Jones it's eerie. The eighty or so guests, dressed in elegant formal attire, mill about, engage in conversation, laughter, champagne.

That's when I spot Beverly, a mere twenty or so feet away. She's wearing a purple silk gown, laughing with absolute ebullience. William stands next to her, watching her in the soft light; his eyes drink her in like there is no one else in the room and that's when I realize this is it. This is what true love looks like, open and willing and vulnerable. Evident and on display like a Picasso or other rare beauty for anyone with the eyes and heart to notice.

I start to make my way over when I see him. Ben.

Something leaps inside of me at the sight of him. And what a sight it is.

He looks so painfully handsome in his black suit that my legs feel weak. He's listening intently to an older man, head tipped, eyebrows pinched, the appropriate engaged nod, like he's entirely absorbed in whatever this man is saying. I watch him for a few gut twisting moments.

"Harlow!" Beverly's unmistakable voice rips my attention away from Ben. She folds me in her arms and smiles. "I am so pleased you're here. And you look absolutely lovely!"

"Thank you," I say. "This is all so beautiful!"

"We were married in this exact spot fifty-two years ago." She flashes a wide, proud smile. "It was Benny's idea. Well, not the tent or the music, but the location. He's always had such a strong sense of place."

I hazard a glance over her shoulder to find him again, but he's gone.

Turning back to the Brandt matriarch, I clear my throat and ask the question that's been on my mind since I received the invitation. "Beverly, your message was so mysterious," I say, treading as lightly as I can so I don't seem like an overzealous interrogator.

"Message?"

"You said you had something to tell me?"

"Oh, that can wait," she says, and before I can ask for more, she excuses herself to talk to a server walking past. Without Beverly there to anchor me, I feel afloat, lost in this sea of strangers. I grip my clutch tighter as I set my eyes on the singer. My cashmere wrap slips off of my shoulder.

That's when I feel it.

Heat on my bare back. It must be one of the indoor heaters, but when I turn, Ben is standing there.

All six foot two of him, every edge and angle of his face and the curve of his lips. He's holding a champagne flute out to me. "You made it."

My breath hitches and I pray he doesn't see. That he doesn't notice the tightening of my throat, the impossible thumping of my heart, the feverish memories of those dreams flashing across my mind that are likely turning my décolleté into a red blotchy mess.

I manage a hello before I take the champagne and sip nervously, looking around the room, at anywhere or anyone but him. And the looming question between us, *why didn't you call?*

To which I have no good answer expect that Laini is right, and I'm a chickenshit.

That's when I notice the flowers on each table. Small bundles of Inca lilies my mom shipped at Beverly's request. She told my mom she didn't want to replicate the bonding bouquet, only the symbolism of the Inca, which denotes longevity and a powerful bond.

"Are they okay?" Ben asks, gesturing to the flowers with his champagne glass.

"Perfect," I say as I swing my gaze back to him.

"But not...under a spell."

I huff out a small laugh, immensely grateful for this little icebreaker. "I thought you didn't believe in magic."

He leans closer, so close I can smell a trace of something intoxicatingly woodsy. He doesn't confirm or deny my statement. Instead, he looks at me expectantly. He wants to know if the flowers are enchanted.

"No," I tell him, devilishly wanting to drag the charade out another second, but not wanting him to suffer from the unknowing. "There is no magic in the bouquets."

Standing taller, he grazes a thumb across his jaw, and stares at me more intently. I swear that gaze could ignite a fire and I have to remind myself, *he's no good for you. He's no good for you.*

And then I remember the foxglove: insincerity, mystery, and deception. Was it a sign to stay away from Ben, or just my dream imagination working overtime?

"How do you know?" Ben asks with genuine interest.

"I might not have the magic of my family," I say, "but I can sense when it's nearby."

"Humph. Does that come in handy?"

If I didn't know better, I would think he's teasing me but his expression is too sincere and earnest. And interested. "Sometimes," I tell him. Like when you think you're being drugged with magical edible flowers.

He takes a sip of champagne and nods slowly, studying me. An awkward moment of silence passes between us and I think this is it. He's going to ask why I didn't call. But then he says, "You're tan."

How does he do it? Say the thing I least expect? Always change the topic to something so benign that still has the ability to spike my adrenaline. "There's a lot of sun in Mexico."

"So, you're still at the farm."

There is a question in his statement, one he doesn't ask directly: *Why* are you still there?

"I am."

"Still writing the book?"

I feel a rush of pride, joy. "Still."

"And that's going well?" Why is he looking at me like that, all soft and dreamy like my book matters so much to him?

"It's going," I say, not sure why our conversation has taken a strange turn. I look away, unable to meet his gaze and quickly change the subject. "This is a really nice party."

"My family are experts at parties," he says with a touch of humor that puts me a bit more at ease.

But then he says nothing. And the silence enfolds us in a space that feels extraordinarily small. So small, I can still feel the heat radiating off him in waves. But how? Am I imagining it? Setting my wrap on a nearby chair, I say, "So, Beverly tells me this was your idea."

He barks out a laugh. I love the sound of it because it rings with surprise and something tells me it isn't easy to surprise this man. "This was *not* my idea. I only told my grandmother that she should have the ceremony in a place that mattered to her and my grandpa. She ran with it."

He has such a strong sense of place.

"Well, it's pretty perfect," I say, keeping my gaze on the fiesta.

That's when I feel his eyes on me again. *Don't fidget. Don't fidget.*

"Hey, you're a writer…" His words linger on the edge of a question I'm not sure I want to answer.

I nod and take another swig of champagne, hoping it will calm my nerves. "Uh-huh…"

"So I have to make a toast and I'm not great with words." I hazard a glance up at him. "Any advice?" His voice is light, his expression pleading. He really is ridiculously beautiful.

I clench the flute tighter, trying to regain some composure here, trying to stay on my mark because if I back up, he'll know he affects me in the most alluring way and I'm not about to be *that* girl. And then my emotions get ahead of me and I'm blabbing, "How about something about true love, the kind that can't be broken, the kind that goes on forever."

"And you believe that?"

Yes! Don't I? Haven't I always imagined a love so deep that it changes my heart in all the best possible ways while still begging the question, *is it all worth it?* The risk, the vulnerability, the baring of your soul set upon the altar of hope.

I'm about to finesse some clever response, when my mouth betrays me. "Don't you?"

Ben looks stricken. The color drains from his face and I realize I've hit a nerve that I wish I hadn't. He clenches his jaw, looks like he's struggling to find a simple answer to a simple question. Then his brows soften. "Maybe... I mean..."

I should save the poor guy from himself, but I'm too fixated on the fact that Ben's stammering. He's human after all.

"It's a simple yes or no," I interject, trying to give him an easy out.

He shifts his feet, looking supremely out of his element. In that split second I catch a glimpse of a boyish charm that is altogether startling and so unexpected it melts my heart.

"Some things," he says, "are more complicated than a simple yes or no."

"Such as?"

"Take dogs for example. You either like them or not. Right? Simple."

I scoff. "Everyone likes dogs."

"But what if you only like small dogs? Or those wiener dogs?"

This man is maddening!

"But love isn't a dog," I argue, standing my ground. "And I think you just don't want to answer the question."

"You really want me to give you an answer?"

I stop breathing. Do I? Do I really want to know? But before I can respond, Ben says, "Love is never simple."

I have to fight the intense desire to blurt, *how do you know? Have you ever been in love?* And then I wonder, what kind of woman would Ben love?

Only ten minutes ago, my biggest worry was blending in, and now? All I want is to know whether Benjamin Brandt believes in true love. And that half-baked answer got me nowhere closer to the truth.

"For the record," he offers, "you look really...beautiful tonight."

I feel a hot vibration under my skin. "Thank you, but are you trying to change the subject?"

"Is it working?"

"No."

He makes a show of grimacing. "That's what I figured. So, how long are you staying in Quebec?"

"A few days." I want to follow that with *why*, but never get the chance because just then a young woman is at the microphone, asking for everyone's attention. She's pretty, with short red hair that shows off her elegant jawline, and she's wearing an emerald green dress that hugs all of her curves like it was tailored just for her.

"We're so happy every one of you could join my family for this occasion," she says with a broad engaging smile.

Family?

But before I can ask, Ben shifts his position to my right and whispers, "My sister loves the spotlight."

I do not see the resemblance, not physically or in personality. Where he's tall, she's short. Where he's all edges, she's all curves. Where he's mysteriously reserved, she seems open and inviting.

"And now," his sister goes on, still beaming, "to spice things up, I thought we could play a musical game."

"You should run while you can," Ben says, his gaze focused straight ahead. The tone of his voice is playful, but there isn't even a hint of humor in his stony expression.

"Is this another bad joke?" I ask.

"No, Harlow," he says. "This one is real."

"Well, I like games."

"You won't like this one."

"That bad?"

"Let's just say my sister dreams up the craziest ideas that are usually," he says, pausing, "humiliating."

Not about to let him scare me off, I say, "I'll take my chances."

"Don't say I didn't warn you."

His sister goes on to explain the rules. Guests are to find a partner and dance until the music stops. When it does, they have to stand as still as statues. Anyone who so much as flinches or blinks is disqualified. The couple left at the end wins.

"Like I said, humiliating," Ben groans.

"Is there a prize?" I tease.

Ben casts me a sideways glance. "Knowing Helena?"

Just then, his sister announces, "And whoever wins will be the lucky recipient of a private boat ride down the St. Lawrence at sunset. Now pick your partner," she sings, clapping her hands together. "And choose wisely."

The crowd applauds; a few guests erupt into giddy laughter.

Then, Helena's gaze scans the room until it lands squarely on Ben. A dangerous looking grin covers her face. "Hey, Ben, why don't you join the competition on the dance floor."

"I'm good right here." His voice is tight, carrying the message only a sibling can deliver. *I'm going to kill you later. In the most painful way.*

All heads swivel in our direction. The air around us feels suddenly charged. Then to my utter surprise, Helena looks at *me.* "You must be Harlow! Oh, this is too good." She's practically bouncing in place. "You have to entice my brother to dance."

I realize Beverly must have told her about me, but I'm too fixated on wanting to crawl under the table to care. There is no way I can dance with Ben. In his arms. Pressed close to his body...and all that heat. I should have listened and run while I had the chance.

"Yeah, Harlow," someone hollers.

My heart jumps. It's thumping so hard I can feel it in my gut.

"Come on, Ben!" another guest shouts.

"Show us your moves!"

I think Ben is going to deny his sister and the crowd, that he will find a way to get us both out of this. But he doesn't. Instead, he is the picture of total composure as he says, "So, Harlow, I have a question."

I stare up at him in complete astonishment. He's going to ask me to dance. Or maybe, *how fast can you run?* Either way, this is not the time for questions!

People are still provoking him with their pleas and jeers when a slow drumroll begins. But he manages to ignore it all like we're the only two people in this room. Then he throws me the unexpected, "Are you competitive?"

Is this another bad joke? A trick question? If he were to ask anyone in my family, they would say I am hypercompetitive, at board games, tennis matches, swimming races, poker. You name it; if there is a winner to be named, the driven side of me emerges ready to collect the spoils *and* the title.

"Uh… I mean…"

Could someone please knock out that damn drummer?

"We don't have all day, Ben," Helena coos into the microphone. The drumroll quickens while Ben waits for my answer.

"I like to win," I manage.

There's a flicker in his dark eyes, something delicious and spirited. He smiles and says, "Good. So do I," before he takes my hand and with long determined strides, leads me to the dance floor.

17

Before I know it, Ben and I are standing in the center of the dance floor surrounded by a few other couples who are already swaying to the jazzy tune.

Ben is still holding my hand, gripping it like a lifeline. He's surveying the growing crowd around us.

"You okay?" I ask, wondering when we're going to actually start dancing.

He swings his gaze to mine. "Just assessing the competition." And then he smiles, a warm, gentle, nearly full grin that steals my breath.

"And?" I say, unable to keep my own smile at bay.

"And I should tell you now that I really don't dance much, but maybe we can wing it…as long as you don't fidget."

"Me?" I sneer. "I'll be still as a statue. It's you we have to worry about."

"I don't fidget."

"You also don't seem like the kind of person who plays by the rules."

"And we shouldn't talk," Ben suggests, surprising me by how into this competition he is. "Mouths moving. Too dangerous."

"You really want to win that cruise."

There's a shift in his posture, like he isn't sure how to hold me, where to put his free hand. And if I didn't know any better, I'd think Benjamin Brandt was uncharacteristically nervous. I inch closer and place my hand on his shoulder. He gives a whisper of a smile and then gently, ever so cautiously, his hand goes to the small of my back, my very bare skin, and I nearly gasp. His touch is light, warm, tender, the grazing of fire.

We begin to move to the rhythm of the music, gliding across the dance floor for one two three steps and just like that, we're out of sync.

"Let me lead," he says.

I thought I *was* letting him lead? Or least I was *trying* to let him. *Who decided that rule anyway?* Laini's voice echoes in my mind. *The patriarchy.*

"You're fighting for control," Ben says, "which means I'm going to step on your foot at some point and you'll be furious and we'll lose the competition. So, Harlow—" he pins me with a dark amused gaze "—either you can lead or I can, but choose."

Yeah, Harlow. Choose.

As much as I want to thwart patriarchal rules, now isn't the time because I have no idea how to lead. "I wouldn't be furious," I say, "But fine, you can lead. This time."

Ben grunts, pulls me closer, so close my hips are pressed against his, my chest is mere inches from his heart and all that heat pulsing off of his very solid body.

An alarm blares in my head. This was a ridiculously stupid decision. To fall into Ben's arms and dance with him, this close. I should just excuse myself, create some distance. Yes, brilliant idea, except that I'm not a quitter.

I'm trying so hard to keep up, to follow his moves, but they're clipped, faltering. Wow, he really can't dance.

Then, out of nowhere, Ben peels himself away from my body so that we are now at near arm's length and you could fit a whole other person between us. I'm utterly confused by this move, but even more so when he begins to steer us away from the others, avoiding inadvertent bumps. We must look like two woefully bad dancers, or maybe a pair of galloping horses.

I choke back an insult because the music comes to an abrupt halt.

We freeze.

I'm gazing right into his solid chest, willing my breathing to slow. Begging my limbs not to tremble, not to give me away as Helena and the other judges walk around looking for one wrong flinch. Miraculously, we pass this first round, and five other couples are disqualified.

The music begins again, slower this time.

I hazard a glance up at Ben.

"Nice job," he says with a curt nod like I'm one of his employees.

"I thought we weren't supposed to talk."

Ignoring me, he adds, "But you nearly moved."

"Did not."

"I could feel it."

Damn! What else could he feel?

"You felt wrong, then."

"You're trying to lead again," he says, clearly amused.

"Am not and this isn't bumper cars," I tease.

"Are you telling me I'm a bad dancer?" Ben cracks a smile.

"Do you really want me to answer that?"

"I'll have you know I took ballroom dance lessons at Ms. Chandler's when I was eight."

I laugh, unable to imagine kid Ben doing the tango or foxtrot.

"Annnnd..." he adds, "I was very good. Or at least until I got kicked out of class."

"How does *anyone* get kicked out of dance class?"

"I thought it would be funny to put superglue in a few of the kids' shoes." He blinks at me. "It didn't go over too well."

A new bubble of laughter erupts from my chest. "Why am I not surprised?"

"But," he says, tenting his eyebrows, "that doesn't mean I didn't learn a few moves."

"Oh yeah?"

He twirls me once, twice, and all the while I'm laughing breathlessly, going with the flow and trying to look somewhat graceful.

In the next instant, he's leading me in a waltz-like move, so fluidly that the floor seems to fall away. With each step he pulls me closer and for the next few beats, I forget we're playing a game, and I get lost in the nearness of Ben, in the rhythm of our bodies.

Then out of nowhere, he says, "You never called."

Not an accusation as much as the question I noted in his tone earlier. He wants to know why.

At the same moment the music stops; we're caught with our eyes locked, staring down the question I can't answer.

How am I supposed to stand perfectly still, gazing into this man's eyes, which are so much more beguiling close-up? A blend of dark and gold and dangerously beautiful.

I remind myself that in my dream he gave me a bloom of *insincerity, mystery, and deception*, but my body isn't having it. It's already lost in his touch, in his lingering scent, in the stack of muscles beneath this suit.

His thumb twitches against my bare back, a barely there caress that ignites every cell in my body. I have this sudden burning desire to kiss him, to press my mouth to his because it is oh so close. And perhaps I want to see if the flesh and blood Ben lives up to the Ben in my dreams.

In that exact fiery instant, Helena appears next to us. Staring. Watching. Waiting for us to make a wrong move.

"Impressive," she purrs tauntingly.

Ben's gaze grows more intense, more focused, like he's struggling against something other than a mere twitch or flinch.

Helena continues to study us. I'm going to blink. Or kiss him. I'm going to blow it. How long can any human be expected to look into those eyes and remain standing?

Lost in his gaze, I barely notice when Ben swallows. When his Adam's apple shifts. Oh, God. Did his sister see it?

She must not have because she says nothing. We've escaped a close call. But then… Ben's eyes…they drop to my mouth and the game is lost.

The instant Ben lets me go, I felt a dizzying relief, but also a strange hollowness. And even now, as we're heading away from the dance floor, I feel like I'm falling.

The music is still playing, the game still unfolding when Ben turns to me. "Are you hungry?"

Hungry? Is he serious? Isn't he going to acknowledge that he lost us the game?

"Ben…"

"Harlow."

"We lost."

"You noticed."

I sigh. "I thought we had it."

Ben works his jaw back and forth. "Yeah, well there were circumstances beyond my control."

"Like your eyes," I blurt. Wow. That came out all wrong. "I mean, they moved when you…"

"It is one hundred percent my fault," he admits. "And to make amends, we can still do the river cruise. If you want to. That is, if you don't have plans tomorrow."

My plans to explore Quebec instantly evaporate, and now all I can see is floating down the river with Benjamin Brandt. And who cares if this is about lust? Or the fact that he is no good for me? It doesn't have to be forever. It doesn't have to be anything other than what it is—an alluring seductive attraction. For once I don't want to choose safe. It always leads to the same outcome: a belief that good is enough. Maybe it's time I spin a new story, something wild, risqué, something that gives me sovereignty over my own life.

"It's not that I didn't think about calling," I tell him, circling back to his unanswered question. "Life just got crazy and the book and…" I take a deep breath.

An expression washes over his face I can't read, but it doesn't matter because it's followed by a genuine smile. Yes, this is the Ben I like. "So you considered it," he teases.

"I did."

"I almost called you too."

"But you don't have my number."

With a small laugh, he says, "I had this whole plan in my mind—I was going to call the shop and leave a message."

I wonder how much that might have changed things. Would I have called him back? Told him his ex had been snooping around the farm, which added a whole layer of complexity and baggage I didn't want to deal with?

Just then a server whizzes past, knocks into a chair, loses her balance and bumps into me, spilling red wine down the front of my ice blue dress.

I gasp, jumping back.

"I'm so sorry…" the young girl cries, setting down her tray and reaching for a cloth napkin on a nearby table. "I… I…here." She thrusts it in my face as tears pool in her eyes.

"Are you okay?" Ben asks.

"It's fine," I say, feeling worse for her than I do for myself as I dab the impossible stain setting in.

"It's red," she cries again. "It won't come out. I... I can pay you."

"Of course not!" I argue. "I've spilled wine plenty of times. Please—don't worry about it."

The server whirls toward Ben as if she's looking for permission. "It was an accident."

Those four words work their magic because Ben mutters something to her, pats her on the back awkwardly, and she picks up her tray and scampers off, apologizing a few more times as she goes.

"That was nice of you to let her off the hook," Ben says.

"It wasn't her fault. Besides, it's just some wine."

Ben is staring at the stain, lips parted, making me suddenly self-conscious. "It looks violent."

"Do you have any club soda?"

"I have a better idea," he says. "Come on."

"Where are we going?" I ask, following.

"You'll see."

We exit the tent in a rush. The air is crisp, clean, and cold. I realize I forgot my wrap inside, but Ben's already shrugging off his suit jacket and setting it around my shoulders. He looks even better with it off; his fitted white shirt clings to him in all the best ways, and I have to pull my mind out of the gutter long enough to ask a coherent question.

"You're not going to dunk me in the river, are you?"

He laughs. "Well, now that you mention it." Then he begins to make his way in the opposite direction of the St. Lawrence.

When he notices I'm not following, he stops in his tracks and turns to me looking confused.

I tell him, "Ben, we can't just leave the reception."

"They'll be playing that game another thirty minutes at least," he says self-assuredly. "We'll be back before they can set out the first course. Trust me."

Trust? Ben Brandt? Not if the foxglove has anything to say about it.

He double backs to me and takes my hand. My hand. In his. Like it's the most natural thing in the world.

Get a grip, Harlow. It's just a hand. He's probably making sure you don't face-plant it in all this darkness.

He leads me down a grassy path, and soon we come to the back side of the farmhouse I saw earlier on my drive in.

Ben opens a wooden door and we step inside the darkness.

"Please tell me this is your family's house," I whisper, "and that we aren't breaking and entering."

"This is my family's house and we aren't breaking and entering," he says, flicking on an overhead light that brightens the tidy mudroom filled with boots, coats, and umbrellas.

"My grandmother grew up here," he goes on as we make our way into a small uncluttered kitchen with low beamed ceilings, dark green cabinets, and stone floors. "It's been in the family forever."

There is a simplicity to the home's charm that puts me instantly at ease. It's as if there is a benevolent energy vibrating in every corner. And for just a moment, it reminds me of La Casa de las Flores y Luz. "It's beautiful."

Ben opens the refrigerator and pulls out a box of baking soda before hunting down a container of salt in a cabinet. He measures each, adding water with precision like this is some kind of science experiment. "Here," he says, handing me a thin towel. "Blot, but don't scrub it."

"So, what're you? A stain master?" Will this man ever stop surprising me?

"Not exactly," he says with a playful smirk. "Helena…she, uh, she got a small wine stain on her wedding dress. It was tiny, but she still made me run to the store for baking soda and salt an hour before the ceremony. It was the only thing that got it out."

"Yikes," I say with a wince. "She must have been panicked." I blot at the stain while he mixes his concoction into a paste. Then he reaches into the refrigerator for a bottle of club soda and turns back to me with an expression of disbelief, like he's surprised I'm still here. "I think this is how we did it."

"Think?"

"I'm pretty sure. We'll find out." He swallows, keeping his gaze on my hands still mindlessly dabbing the stain. Then he looks up at me, a small frown creasing his brow. "You should probably take off the dress."

18

Heat rushes my cheeks, my neck, my chest, radiating down down down.

And Ben? He's just standing there, holding me with an impatient gaze like he didn't just ask me to take off my clothes, and yes, I'm aware that it was a utilitarian request, but still, the words sounded so intimate in his mouth.

The old wooden stairs creak noisily as we make our way to the second floor. Ben leads me to a tidy bedroom with antique pine furniture that looks like it came from an English estate sale.

I stand near the doorway while Ben goes to the dresser and tugs out a couple of T-shirts and a pair of sweats. "This is all I have," he says, offering me the stack of clothing. "They're old. From when I was in high school, but they should be good enough."

I take the clothes and look around the room, thinking it's perfectly poised for the pages of some minimalistic design magazine.

"I'll wait outside," he says.

After Ben leaves, I shed the dress and my shoes and look at my choices of T-shirts: Nirvana, Dr Pepper, or the San Diego Zoo. I go with the polar bears. As I pull it over my head, I get a whiff of Ben, of his signature scent: rain-soaked earth. I inhale sharply, breathing it in. How in the world does it manage to linger in the fabric after all this time?

The sweats are too big, so I roll down the waist a few times before I open the door with dress in hand. "Okay, doctor. Now what?"

Ben's mouth curves into an entertained smile as he takes in my grunge look. "You picked the polar bears."

"Not a fan of Dr Pepper and never listened to Nirvana."

Ben pulls a face to make sure I see his shocked disappointment. Then he starts to sing in an upbeat tone while playing air drums "Hello, hello, hello..."

"Never heard it." Although I think I have. "Are you sure you're in tune?"

He just shakes his head. "Blasphemy."

I laugh and soon we're back downstairs and he's dispensing club soda onto the stain, letting it soak in before he applies the baking soda–salt paste with such exactitude you'd think a life is at stake and he's got one shot to save it. Cautiously, he steps back. "Okay, now we let it dry."

"And then what?" I ask, staring at the four-hundred-dollar mess helplessly.

"We hope for the best?" His voice isn't the usual tenor of confidence and dammit if I don't find it so endearing, I want to kick myself. I lean against the counter, and that's when I notice a vase of porcelain containing an Inca lily enveloped by sprigs of lavender.

Ben's gaze follows mine. "Beverly got those from your mom. Something about energy and the walls and..."

"Lavender is good to ward off the evil eye."

Ben folds his arms over his chest. "So we have a magic bouquet under our roof because of an evil eye?"

I touch the blooms. The flowers pulsate with warmth; their vibrant energy seeps into my fingertips and courses through my veins. "Do you want the good news or the bad news first?"

"Definitely the bad."

I laugh. "So you're one of those."

Ben stiffens like he's preparing himself for a great blow. "I like things to end on a good note. Okay, so go ahead. Lay it on me."

"The lavender is enchanted," I say as casually as I can.

"And the good?" The words explode out of him like he can't get to this part fast enough.

"You don't believe in magic," I tease, holding back a laugh, "so it shouldn't be a problem."

Ben swallows, clears his throat. His eyes land on the flowers, and I can see the wheels turning in his head. "Well, let's just say I'm curious," he says, "why put the lavender *with* the lily?"

"The lavender symbolizes constancy and devotion, and the lily bonded love, so maybe Beverly wants to bless the memories of this house, enhance the devotion and love or…something like that. Maybe since her and William were married here?"

"Yeah, sounds like her. But can we get back to the evil eye?"

"It's not exactly evil…it's more of an energy thing, like to clear the space of anything negative."

"Right. She said something about clearing the energy before we start renovations."

"You're renovating the house?" I don't know why this takes me aback, but the idea of touching what already oozes charm seems a downright sin.

Ben rubs the back of his neck and looks around. "My grandmother hates dust and change, in that order, but the roof is leaking and the plumbing is old and…" He shakes his head and blows out a long breath. "So it's a good time to renovate, which means I'll be staying here for a few months to oversee everything."

"What about your job?"

"I can do most of it remotely."

So you'll be all alone in this dreamy house on this dreamy island? I want to say, but instead, I tell him, "Sounds like a lot of work."

"I actually..." He glances up at the timbered ceiling like he's searching for the right words. "I guess I'm really into the idea of tearing something down to build it back up."

There it is. The smile. The warmth. The passion. This—*this* is what was missing when he talked about the hotels.

"Do you want something to drink?" Ben asks, poking his head into the refrigerator. "I've got wine, water, wine and...water."

"Well in that case," I say, "I'll have some wine. White, please."

A few minutes later, with wineglasses in our hands, he's touring me around the house, showing me what he wants to change. We navigate our way through hanging tarps, layers of sawdust, and stacks of tools randomly tossed here and there. His entire demeanor has shifted; there is a palpable excitement in his voice, in the rhythm of his movements. "I want to knock down that wall," he says as we enter a small low-ceilinged library. The old shelves are empty, and I'm about to ask why when Ben tells me he's clearing things out to make space for the demolition and the dust.

"Please tell me you are not getting rid of the library," I say, sipping my wine.

"No way," he stresses, "I want to expand it into the sunroom next door, so it feels more spacious. You should see the light in here during the day. It's the perfect place to read."

I admit it. I'm sort of blown away by this Ben. He's so relaxed, natural...maybe more like himself. Or at least I hope so. "You like to read?"

He hesitates, takes a drink of wine. I expect him to say no. But he doesn't. He just smiles. "Depends if the story is worth it."

A beat of silence passes over us, and I'm picking apart his

words, wondering what he considers *worth it* when he rushes in with, "And check it out."

He presses on a bookcase and it swings open to reveal a tiny closet. "I used to spend hours in there as a kid, pretending it was my own bat cave."

I stifle a laugh.

"What? No hidden doors in your family's house?"

"One," I admit. "Under the stairs."

"And?"

I know what he's asking, but I stretch out the game another beat. "And what?"

He stares at me expectantly.

"Okay, yeah, I pretended I was a genie…locked in a bottle."

"Interesting," he says, making a show of stroking his chin. I hate how adorable he looks right now.

"Dance lessons and Batman," I say. "What other surprises do you have up your sleeve?"

Ben huffs out a snort. "Yeah, I don't do surprises. I like to know what's coming."

"Kind of ruins the fun, doesn't it?"

"The fun of what?"

"I don't know." I grip my wineglass with both hands. "I guess waking up every day and wondering what good surprises are around the bend, big and small and even the life-changing ones. I mean, if you look at it like that, then I guess you're always one step closer to something amazing or some revelation…"

"Or you can make your own amazement."

I laugh lightly, warmed by the wine. "Then no one would ever need magic." The words, spoken like a spell, seem to linger in the quiet dim space. And I realize it's true; if everything always went as desired, if life turned out as expected, then magic would have no place in the world. Isn't that why people seek it out? Because they need a spark of possibility? A hint of good fortune?

We lean against the empty shelves, shoulder to shoulder, both taking in the space before us, and the possibilities of what it could be.

"Just think," Ben says quietly, "someday your book will be on people's shelves." He taps the cabinet to make his point.

His comment is so unexpected, I have to take a moment to process the enormity of it. Not his words, but his belief. In me. "That would be incredible."

"And true." His tone is low, almost intimate.

True.

My bones vibrate with the power of that word as I cling to the belief. Each guy I've been in a relationship with (all two if you count my high school love) were easy to dissect. I never had to look far to discover what made them tick, to determine who and what I had to be to earn their acceptance, their admiration, their love. But it was never *real.* Christ, I never even told Chad I wanted to write a book; I was too lost in building a life that fit him more than it fit me. In the end, I think I was too much of a coward to confront his doubt in my abilities. His all-knowing smirk, right before he launched into the statistics and odds that spelled out *his* truth, not mine.

And now I am standing next to a man I barely know, basking in the glow of his confidence in me. I can hear the distant music of the party, an upbeat rock tune that feels like an intrusion of the outside world, one I want to shut out, but I can't.

"So tell me about it," Ben says, "the book. Or at least the plot."

"Hmm…it's about a woman who inherits a magical piece of land from an estranged aunt."

He stares at me intently. "And then what happens?"

"She gets to the farm and is totally out of her element," I say, "made worse by all the mysterious things that start to happen."

"Like what?"

The words are coming fast and easy, ideas that I haven't written yet. "Like flowers dying at her touch."

"So it's a horror book?" he teases.

I laugh. "Definitely not, but she has to find her way, to learn to speak the language of the blooms, to unearth the family secret."

Ben is leaning closer, toally engaged. "Which is what?"

"You ask a lot of questions."

"But it's going to have a happy ending?"

"I have no idea."

Ben scowls. "I assumed you were an ambassador for happily-ever-afters."

A chuckle rolls out of me. "Ambassador?"

"Aren't you?"

Am I? I mean, sure I want to believe in them but that doesn't mean I'm going to lead some HEA crusade. I press my lips together, thinking. "I guess that's why I write. It's a place to put all my thoughts and feelings, a place I can ask the big questions, figure things out."

Ben shoulder bumps me. "Well, then, I guess I can't wait to find out how it all ends."

Even if it doesn't end happily? But I don't ask. "We should check the dress," I say, regretting the fact that we have to leave this space, this moment.

"First..." Ben takes a swig of wine and sets the glass down on the shelf. "There's something I need to tell you."

A tremble makes its way up my legs, and I'm eternally grateful for the solidity of the bookcase right now. "That sounds ominous."

Rubbing the back of his neck, he says, "I don't mean for it to."

Each word is layered in tension, and I admit it, I'm nervous. "Then what do you mean?"

He doesn't immediately answer, and I feel a fresh panic blooming in my chest. An excruciating few seconds later, he takes a deep breath. "Never mind. It can wait."

"Ben..." I utter through a nervous laugh, "now you absolutely have to tell me."

For a nanosecond I think he's going to shut down, change the subject, leave me spinning.

"I lied to you about Alicia." He spews the words like they are hot pokers. "When I told you that it meant more to her than to me."

Is this it? Is this what the foxglove from my dream was trying to tell me about deceit? "Okaaay." My pulse is pounding double-time. If this is a confession of his love for her, I absolutely do not want to hear it. Now or ever.

"What I mean is," he goes on, "I think what I told you was kind of misleading."

We spent some time together. It meant more to her than to me. End of story.

I wait for the guillotine to fall as Ben says, "She wasn't in love with me or anything close to it. She was more interested—" his eyes flick to mine "—in the story of the magic flowers."

My heart goes still.

"Alicia told me that she overheard my grandmother on the phone one day and after that she became obsessed with the idea of writing about the farm." He rubs his forehead. "It's the reason that she followed us down there, why she wanted to get her hands on the bouquet."

"I know."

Ben looks surprised.

"She came to the farm. Interviewed some people in town about my family," I tell him, offering the details down to the bee sting. "Then she went home so maybe now she'll let this whole thing go."

Ben places his hands behind his head and inhales. "She won't give up that easily."

I swallow the anxiety coming up like bile. "What do you mean?"

"I mean, she wanted to use the bouquet to prove the magic was real, and since that didn't work, she'll find another way."

"Well, she won't find anything." I wish I felt more confident than I sound. And now I'm filled with a bottomless worry that maybe my family isn't out of the woods yet, that if Alicia is still snooping, maybe my book *could* hurt the farm in some unintended way. But why would Mayahuel give me the beginning, open my heart and mind to a story that feels right for me when it is clearly so wrong for my family? It's a contradiction that I can't untangle.

"Why did you tell me all of that, about Alicia and her intentions?" I ask.

He casts a sideways glance at me; in the lamp's soft light, his eyes are undeniably warm, the color of whiskey. "I guess I felt responsible for her finding out. And I didn't want there to be any lies between us. I wanted the air clear so..."

"So what?"

Ben runs a hand through his hair and attempts a smile that looks more agonizing than anything else. "I think your dress is ready now."

I push off the shelves and face him. "You're not going to tell me?"

A low groan escapes his mouth. "I'm really bad at this stuff."

"What stuff?"

"This."

I fight the urge to roll my eyes. "That's clear as mud."

"I hate lies," he blurts before the dam breaks. "They ruin everything. I hate being manipulated like Alicia manipulated me. And I—I don't want that to ever be between us. I want us to tell each other the truth from the start."

There are so many ways for me to interpret his words, but I can't manage to because I'm trying to process it all at once.

Between us. From the start. There's a promise in there, one that feels a lot like the beginnings of something that both terrifies and exhilarates me. I want to press, but Ben already looks so pained, and something tells me he's being brutally honest, that he really is no good at communicating how he feels. Or at the very least, he's not used to it.

"Fine," I tell him, letting him off the hook for the moment, "You have a deal. Only the truth."

He looks surprised. "Yeah?"

"For sure."

He offers me a wry grin. "That was easy."

"I could make it harder," I say, socking him in the shoulder; the action sparks a laugh as he hunches down like he's bracing himself for more.

"Kidding. It was a joke."

"There are a lot of adjectives I would use to describe you, and funny isn't one of them."

"Like what?" He's amused, I can see it in his eyes, in his expression, in the way he holds his body.

"Truth?"

"We just agreed…"

I sigh. "Okay, fine. How about this…" *Generous and thoughtful, surprising in every conceivable way, hilariously competitive.* I could go on but he's staring at me, waiting for an answer, and of course I can't say any of those things, truth truce or not. So I go with, "Good with stains. I think."

Ben laughs. "Well, I haven't proven myself yet." He polishes off his glass of wine, and pushes off the case. "Let's go check it out."

I walk across the wood floor; it's cool beneath my bare feet. In between the next steps, I see a nail pointed up and jump back to avoid impaling my foot. Ben throws out a hand to steady me and then whatever happened next is a blur because I am somehow encircled in his arms.

I freeze. Too afraid to move, to even flinch. He's frozen too, and he's looking down at me. There is a strange distant light in his eyes as they circle my face. Warmth radiates off his body in all-consuming waves.

It's an agonizingly slow moment, one for the storybook of my life, which I will relive countless times with renewed mortification.

The decision is no decision at all. It never even gets filtered through my brain. Instead, my mouth is moving toward his and he isn't stopping me so I do it. I kiss him, just to get it over with. Well, *kiss* is a relative term. In this case I smash my lips against his. Teeth might have been involved. His spine goes rigid. My God, it's the worst first kiss in all of history, destined to be our last. A tidal wave of humiliation threatens to pull me under and kill me slowly.

But then, Ben doesn't laugh like I expect him to, he doesn't push me away or let me down easy. He does the one thing I don't expect. Of course, he does.

He inches me up against the bookcase and says, "Truth?"

I manage a nod. Christ, could someone open a damn window?

"I don't think… I should kiss you."

I really hate this new truce of truths right now.

"I didn't mean…" I say shakily, unable to finish the sentence because what's the point? I took a risk; it blew up in my face. Exclamation point inserted here. I try to extract myself from his embrace. But he doesn't let me go.

He leans in, a fraction of an inch. "This is…"

Closer…

"…a really bad…"

"Idea," I finish just as he drops his lips to mine. Soft and gentle like summer's first rain.

His body goes rigid like he's second-guessing this. I throw up my guard, unwilling to be humiliated a second time. But then comes the warm pulsation, the familiar vibration; it cuts through me like a knife, and I know he feels it too because his muscles loosen, his mouth yields. I taste the sweetness of wine still on his tongue. And then I'm lost.

Drowning in his touch, I drink him in while he kisses me hungrily, urgently like he might never kiss me again.

I'm shocked at the current coursing between us, strong and powerful, like the ocean. And in that moment, I feel Ben in my entire body, his want, his desire, his desperate longing for more.

It's too much *truth* to handle.

Somewhere in the distance, in another time and place, a door slams. A voice calls out, "Ben?"

We break apart. Chests heaving, hair tousled, eyes ablaze. He holds me with his gaze.

"I… I…" He looks lost, unhinged, unable to speak a coherent word.

My pulse has hit full on turbulence, and all I can manage is, "I know," just as Helena walks into the library, takes one look at us and says, "Should I even ask?"

19

❦

I wake languidly the next morning buried in sumptuous Egyptian sheets. Warm sunlight spills into the room, illuminating speckles of dust that drift in the air.

For one...two...three beats, I'm floating, remembering.

Ben. Those eyes.

And that kiss, his struggle, his surrender. All of it so delicious and also confusing, the push and pull, the yes and no. It was as if a force of nature was drawing us together.

I don't think I should kiss you. Not the same thing as I don't want to kiss you, I reason.

And yet...

After Helena caught us in the act, and graciously didn't pry, I quickly put on my barely perceptibly stained dress and returned to the party. Ben and I mingled, we ate, we smiled, and all the while, I found myself resisting the urge to take his hand, to lean against him, to do all the things "couples" do, but one kiss doesn't exactly make us a couple. Not even if it was the most incredible kiss of my life. And there's no denying that the moment we both yielded something shifted in me; I felt that tug deep in my heart, the same one that tells me when magic is present. Except that Ben isn't magic (well, not in the literal sense) and neither am I.

When the night was finally over, he walked me to my driver's car. Others were departing at the same time, making the area too crowded for another kiss. So he merely gave me a tight hug and whispered into my ear, "Thank you."

I thought it was an odd thing to say, and wasn't entirely sure what he was thanking me for. Coming to Quebec? Agreeing to our truth pact? Not giving him a hard time for losing the dance competition? Surely he wasn't thanking me for the kiss, right? That would just be weird.

By the time I got back to the hotel, I was floating in a strange fog of possibility and hope. Too wired to sleep, I found myself bent over my journal, hand flying across the pages, unable to keep up with the story.

Violeta felt like she could breathe for the first time in her life. The air at the farm was clean and sweet; it held the promise of a new life.

I stayed up late building Violeta's story, word by word. I don't even realize time is passing. I stretch my arms over my head just as the hotel phone rings. My smile is instant.

I sit up, clear my throat, and answer the cordless phone.

"Harlow?"

"Beverly...hi." My heart sinks a little, wishing it were Ben.

"I'm so glad I caught you," she says. "I wanted to know if I may take you to breakfast. So we can talk...about the message."

I glance at the clock. It's 8:15 a.m. "Of course. What time and where?"

"Downstairs, lobby level. Does an hour give you enough time?"

"Sure. I'll see you then."

I check my cell phone and find a text from Ben from twenty minutes ago: Good morning.

Smiling ear to ear, I return the message and begin to unpack what I didn't have time to last night. That's when I find a single bloom of canto in a side pocket of my bag. There's also a note from my mom. "A piece of the farm to take with you."

I bring the bloom to my nose and inhale its sweetness that is both distinct and subtle. "What are you trying to tell me?" I whisper just as my phone vibrates.

It's another message from Ben. Sleep okay?

Would rather have had my nightly dreams of you, I think as I type out, like a log.

And before I can type anything else my phone is ringing. It's Ben.

"Hi," I say. My voice has traces of morning husky, and I wish it didn't sound like I was trying to be alluring.

"Hi." Oh my God. He's smiling when he says it. I can tell. Then comes a bone grating noise of what sounds like an orchestra of drills, hammers, and saws. "Sounds like a construction party over there," I say.

"It's a mess. How's the hotel?"

"Beautiful. Quiet."

"Don't rub it in."

I glance at the clock. "I better get going," I tell him regretfully because I'd love nothing more than to crawl naked back into the soft clouds of this bed and talk to Ben for the next few hours. "I'm having breakfast with Beverly."

"And I wasn't invited?" he asks. He's still smiling.

I never told Ben about the note his grandmother had included with the invitation. And now I'm not sure I should say anything at all. What if Beverly doesn't want him to be in on whatever she has to tell me? I bite back the words climbing up my throat, and steer clear.

"Sorry, girls only."

He chuckles and I delight in the sound of it.

"So about today…" he says, his tone shifting, which raises my guard. All giddiness drains out of me as I brace myself for a rain check speech.

"Yeah?"

"The construction workers knocked into the library wall, they burst a pipe and it's a mess."

"Ben, don't worry about it," I say as I fill a glass with water. "I know you have to take care of things at the house. We can do the river cruise another time." And my brain means it, but my heart wants what it wants, and I'm supremely disappointed that I won't be spending the day with him.

"But we'll be done later," he adds, "and I was thinking maybe we could have dinner. Here on the island or…"

A knot of anxiety and excitement tightens in my belly. Are we really doing this? Dancing and kissing and dinner? I usually take things slow in a dating situation, but now? I feel like I skipped a step or two.

"I can come get you about 5:30?" he says.

"Of course not," I tell him.

"Is that a no?"

I chuckle, realizing how my comment must have come off. "I meant…if we're going to be on the island for dinner, it makes sense for me to come to you."

A man shouts, "Yo, Ben," in the middle of pounding and drilling, but Ben ignores him and says to me, "Okay then. See you tonight. And it's casual."

After we hang up, I set the nearly wilted canto inside the glass of water. All I can see is Ben pressing me against that bookcase, the sharp angles of his jaw as he leaned closer, his mouth parted ever so slightly right before it met mine. Coming back down to earth, I realize that I've brought my fingers to my lips and I'm smiling. Again. I look at the canto. And in that instant, its silky petals unfurl right before my eyes.

Place Dufferin is a relaxed but elegant restaurant made even more appealing by its sunroom that overlooks a wooden promenade and the St. Lawrence River. This is where I find Beverly, sitting near a window, gazing out at the boats cruising by.

"Good morning," I announce cheerily, hanging my purse on the back of my chair.

She's up and out of her seat before I can say another word, and she's pulling me into her arms like we're family, like the ties she has to my grandmother have extended to me.

After we order coffee and some croissants, she says, "Did you enjoy last night?"

I feel a rush of heat beneath my skin because last night will always represent the first time I kissed Ben Brandt. "It was so nice," I say. "I'm really glad I came."

Her eyes nearly glitter when she says, "And Ben?"

I'm going to choke on my own spit. Where did that question come from, and why does the question have to be so vague? Truly, it could mean so many things, none of which I want to take a stab at. "Ben?" I say with just the right inflection as to not be too coy or invested in this topic.

"I saw you two dancing and then you left and…" There's that gleam in her eye again "Is your dress okay?"

Shit! Did Helena tell her what she walked into last night? Are they *that* kind of family? The kind that tell each other everything, that blur the lines between privacy and all-out truth? In other words, are they like *my* familia?

The word *mortified* doesn't begin to convey what I'm feeling. As a matter of fact, I am certain there is no word in the English language that does. I begin to search for one in Spanish, coming up short.

"It's fine," I say, playing it off as the skin of my décolleté begins to erupt with those diablo blotches. I'm grateful I'm wearing a crewneck sweater to hide the devil's truth.

"Ben will surprise you like that," Beverly sings.

Please speak in clearer terms that my foggy kiss-hangover brain can understand. Guessing her meaning, I go with, "He's a regular stain magician."

She's nodding, like she's expecting me to say something else; I decide to stay in safe territory and avoid any and all borders with Ben's name on them. "And your farmhouse is so beautiful. There's a charm to it that reminds me of…"

"La Casa de Las Flores y Luz?"

"Exactly." I feel a sort of bond between me and Beverly, a shared memory of someone we both loved, a place we both adore, and a belief we both live by. Magic.

The canto flashes across my mind, the way its petals unfolded, and I wonder if my mom enchanted the flora so that it would only bloom when I laid eyes on it. I make a mental note to ask her later.

A server pours our coffee, and a few minutes later our plates arrive. Unable to keep my curiosity in check another second, I get right to the point. "So your message."

Beverly nods, sets a chocolate croissant on her plate, and begins to pick at its edges. "I hope I'm not crossing a boundary here, Harlow, but I'm worried about William."

"Is it the bonding?"

"No, he remembers everything about our lives together and is so connected to me, like I'm his very lifeline." She takes a long breath in, but I swear she never exhales. "It's just that…he…" The corner of her mouth trembles.

"It's okay," I say gently. "You can tell me."

"My William is a man of many layers," she goes on, recomposing herself. "Much like Ben. There is a complicated structure there that no one understands. Oh, dear. I'm afraid I'm not explaining this right."

"I think I understand," I say, thinking about Ben.

Complicated. Layers.

"Well," she says, "I feel as if those layers are being peeled away one by one and vanishing and pretty soon…" She chokes back a sob. "I worry they'll all be gone and there will be nothing left."

I reach for her hand, trying to process what she's telling me. Yes, the magic has done its job, but it isn't enough to keep William from floating away. And *I* don't have the power to do anything either, so why is she telling me all of this? And then I remember. The lavender and lily in the kitchen. It was her way of protecting something that the house holds: her and William's story, their love, their beginnings.

Beverly stirs her coffee over and over and over, blinking away fresh tears.

"I'm so sorry." My voice is nearly a whisper. *But how can I help?*

She must sense the question I'm harboring because she says, "Your grandmother was such a force in my life, her very presence pure magic. And I haven't felt that energy since…well, until I met you."

I feel a stab in the center of my gut. My grandmother Azalea was everything I always wanted to be, a pioneer in every way, breaking all the rules, charting her own course. Seeing what others couldn't. Beverly is right. She was a force, taken too soon.

Azalea used to tell me that it didn't matter what name the goddess had given me, that *heap of stones* could be its own magic. I, of course, argued with her. Stones were for throwing; they were drab, colorless things that sank in water.

She had sighed as her hands were doing their usual busywork of braiding baby's breath into my hair, a symbol of her love for me. "Ah, Harlow," Azalea had said, "stones can also be polished."

"And that's what I want to talk to you about," Beverly says, gazing at the island across the water. It's even more magnificent in the light of day. Rolling green hills, trees bursting with golds and rusts and reds, the shore dotted with impressive historic homes.

Without turning to me, Beverly says, "When you were born, Azalea called me. She wanted to tell me how special you were." Her voice takes on a wistful tone while I try to catch my breath. "She said that she had seen something, about your future."

"What?" She performed a divination? I can hardly believe my ears. Why would my grandmother have looked into my future? Why would she risk depleting the crops? And why hadn't I ever heard about it?

Beverly turns to me now. "She told me that you and I would share a future, and when I pressed she couldn't tell me more, only that I would know at the right moment and now I see that it was no accident that our paths collided. That you were meant to come into our lives."

I don't know how to begin to process what she's telling me. "But why did she tell you?" I finally ask. "And not my mom or my aunt?"

Beverly twists her napkin between her fingers. "She didn't want anyone to know about the divination, but she told me that the second you were born, she knew she needed to look into your future, to understand why you weren't named for a flower."

My pulse pounds in my ears. "And did she find out?"

"She never said."

Anger seeps into my bones. How could Azalea not have told me, not have told the family? Why keep it a secret?

Beverly switches topics too soon. "I said that I wanted your energy nearby. Not because I think you can fix what's broken, but because I needed a piece of Azalea with me."

"I understand." And I do. The Estrada women carry every ancestress in our blood, in our hearts and spirits. We carry their burdens, their sorrows, their triumphs.

"And because I made a promise to Azalea, to tell you what

she shared with me so many years ago. She said I would know the right time, and that it would mean something to you."

Except that it doesn't.

Beverly adds, "She said that no matter how hard it gets, you must press on, that when all has been destroyed…"

"The goddess shall rise," I whisper. I have absolutely no idea what to do with any of this. But the last thing I want to do is make Beverly feel bad, so I say, "Thank you for telling me."

"And now that you're here," she says, dabbing her eyes with her napkin, "we'd love to take you to dinner or lunch…maybe tomorrow?"

How is it that a once-stranger can so quickly become a part of your life, as if they've been in it forever? "I'd love to."

Back in my room I call my mom to ask her about Azalea and the canto she placed in my bag. But before I can get mention it, she launches in with, "Are you enjoying Quebec?"

"The party was nice and I'm headed out for the first time in daylight now, so I'll report back. And thanks for the gift."

"It arrived safely? Not smashed?"

"It was a little sad when I unpacked it," I say, tracing my fingers over the flower next to me. "But then your enchantment went to work and now it's perfect."

"Enchantment?"

"To make the petals unfold."

Another bridge of silence. "Mom?"

"Yes, I'm here."

I think about how Azalea had peered into my future and I'm on the verge of asking my mom about it, but then I realize that there must have been a reason my grandmother didn't tell the family, that she only told Beverly. But what did she see in my future? It's hard to accept that a ghost has the answers I'm looking for, answers I might never find on my own. I decide to keep it to myself…for now.

"You seem distant," I tell her. "Is everything okay?"

She hesitates. "We can talk when you get home."

"We can talk now," I say, suddenly unnerved. "What's wrong?"

"That journalist," she says, "she's been calling past clients."

"What!" If I was annoyed before, I'm infuriated now. Ben's words echo through me: *she won't give up that easily.*

"They of course have said nothing," Mom goes on, "but how did she find them, Harlow?"

I press the bridge of my nose. "No idea, but… I mean it's good no one is talking."

Mom's silence is overpowering, sending me the message she doesn't want to verbalize: *you can't write this book.*

"Claro. Go. Have a good time. We'll handle this."

I feel queasy, thinking there has to be a way to deter Alicia, but how?

A few minutes later, I exit the hotel and am met by a fierce blast of cold rolling in off of the water. The street is filled with wanderers like me, as well as tour buses, street musicians, and the occasional horse and carriage. Near the waterfront I find a tucked-away staircase, leading down to what can only be described as a fairy tale.

The lower city is enchanting with its little boutiques, storefront galleries and restaurants, and cobblestone roads. One road leads to another, sometimes opening into a historic square; the occasional open space is festooned with pumpkins, piles of haystacks, scarecrows, and brilliant orange and gold foliage.

Everywhere I go I take in new colors, scents, accents, and languages. It's a feast for the imagination, and soon I stumble upon a bench soaked in sunshine just outside a café, and for the next few hours, I write in my notebook.

It's three o'clock when I head back to the hotel with a small bag of caramel popcorn that I picked up along the way, which is a pile of crumbs by the time I reach my room.

I check my phone, which I've had on silent, and find a hope all is well text from my mom, one from Beverly about the restaurant tomorrow, and a series of texts going in my group chat with my sisters.

The last text is from Laini. Well? How was the party? Was he there? Details!

I laugh and shoot her a response: Great. Yes. Details forthcoming. Promise.

It won't be enough to feed her curious appetite, but it will hold her at bay until I can process what to even tell her. He was there. We danced. There is an inexplicable energy between us. I kissed him. In a dusty library. It was delicious.

After a long hot shower, I decide on a pair of black jeans and a white T-shirt paired with a cashmere duster and some ankle boots. I do a once-over in the mirror, run my fingers through my hair, air-dried into loose beach waves, and am downstairs and in a cab in under ten minutes.

The sky has softened to a pale shade of blue, and the waning sun casts an iridescent gold glow over the water as we cross the bridge.

I'm lost in the beauty of this place when my phone vibrates in my pocket. It's Lil. I almost don't answer until it's followed by a text, please pick up. It's important.

"What's up?" I ask, hoping nothing is wrong.

"How's Quebec?" she asks. Immediately alarm bells go off in my head. My sister is the worst small talker of all time and isn't really asking.

"Fine. Why?"

She takes a deep breath. "Okay, so I wasn't going to tell you, but then Cam said I have to but I don't want to ruin your trip, so you decide."

"Jeez, Lil, how about a little more detail?" My voice may sound in control, but my heart is about to lose it.

"I had a dream. About you."

"Missing me that much?"

"Bean, I'm serious."

"Okay, but can you tell me later, I'm heading out right now." Oof. I wish I hadn't said that because it's only an invitation for her to dig.

But surprisingly, she doesn't. She says, "I have to tell you now."

"Then why did you ask me to decide?"

"Because I'm democratic."

The driver makes a right onto the road that leads to the Brandt home, which means we are less than two minutes away.

"You were drowning in a lake, and the water," Lil says, "it turned into a bed of flowers. They were everywhere and they were pulling you under."

"What kind of flower?"

The driver turns into the Brandt vineyard. From here I can see Ben on the porch. He's sitting on an old wooden bench, wearing a white button-down and dark jeans. He definitely got hotter overnight. Damn him.

Just then he looks up, gets to his feet, and waves.

My stomach does this weird flip. And I've forgotten Lil is still on the line. Until she says, "Foxglove. You were drowning in foxglove."

20

I'm out of the car and walking toward Ben, who is already down the porch stairs headed my way. And with each step I take, I see myself in Lil's dream, drowning in foxglove, in deception, insincerity, and mystery. But why would a flower that also has the magical power of protection be trying to kill me?

Beverly's words reverberate through me.

You were meant to come into our lives.

A clear contradiction to the foxglove's message. But why?

My time with these disturbing thoughts is up because Ben is now pulling me into his arms, and I lean in effortlessly, hugging him, wishing I could rest my head on his chest and pretend away the world of dreams and magic.

He's smiling as we break apart as naturally as we came together.

"Hey," I say, quickly searching for a safe topic so I don't have to stare into those whiskey eyes in total silence. "How's…the wall?"

He shoots a backward glance at the house. "Well...it's, uh, down."

"And?" I ask, unable to contain my curiosity. "Does it look how you imagined?"

Ben throws me a smirk; it's a playful one.

"Do you mean the dust or the flood or—"

I laugh. "I mean the light." The perfect light for reading that you promised me.

"I think so, but." He stops midsentence and looks at me. His mouth curves up gently and he says simply, "You look beautiful."

And just like that, I've forgotten about the light and the library and the foxglove.

"Thanks," I say, wishing I had a better response or was half the flirt that Lil is. She has this astonishing ability to say the right thing at the right time with the right expression that always gets her what she wants. It's annoying, but also? Very impressive.

"Hungry?" Ben asks.

"Famished," I tell him, realizing I've only eaten a croissant and a bag of caramel popcorn—not exactly sustenance. A minute later, we're approaching an old silver truck that looks like it's seen better days. Beyond the few dents, there's sun-damaged signage on the door: Vineyard Couer.

"Is this okay?" he says as he opens my door for me.

"Why wouldn't it be?" I tell him as I climb into the cab.

He hops in the other side and I catch a brief trace of his signature scent. "Not exactly first date wheels," he says as we drive onto the empty road.

First date? Is that what this is? He must see the look on my face in the fading light because he autocorrects with, "I meant..." Seeing Ben Brandt panicky is akin to watching a wild animal locked in a cage. It's not natural, and something about it is even painful.

I keep my gaze out the passenger window, watching the

greens and golds and reds blur by. "I learned to drive in an old Ford like this one, on the farm actually."

"Oh yeah?"

"When I was eleven—" I stare out across a picked-over pumpkin field, its scarecrow limply clinging to a stake of wood "—my gram said every girl should know how to drive early and well, so she took us around the farm," I say, savoring the glow of Azalea's memory.

"Sounds like how I grew up," Ben adds. "I spent my summers here and learned how to drive anything with an engine by the time I was twelve."

I'm taken aback at how at first glance Ben and I appear to be polar opposites, but if you look close enough, if you peel back enough layers, we're similar in so many ways. Both entrenched in loyalty, both tied to an inheritance we didn't ask for, and both deeply rooted to the land.

He turns down a dirt road through an apple orchard. There are rows and rows of lush trees and a few wooden ladders propped at various angles.

"We're eating apples for dinner?" I tease.

"You'll see."

The sky is nearly dark with the first pinpricks of starlight coming into view as Ben pulls the truck into a little dirt lot next to a few other cars and what looks like a stone barn, its ramshackle doors are strung with pink and orange lights.

The moment I'm out of the truck I'm struck by the scent of fresh baked bread, and garlic sauteed in butter; my stomach rumbles.

"A friend of mine opened this place last year," Ben says, steering me inside. Okay, it's not a barn. It's more of an intimate space with stained concrete floors, wooden crossbeams, antique chandeliers, an entire wall of wine bottles, and a scattering of stone-top tables with mismatched chairs. Its charm is unpretentious, unassuming, and absolutely perfect.

"This place is amazing," I say as the hostess greets Ben with a smile and leads us to a table tucked in a back corner near a small stone fireplace.

"I was hoping you'd like it," Ben says, pulling my chair out for me before I sit. On one hand I'm surprised at the gesture, but then I remember Beverly raised this man for the most part and so it makes every bit of sense that he has manners. "So, here's the deal," he says with a note of excitement that's contagious, "there isn't really a menu. It's basically chef's surprise. Vegetarian or nonvegetarian."

"Kind of like eating at home," I say, secretly thrilled I don't have to make any decisions. But then a new panic sets in. What if the dish is pasta with extra garlic? Or some unmanageable sloppy sandwich? I could write a book on what *not* to eat on a first date: slurpy soups, ribs, crab legs. Pretty much anything that stinks, makes you look like a slob, or ruins that movie-worthy kiss. Not that I expect to kiss Ben again. Actually, I do. I absolutely expect/hope/plan to.

Just then a stocky guy comes over, sporting a stained apron and a ratty baseball cap planted on his head backward. "Yo, Ben."

Ben is on his feet, shaking the guy's hand. "Abe!"

And just as Ben gestures to me like an introduction is coming, Abe fixes his hazel eyes on me and smiles wide. "You must be Harlow."

This simple sentence could mean so many things. Why do I do this to myself? Try to interpret every little nuanced word, every gesture. It's maddening and it's ending right now. I'm doing things differently with Ben. I'm a grown woman, and I don't need to play games. Besides, we made a truth pact, and I'm sticking to it.

"Hi," I say as Abe spins a chair around and straddles it. Then he leans into the table like he has a secret to tell. "Good to meet you," he offers, backslapping Ben in the chest while holding my gaze. "This guy's told me all about you."

I give up a playful smile and glance at Ben. "Should I even ask?"

Ben folds his arms over his chest and reclines back in his chair. His mouth is on the verge of a grin, and if I didn't know better, I'd think he was totally enjoying this.

"So, you came all the way to our neck of the woods from Mexico?" Abe asks. I like him immediately, his directness and energy.

"I did," I tell him as the fire crackles, warm and inviting. "It was such a great party."

"Yeah, sorry I missed it," Abe says. "Had a big event here at the restaurant last night."

"So, this is your place?" I ask, glancing around. "It's really incredible."

Abe beams with an expression of pride. "I can see why you like her," he tells Ben.

I feel a pinch in my gut and am suddenly afraid to look at Ben, to watch him correct his friend, and maneuver his way out of *liking me* with a few single words. But Abe is talking again before I can hazard a glance. "Although I have no idea why *she's* hanging out with *you*."

Ben doesn't correct him and he doesn't maneuver. He merely chuckles and says, "Yeah, me neither."

I feel a flood of heat racing over my skin, my cheeks and chest. Please please please no red splotches. Not now. *I will forever have to wear turtlenecks with this man.*

Ben smiles as he turns to me. "Abe is my oldest friend. We grew up together," he tells me, helping to fill in the gaps of their banter.

"Oh, really?" I focus my attention back on Abe. "That means you have all the good dirt on Ben."

"So much dirt I could fill in a playground," Abe teases. "Buy me a beer sometime, and I'll tell you every single story."

"No one's buying anyone a beer," Ben declares, trying to

hold a stern expression but failing miserably. "But could we get some dinner?"

Abe removes a cigar from his apron pocket and puts it in his mouth, but doesn't light it.

"I thought you quit," Ben says.

"Doesn't mean I can't enjoy the taste."

"Abe just got married," Ben tells me by way of explanation. And clearly Abe's spouse doesn't like his smoking habit. Got it.

"Congratulations," I say. "When?"

"Eight blissful months ago. Ben was my best man, got me drunker than shit the night before so Leeza hasn't really forgiven him, and she's got a loooong memory."

I throw a teasing glare at Ben. "How could you?"

"Tell him!" Abe nearly shouts through a snort of laughter.

"It's a rite of passage on this island," Ben says matter-of-factly as he studies me. "No way was my best friend going to the altar without some sustenance in his blood. And Leeza still owes me for getting her out of jail senior year for setting off all those fireworks at the Hoover Farm."

At this Abe rolls his eyes. "Man, you have such a bad memory. *I* got her out of jail, which is why she married me and not you."

I'm loving how this night is starting, seeing Ben through the eyes of his oldest friend, and the warmth that exudes from him as a result. But another part of me is afraid, afraid that I love it too much, that I'm trapped in a mudslide and it's too late to turn back.

Abe turns to me, holding up his hand so I can see a nasty three-inch scar on the underside of his wrist. "See this?"

"Here we go," Ben says.

"This guy." Abe points to his friend.

"Look," Ben argues, "it's not my fault you can't climb a chain-link fence."

"I have to hear this," I say, already on the edge of my seat.

Shaking his head, Abe says, "Old Ben here thought it would be a good idea to steal some tires from a junkyard."

"Borrow!" Ben corrects him.

I laugh as Abe waves him away. "We were ten maybe eleven, and he was in love with Shayla Montcler."

I try to contain my laughter. "Shayla, huh?"

"She was nothing compared to you," Ben teases, and I relish in the playful praise.

Abe shakes his head. "Anyhow, she was trying to build a go-kart and Ben had her convinced he was Mr. Handy."

"I was in woodshop!" Ben argues.

Ignoring him, Abe goes on, "So he tells Shayla he'll help her, but she was short the tires, so..."

I throw a glance at Ben "You thief."

He grunts. "We didn't even get the tires because this guy was bleeding to death."

We're all laughing now and then someone calls Abe's name from the kitchen. He mock-puffs on his cigar before he gets to his feet. "Duty calls," he says. "Great to meet you, Harlow."

"Likewise," I tell him. "And someday, I will definitely buy you that beer."

Ben groans.

"Deal," Abe replies. "And hell, maybe I'll even light this."

As I watch him go, my eyes alight on the wine wall, drawn to one bottle in particular. I go over and tug the bottle free, and bring it back to the table. The simple cream-colored label is inked with black lettering, Vineyard Couer, and a sketch of the Brandt house surrounded by the vineyard.

"This is your wine," I tell Ben as if he doesn't already know.

"My family makes small batches," he says, staring at the bottle then back at me. "Abe's nice enough to carry it."

"I like him," I say. "I mean, if he's willing to go on a heist with you to impress a girl, that's true friendship."

Ben's smiling, leaning back casually with his arms folded over his chest. "He's the best guy I know."

Turning back to the wine, I ask, "What kind is it?"

"A sparkling wine. We have to grow hybrid-grape varieties that are hardy, can survive freezes, but really you should ask Helena. It's her baby."

Just then a server arrives and sets two small white plates in front of us. "Amuse-bouche to begin," he tells us in a thick French accent.

I don't speak French, but I learned the term *mouth amuser* or *amuse the mouth* on a trip to Paris when I was a teen. I never forgot the translation because Lantana and Camilla spent the entire trip coming up with lurid jokes about it.

This particular pleaser is a petite pastry with salmon and dill fronds, paired with unoaked white wine that is dry, crisp, and bold.

"I thought you said this place was casual," I whisper to Ben like it's a secret.

"It is," he whispers back.

"A multicourse meal isn't casual," I tell him. "Not where I'm from."

"You have to know Abe." He takes a drink of wine. "He opened this place with nothing, only a dream. I really admire the guy. His entire business plan was one line—'I want to make whatever the hell I want as long as its local.'"

Okay, now I like Abe even more.

"I can't believe you got the poor guy drunk before his wedding."

Ben looks affronted. "There's always more than one side to a story."

"Like who got Leeza out of jail."

I think I hear a laugh, but he bottles it up with a deadpan stare that feels like a challenge.

"Exactly."

After three courses of salmon confit, beet purée, and pan-seared scallops in ginger sauce, I'm skating the edge of a delightful warm buzz. I've already had four half-ish glasses of wine, each paired masterfully with our dishes. My mouth is definitely pleased.

Over the course of dinner, Ben has managed to scoot his chair closer and closer, so now we're sitting side by side, knees touching.

"This food is amazing," I say, licking the last of ginger sauce off my spoon.

"I'm glad Abe got his dream."

"And you," I say, emboldened by the wine, "tell me more about the land...your soul truth."

"It's something I haven't told anyone." His voice is low, unsure.

I brace myself with another swig of wine.

"We have these behemoth hotels and they feel so corporate, so impersonal." He scrubs a hand over his face. "They feel lifeless to me."

I don't ask why he does it because I already know the answer. Loyalty. Family. Honor. Christ, he must feel trapped.

"It's weird, you know? To be locked into something and don't get me wrong. I'm lucky, I know that. Lucky to have so many resources and..." His voice trails off and I wonder if he's thinking about his mom and dad, the loss, and every loss since that has defined who he is.

"So I have an idea," he says, brightening a bit. "And I want your opinion."

I'm flattered. Really, but— "I don't know anything about hotels, Ben."

"But you know about other things that matter, like—"

"Please do not say flowers."

"I was going to say *life*."

I make a sound between a snort and a gasp. Waiting for Ben

to laugh, to tell me it's another bad joke, but he's staring at me with utter sincerity.

"You'd have to," he goes on, "to be able to write an entire book."

"Not entire," I say. "It's not done yet."

His expression is so earnest. "But it will be."

I adore this man's belief in me.

"Okay," I say, "I'm all ears."

Maybe it's the afterglow of wine, or our close proximity, but for a split second, Ben looks like a little boy, his face painted with a hope.

"I want to start a new concept under our brand," he says, "something that symbolizes this island, a place people can reinvent themselves." He's talking with his hands, his eyes, his entire body. "So not exactly a hotel or a resort, but smaller scale, something that uses local businesses for all its needs from furniture to the menu, you know? An experience. A place that feels like home but also like a dream."

A dream. Like mine and Lil's with foxglove? A warning about Ben? And yet he's trusting me with his secret. Hardly *deceitful and insincere.*

The heat from the crackling fire warms my cheeks and casts a golden light on Ben that highlights the beginnings of crow's-feet around his dark eyes.

"You hate it," Ben says, not knowing my mind is churning over the meaning of the foxglove.

"Truth?" I say.

He swallows. "That was the deal."

"So something really farm to table," I tell him, wanting to show him I understand and I believe in him the way he believes in my book. "A place that feels more personal. I love everything about it."

"Really?"

"Really."

Ben's entire expression shifts, and he's on his feet before I can take my next breath. "We need to go."

"But..."

He's already taking my hand and leading me outside. I barely have time to grab my purse. "Ben—we haven't paid, and isn't there another course and because..."

Outside, he turns to me, cups my face. "Because inside, I couldn't do this."

And then he kisses me.

It's nothing like the other night. There is no hesitation, no awkwardness, no push and pull. Only the desire to be closer than our bodies allow. I can feel the raw energy pulsing from every inch of him, and before I know it my arms are around his neck, my fingers threading his hair, wishing, yearning for more. His breathing is hurried, his touch both gentle and desperate. And the deeper we go, the longer I cling to him, the more I open myself to him, the farther I fall.

My heart is pounding against my ribs when he lightly breaks away. I suddenly hate the inches between us. With a half sigh, half groan, he presses his forehead to mine. "Truth?"

I nod.

"I think I'm in a lot of trouble."

21

We never go back into the restaurant.

The air is too crisp, the sky is too beautiful, and the moonlit orchard is too inviting.

Before I know it, we're walking and talking, about anything and everything, and it's as if our sentences meld one into the other, as if, together, our words make up one story.

I'm sure I won't remember everything that we say, or how often we've laughed, or the ache in my cheeks from smiling too much, but I know, in that moment, I *know* I will always remember how easy and natural this is, this feeling of connection and trust. Especially when Ben tells me, "It was the hardest moment of my life." He's talking about his parents' death. There is the slightest tremor in his voice, one that triggers an auto-hug response in me but I resist because something tells me he just needs me to listen.

"I'm lucky I had Helena and my grandparents to get through

it," he says, like that's what's expected—this glass-half-full at-titude. "But there was all this guilt."

"About what?" I ask.

Ben stops in a patch of shadow, his gaze fixed on something over my shoulder. A wedge of moonlight spills through the trees, enough that I can see the pain on his face. "My mom…she, uh, she never loved my dad." He scoffs then pauses, and I can only imagine how hard that was for him to say. "It was all about the money for her," he adds with a half-hearted shrug. "I guess I always knew it and I…" He glances at me like he's gauging my response, my judgment, determining if he's going to divulge the full truth. "She had this way of manipulating him, and he just couldn't see it."

His tone is one of frustration, fresh resentment as if these events just happened, and that's when I know that he's never talked about this before.

"Then I was on her phone one day," he adds, "and I found these texts messages. And… I hated her for it." His chest sags with the weight of those words.

That's all he needs to say for me to know how the story ends. I reach out and touch his arm, trying to imagine how hard that must have been to experience as a child.

"So when they died," he goes on, "I felt like this horrible per-son that I ever hated her. That I never told her I saw the texts, that she never even knew the truth."

"Except you didn't hate her," I say, guessing that what he was really feeling was anger. *Is* anger.

Ben runs a hand down his face, clenches his jaw. "Maybe not, but I really wanted to, and that night I refused to tell her good-bye. I don't even remember what my deal was, but she asked me for a hug and I wouldn't give her one."

I feel the weight of his pain in the center of my chest. To be so young, to have lived with all this guilt for so long. "The day be-fore my grandma died," I say gently, "she told me something I've never forgotten. She said that the mind doesn't know what the corazón knows, that it's the heart that carries all the memories, and that when we die, in that last breath we see all the truths, we feel all the love so that nothing is really left unknown."

Ben looks at me. His eyes are filled with emotion, tenderness. "I think I would have liked Azalea."

"Me too."

He stuffs his hands in his pants pockets and glances down at the ground. "I think it's why I'm so bad at relationships."

The territory we haven't broached.

He's waiting for me to say something, but the words are piling up in my mind like a traffic jam, and alarms are blaring, and I don't want to say the wrong thing. What would Dahlia tell him? God, if ever I needed her relationship expertise it's now. "What do you mean?" I ask.

Ben huffs out a breath, then tilts his head back to look at the treetops. "I've been told I'm not a great communicator." He pauses, lets the words float between us. "And I never really let anyone get close to me."

I may not have lost my parents tragically, but God, I understand his need for armor. And I realize we're all wearing it, just different versions and weights.

"Okay, so what's your longest relationship?" I ask, thinking he's likely exaggerating how bad he really is.

He squints one eye closed like he's calculating. "Uh...a few weeks?"

Oh. Yeah. That's not even in the realm of relationship. "Seriously?" The word slips out too easily.

"I told you I'm bad at relationships."

Is he trying to tell me that *this*, me and him, that it's going nowhere north of a few weeks? Is this what the foxglove was trying to tell me?

"And," he goes on, "I'm not exactly the Mr. Romance happy-ending kind of guy."

My heartbeat is picking up speed, but I say nothing because it's not my job to change him, to make him believe in something he doesn't, which only fills me with a terrible disappointment. I thought I saw something in Ben, some shining light behind his armor.

He softens his gaze. "I don't know. I really want to think people get happy endings. I mean look at my grandparents."

The knot in my stomach loosens as I cling to some weird kind of hope that Ben can believe in happy endings, in magic, in a forever kind of love.

Ben narrows his eyes, taking me in as his mouth curves into a boyish grin. "Did you know they met in Ventana and that he proposed after a week?"

"A week?! Wow."

"My gramps always told me he knew the second he saw her," he says with a laugh. "She had fallen off her bike and was sprawled out on the sidewalk surrounded by flowers from your family's store.

"So he goes running over to help her up," Ben continues, his eyes dancing with the retelling, "and she's pretty banged up but she kept pushing him away, telling him to not stomp on the flowers."

I'm smiling, imagining the scene, wondering how a boy can grow up with such sharp contrasts of love and still choose to focus on the one of betrayal. Is that what we humans do? Choose the dark instead of the light, choose denial instead of hope?

"*That* is a story that should be in a book."

Ben laughs. "Yeah? Well, just send me the royalty check."

"Deal," I say. "And see? Happy endings exist."

Ben's grin fades. "But is it a happy ending? I mean..." He hesitates and I know where his resistant mind is going. But I don't have the answers either, only this. "Everyone has to say goodbye eventually, but it's the time they spend together when they have each other. That's what matters most." To remember the love not the loss.

He nods. "I like your optimism."

"I mean you are the guy who wants my book to have a happy ending."

"But that isn't real life."

I have no idea what I can say to that. How to begin. But somehow the words find me. "I know trust can be a hurdle. And not letting anyone in? I get it. We all have our reasons…"

I can feel his eyes locked on me now, but I'm too afraid to look up, to see something I don't want to. "How about an apple?" I suggest cheerfully, tugging one from a hanging branch.

"Are you trying to change the subject?"

I hold the apple out to his amused face. "No. It just…looks really good."

"Harlow, I'm a pro at changing subjects, so believe me, I recognize it when I see it." He takes the apple and bites into it. "There," he says around a mouthful. "We are officially kicked out of the Garden of Eden."

"Ben, things didn't work out too well for Adam and Eve."

He pinches his brows together. "Probably because he wasn't a happy-ending, romantic guy."

"Define romantic," I say, a hint of challenge in my tone. Maybe I want to make him see himself in a new light or maybe I'm trying to see something that isn't there.

He cradles the back of his neck with both hands. "I don't know. Roses and poems and sunsets, and love notes…stuff like that."

I'm scared. So scared to say the thing I want to say, to have him reject it, but regardless of whether we even see each other after tonight, I guess I really do want him to see himself through my eyes.

"Or…dance competitions, first kisses in dusty libraries, out of the way restaurants, walks through orchards," I tell him.

He freezes. There's a battle going on behind those eyes, one that might not be won tonight or any night, but he's heard the words, he's registered them and now I wait to see if he ignores them, scoffs at them, cracks a joke or...

He wraps his arms around my waist. He doesn't clasp his hands, just lets them rest there. "You must be a really good writer, or something,"

Relief floods my body. "Or something."

Not letting me go, he asks, "What about you?"

"What about me?"

"Your relationships."

"Bah..." I tug out of his embrace, batting a nonchalant hand through the air. "Boring, dull, not worth talking about."

"Oh, come on," he pleads, "I want to know. Tell me about the last guy you dated."

I'm about to shut down this conversation; it'll make me too vulnerable, and I already feel so exposed. Just as I open my mouth to do so, that small voice inside of me rises on a whisper, *if you are ever going to be the sovereign over your own life, you have to own it.*

So I tell him. All of it. And when I'm done the earth is still beneath my feet, I haven't gone up in flames, and Ben is still standing here. Staring at me with those enchanting puppy-dog eyes.

Please don't pity me. Please don't pity me.

He shakes his head, then he grunts, "That guy needs an ass kicking."

"Well," I chuckle, "he did get a martini thrown into his face."

At this Ben's whole face breaks into a smile, and his gaze drifts off like he's imagining the scene before cutting back to me. "So why did you stay with him for so long?" The question catches me off guard, and it takes a moment to regain my balance. I search for the truth, the one I feel and know today, not the one that is buried under a pile of excuses that villainize Chad and makes me look like the injured party.

"He was safe," I say. "He didn't expect too much from me and it was easy to get swept up in his world, so I guess I didn't have to try to create my own."

A breeze floats through the orchard; the trees sway with a susurrus whisper, one that reminds me of the farm's magic and instantly I'm homesick.

"Do you mean writing?" he asks. His voice is gentle, encouraging.

I nod, meet his gaze, thinking how utterly bizarre it is to be so open and honest with someone, to show them all the parts of myself that I usually keep hidden away, the scared, lonely, and insecure parts.

I lean into Ben's chest, feeling lighter than I did a few moments ago. I can feel his heart beating, a tender *thump thump thump* that seems to reverberate through me, telling me he gets it. He gets me.

Just then a crack of thunder makes me jump.

"We better get back," Ben says, but it's already too late because in an instant the sky splits open and we're caught in a torrential downpour. I squeal, laugh—I think Ben is laughing too, but the rain is loud and the thunder louder. And we're running.

Over the now muddied ground, between the trees. The rushing sound of the rain hitting the leaves and branches and earth.

"This isn't the way," I shout.

"There's a place up here." Ben's tugging me along and before I know it, he leads us to a small toolshed. He yanks the wooden door open and ushers me into the dark.

"Oh my God!" I'm still smiling, wringing out my hair, wiping off my face. "Where did that come from?"

I hear a click. A small light bulb flashes awake above us. Ben gives me a once-over. "Your sweater is soaked."

I glance down at my cardigan, now clinging to my skin, thinking I would give anything to be in a warm, rose-petaled bath right now.

"You should take that off," Ben says.

"Not this again," I tease as I shrug it off with a shiver, grateful my T-shirt beneath isn't saturated too.

And then I look up. Remnants of rain trickle down Ben's cheeks, his dark hair is sticking up, a messy heap of chaos. He looks ridiculous and amazingly hot all at once. And while I'm thinking carnal thoughts, Ben is glancing around. He tugs a striped wool blanket off of a shelf. After a quick sniff he wrinkles his nose and says, "Er…it smells a little like sheep. Maybe you don't want to dry off with it."

I catch a whiff. "It doesn't smell *that* bad." I spread it out on the floor and plant myself there, rubbing my arms vigorously.

Ben sits too, and I don't know if it's because I'm freezing or we've hit a new plateau in our truth truce, but I scooch between his legs as he leans back into the wall and wraps his arms around me.

Heat instantly radiates off of him, enfolding me in cozy warmth.

"You're a human heater," I tell him, snuggling closer.

The rain thrums against the roof, lashes the crooked window framing the storm.

"Question," I say, tilting my head back into his chest. "How long do these rain storms usually last?"

"Mmm…we could be stuck here for days."

I'm about to return his sarcasm with something quippy, but the rain is unrelenting, the sky is flaring, and Ben's arms are tight around me. In the same instant I feel a tug, a faraway vibration. The same one I sensed when we kissed last night, when we danced. The one that signals magic.

I grip Ben's hand, hold it up with my fingers entwined in his. A perfect fit. I reposition myself, leaning into his left shoulder so I can see his face. "I have another question."

He kisses the tip of my nose. "Okay."

"The day we met, in the café, you wrote something in the First Impressions book..."

A ghost of a smile. "I did."

I wait, thinking he's going to tell me, but he doesn't say anything else.

"And?" I ask, feigning annoyance.

"And I'm not going to reveal that secret."

"Ben!" I groan. "What happened to the truth pact?"

"Doesn't include past events."

"You can't just change the rules like that." I turn and face him now. "Why won't you tell me what you wrote?"

He pushes a stray hair out of my face looking more amused than he has any right to. "How about this?" he says. "How about I promise to tell you someday, but not today."

I push aside my frustration, deciding he doesn't get to have all the fun *or* make all the rules. With a resigned sigh I lean closer. I kiss him softly. "How about..." My lips fall to his chin. "You tell me..." Down to his neck. "Now."

Ben clears his throat. "If you keep doing that, we're going to spend the night in this shed."

I love the effect I have on him, on his pulse, his breathing, the way his voice drops low and quivers when I'm this close. There is power in that, a power that feels intoxicating, and I can't stop myself when I run my hands down his chest, stopping at the top of his jeans.

"Harlow." My name is an aching whisper on his lips. In one smooth move he spins me around and I'm on my back staring up into his eyes, the light silhouetting his tousled hair.

Instantly, a floral earthy aroma fills my nose, envelopes me. Something divine, seductive...something...

"I know I said..." he begins, takes a long breath, "I know I said I'm not exactly romantic..."

I slide my fingers through his hair. "Mmm-hmm."

"But when we do this..."

"This?" I tease.

He closes his eyes, tenses the one arm that's holding him up. "It's not going to be on a sheep smelling...blanket...in a shed on...Abe's farm."

Disappointment swells, but the fact that he said *when* flicks a light switch inside of me and something tells me that sex with Ben isn't going to be a two-minute unfulfilled roll in the sheets.

His eyes glaze over as he looks down me, a gaze so heady, so filled with desire my body reacts before I can stop it from pressing deeper into him.

"That's just mean," he says.

The aroma is subtle, mysterious. A shadow of a bloom I can't name. Why can't I name it?

And then I feel that tug again. Powerful. Alluring. A kinetic spark that ignites every cell in my body.

Everything goes still, silent. The intoxicating scent is everywhere now, in the air, on Ben. Sensual sandalwood blended with...

"I think it stopped raining," I mutter.

"Harlow," he breathes again.

My God, I've never wanted someone more.

A phone rings.

Ben's fingers trace my bare stomach. They hover near my bra, then slip the seam. He cups my breast and then his thumb, oh, God his glorious thumb traces my nipple so delicately, so tantalizingly I think my body will never be able to contain the pleasure of this man.

"You're so..." He kisses my neck with a whispering cruelty, his lips...his breath...his tongue all so luxuriously warm on my skin. "Beautiful."

He says this as his body is yielding to me as his phone continues to ring.

I rip at Ben's shirt like a feral animal. With one hand, he helps me get it over his head. I spread my hands over his skin, touching as much as I can, wanting nothing more than to trail my fingers, my mouth over every inch of him.

The heady scent—it's coming from him, I realize. Emanating from his bare skin. Spicy. Warm. Decadent. An aphrodisiac created just for me. But I'm too far gone to even try to identify the flower.

Now his phone pings with a maddening little bell sound. Once. Twice. Three times.

Ignoring it, he begins to lift my shirt, never taking his gaze off of me. A centimeter, another… His eyes fall to my stomach, he sucks in a breath as they trail my body excruciatingly slow, watching his fingers bunch the fabric, raising it higher and higher…until…

Another ping.

"Ben…" My voice is a ragged whisper ripped from my lungs. "Your phone."

"Ignore it."

In the greatest show of willpower of my life, I tug my shirt down. "It could be important."

He drops his head to my chest and growls. "Fine. But do not move."

Sitting up, he jerks the phone from his pocket. His eyes scan the screen as his thumb scrolls.

"Shit!" And in an instant, he's on his feet, pulling his shirt back on.

"What is it?" I say, panicked.

"My grandpa's in the hospital—come on."

22

Bits of rain lash the windshield as we drive down the darkened road. The texts had come from Helena, messages about William and his fall, his transport to the hospital, then a voice mail pleading for Ben to hurry.

Now Beverly's voice fills the truck, adding to the panic I feel rolling off of Ben who hasn't stopped white-knuckling the steering wheel.

"Oh, Ben," Beverly cries, "it was so careless and silly and his head...it was bleeding." She takes a long inhale, punctuated by a sob that she manages to swallow before claiming an unexpected poise. "He's going to be okay," she chants. "He's going to be okay."

"Of course he is," Ben says calmly, although I can hear the tremor in his voice. "Is he conscious?"

I hold my breath, waiting.

"Yes, he's awake, and he's mad that I called the ambulance.

You know how he is, hates hospitals. I've never been so happy to be on the receiving end of his anger."

"Are you with him now?"

"Helena and I are waiting in the ER while he has some scans. Are you on the way?"

"Be there in twenty."

My stomach twists painfully, and an inner voice rises before I can stop it. *This is how it starts.* I try to shake off the dark thought, but it turns like a kaleidoscope bright and vivid. After Azalea fell and broke her hip, she was never the same; it was as if the break wasn't about bone, but about will. Silently, I reach for Ben's hand. And I hope as he tightens his grip.

The ER is eerily quiet; a few nurses shuttle about. The hall has an antiseptic smell, lingering and old, and many of the rooms we pass are vacant. Behind a closed door, there is a dull chorus of indistinct voices, and I wonder what emergency disrupted their lives and brought them here.

When we reach William's windowless room, we find Beverly and Helena, both sitting in beige vinyl chairs. Helena is scrolling through her phone while Beverly flips through the pages of a magazine too quickly to be registering anything.

The moment she sees Ben, Beverly jumps to her feet and pulls him in to a fierce hug. And then her eyes alight on me. "Oh, Harlow. I am so happy you're here."

I embrace her, wishing there was something more I could offer while Ben launches in with a series of questions that all ask the same thing: *Is he going to be okay?*

Helena, calm and cool under the circumstances, delivers the same report Beverly had given but with a directness that sticks only to the cold, hard facts. She reminds me of Lil in that regard. If there is ever an emergency, anyone would want level-headed Lil by their side. Her composed demeanor is probably what makes her such a good doctor.

"Anyway," Helena says with a sigh, "it was dark and anyone could have tripped on the step. I'm just glad the restaurant was so close to here. And thank God he didn't lose consciousness."

Just then, a nurse pushes William into the room in a wheelchair. He's wearing a bandage on his right temple, and has a few scrapes on his cheeks and his hands, but other than that he looks like William, a very exasperated one.

"Hey, Gramps," Ben says, feigning good cheer. "You doing okay?"

William twirls a hand uselessly in front of him. "I didn't need to come here. I told them I was fine. Such fuss for nothing."

Ben's flat expression is a veneer masking so many emotions I know are brewing inside of him. "Well, you look great," he says as he and the nurse help William onto the hospital bed.

"I won't stay the night here," William grumbles. It's then that I notice how frail he looks, how much thinner and paler than he did just two nights ago.

Helena is fluffing the pillow under his head. "Let's just see what the scans say."

William's eyes find me and I expect him to smile, to say hello, but instead he studies me a moment before he asks, "Who are you?"

My throat tightens, but I manage a friendly smile. "I'm Harlow."

"She was at the ceremony last night," Ben puts in, but there is a misery in his voice, one that pains me, but not as much as the distant look in William's eyes.

"She's Ben's friend," Helena says, emphasizing friend with a teasing lightheartedness that earns her a scowl from her brother.

William nods, pulls his sheets higher. Unflinching, he stares at me. "You look like someone I used to know." He turns to Beverly who is at his side, clinging to his hand like a lifeline. "What was her name? Your friend that summer...the one with the plants...or no, the flowers."

Beverly nods, never taking her gaze from William. "Azalea. This is her granddaughter."

I wait for a dawning comprehension, but there is none. Only an expression of pained confusion that washes over William's face. He's trying to place me, to find the memory he knows is there, but it eludes him like so many others he will never possess again.

At least his memories of Beverly are strong and bright, I think just as a low hum begins in my chest, warm and familiar. It's the magic, the preternatural bond between William and Beverly that vibrates through me like a plucked violin string, offering me the smallest semblance of comfort until...it ebbs, bit by bit leaving in its wake a cold and disturbing shudder.

A sense of panic rises in me; I'm not sure what it means, to sense the magic in one breath and to lose it in the next.

Just then a doctor, middle-aged and heavyset, comes in. Her gray hair is pulled back in what can only be called a ratty knot. Her gray eyes shift about the room like she isn't sure where to begin or who to kick out first. I begin to step out when Ben grabs hold of my hand and silently holds me in place.

But all I want is air and to call my mom, to ask her about the receding magic, to hear her comforting voice.

"Your scans look good," the doctor says flatly.

There is a collective sigh of relief that fills the room.

"I told you," William says to no one in particular. "Can I go home now?"

"You're lucky you didn't break anything," the doctor goes on. "Although you do have a hairline fracture in your pelvis, more specifically your pubic bone. You need to rest, take some vitamin D and calcium supplements and since you're traveling in the next week, I'd like you to be on aspirin to avoid any chance of a blood clot."

Beverly is nodding, taking mental note while William stares blankly like he'd rather be anywhere but here. "And," the doc goes on, "I'd like you to use a cane for a bit, just to make sure you're stable and we avoid any more falls."

"Absolutely not!" William argues, shifting around in his bed like he's going to leap out any second.

"William," Beverly begins at the same moment Ben rushes in with, "It's for the best," but it's the gentlest voice that gets William's attention.

"Grand-père," Helena says, stroking his white hair softly. She speaks two small words in French, "pour moi."

For me.

Simple in its request, powerful in its love.

William hesitates, then huffs out a grunt and nods. "Very well. Can I leave now?"

"We just need to complete some discharge paperwork," the doctor says.

There's some bustling about the room, bodies shifting, moving toward the door to give him some privacy to get dressed. When I take one last glance at William he says, "Can I talk to you? Alone?"

The question freezes Ben, Beverly, and Helena in their spots. But the moment I say, "Sure," they exchange curious glances and head out.

Alone with William, I feel a sudden nervousness, further compounded by his words, "I remember you now."

A small and cautious smile spreads across my mouth. "That's great."

"When I hit my head, I saw you..."

My insides go cold. "Saw me?"

"You were there, and had all these flowers growing around you, white if I remember, and you were whispering something but I—" he frowns deeply "—I can't remember what it was."

So, he'd had a dream. Maybe on the way to the hospital and he just doesn't remember dozing off.

"And then the flowers, they swallowed you."

It's a coincidence, I tell myself. I don't really know William, so how could he be dreaming something so similar to what Lil told me?

"Do you remember what the flowers looked like?" I ask weakly. "I mean the details?"

He shakes his head. "But when they swallowed you…you became one of them." He scratches the side of his head. "Does that make sense? Probably not."

The room suddenly feels smaller, and the air is so thick I feel like I can't breathe.

"Can I show you something?" he asks.

I nod as he gestures toward a counter. "My wallet, please."

I retrieve his soft leather wallet and hand it to him. When he opens it, there is a bifold photo insert. He points to the first photo, a young man with dark wavy hair and hauntingly dark eyes staring into the camera like he was caught off guard. "This is my boy," William says with a hitch in his voice.

"Ben's dad," I say.

"He was twenty-four here, had the world by the tail." William's mouth twitches a little when he turns to the next photo. "I look at these every day. To remember. These are the people I love most, the people this *thing* can never take from me."

It's like music, his voice. The notes and tune perfectly spaced, effortlessly harmonized when he talks about his family. And I suddenly wish I had had the chance to know him before parts of him started disappearing into forgetfulness.

The next photo is of a younger Beverly, maybe in her forties. She's looking over her shoulder at the camera; a strand of her auburn hair slips in front of her wide smile. I feel a sharp stab in my chest, and all I can think is that this man was given so much and yet, here he is, his frail hands gripping the last shreds of his life.

After he shows me the last few images, including what looks like a more recent one of Ben standing next to a snowman, he takes a shaky breath. In a moment of absolute lucidity, he looks up at me and says, "It's falling away."

I'm suddenly scrambling to piece together what he's telling me and the moment my understanding dawns, he says, "The bond... I can feel it."

And then I recall Beverly's words from breakfast. *I feel as if those layers are being peeled away one by one and...pretty soon, I worry ...there will be nothing left.*

I hold steady but my pulse is starting to pound. Does he know that he's slipping away, that no amount of bonding can stop that?

"I'm sorry," I tell him, wishing I could comfort him in some way. I search for the spark, for the gleam in his eyes to tell me the magic is still there, but these unnatural fluorescent lights make it impossible.

He nods, then with trembling hands, he folds his wallet closed carefully as if it contains the most fragile bit of china.

I place my hand on his; a ribbon of feeling moves between us silently.

"Can I go home now?" he asks.

An hour later, after we make sure William is settled in his hotel suite, Ben and I catch the elevator to my room one floor down.

I stand in front of my door, suddenly exhausted from the emotional highs and lows of tonight. If I close my eyes, I'm back in the shed safe from the storm, wrapped in Ben's arms. That's where I want to be, lost in the memory of his hands and mouth and eyes, of that seductive fragrance I can now no longer recall, only that it was intoxicating.

"Where are you?" Ben asks lightly; his voice sounds hoarse like he's been out in the cold too long.

I shake my head and meet his gaze. "Right here."

He puts his arms around me, kisses my forehead lightly. "What did you and my grandfather talk about?"

There it is. The question I know he's been dying to ask since we left the hospital. Do I tell Ben the truth? That I think the bonding magic is fading, and I worry that it means that William is too? And even if I knew with absolute certainty that this were true, should I tell Ben?

"He wanted to show me some photos," I say.

"The ones in his wallet?"

"You look like your dad."

Ben smiles briefly. "And?"

He knows there's more, and I'm suddenly too fatigued or maybe too bewitched to craft a lie so I reach for a half-truth. "He had a dream about some flowers," I say, "and he wanted to ask me about them."

I'm afraid Ben is going to ask more questions, but thankfully he doesn't. Instead, we stand like that for a long moment, embracing one another simply, easily, tenderly. Then, as we break apart our eyes lock.

He slides one hand softly up my neck into my hair. I don't move, simply accept his mouth on mine. I dissolve into Ben. His kisses are like the wind, forever changing course, and this one is deliberate, exploratory. He's looking for the same thing I am. An answer to the question neither one of us wants to ask: *What is this thing, this vibration, this magic between us?*

He pulls back, stares at me in the shadowy light. "Good night."

And just as I enter my room and turn to close the door, he inches it open and whispers, "Harlow?"

"Yeah?"

"Don't make any plans tomorrow." His fingers touch mine lightly. "I want to show you something."

23

In the morning, I'm in a deep sleep, floating in a world of fragmented dreams when a hypnotic floral fragrance, so overwhelming, stirs me awake. It's as if someone has walked into the room after a fresh spritz of the loveliest perfume.

I open my eyes lazily and take another breath. The aroma is coming from the canto. Blinking away my drowsiness, I sit up to inspect the flower. It's grown taller, and its double ruffled bloom has blossomed even more, expanding into an unimaginable beauty.

I trace a single finger over the fragile petals, swept away by their simplicity, their elegance. A singular promise that beauty will always endure.

My phone is on the nightstand, message light blinking. The text must have come in from Tía last night.

Your mom told me about the canto. We need to talk.

Rosa has always been the family carrot dangler. Delivering cryptic one-liners that get you to do the thing she hasn't even directly asked you to do, which in this case is to call her.

It's 7:00 a.m. here and she's an hour behind, but thankfully she's an early riser.

"Harlow!" she answers on the first ring. "Why did you take so long? I could have died of waiting." Did I mention she's also muy dramatic?

I laugh lightly, choosing my words with the utmost caution so as not to invite questions I don't want to answer. I'll tell her and Mom about William and the hospital visit—including his dream of me—when I get home. If I told her now, she'd only worry, call Beverly, make it a thing it doesn't need to be. "I'm sorry, I, uh, got sidetracked writing and sightseeing, and I didn't get the message until it was late."

Thankfully, she doesn't dig any further. "The canto. It's everywhere."

"Still?" She's caught me by surprise, but what did I expect? That the mysterious flower would suddenly shrivel with me gone?

My aunt must be doing her farm rounds because I hear the birds chirping, the rustling of leaves, her footsteps crunching along the gravel.

Her voice cuts in and out. The farm's dead zones are to blame. "Rosa? Are you there?"

"Ay, damn cell phones," she growls. "Yes, I'm here and this flower has a message."

I rub my eyes. She's only repeating what I already know. If this is the reason she called, she's a little too late. My mom beat her to it.

"When a bloom is this insistent," she says, "well…"

"Yeah, I know, it has a message."

There is a stretch of silence and I think I've lost her again, when she says, "I think something is coming, amor."

I feel a painful twist in my gut. "Something? Like what?"

"I tried—" her voice is hurried between the call's broken gaps "—and the flower…but I'm sure…"

I comb my fingers through my hair. "Rosa? Sure of what? Hello? Are you there?"

"The magic…" are her last words before the call goes dead.

I try calling her back but there is no answer. Then I try my mom, and of course it goes right to her voice mail. I shoot off a few texts for Rosa to call me back or text me. Maybe my sisters or cousins are in the know, but it's way too early to bother them. I'd only be on the receiving end of their ire if I did.

My phone pings and I jump. But it's not my aunt. It's a text from Laini, demanding an update followed by CALL ME!

I don't even know where to begin: With the party, the kiss, the shed, William's dream? So much has happened in the last forty-eight hours and to try and put it into a short conversation let alone a text feels daunting. Still, I have to tell Laini something. So, I go with the one thing I know she'll accept.

I send her a voice text: "Sorry to be absent. It's just been really busy, but the party was so nice. Quebec is beautiful. Anyway, I'm so inspired by this place that I'm treating it like a mini-writing retreat, and turning off the phone which means I'm getting so much done on the book." I pause, grimacing at the half-truths coming out of my mouth before I hit send.

She immediately sends me a few grumpy faces followed by, the wait better be worth it.

I immediately text back, I promise I'll give you all the details when I'm home.

Home.

Suddenly, I ache for the farm, for family and familiarity, for the essence of magic that breathes across our land. A wellspring of emotion moves through me and before I know it, my journal is open and I'm filling the pages. Words are pouring out, punctuated by something else, something beyond my control.

I don't stop. I don't think or judge. I don't lift my hand.

But like a river changing course, the story has shifted.

The man doesn't know that the magic that exists in the soil is uniquely tied to the heroine, that the land only answers to her voice, her presence, her very spirit. And now, the moment he is ready to claim victory, he realizes the price of his greed and betrayal. Now all he possesses is an expanse of absolute nothingness. And she, well, she holds all the power.

I lift my eyes to the canto on the nightstand, the flower that's been watching me sleep and dream and write—a guardian of creativity. "Is this the something?" I ask it. "The piece of the story?"

The flower doesn't answer, merely sheds a single petal that falls to the floor.

Ben is downstairs in the lobby at 8:00 a.m. as we planned. He's wearing a thick army-green jacket, hiking boots, and a pair of old jeans that look like they've seen better days.

The moment he sees me, he comes over, smiling, and presses a light kiss on my cheek. Damn he smells good. "Good morning," he says.

"Morning." I gesture to my outfit: a pair of leggings, flat ankle boots, and a chunky cardigan sweater. "Is this okay for wherever it is that you're taking me?"

Ben tugs on the knitted beanie I'm wearing, fighting a smile. "It's perfect."

Before we met this morning, I tried to sway him to reconsider his plans, to instead spend time with William. My attempt was futile and any further pressing would have resulted in Ben suspecting something. And how could I possibly share with him what transpired last night? The secret feels too big to contain, but I rationalize it by telling myself that what I felt yesterday, the waning of magic, could very well have been just a moment in time, not an indicator of William's health or future.

Plus Ben tells me that his grandfather is doing "remarkably" well this morning and reminds me we're supposed to have dinner with the entire family tonight. I do my best to cast my worries aside.

Outside the sky is a mottled gray and the air is fresh and brisk. Ben leads me to a parked SUV at the far end of the valet station and opens the passenger door.

"Where's the truck?" I ask.

"The old beater might not make it, so I rented this."

There are two steaming coffees resting in the cup holders.

"Black, right?" Ben says as we buckle up.

"You're my hero," I tell him, sipping the dark brew, wishing I could put the caffeine straight into my veins.

"Oh, and I stopped by Abe's for some pastries," he says. "I wasn't sure if you're a breakfast person or not, so I uh…bought a bunch."

This is the dance couples do. Maneuvering the mysteries of the other's tastes, desires, habits until they know enough about each other that there's no guessing involved—only simple acceptance of each other's likes and dislikes.

"Do I smell chocolate?" I retrieve the goodies like a little kid and begin rifling through the bag, which is filled with croissants, brioche, pain au chocolat, and several other flaky pastries that look and smell divine. "Oh my God! I love pain au chocolat!"

Ben is smiling ear to ear. And it changes him, softens him.

"Which do you want?" I ask, trying to ignore how adorable he looks.

"Oh, I don't like breakfast."

I huff out a surprised laugh. "Ben! Then why did you buy all this? I will never eat it all."

He offers a side-glance, and even then, even in that brief

glance, his dark eyes are arresting. "I didn't want to guess and get it wrong."

Code for, *I wanted you to be happy.*

I tear off bits of the flaky pastry and pop them into my mouth. "I take it back," I say around a mouthful of perfection. "Abe is the hero!"

Ben laughs. "I'll be sure and tell him."

A few minutes later, we are on the Sainte Anne de Beaupré highway. Soft rock plays through the speakers as we head west.

"You should absolutely serve this kind of deliciousness at your new..." I pause, searching for the right word. Not hotel, not resort, not lodge. "Your new place."

"I've got an idea," Ben announces, thrumming his fingers on the steering wheel. "When I find the right land, the exact right spot, will you help me with the details?"

Something flutters in my chest. I don't know why I had assumed his dream was further along, but it's only the beginning. "I'm not sure how much of the details I could help with, but if you need a taste tester, I've definitely got your back," I say, gazing lovingly at the pastry.

Ben laughs. "Okay, taste tester, you're making that look way too tempting. How about you share a piece?"

I tear off a bit of the flaky pastry and set it in his waiting mouth. "Awesome, right?"

After he chews a few bites, he swallows and gives me a sideglance. "Abe is definitely on his game."

Smiling triumphantly, I switch topics. "You should talk to Camilla, my sister. She has this amazing beach inn in California. I mean, I know you're an expert on hotels but she has this knack for the tiniest of details."

"Actually, I'm not an expert. I used to be in accounting, the great number cruncher until my grandfather got sick." He offers a tight smile. "But thanks, that would be great. I just—I really want this to work."

"It will," I say assuredly. "I have a good feeling about it."

Ben takes my hand and squeezes gently.

I kick off my boots, prop my feet on the dashboard just as the sun pokes its head through a scattering of clouds.

"At least tell me how far we're going," I say as the town drops away, replaced by a stretch of highway flanked by a thickening forest made up of amber and gold.

"Harlow."

"I'm only asking how far, not the details."

"If I tell you, will you promise to quit asking me questions?"

"Deal."

"Thirty minutes. Happy?"

"More like…satisfied."

I'm tempted to google points of interest within thirty minutes of Old Quebec, but underneath it all, I don't want to ruin what Ben has planned. Still, the more I think about his *something*, the more I'm reminded of Tía's warning that *something* is coming.

No, I won't let my aunt's ominous tone ruin this day. She could have been trying to say something really good is coming. I can't always be getting in my own way thinking worst-case scenarios. And then I think of Lil's dream, of the foxglove drowning me, which quickly morphs into William's dream, where the mysterious white flower swallowed me, changing me into a bloom.

My anxiety spirals and my mind becomes a dark attic of cob-webs and stacked boxes, old photos, and discarded items no lon-ger useful. And I'm rattling around, searching for a window, for air and light.

Why do I do this? Why do I clutter my mind with questions and worries instead of living in the moment? It's as if I'm pro-grammed to forecast *what could go wrong*.

The rest of the drive is without words, my hand resting lightly in Ben's, our eyes on the world outside, each lost in our thoughts.

And there is something comforting in this, that we don't need to fill the gaps of silence. That this is enough.

Not today. Today is for something good.

I sit up straighter, squeezing Ben's hand and earning a melting smile. It isn't long before Ben pulls off the highway and drives down a country road that leads to a ranger's gatehouse. The sign reads: Jacques Cartier National Park. My stomach is a flurry of expectation as Ben presents a digital ticket he apparently bought ahead of time, and the ranger passes us through.

We turn onto a narrow, wooded road, edged with tall imposing trees that boast the most vibrant yellow and tawny leaves.

Ben turns off the music and opens the sunroof. He's driving slow now. Up ahead there is a magnificent shower of spiraling russet and gold. The fallen leaves twirl and dance before us, looking more like a flurry of butterflies suspended on the breeze.

It's a postcard moment you want to press between the pages of a book and save forever, for the cold moments when only a warm memory will do.

A single leaf drops through the open sunroof, landing on my lap. And for that single instant, I feel as if I've been touched by this forest's magic.

"This place is incredible," I whisper as I turn the leaf over in my hand—if not for the fissure down the delicate center, it appears entirely whole.

"Feuille morte," Ben says, gesturing to the leaf.

Morte sounds like *muerto* so I wager a guess. "Dead leaf?"

"That's the literal translation but it specifically means a brownish or yellowish-orange color."

"I love that." When words hold a deeper meaning, something more than their face value.

It seems like forever until Ben finally pulls into a small inlet. I've been so captivated by the beauty of this place, by the enchantment that seems to breathe from every silhouette, that the journey seems like the surprise and I've forgotten all about the destination.

Once we're out of the car, we hike down a winding trail. I hear the sound of a gurgling brook as we maneuver around the moss-covered rocks and across the muddied path littered with gold, brown, and the occasional red leaf. Along the trail's edge there are ferns and tiny sprigs of pines popping out of the shaded moist earth. I turn my face upward, finding only glimpses of distant green at the very tops of trees where the gold hasn't touched yet.

"This is one of my favorite places on the planet," Ben says. "I spent so much time here as a kid with my dad. We'd hike and fish, and in the winter, we'd sled until our entire bodies were numb."

I smile at the memory of a kid Ben, picturing it perfectly, his dad young and vibrant like in William's photo, and Ben, stomping across this verdant playground without a care in the world.

Then, to my surprise, Ben says, "We're almost there."

"This isn't it?"

"Nope."

Impatient by nature, I want to ask, *how much longer?* How many more steps will I have to take? Deep down, I think I just really want all this secrecy to be worth it. And maybe even deeper than that, I want to believe that Ben, a self-professed not-a-romantic-guy can be.

Just then the trail ends and I nearly gasp.

24

The path opens to a wide, dramatic view of a majestic river that meanders through the vast mountain plateau.

Ribbons of mist cling to the land like bits of cloud have dropped from the sky. The dark waters decant a golden autumn light. The word *awe* doesn't come close to what I'm feeling. I've seen so many beautiful places in the world but this…this is something entirely different; it's as if this place has never been seen before now, has never been touched by the hands of time.

My writer's heart tries to find the right word to describe it. Then it drifts to me as if it had been waiting for me to pluck it straight from the air.

Ensorcelled.

"Ben." My voice is barely a whisper.

Smiling, he tugs my arm. "Come on."

"Wait, this isn't the surprise either?" How could anything be better than this spectacular view?

He merely laughs and shakes his head.

I'm like a child, skip-hopping behind Ben along the river-bank, a ball of nerves and excitement, wishing I could stop for every stone, every leaf, every tiny flower head. But Ben's strides are long and purposeful, and I'm not about to slow him down.

Up ahead I spy something red. A rowboat, I realize as we draw closer.

"All aboard," Ben announces.

"This is *your* boat?"

"No, Harlow," he says with a lighthearted grin, "it's just luck we came upon it."

"Well, you *are* a known thief."

He chuckles as I step inside the watercraft where there are two cane bucket seats and a couple of blankets. When did he park this out here? As if he can read my mind, he says, "Abe helped me this morning."

How can this man claim he is unromantic? I'd give up a life-time of roses, poems, and chocolates just to have a single one of Ben's surprises.

"Now I really have to know," I say. "Where are we going?"

"You really are impossible."

I groan dramatically as he pushes the boat off the bank and hops inside before he sits in the seat at the bow, then grabs the oars, sets them in place, and begins to row.

"Can you tell me if it's far?"

With a sigh, he shoots me a mischievous glare.

We glide through the gently rolling water, reflecting a smat-tering of cumulous clouds as warm sunlight presses through the gray. The effect is mystifying, and if I let my eyes go out of focus, I can't tell which image is the real one.

Ben sheds his coat and continues to row effortlessly, leaning forward and back with each turn of the oars the fluid move-ment reveals his very solid biceps. It's all I can do to not stare so I offer to row, anything to admonish the carnal direction my imagination is heading.

"Have you rowed before?" Ben asks.

"Uh…does a rowing machine count?"

He smirks and hands over the oars.

"Okay, so the trick is to feather the oars," he says, "so they turn sort of sideways and you don't drag a lot of the water."

"This is way harder than it looks," I admit, struggling to find the right angle and rhythm.

"I think you're doing great."

"I think you're a liar."

Ben laughs. "Look, we're moving, aren't we?"

Birds sing and soar over the gurgling river, as it narrows and widens and bends. And with each shift, the landscape changes, colors fade, and deepen. If not for the fluttering leaves, the gamboge trees look like a painting.

After a few minutes of frowning and grunting, I find the rhythm, leaning forward and back in long even motions, my abdominal muscles doing the most of the work. Okay, this is not like a rowing machine. It's much harder.

"We're almost there," Ben says eagerly, looking ahead to where I can't see since I'm rowing backward. "I'll take it from here."

I give him command over the boat again, glad to give my arms and abs a rest.

"Can we just stay here forever?" I utter as I tilt my head back and close my eyes. Soon I'm lost in the peaceful swishing sound of the oars sliding through the water. I must doze off for a split second because the moment the boat stops, I startle and open my eyes.

I freeze.

All around us is a fine mist. Gone is the forest, the water, the autumn sky. It's like…

We're floating in a cloud.

"This is as close to magic as I've been," he says, glancing

around, "so I thought if I showed you this that maybe someday, you'd give me the full tour of the farm."

Someday.

I'm already saying yes in my mind, envisioning long walks through the fields, leading him to my garden, letting him fully into my life.

"Are you saying that you believe in magic now?" I ask, my tone skating the edge of humor, but my intention is something more serious.

"I'm saying that maybe everyone has their own version of magic." He holds my gaze for just a moment, then leans forward and kisses me softly, an answer that screams a thousand yeses.

I feel a jolt in my solar plexus, like I'm standing at the edge of a darkened cliff, knowing there isn't going to be a first step because I'm already falling.

So *this* is what it feels like.

Ben brings the oars inside the boat, allowing us to simply drift. "I have something to tell you. And if I don't tell you, I think maybe I'll lose it."

My body tenses.

"Ever since that day at the hotel in Mexico," he says, looking around as if he can see through the fog, "I haven't been able to stop thinking about you. It's like...like you're everywhere— in my mind and dreams." He laughs lightly, then drags a hand down his face. "Sometimes I even catch your scent, and it's like you're in the room with me."

I go completely still, unsure what to say, how to respond to this declaration. And that's what it is, isn't it? A declaration of the feelings I share too? The utter madness at how quickly I've... *we've* fallen. How he's not only been in my mind and dreams but between each breath.

I scoot closer until he's inches from me. Wrapping my hands around his neck, I gently rest my forehead against his.

"Is that crazy?" he asks. "Because it feels like it is."

"It's not crazy."

"You're sure?"

"One hundred percent."

"How do you know?" I think I feel him tremble.

"I'm the one from the magical family, remember?"

He shifts his weight, leaning into me.

Then softly, slowly our lips meet. The kiss is warm, electric, pulsating with an inexplicable energy that vibrates through my entire being. This is more than attraction, more than want or desire.

Ensorcelled.

With every passing second the kiss deepens, growing more fervent until all I can feel is his hunger; all I can taste is his want. His hands slide down my body and I'm urging him closer, drowning in that rich dark mysterious fragrance.

The boat bumps against something, and I realize we've hit land, a small sandy inlet. We both laugh at the intrusion, but there is an urgency burning in his eyes, one that asks a question I answer by disembarking with blanket in hand, which I spread on the little beach before we sit down. Ribbons of fog swirl all around us, robbing me of any view other than what's right in front of me.

Ben takes my hand in his, staring down at our entwined fingers with a look of fascination that puzzles me. I lean my head on his shoulder, wanting nothing more in this moment than to be with him, near him.

"You said you could smell my scent," I say softly, allowing the reality of those words to hit me for the first time. How could Ben smell someone who isn't there? "What does it smell like?"

"No way."

"What?"

"I'm terrible with words, remember?"

I shoulder bump him playfully. "Just try."

"I don't know like…something mild, clean…like fresh sheets but with a little bit of some flower too." He sighs. "See? Awful."

Clean. Floral. Fresh sheets.

"That totally makes sense."

"Now you're just being nice."

I trail soft kisses down the column of his neck. He drags in a breath, and before I know it we've eased down onto the ground so that we're lying side by side.

Slowly, he peels off my beanie, letting my hair spill around my face. "Better."

My fingers sift through his hair at the back of his neck. And I'm swimming in those eyes.

Ben swallows. A muscle jumps in his jaw.

"Thank you," I tell him. "For doing this. I'll never forget it."

He kisses the tip of my nose.

"And," I add, "don't ever tell me you don't do romance again."

He grunt-laughs. "But I wasn't *trying* to be romantic. I just wanted to show you something that was important to me, something I thought you would love."

And maybe that's where everyone gets that word wrong, I think.

"It won't last," he says, jutting his chin out in a small nod.

It takes me a moment to realize he's talking about the mist, causing my heart to skip a beat.

"Are you cold?" he asks, wrapping his arms around me.

"Surprisingly no," I say, sinking further into his warmth, his embrace. "Can I tell you something?"

He nods.

"I used to hate the mist…on the farm. My sisters told me it was an army of ghosts coming to get me, so I always stayed inside, hiding with the windows closed and covered." I roll my eyes, chuckling at the memory.

I feel the vibration of Ben's voice in his chest when he says, "So what happened to change your mind?"

"I guess I just learned to sort of love it. The mystery of it."

"I am very glad you aren't afraid of the mist anymore."

"It would definitely have ruined this surprise."

"Definitely."

His lips are soft breaths on my neck as he places a warm hand on my bare stomach, toying with the hem of my cardigan sweater before trailing his hand up to the top button. "These are really tiny."

I nod, holding my breath as he unfastens the top button. Then the next. "I can't remember the last time I felt this nervous," he says.

"I know how you feel."

One side of his mouth lifts into an adorably crooked smile. "I doubt that."

When Ben releases the last button, he angles back, staring down at me, at the lace bra that leaves nothing to the imagination. His heady gaze consumes me.

Goose bumps sprout all over my body, but I find warmth when my hands reach under his shirt, pressing against the bare skin of his chest, urging the damn thing off of him. In one swift movement, he removes it, keeping his eyes locked on mine.

And just like last night, waves of his overwhelming sandalwood fragrance find me, the scent so alluring, so seductive I'm breathless, lost in the want of him, the want of his touch, of the desire to feel him moving inside of me.

I'm sinking, surrendering.

He presses against me, whispers in my ear, "Is this okay?"

I'm still sinking when my hand unhooks the front clasp of my bra. I want to feel his heat against my bare skin. For one millisecond, I sense his tension, as if he's trying to hold back, but this simple movement undoes him.

Ever so lightly, he swirls his tongue, warm and sensual, across my breast, teasing out the moment, until unhurriedly he takes my nipple into his mouth. I gasp, cling to him as if this is all there is, all there will ever be.

I can feel the length of him, hard against my thigh as I unbutton his jeans, as his mouth trails down to my bare stomach. "Are you sure…" I breathe, "you won't tell me what you wrote…in that…book."

I think if there is ever a moment, he will yield to me, this is it, but he merely says, "Not yet."

We both laugh, our bodies clinging to each other.

The mysterious signature scent of him is everywhere, a physical thing that I can reach out and touch if I just try hard enough.

Slowly, he tugs on the elastic of my leggings, peeling them down, but just barely. His lips trace my pelvic bone with a featherlight touch that sends an unbearable ache through me.

My fingers are tangled in his hair, my breathing quick, on the brink of a delicious moan. And all I can think is faster slower faster.

Ben raises himself onto the weight of one arm. His eyes sweep over me; lost in the now, in what comes next.

"Are you sure?" he asks again.

"I thought the bra was the first clue," I say as my gaze devours his entire chest, the chiseled lines of his body with more want than I knew existed. Still, I need to ask, to find out if we're safe to do this…if…

The mist parts. A single sunbeam shines through.

I look up at Ben. I want this. Him. Those sunlit whiskey-colored eyes. So deep, so rich, so—

At first, it's a mere flicker. But then…

An uncommon spark of light right there inside his pupils. Like the strike of a hateful match flaring, then dying out so quickly I nearly miss it.

The magic is unmistakable. Lighting me up, burning me from the inside.

My mind is a storm of chaos. It can't be. No. No!

Something is coming.

It's a trick of the light. I blink, look again. I don't want to see it. But the spark of magic in his eyes is unmistakable.

"Harlow?"

How...how... HOW!

Ever since that day at the hotel in Mexico I haven't been able to stop thinking about you.

My heart plummets.

"What's wrong?" Ben asks, blinking once, twice. The magic flickers within his pupils each time he blinks.

I lean closer, praying I didn't see what I'm still seeing—that glint of light.

And that's when I know—Ben Brandt has been magically bonded to me.

25

Fake. All that I felt, all that he felt. Fake.

This entire relationship wasn't real. All that we'd felt for each other was a magical mirage.

I gasp. There is no *we*.

I'm raging against the cruel and sudden blow, a shock that has left me sick to my stomach. And I'm scrambling, desperate for a way out, but I have nowhere to go because all there is is this little beach, and Ben staring at me with bewildered eyes.

I'm trapped.

The irony of that word crashes down on me with the weight of a thousand stones. I'm not the prey. *I'm* the predator. My family's magic did this to Ben.

It's like...like you're everywhere—in my mind and dreams.

Did it happen when we both touched the bonding bouquet? No. I remember now, the way he set those five petals in my hand so delicately—I remember the exchange of energy and the unnameable magic. It must have happened then.

With trembling heavy limbs, I manage to dress.

"Was I going too fast?" Ben asks, but his voice is just this faraway thing that cuts away at my resolve.

Tears spring to my eyes, and a sob climbs up my throat, demanding release. But if I fall apart now, Ben will ask questions, questions I'm not ready to answer. I clench my teeth and inhale sharply, managing the painful facade.

"I just feel really sick all of a sudden."

My entire being is vibrating with disbelief, denial, fear, and even a touch of madness. There is no explanation, not that magic ever needs one, but this? How could this have happened and I be so completely unaware?

He reaches for me, and for a microinstant I consider it, his touch, the way his arms felt around my body, and I want nothing more than to get back to that place before, that single moment before everything was destroyed. I shrink away, getting to my feet.

"Harlow...talk to me."

"I think...maybe it was the pastries," I lie, going back toward the boat.

A cool breeze whispers through the trees, the susurration is both beautiful and haunting.

Ben throws his shirt on. "Har, are you sure?" His tone is so perplexed, so forlorn, I think I'm going to split open.

"Yes."

A broken heart is such a violent thing, in want of sharing the agony by lashing out, but I refuse to go down that road, to make Ben suffer with barbed words that would surely drive a wedge between us, a wedge to incite his anger. Because anger is always easier to battle than pain.

His eyes soften, warm pools of kindness. "I feel like I did something wrong."

"Ben, you didn't. Really. I just feel nauseous."

He doesn't believe me. I see it in the tautness of his body, in the clench of his jaw. But he doesn't know the truth of what I'm saying. I *do* feel sick to my stomach. He *didn't* do anything wrong.

The beam of sunlight is gone, vanished into the mist, and I long to believe that the flicker in his eyes wasn't magic. My God, I want to believe that with all my heart. That all this time spent together, all of his declarations, and his openheartedness was true. But the only truth I know is the one staring me in the face.

The mist now feels like a swarming monster, clinging to me in bitter whispers. *How could you think the feelings between you were real? How could you so recklessly disregard the signs right in front of you?*

The landslide of truths I didn't pay attention to are everywhere now.

The inexplicable force of nature that drew us together.

That first kiss. His initial struggle, his eventual surrender.

The earthy seductive aroma, coming off of him in waves.

The intense energy radiating through me when he was near me.

It was all magic.

We're settled in the boat and Ben is rowing us back now, back to reality; his gaze is firmly set on me. But I avoid his gaze, terrified the sun will make a reappearance, that I'll see the truth in his eyes again.

"I'm really sorry," I say as I draw myself up, keep my eyes only on the water because if I look at him, I'll dissolve, I'll drown in a love that never existed.

"Har," he says quietly, "it's not your fault." Then with a forced laugh he adds, "We might have to sue Abe for food poisoning."

I nod absently, sensing the questions that must be overwhelming him, the crushing bafflement he must be feeling, but I don't have the answers that he wants.

As we glide through the water so excruciatingly slow, as I try to deny the bitter shock of it all.

And all I can think about is, I need to find a way to break

this bond. I'll do whatever it takes to make this right, to give Ben back his life—and his heart.

The hike and the drive back seem like an eternity of awkward silence, every breath a struggle, every heartbeat painful. And every time Ben tried to help me along, to offer some sort of comfort or support, I found myself withdrawing from his touch.

When we finally get to the hotel, I jump out of the car. And before I can take a single step Ben is out too.

"Harlow...wait. Can I help?" He shakes his head, imploring me with those eyes. "You know you can tell me anything."

The tears, the sob, they're winning the race and, in another blink, I won't be able to contain them.

To keep Ben from following me, I manage, "I might throw up. I'll text you." And then I rush inside and into the elevator. My legs nearly give out, and I collapse against the wall, fighting the tears.

Not yet. Not yet.

Once I'm in my room, the world stills. All sound falls away except for the pounding of my pulse in my ears and throat and chest. I slump onto the bed, my mind spinning with the memory of the magic flaring to life in his eyes.

The tears come fierce and heavy, a heap of sobs that shake my body so violently I can't breathe. How could I have been so stupid? Why didn't I see the flicker earlier? Or the signs of magic that are so obvious now, signs that would have saved me from falling so hard.

My God, I feel so incredibly foolish to have gotten caught up in his affections, his attention, his dreams. How could I have believed that this unfathomable connection between us was anything but magic?

I was attracted to him from the moment that I saw him at Pasaporte. His angles, his voice, that ridiculous wrinkled shirt. Was that the real Ben? That guarded distant mysterious man?

Or is he the playful, kind, generous, romantic man I've come to know in the last few days?

And that's all it's been—a few days. Why then do I feel as though I'm losing my best friend of a lifetime? Why does a life without Ben feel suddenly unbearable? Unless the bonding also worked on me, but that's impossible. Although it would explain the same symptoms: he was in my thoughts and dreams too, and whenever I was near him it took all of my willpower not to draw nearer, to touch him, to breathe in his entire essence.

I sit up, wipe my face, and begin to clear the cobwebs from my mind.

Okay, Harlow. What do you know?

I know that a bonding can be powerful; it can open hearts, it can enchant even the most miserly. I know that a magical binding is more powerful than even love. It creates an unbreakable connection between two people who become one. Where love is complicated, a bond is elegant in its simplicity. Where love is ambiguous, a bond is exact. Where love is breakable, a bond is forever.

I glance at the canto. Gone is the beautiful bloom. All that remains is a pile of petals on the floor. Carefully, I retrieve them, hold them in my palm. "Is this the something coming?" I ask, already knowing the answer.

And then I remember the foxglove, the one Ben gave me in my dream, the same one Lil and William dreamed about. All this time, I worried that the bloom's meaning of *insincerity, mystery, and deception* was a warning to stay away from Ben, but now I realize with painful clarity that I was entirely wrong. The threat was never Ben. It was me, my family's magic, and a spell neither of us asked for.

Exhausted, I tug my phone from my bag. I'm expecting an onslaught of messages from my family given the current emotional hurricane of my life, but there is nothing. How is that possible?

I want to call my mom, to tell her what's happened, to ask her how any of this is even remotely conceivable, but this is a conversation that needs to happen face-to-face. I need to go home.

I'm so relieved when I find a flight for later this afternoon. For the next hour, I force myself through the necessary steps, moving about numbly, mindlessly tossing my things into the suitcase, generating the same thoughts and memories over and over. The dance, the library, the orchard, the shed, the mist. I can hear his laughter, feel his warmth, nearly smell the magic of his scent.

Sometimes I even catch your scent, and it's like you're in the room with me.

Was that part of the bonding spell? To ensure I lingered not just in Ben's imagination, but in his very breath? My God, it's all so twisted, I can't begin to make heads or tails of any of it.

My phone alerts me to a new text. It's from Ben. I can bring you soup or medicine. Anything you need.

My heart sinks further. It's ironic, really, that Ben is the source of my pain, and yet he's also the remedy. If I could just hold him one more time. But deep down, I know there will never be *one more time*, and the hopelessness of it all makes me want to scream.

I send him a single response: I'm okay. I'm going to sleep. Will text later.

The lie is bitter and sharp, but it's necessary because the last thing I need is for Ben to come by to check on me.

It isn't until I'm through security at the airport that I finally breathe. I feel like a coward, slinking away into the night, but how could I possibly explain the truth to Ben right now when I don't understand it myself? Or how to make it right?

I wait until I've boarded my flight to text Beverly and offer my sincere apologies for not making dinner tonight. And then, through a blur of tears, I thank her for some of the best few days I've ever had.

Next, I text Ben.

I know you won't understand and I promise to explain when

I can, but I've gone home early. Not wanting to risk a response from him I turn my phone to airplane mode. Then I lean back and close my burning eyes.

And for the first time, I let the all-consuming fatigue take me.

26

In between flights, I arrange for a car service to take me to the farm. And now, as I watch the darkness outside the windows in an inky blur, I realize how desperately I needed these moments to myself, to process, to try to find a modicum of understanding, because once I reach beyond the pain, I'm only left with the *how* of it all.

When the sedan pulls in through the iron gates of La Casa de Las Flores y Luz, I feel soothed for the first time in many hours, as if our hacienda is opening her arms to embrace me, to hold me close, away from the dangers of the world, and my own broken heart.

With suitcase in hand, I stand outside the thick hand-carved doors. Each of the eight panels is carved with the face of a saint, but their identities elude my memory. The irony of the moment hits me with the weight of a thousand stones. I stood on this same threshold just a couple of months ago, suitcase in hand, running from a man, from myself. Except that I'm not that same person this time; I'm not wondering who I am or what I want. I'm painfully aware of both, and maybe that's what makes this so agonizing. Because I don't want to be running from Ben. But I can't have him, at least not his real love.

The moment I step inside the house, the clean, sweet scent of hyacinth surrounds me. A flower with so many meanings depending on the color. But here in the foyer, there is an enormous bouquet of blooms tastefully arranged in a silver urn, purple for sorrow. How appropriate, I think.

Wheeling my bag over the uneven stone floors, I park it in the corner near the stairs. And then I go searching for my mom. The scent of cumin and poblano peppers floats from the kitchen where I find stacked trays, dishes, and cooking utensils. The faint sound of music leads me outdoors, and it isn't long before I hear Mom's voice coming from the rooftop terrace. I rush up the Talavera tiled staircase like an eager child, and when I reach the top, she is already ending her call, walking across the small garden, and pulling me into her arms, as if she knows.

I collapse into her solid embrace, held up not by my own volition, but by her strength. And maybe that's what buoys me, or maybe all my tears have been spent, but either way, I have never been more grateful for my mother's touch than I am right now.

There are no words between us for several seconds until she says, "You're home a day early."

"Mom…"

"Jita, what is it?"

I pull free and walk to the roof's edge and lean against the half-wall to collect myself. The air is warm and welcoming, and if not for the moonlight, the flower farm below would be a sea of darkness. Instead, it is only familiar bursts of color. Dramatic anemone, billowy peonies, bright canterbury bells, ruffled daffodils, surges of sweet rocket, and unimaginable clusters of blooming shrubs and trees. A landscape of pure magic thriving in our blessed soil.

And in between it all are the erratic patches of canto; the bunches of snowy-white blooms look like tiny moons, rising out of the earth.

I feel a painful stab between my ribs. I love my family's legacy, and yet at this very moment, I hate it. What the magic has done to me, to Ben. What its absence has meant all these years.

I turn to my mom, arms wrapped tightly around my torso. I've practiced this conversation my entire journey home, what I would say, how I would say it. There is a shame in admitting the truth because it reveals my initial mistake with the bonding bouquet. But more devastatingly, I feel my own foolishness for believing that Ben's feelings were true. The words that come next are unrehearsed, the simplest truth I can find right now. Anything more feels too arduous.

"Ben is somehow…bonded to me."

Mom, in her slimming jeans and crisp white blouse, blinks, and I watch as her expression goes from one of confusion to sympathy but not the distress I expected. And when I explain the light in his eyes and the five petals from William and Beverly's bouquet that he retrieved and gave to me, she merely steeples her fingers in front of her mouth. Then she begins to pace, her eyes scanning the ground restlessly. With each step she takes, my pulse pounds more violently.

"Mom?"

Finally, she looks up, and with a long sigh, she says, "Harlow…"

There is a painful hitch in my chest. Oh my God, she knows something.

"How did this happen?" I nearly shout. "How is it even possible? It was only five petals! Did…did you know?" Please tell me no because my heart cannot take one more crack.

"Come," she says gently, "sit down,"

But I stay put, wishing I could bury myself in the bougainvillea vines climbing wildly up the half-walls and over the roof-top. "You're scaring me."

"I don't mean to scare you, and if you will come and sit, I will explain everything."

"Did you know!" I demand as tears spring to my eyes, blurring the jacaranda tree, potted hydrangeas, and wide succulent beds that blanket the rooftop garden.

"Of course not," she says, and I feel a relief so immense I almost collapse under the weight of it. I walk toward the lounger and take a seat across from my mom. It's only then that I notice the pine dining table under the trellised portal is scattered with used dishes, discarded cloth napkins, empty margarita glasses, and the afterglow of dying candles.

My mom follows my gaze. "We had a few friends over tonight," she says almost wistfully. "Pobre Rosa had to drive a couple of them home."

Not surprising given the three empty margarita pitchers.

My mom's dinner parties are notorious; she makes friends faster than anyone I know. If she meets a poet, or a nun, or a baker at the market, the next thing I know they're being invited to our house for "conversation." I've never known anyone as curious about and intrigued by the lives of other people as Mom is.

"Why do I think you know something?"

Ignoring the question, or maybe my accusatory tone, Mom folds her hands in her lap. "The first clue was when you messaged me in Italy and asked if I had enchanted your food, which of course I hadn't."

"First clue of what?"

"And then the canto, out of nowhere, began to spring up," she goes on. "A flower of endings but also beginnings, and immense creativity."

"So?" I'm growing impatient.

"And now you tell me the bonding flowers, five mere petals, have bonded a man to you."

"Mom, please be clearer," I say, feeling suddenly flushed and dizzy. "I have no idea where you're going with this."

"You have lived your life believing you have no magic, and so did I, but the truth is..." She hesitates. "Rosa and I believe that you are an encantadora."

"An enchantress?" My voice is a long shiver, verging on a maniacal laugh. I cannot begin to fathom the enormity of what she's telling me. I've always known magic, felt it there, just beyond me, but never once have I possessed it, never once have I caressed the shape of it.

"You enhance magic," she says. "It's the only explanation. Think about it. The flowers you ate were not enchanted, but once they were in your blood, their power was realized. The canto, I believe, grew in response to your creativity, and the petals..." she says softly, "laced with mere traces of magic meant for another, empowered by your very touch." She plucks a white hydrangea bloom from its stem, rolls it between her hands until it looks like a wet ball of paper. She places it in the palm of my hand. "Close your eyes, will some life into it," she says softly.

I stare wildly at the mess. Then I do as she says, and in a few seconds, I feel the vibration of life in the hydrangea; slowly I connect a thread of magic to it. The flower pulses as I open my eyes and watch it unfold into a healthy bloom.

I've seen magic my entire life, but seeing it in my own hands, feeling it in my own blood—that's something altogether new.

My mom is smiling as she takes the hydrangea from me and sets it aside. "Do you see?"

I feel the strangest flicker of pride quickly chased away by fear and confusion and utter disbelief. Then I relive my last few minutes with Ben, the dreaded magic spark lighting his pupils, the hurt in them when I left him so suddenly.

I did this to Ben.

The realization is a punch to the gut. Hot painful tears gather in my chest.

"Corazón?"

The term of endearment is loaded. My mom is asking me if I'm okay, if I want to talk about whatever is in my heart, but there are no words, not when it comes to Ben.

Is this what my grandmother saw in my future? Had she known all along that I'm an enchantress? Desperate for answers, I tell my mom everything Beverly told me, and if she's surprised she doesn't show it.

"But if she saw the truth why keep it a secret?" I ask.

My mom locks her fingers together and sighs. It takes her a moment to gather her thoughts, and I'm half expecting a long shrug, but then she says, "If she had told you or me, you wouldn't have experienced the goddess rising within you."

"Why?"

"Because we must move through the darkness alone—navigating all the pitfalls. Knowing what's on the other side defeats the purpose."

When all has been destroyed, the goddess shall rise.

"But why tell Beverly and not you or Rosa?"

She laughs lightly, sweeping a lock of hair from her face. "Because the temptation to relieve you of your suffering would have been too great," she says.

"But what if I could have avoided all of this? Ben and..."

Mom says nothing, allowing me to come to my own conclusion. I wouldn't have come into my magic, or realized my true self without the pain and heartache.

I tell Mom about the foxglove dreams, about the meaning I had gotten all wrong. "Why would William have dreamed of me? That part doesn't make sense."

She chews her bottom lip, sighing, processing. "I'm going to guess that there was a thread of magic between the two of you because of the bonding bouquet and your connection to it."

She takes it all in with a calm I wish I possessed. "And the night the flowers chose you as guardian...did you dream?"

I had forgotten until this very moment. A vague dream that meant nothing at the time, but screams with meaning now.

I'm climbing a steep mountain, searching for something I can't name. I hear laughter echoing in the distance. My laughter. And then my own voice hums with a frequency of…magic… A woman's voice I don't recognize, tells me, "It's time for the beginning."

"The goddess spoke to you."

It was all right there in a single dream. The climb, the hum of magic, Mayahuel telling me of a beginning. "But in the dream, I was laughing," I say. "Why would I sound happy when nothing could be further from the truth?" If anyone would know, it's my mom, gifted with dream magic.

"I believe a part of you is joyous to realize your full potential, to write, to become the woman you were always meant to become, and," she says softly, "to finally touch your own magic."

I'm not sure if there is space for both joy and grief in my heart right now. But strangely I feel a confusing blend of both.

"That night, after I had eaten the hibiscus tacos," I say, recalling the vivid details, "I ran to my garden and I was… I felt like I was drowning in so many emotions, and I mourned for some older version of myself."

My mother, her expression inscrutable, but for the small smile curving her mouth as she says, "An awakened consciousness."

"Consciousness?" I growl. "I just… I blew up my entire heart and learn I have magic and now there's something about an awakened consciousness? It's all too much!"

"I understand."

Does she always have to be so damn calm?

"It is a lot to take in, but you have no other choice, do you?"

I hate that she's right. I have to take it in, examine it, figure it out. I consider her New Agey term, awakened consciousness.

Is that what it was? Had I been asleep, navigating this life, this world with my eyes and heart closed? Shutting myself off from the possibility of pain because I had known its bitter taste;

I had felt its agony. I had held it close from a very young age when I realized I possessed no magic, that I wasn't worthy of a name that tied me to our land.

I see now that it was then that the power of my imagination was quieted, that my voice was stifled, and my dreams were subdued, denied.

Looking at my mom, I see a generous spirit with so much unconditional love that it gives me the courage to continue. "The goddess…she whispered to me in a dream."

My mom searches my face, waiting for Mayahuel's words as they were spoken to me. But there was only one. "Begin," I whisper. "And that's when I began to really write. It was almost as though that night, that moment gave me the story."

And isn't that what I wanted? To possess magic? To become a writer, to carve a new path? I guess I just didn't realize the price of it all. I guess none of us ever do.

"Do you see now," she asks encouragingly, "that when the magic of this land felt your rebirth, your new beginning, the canto bloomed, gifting you with the beauty of heart song and all of its creative power?"

"I still don't understand why," I say, grasping at any thread of understanding. "Why now? I've gone my whole life with… nothing."

My mom hesitates, considers, then says, "I don't know why the magic was dormant for so long."

"Dormant?"

"Sometimes," she says softly, "magic needs to sleep."

These words hold power; a slow understanding begins to unfold inside of me, confirming what I already know. *It wasn't just the magic that was asleep. I've been asleep too.*

"Rosa has a theory about the timing of it all," Mom adds, "and I think she's right."

"What's her theory?"

"When you left New York that night, when you had had

enough, when you chose a different more challenging path, the magic, like your consciousness, was awakened."

I suddenly remember the words I whispered aloud: *I want to find the better and truer way.*

"One decision set this all in motion?" I say.

"A single decision always has a ripple effect."

I hear her every word, but it's a hard thing to live your entire life with a belief, realizing a vast truth and then in an instant, watch it evaporate before your eyes.

"So how does it work?" A fiery heat pulses through my veins. "Do I just touch a bloom and bam it's supercharged with that flower's magic? That sounds like a terrible way to go through life, Mom. There have to be some rules, some controls."

"And you will learn them," she says confidently. "Think about each time you enhanced a bloom. What did all those times have in common?"

I consider the moments; each was one made of strife, trauma, confusion. "Intense feelings," I say quietly.

She comes over and sits next to me, placing a warm hand on my arm. "What you have gone through, it's a union of a wild and creative power. It's no easy thing, and I'm so sorry for the suffering but I am also so proud of you."

At that I lean my head on her shoulder as tears prick my eyes. And I think of Ben. "Is it possible," I say, "that I bonded to Ben as well? The way he bonded to me?"

Stroking my hair, Mom says, "It seems there are many possibilities of magic where you're concerned." Her voice is light and soothing. "But I'm not sure."

My insides clench tighter. If I *am* bonded to Ben, do I want to break it, to destroy what feels so right? And in doing so, what will happen to the memories? Will those, like a rose, die on the vine without any love to sustain them?

"Let's go inside," she says. "I'll give you some rose vervain oil."

A healing concoction to soothe a broken heart, to offer light in the darkness.

"I would only increase its magic." The words are hardly recognizable, so immense in their truth I find breathing a challenge.

"Don't you want that?"

I shake my head, already having made the decision. As much as I don't want to feel this heaviness in my chest, this agony of truth, to diminish it in any way might dilute the courage I'm going to need.

"But I do want to know something else," I say. "During all of this turmoil, no one called, no one sensed what I was going through. Do you think somehow all of this is related?"

"You have never liked giving up your privacy."

"It's pretty invasive."

"Jita, that thread is one of magic, and now that you have found your own, it makes sense that you severed that connection, even if you didn't realize you were doing it," she says. "I think you knew at some level how much you needed space, some solitude."

She's right. Interrogations from my family would have felt like a tipping point.

"I feel so awful, Mom." The tears fall slowly, rolling down my cheeks. "And so stupid. Like I really believed..."

She presses her hand right above my heart. "I know it's broken and I wish I could mend it for you." I think about Lil's powers of memory, how they could help me forget. But then what? I'd be giving up too much, not only how Ben made me feel, but who I am when I'm with him.

"But this is your journey," Mom goes on, "and only you can decide what to do next."

"There's nothing to decide," I say willfully. "I have to end this. I have to break the bond."

"Harlow, it's nearly impossible to break a bond. A magical bond is like a deep-rooted vine."

I pull back and face her now. "Mom, please. There has to be a way."

Her expression goes tense; she looks away then back to me. "You…as an encantadora, *you* have the power to do it."

I stiffen. How ironic that the magic flowing in my veins gives me the power to destroy what I so desperately want to keep close. "Tell me how."

"Are you absolutely certain?"

I nod. My mind is sure, but my heart is rebelling with the force of a million noes.

But then a new idea blooms, one so out there and impossible I nearly dismiss it. "Do you think that maybe after I break the bond, that we could start again? Is that possible? I mean, things don't have to be over over, right? Or…will I even care?"

My mom goes silent, and it's in her silence that I feel suddenly hot and dizzy.

"Oh, Harlow," she says, "because of your power, when you sever this bond, you will likely destroy *all* of the love between you."

I look at her, blinking away hot tears, not fully understanding.

Seeing the question on my face, she explains, "It's possible real feelings grew during the time of the bonding. And that means he will also lose any real feelings he has for you."

"What!" I gasp "No, Mom! How is that possible?" I'm about to combust.

"It's why we are so careful with bondings."

"And what about me? My feelings?" I cry. "If I'm bonded…"

"I don't think that the magic will destroy any true feelings you have."

"Why not?"

My mom pulls a face, blows out a whoosh of air. "Because the magic comes from inside of you, and now that you are aware of it, it won't do anything to affect you without your permission."

I get to my feet, wishing I could crawl out of my own skin.

My mind is a cyclone, spinning, searching for a way out of this, for a happy ending, but the possibility is only a dismal dead end.

The very power that created the emotions is the same power that will destroy them.

All my life, I have wanted an inheritance of magic. To feel connected to something so much greater than myself. And now? I see the complexities of it, its conflicting nature, and the price it asks you to pay. It all feels unfair.

In a moment of desperation, I think I could perhaps use a truth bloom to see if maybe he has genuine feelings. But then I remember, people can't be double spelled. As much as I want to live with this lie, to pretend that what Ben and I have is real, I know I can't do that to him, to me, to both of our futures. Every time he'd kiss me, look at me longingly, I'd wonder if he were just under some twisted spell.

I manage to draw myself up. "Then I guess I have to do this. Just tell me how."

"If you are sure. There's a recipe for an elixir. You will infuse it with your essence, and then you both have to drink it."

"I have to see him?" I don't know why I'm so stunned. I guess I presumed that I could do the bond severing long distance, that I wouldn't have to face him again.

"Yes, and Harlow, there is no going back once this is done. Do you understand?"

And with that my heart breaks even more.

27

The next afternoon I'm sitting in Pasaporte staring at my phone like it's a bomb ready to explode.

I haven't had the courage to turn it on for fear of seeing messages from Ben, or Laini, or my sisters and primas. Each relationship comes with its own rules of engagement, requiring more than I can give. Right now, I need separation; I need to process and think about the enormous turn my life has taken and what happens from here. Thankfully, Mom promised she wouldn't tell the rest of the family about my newfound magic, saying that it was my story to weave. A story I have no idea where to start because the beginning feels so far away, from before I was born and even long before that.

I think about Mayahuel, about the price she paid to become her truest self. I think about her inevitable destruction, about how even then she rose—to love, to create, to command. I imagine my ancestor walking these lands when Mayahuel found her and asked her if she would carry the goddess's legacy, when she told her there would be a cost to the magic.

What kind of cost?

That is for each soul to discover.

The understanding comes slowly, in bits and pieces until I realize fully that all my life I *hadn't* been unnoticed or excluded. I had been protected. All these years I have mourned the absence of magic, but what if it had been a blessing all along? What if the cost is greater than the power?

I close my eyes, center myself with deep breaths as I seek the goddess, wondering if she can hear my pleas, if she can feel my pain, my hollowness. But she is silent.

I take a sip of dark iced coffee, anchor myself to the seat with unflinching determination before I turn on my cell. A few messages from Cam pop up, photos of the inn's newly created garden. It's a stunning enclosed jardín, with a brick walkway, a three-tiered stone fountain, and an abundance of red camellias that conceal a wooden gate original to the property.

After I shoot her a quick text to tell her how gorgeous it is, I brace myself for an onslaught of messages from Ben, but there is no onslaught only one text from yesterday—a response to my admission of going home.

Okay. Be safe. I hope we can talk soon. I want to understand.

And another from this morning, a photo of the delicate leaf that had fallen into the car now resting in the palm of his hand. You forgot this.

I close my eyes against the inevitable tears, and the image of him finding the leaf when he returned the rental, of him carrying it with him, knowing it meant something to me. A sudden agonizing emotion burns through me, igniting a flare of not sorrow but grief.

I stare at the photo of the yellowed leaf, at the crack threatening its wholeness in Ben's hand. And I know I have to let go. Because if I don't, then I will forever be drowning in the what-ifs.

My text is short and simple: I need to see you.

His response is immediate: Can you talk?

I so badly want to tell him no, but he deserves more than a coward. With trembling hands, I text back, sure.

My phone rings two seconds later, and my heart is thrashing so hard I can feel it in my throat and limbs. I take a deep breath, and answer, "Hey."

"Hey. How are you?"

I'm not sure if he's asking about me or my feigned illness. "Better," I lie. "How are you?" I cringe the second the words are out of my mouth. Such a stupid question to ask under the circumstances.

Oh, I don't know, Harlow. He's probably miserable and confused and thinks you've lost your mind.

In typical Ben fashion, he skips over the question and gets right to the heart of the matter. "I'm glad you want to see me."

I squeeze my eyes closed, trying to ignore the bitter truth that I know is coming before he does and something about that feels so wrong and unfair. "When are you going to be back in the States?" I ask, wishing my voice didn't sound so high and tight.

I'm surprised when he says, "I have to go to New York in a couple of days for some meetings."

"What about the renovation?"

"It'll run fine for a few days without me." He pauses, and I imagine Ben standing in the library now; I imagine its shelves are filled with books. Maybe it's midnight, and he can't sleep and the moonlight is pouring in through the windows and—

"I can come to Mexico after my meetings," he says.

"No... I can come to you," I insist, thinking I don't want any bad memories of Ben lingering on our land. I quickly add the lie, "I have some things to do there anyway."

Ben hesitates. I hear an inhalation of breath. "Should I be worried, Har?"

An impossible question with only a heartbreaking answer that I'm not about to give. But what am I supposed to say? No? Yes? Christ, this is so screwed up. "Ben…listen, there are just some things I need to tell you, to explain. I mean—I ran out on you and I'm really sorry about that, but please don't ask me to explain on the phone."

"Fair enough."

My chest squeezes painfully. "I'll call you when I get to the city?"

"Okay. Oh, hey, did you get the photo?"

"Yeah." A smile sneaks onto my lips. "I'm glad you saved it."

"I'll bring it with me." He's smiling too, and my heart feels like it's being wrenched from my body.

The next night I'm in the kitchen with my mom and Rosa, watching them as they set out the flowers that I'll need to break the bond. I gave my mom permission to tell my aunt, knowing I would need her support too. What would ordinarily look like lovely blooms, now appear to be nothing more than stems and petals of poison in my eyes. "What are those?" I ask, pointing to a cluster of dark violet blooms shaped like tiny trumpets.

"Dark root," my mom says.

"I've never heard of it."

"It's our own creation," Rosa says as she pours us each a shot of añejo. Then lifts her own glass. "A shot to courage."

"To courage," I repeat, and tip the amber liquid back. The heat of the tequila explodes across my tongue, and the aftertaste of the agave sends waves of warmth through my body.

"What's the meaning of dark root?" I ask.

"It means, *let me go*," Rosa says, pouring another round. She has always been the most direct Estrada with a can-do spirit to rival any champion. So when she spits out the words so matter-of-factly, I take no offense, but my corazón? That's a different matter.

"I'm including a pinch of cascuta," Mom puts in. "For healing."

"Also known as devil's hair," Rosa says, raising her shot glass for a second time. "Harlow, what do you want to toast to?"

"Shit days?"

No one challenges my self-pity, and instead embraces it as we all say in unison, "To shit days."

My mom sets her glass down and unwraps a piece of velvet I hadn't noticed. There, in the center of the fabric, is a single black rose petal. It is a rare beauty, and one of my favorite shades. Until now.

"For death?" I ask, knowing it's merely symbolic, but the word, the meaning is a dagger to the heart.

"And a final goodbye," Rosa says, taking another shot.

"How can anything so beautiful be so ugly too?" I say, wishing I could touch the silky petal. But my mom has warned me not to touch any of the ingredients until I make the elixir, for fear that I might alter their magical properties.

"I need another shot," I say miserably, pushing my glass across the island toward Rosa who happily obliges.

"And don't forget," my aunt says, pointing to the small bag of dark chocolate filled with disks no bigger than dimes, "the cacao must be brought to a slow boil."

My mind is a machine, rotating levers and gears, trying to figure out the logistics of this. If I have to cook this concoction, that means that I can't just meet Ben anywhere. Maybe I can use Laini's apartment. The thought of luring him to her tiny pad and offering him this drink feels like something out of a wicked fairy tale. And I'm the evil witch.

"Is the chocolate for taste?" I ask, downing my tequila with way too much gusto.

"It's for harmony and friendship," my mom says. Is that what she thinks? That Ben and I could ever be friends? That any of this could ever end harmoniously?

"Severing a bond is dangerous," Rosa says, "and often turns bad rapido. You could end up hating each other, so this is a safeguard."

My heart twists painfully, and a new anger surges. A part of me is still shell-shocked, thinking that this is just a nightmare I'll wake from, but it's not. It's my reality, one that's insisting Ben and I pay the price for a magic neither of us asked for.

"What will it feel like?" I ask. "I mean, once we drink the elixir."

"Like all your bones have dissolved," Rosa offers.

My mom sighs and shoots her sister a glare. Then to me, "It will likely feel exhausting, like you've woken up from a vivid dream."

"You mean nightmare?"

"Is there a difference?" my aunt asks.

"Of course," I argue. "One is pleasant and the other is awful."

Rosa shrugs. "Ah. Well, my dreams are not always pleasant and my nightmares are sometimes delicious."

For the first time in days, I laugh. We all do, as if this is a normal evening and I'm watching spells being constructed the way I have many times before. But then my fear comes roaring back, and I curse myself again for not recognizing the signs of magic. For making myself believe that the extraordinary spark between me and Ben was somehow real.

"A bond severing is a brutal act," Rosa says, sipping at her tequila. "Have you really thought about this? About the consequences? Truly, Harlow. Why break your heart when you don't have to?"

"Tía—I can't live a lie! I can't do that to Ben, or myself." How could she even suggest it?

Mom tsks. "Rosa, you've had enough to drink."

But my aunt isn't drunk. Her eyes are too clear, her stance

too strong. She actually believes leaving the magic untouched is the solution.

"It's not a lie," Rosa argues, "it's more like a colorful version of a life you get to paint. Amorcita, you are an encantadora! You have more power than you know. But that doesn't mean you have to use that power for this."

"And it doesn't give me the right to control someone else's life either."

"I wonder," she says, narrowing her gaze, "if you gave him a choice, what he would choose?"

I'm screaming inside, raging against the magic, my heart, her question. Ben hates lies, any kind of manipulation. Wouldn't he want to cut away at this magic to get to the truth as much as I do? I have no idea.

Which begs the question: How much will I tell him? Risk his refusal to break the bond? Or will I leave him in the dark where he doesn't have to suffer the pain of knowing? He'll feel like he's woken from a dream like Mom said. He'll never know why his feelings for me have vanished, only that they're gone. And isn't that better than grieving the loss of something that was never real?

Mom wraps all of the ingredients up in linen, securing the bundle with a silver ribbon. "You melt the cacao first, and then add each ingredient slowly, always stirring."

"And as you stir," Rosa says, "do not hide your feelings. Let them come to the surface. Let them be a wave to carry your magic forward. You'll need it."

"No specific order?" I ask, feeling suddenly exhausted, as if the events of the last few days have finally caught up to me, as if they have coalesced into a violent thing hurtling itself through space and all I can do is wait for impact. And then what? Will I find peace? Happiness? Calm? Will anything ever be the same again? I haven't even had a moment to process the magic that has awakened inside of me, a magic that has given shape to my life, my dreams. To a living nightmare.

"No order," Rosa says, "only that the black rose petal has to be last."

I don't need to ask why. I know the answer.

For death and a final goodbye.

28

I have exactly five days to hone my skills, and gather my nerve. Both feel impossible, but my mom and aunt are determined to help me embrace my magic. I'm not so sure I can begin to embrace it until I fully accept the truth of it.

I'm an encantadora.

Either way, I'm too worn-out to fight them when they insist I rise at dawn the next day. I roll out of bed bleary-eyed and throw on some shorts and a tank top. By the time I get downstairs, my mom is already in the fields and my aunt has brewed some coffee, which I drink gratefully.

"So what's on the agenda, Yoda?" I tease as the caffeine hits my system.

My aunt throws me a curious stare. "Who's Yoda?"

"*Star Wars*," I say, thinking she's kidding until I see the confused expression on her face, so I add, "*Empire Strikes Back*? Little green Jedi master?"

Rosa gathers a basket of gloves, sheers, and some seed pack-ets. "Doesn't strike a bell. Vamanos."

"You can't be serious," I say, trailing her out to the south garden.

When we arrive, Mom is hoeing weeds from a dry patch of dirt no bigger than ten by ten feet. She's wearing a wide-brimmed sun hat that flops around her face. "Good morning!" she says, turning to me.

I wave because I'm not sure why I'm here, and it better not be to offer some free labor in the name of magic. Rosa sets down the basket, hikes up her pants and squats. She rips a spiky weed from the soil. "Bah! They just won't give up."

The weedy patch of land is adjacent to a small field of bloom-ing peonies, azaleas, bearded irises, and delphinium.

Mom eyes me up and down. "You should have worn pants."

"Why?"

She hands me the hoe and wipes her forehead with the back of her hand. "I need some tea."

I watch as she goes over to a shady spot between two trees, where there's a small wooden table and a couple of chairs, and pours herself a glass of tea. "Damn weeds," she groans.

Rosa nods. "Damn is right. Go on, Harlow—rip them up."

With a frown, I say, "Is this part of my training? I mean, I'm an enhancer not a killer so..."

"This part has nothing to do with magic," Mom says, fan-ning herself. "I just need a break."

"I thought you two were going to teach me about my magic and how to use it."

"We are," Rosa says, throwing her hands on her hips and sur-veying the overturned earth. "But first we get rid of the weeds. Roots and all."

With a groan, I begin jamming the sharp bladed tool into the ground and jerking the invaders from the earth while Rosa and my mom chat in the shade. A few minutes later, I've completed a single row. By the time I've finished the third row, my shoulder blades are burning, my hands are stinging, and my neck is sweating. I'd forgotten how good physical work feels, how it invigorates the body and distracts the mind.

Mom is at my side, taking the hoe from me. "You're crying," she says.

"What?" I bring my hand to my wet cheek. When did that happen? And how did I not even recognize it?

Rosa says, "Ay! You truly are powerful."

I glance at my mom. "What's she talking about?"

"You're not weeping for yourself," she says.

"I didn't even know I was crying!"

"It's the weeds," Rosa says. "They're communicating through you."

"Are you seriously telling me the weeds are crying? Oh my God! I'm a monster," I nearly shout.

Mom pats my back while Rosa tells me, "Weeds are quite sensitive."

"Well, maybe we should just leave them," I suggest.

"Our soil is for magic and flowers," Mom says, "not unrelenting invaders."

We spend the next hour tilling the land before watering it. A pleasant sweet earthy scent fills the air as the sun rises higher.

"Now," Rosa says, sprinkling packets of wildflower seeds onto the land, "most would have to wait a couple of weeks for the planting, but they don't have your magic, Harlow."

Mom kneels into the earth, gesturing for me to follow. "This is why I wanted you to wear pants," she says. But truth be told, I love the cool moist soil against my skin. I press my hands into the earth, and feel a jolt of joy. I know that bacteria in the soil releases serotonin in the brain and lifts moods, but this is different—I can feel the magic pulsing across my fingertips, vibrating through me.

I grab a handful of the wet earth and rub it between my fingers. "Now what?"

"You have to breathe on the seeds," Mom says, "and the rest? All instinct."

"Well," Rosa interjects, "not entirely. You must follow the path of the magic as it vibrates through you."

"Like I said," Mom offers, "instinct."

Rosa looks like she's about to argue but then closes her mouth and smiles at me.

I lean closer to the loam, and as my mom instructed, I breathe. Inhale. Exhale. But nothing happens. "What am I doing wrong?" I ask.

Mom pushes her hat back and sighs. "I can't teach you how to channel the magic."

"Relax you must," Rosa says.

I shoot her a glare. "You said you had never heard of Yoda."

My aunt laughs. "I said the name didn't ring a bell and now it does."

I toss a handful of dirt at her. She jumps out of the way, and in a single swift motion, she picks up the hose, turns the nozzle, and sprays me.

"Rosa!" Mom shouts as I shriek and leap back.

My aunt rolls her eyes and points at me. "She started it."

Mom huffs, takes the hose from her sister, and turns to me. "The other times you experienced your magic, you were feeling heightened emotions."

"You think that's what's missing?" I ask, wiping the cool water from my face.

"Anything is possible," Rosa puts in. "And I need a shower."

After she leaves, I make a few more futile attempts to grow the seeds into blooms when Mom finally says, "Maybe you need food. Want some breakfast?"

I want to refuse, to keep trying my hand at magic, but I know there is no forcing it.

We spend the rest of the day walking the farm, checking on the crops, making bouquets of blue thistle, lilacs, and gladioli. I try my hand at enhancing the potency of some dried herbs, but I feel blocked, or maybe I'm just putting too much pressure on myself.

That night, my body is exhausted but when the house goes silent, I slip out of my room and back out to the newly seeded jardín. The moon is a mere sliver, but the farm is dimly lit with garden lights that guide my path.

When I reach the patch of land, I sit at the edge, sifting dirt through my fingers. I think about Ben, about what's in front of me, about the truth or lies I'm going to tell him. I think about the trust in his eyes, the warmth of his skin, and that signature scent that feels like more than a memory.

Tears burn my eyes, and soon my body is vibrating with magic—with a power I never asked for. I realize the fear it induces, the resistance I have felt to its presence as if I can't trust it, but isn't that saying I don't trust myself?

Closing my eyes, I take a deep breath, and I let the magic rise. I give myself over to it, as well as the grief stirring inside of me.

With a long exhale, I press my hands into the soil. There is no effort, no will, no resistance.

I let go.

Heat spreads across my chest. My body hums with power.

When I open my eyes, I see a tiny pink bloom growing from the earth, stretching itself toward me.

And I smile through the pain.

29

For the next four days I try my hand at magic.

Sometimes it works, like the seeds, and sometimes it's utter failure, like when I try to empower sleep herbs that have the opposite effect and leave Rosa tossing and turning all night. Mom keeps telling me that magic is like breathing—you don't tell your lungs what to do, they just know.

I spend my last day in town at Pasaporte getting out of my own head and into Violeta's world.

Violeta spun to see Jack standing before her, his face shrouded by the backlight of the sun.

"Jack," she began, wanting to start off on the right foot, "I'm..."

"I know who you are," he said. "How about we sideline the niceties and get to the point." He stepped closer, enough for Violeta to see the face that belonged to the anger.

It was a face she would never forget.

I set down the pen, staring up at the gathering clouds, wondering what's so unforgettable about Jack's face, which makes me think of Ben. His angles and smile—those eyes and hands.

For the umpteenth time, I go in search of that damn First Impressions journal he wrote in. But as usual I come up empty-handed, as if the journal knows I'm searching for it and is purposefully staying hidden.

That night I can't sleep. I'm too wound up about getting on a plane tomorrow, flying back to New York, to Ben, to heartache. There are moments I don't think I can do it, that it's too much for the magic to ask of me. Would it be so terrible to keep falling? To stay blissfully bonded?

Lying in the dark, I feel both unsettled and spent. I need air, space. I'm reminded of a line from Rilke's poem "Lament": "I would like to step out of my heart and go walking beneath the enormous sky."

If only I really could step out of my heart. If only.

Wrapped in a robe, I make my way outside. The air is still, gentle, like an eternal spring, and the sky is a cloak of velvet. A half-moon hangs high and faraway, but not as distant as the stars, bright burning things, many long dead.

The garden lights are soft, dim, just enough to cast shadows. As I stroll, I spy the canto that has sprouted up in little clusters here and there, even through cracks in the stones. As I pass each bunch, the white silken flowers sway, slanting toward me as if in a show of solidarity. I stare at their loveliness. At their diaphanous petals, so fragile and yet sturdy.

When I reach my own garden, I expect to see the bloom in abundance but the plot is exactly as I left it, barren and seemingly deserted. Squatting, I press my hands into the cool earth, turning it over in my hands mindlessly. And I know why this tierra has remained empty. Because even the rising of my magic can't fill the hole inside of me.

A mild breeze sweeps across my face, through the fleshy

stems of the Hylocereus. The Night Queen stretches her angular arms toward the sky like an offering of its white fragrant flowers. The blooms seem to glow; their scent is one of ripeness and hope. But how can there be hope when the bloom's life span is a matter of hours?

I imagine Azalea and Beverly rushing toward the tree for its magic, to divine Beverly's future. The plant's symbolism is one of endurance, determination, strength in the face of adversity. A beacon of light and utter beauty.

I can see my grandmother plucking a flower in the moonlight and handing it to Beverly.

The single bloom that would decide Beverly's fate and tell her if William was worthy.

I think now of the bloom that will decide my own future: the black rose petal.

Death and a final goodbye.

Filled with a strange longing, I walk toward the Queen. Slowly, I reach up and caress the edges of a waxy petal. Its warmth surges through my hand. Instantly, I feel its strength, its endurance, and light, coursing through my veins. I hold tight to the blossom, drawing on its strength, pulling it into my spirit as I inhale its honeyed fragrance like it's my last breath.

The realization isn't a dawning, but a shock to my system. My abilities don't merely enhance the potency of a bloom.

My power allows me to *draw* magic from the flowers.

I shudder, imagining the possibilities. And then I see Ben's eyes, his smile, I feel the tenderness of his touch and wonder if my perception of him was masked by magic. And if it was, what would it be like to see him, to feel him, to know him without enchantment?

Remorsefully, I release the magic, letting it flow back into the Night Queen. Because as much as I want all of her courage, I know I can't face Ben with a false strength.

If I'm going to do this, I need to do it my way. With all my grief and messiness and hopefully, with a modicum of kindness.

The whisper rises inside of me slowly, bitterly—

As if there is any kindness in death.

30

The New York sky is a breathless expanse of stone-cold gray. I'm in the cab, staring out at a place I don't recognize anymore, a world that now seems like a faraway memory.

The city streets are crawling with the drably dressed masses. A collection of humans moving in various directions, all with the same determined look that tells the rest of the world they have somewhere important to be.

I guess we all do in some capacity, a place, a goal, a dream we're moving toward. Most of us are consumed with these thoughts, forecasting outcomes we can't possibly know, and all the while worrying ourselves about the wide chasm between the here and there, the present and the future.

I step out of the cab in front of Laini's apartment on Washington Place in the West Village, and my heart begins its chaotic dance. A thumping that will soon become a pounding if I don't take a few deep breaths and get some semblance of control over my nerves. But how can I? When I'm back in a city that only reminds me of a false life. A city where I have to destroy the one thing that seems so real.

A city that will now always feel like goodbye.

Laini had a meeting at work and won't be home for another hour or so. I use the spare key I still have to let myself into the old art deco building before I schlep up to her apartment on the second floor. The living room and kitchen make up the unit, other than a narrow passage that leads to a single bedroom no bigger than a closet and a bathroom where you have to step over the toilet to get to the shower. Space is not a necessity for Laini, not as long as she's in the middle of the action.

I set my bag down and tug free a small arrangement of dried heather tied with a black silk ribbon. It's a small token of my appreciation for Laini letting me crash here. After I set it on the coffee table, I flop onto the pink overstuffed sofa. The radiator hisses and spits; the familiar hum of late-afternoon traffic outside makes me yearn for quiet, for wide-open spaces and brilliant blue skies. I've already told Laini everything. I had to. First, there was no way I could come here and hide the truth from her; she would know something was wrong the moment she saw the doom and gloom all over my face. I wasn't blessed with the same mask Cam and Lil have. They can conceal their emotions so flawlessly that no one (other than an Estrada) would know they were suffering from a broken heart.

My emotions, on the other hand, are as evident and capricious as the sea: calm and languid one moment, stormy the next. My mom always told me I have a poet's soul and that someday my heart would translate to the page. *Lost Soul* is halfway complete now; its edges have grown sharper, cutting more deeply. And I love it—all of its messiness and darkness, its light and promise. I realize now that I wrote this story to uncover a truth, to answer a question: Can love forgive all?

After a glass of wine, I text Ben. I'm in the city. Can you meet at seven?

Then I unzip my bag and retrieve the linen bundle that holds my future. The rich scent of chocolate overwhelms the flowers' fragrance, and my heart sinks with a burden too big to contain.

Just then my phone pings: Seven is great. Are you hungry? Dinner?

I was thinking you could come to Laini's. She lives on Washington between sixth and seventh. Where are you staying?

Helena's apartment. Upper east side.

His sister has an apartment here? A new plan unfolds at the speed of light. If I went to Ben, I would be in control to leave at any moment. I won't have to wait awkwardly for him to make his exit once he wakes from the "dream." And if I decide to tell him the truth, he'll likely slam the door on his way out.

I feel like a snake when I text back: I'd love to see her place. I can come to you?

Perfect.

He sends me the address along with, I can't wait to see you.

Just then I hear keys in the door. Laini comes in. She's dyed her hair a deep red and it looks so gorgeous. I'm envious for all of the four seconds it takes her to cross the room and pull me into a giant hug.

Feeling smothered, I try to break free but she won't let me. "Lain..."

"I don't care that you hate hugs. You need one."

"Uh, I really don't." What I need is to rewind time and prevent the damn bonding.

Laini releases me, her deep-set eyes rove my face, then her hand is on my forehead like she's checking my temperature. "Do you feel different?"

"It's magic," I laugh. "Not the flu. And your hair looks amazing!"

"Do not change the subject, but you really think so?" She smiles and flips a strand over her shoulder while batting her eyes dramatically.

"How do you pull off every single color better than the last?"

"True, I'm a chameleon but you…you are an enchantress. What a dynamic duo we are."

"Actually, I think I'm the villain of the story."

"Harlow, you did not do anything *intentionally*."

"Doesn't mean it won't hurt."

Her gaze falls to the empty wineglass on the coffee table. "You need a drink."

"And a long hot bath."

"Not in this apartment."

We both laugh and make our way to the kitchen bar. Laini gets busy mixing some concoction that I'm not even paying attention to because my mind is focused on one thing. Ben. It's only been five days since I last saw him, but damn if I don't miss everything about him: his earthy scent, the way his mouth curves slowly when he's about to tell a bad joke, the way his fingers entwine with mine so perfectly. And his kiss. If I'm bonded, will the severing really take all that away?

Laini pushes a glass with silver liquid and a lime toward me. "I call it Heartbreak Hotel. Sorry. Super on the nose, but we shouldn't sugarcoat it." She inches back and offers me a hesitant smirk. "Right?"

With a nod, I say, "Look, this is the hazard of having a heart." I'm trying to put on a brave face but failing miserably. "It gets broken, shattered even." Tears fill my eyes, and I want to throw open the door and go running down the street screaming like a banshee.

"Oh, hon." Her voice is soft, feathery. "You really fell hard."

"It could just be the bonding," I argue. "I won't know until I drink the elixir."

"I would ask about him, but that might make it worse, so don't tell me. I mean unless you absolutely want to, or at the very least if, you know…" She leans closer. "Did you sleep with him?"

I shake my head miserably.

"You had to have been bonded then."

"Why do you say that?"

"No way could someone fall this madly if they hadn't had sex, right?"

I might have once subscribed to her cynical view but that was before I met Ben, before I felt his touch, before I experienced the way he made me feel seen. Heard. Understood.

"Not everything is about sex, Laini."

"That's only true for bad sex."

I can't help it. I laugh. I know this is her MO. Use humor to diffuse the ache. I swipe the tears away. "I'm fine. Okay not really, but I will be. I just need to get this over with."

Laini's expression softens into something between pity and compassion. She lifts her glass. "To useless little hearts."

Clinking my glass with hers, I add, "May they be made of stronger stuff in the future."

I down the drink; it's both sour and citrusy with a smoky aftertaste that instantly warms my weary bones. "Lain, this is really, really good."

She beams. "So…what time—"

"Seven," I say. "I'm going to his sister's place so you don't need to cut out tonight."

"What can I do to help?" she asks.

"Just being here?" I sigh. "And maybe a few more rounds of these later?"

"Well, um…" She taps her fingers along the counter, avoiding my gaze. I feel a pinch of anxiety. I know that nervous look. And it almost always means I should worry.

"Spill," I say. "What are you hiding?"

She balks. "Nothing."

"Laini."

"Okay, don't be pissed but Lil called me. She said she knew something was up with you, something about the dreams she's been having, and she totally sucked the truth out of me. Actually, she tricked me into thinking she already knew." Her eyes go wide. "I swear."

"How much does she know?"

Laini scrunches up her face. "Everything?"

My body goes cold. If Lil knows, then so does the rest of the family. Not such a horrible thing except that I wanted to tell them on my own terms. Although, maybe this is better. It saves me the burden of having to retell the same story, and truthfully? That sounds like torture.

"Why didn't she just ask me?" I say.

"She said she was worried you would try to hide it, and you know how much she hates being kept in the dark."

The sudden image of me and Laini in my old apartment burns bright in my mind's eye. It was the night of Chad's promotion party and my biggest problem was being fired and trying to figure out what I was going to wear to a party I didn't want to go to. In retrospect the rejection, the pain, even the breakup all seems so insignificant now. "It's okay," I say. "Lil was going to find out eventually."

"Right..." There is a tremble in Laini's voice that makes me nervous. "Except that she told Camilla and your cousins, and they all drew straws."

My pulse skips a beat or two. "Straws?"

"Like metaphorically."

"English, Laini."

"Don't lose your shit, okay? Promise?"

"How can I promise when I don't even know what you're going to tell me?" But I do. I absolutely know what she's going to tell me, and I've barely completed the thought when she says, "They all wanted to come, to help you pick up the pieces. Lil won. She's on her way and will be here at—" she glances at her phone "—eight o'clock."

Of course she did. She's the family fixer. "Please tell me you're kidding."

"I'm not," Laini says, lifting her chin into a defiant stance I usually love, but at the moment all I want to do is strangle her. "Look, I'm not an Estrada," she says. "I don't pretend to understand your guys' connection but I do know you, and I know you're going to need your sister tonight."

I feel a release, a lock unlatching deep within me. Laini is right. Tonight is going to be unbearable, and I can't begin to know the outcome other than it's going to hurt like hell, and I'm going to need Lil, her energy, and maybe even her memory magic to help me forget.

"I can have your luggage sent to the hotel," Laini says, "which happens to be the Ritz Midtown. Way better place to heal your heart than this shabby apartment."

I offer a tremulous smile, knowing there is no place on earth that is going to make this any easier.

Two hours later, I'm in a cab headed toward uptown, fidgeting with the silk belt of my dress. The stone-gray sky has given way to the blackness of night. As the driver pulls up to a handsome town house, I wrap my hands around the bundle of magic in my bag.

It hums and pulses, vibrating with an energy that wants to be set free as I pass the doorman, walk across the elegant lobby, climb into the elevator, and head up to the tenth floor where I walk down the plush carpeted hall to the corner apartment and stand in front of the door.

I wait, slow my breathing, close my eyes. And I sense it. The thread of magic that ties me and Ben together. It's warm, like a beam of sunlight on a wintry day. I feel it from head to toe, igniting heat and fear and want. So much want.

Lightly, I knock. Once, twice.

I hear footsteps, a click of the lock.

And then the door swings open.

31

B en.
  He's standing two feet from me. And even from here I
can smell his intoxicating scent, even from here I can feel the
heat radiating off of him, even from here I want to fall into his
arms and...

Pretend. It. All. Away.

But he's already reaching for me; his arms are around me, his
face buried in my neck, his breath warm against my skin. His
voice a whisper in my ear. "I've missed you."

My eyes burn with unspent tears. And for just a moment I let
myself sink deep into his orbit. We stay like this for a few heart-
beats. Ben embracing hope. Me cursing the lie.

When we break apart, I can't look into his eyes, but I feel the
weight of his stare. "You look beautiful," he says softly.

At this I smile and meet his gaze. "Liar." I got a good look
at myself in the mirror before I came over, and even a subzero

spoon wasn't going to improve the puffy dark circles beneath my eyes. "I look like a swamp witch."

Stroking his chin, he smirks playfully. "A very beautiful swamp witch."

I step into the sophisticated apartment, the epitome of style and refinement. The walls are painted a light blue; the elegant furniture is well curated, but I can't help but feel as if I'm walking into a hotel suite and not someone's home.

Ben is wearing a pair of jeans and a black Henley. His jaw is even more chiseled than it was five days ago, or maybe he trimmed his scruff—either way he's as attractive as ever.

"Helena lives here?" A tremble moves through me as we walk into the living room where a fire simmers in a stone fireplace. There's a table near the window with several silver framed photos. Even from here I can make out Ben's young face, the smiling boy with the broken heart.

"My grandparents bought it forever ago," he says, "and then Helena just sort of adopted it, made it her own, at least when she's in town."

You can tell a lot about a person by their abode. Their tastes, interests, organizational style, their preferences for comfort. Helena is a woman of great taste; her interests likely include art, given the number of paintings on the walls. She is hyperorganized because there isn't a thing out of place, and she prefers style over comfort because the stylish furniture looks stiff and uninviting.

"Good for her," I say.

"If you like that sort of thing."

"And you don't?"

"I'm not a big fan of the city."

I'm curious now. "What don't you like?"

"It's a long list."

"Then give me the SparkNotes," I say, with a light laugh, trying to forget what's ahead of me.

"SparkNotes, okay," Ben says humorously, like he's up for the challenge. "Concrete, steel, always loud and awake, too many shadows."

"You forgot no wide-open sky."

"You said the SparkNotes version," he says, grinning. "It's hard for me to imagine that you ever lived here," he adds.

"Well, you named the not-so-great stuff, but there's also cool restaurants," I argue, "and cafés, and the theater, and museums, and diverse cultures, and an anonymity that lets you get lost in all the bustle." I know I'm stalling with the chitchat, but I can't help myself. I don't want it all to be over—not yet.

"That's all true, but the no sky part? Deal breaker," he says. "And you for sure seem like you need the sky."

"Why would you say that?"

"Because you're always looking at it."

Oh.

Ben claps his hands together. "So, what are you in the mood for? Dinner? We could order in. There's a great Thai place around the corner. Or you know, whatever you want."

"I'm not really hungry," I tell him, "but, if you are…"

"I'm good," he says, running fingers through his hair. His nervous energy is palpable, and all it does is crush me more because he's trying so hard to act as if everything is normal.

There is an awkward moment of silence when all I can hear is the hum of traffic, a reminder that a world exists outside of this space, outside of this moment. I should have planned better, rehearsed this more. "Can I see the kitchen?"

He raises a single brow. "Uh, sure."

We walk across a short hall to a small but modern kitchen with a breakfast bar, stainless-steel appliances, and a small window framing the darkness.

Ben leans against the counter, folds his arms across his chest. "Listen, you can tell me anything. You know that right?"

Careful what you wish for.

I nod, swallow past the lump in my throat that is throbbing with a dreadful ache, reminding me to just get this over with. "I brought something from the farm," I tell him, starting with incremental truths. "It's a drink I want to make you."

"Sounds ominous," he teases.

"I just need a pot."

Ben pushes off the counter, breezes past me, and retrieves one from a lower cabinet. I go to the stove, but end up blocking him in, and because the space is so tight, there's no way for him to get past me without our bodies grazing.

"Can I watch?" he asks, his grin waning as if his instincts are catching up.

"How about I just bring it to you in the living room?"

"Are you trying to bewitch me?" He leans closer, and my body is tilting forward, my heart yearning for his touch. In a moment of weakness, I drop my head to his chest.

"Ben... I..."

"Heyyy." He folds me in his arms. "I don't know what happened in Canada, if it was too much too soon, but I don't want you to be feeling bad or upset. Whatever it is, we can figure it out."

His kindness, his utter openness unhinges me, and tears sting my eyes. Couldn't we just stay like this? Maybe Rosa is right. Maybe I don't have to do this. Maybe I'm rushing it. I let the maybes pile up until I'm filled with doubts.

My body is on auto-drive, operating on sheer emotion when I tilt my head back and kiss him. An urgent fiery kiss that is all-consuming, so that it's just me and Ben, clinging to each other.

He returns the passion, the heat. Soon he's trailing his mouth down my throat, his hands are all over me, caressing the length of my body. This can't be wrong. This can't be fake.

My mother's voice slices through the moment.

You enhance magic. The petals...empowered by your very touch.

Ben lifts me onto the counter. His breathing is ragged; he repeats my name like a new language he's only learning now. And I empower him the same way I empowered the magic. I let him touch me, kiss me, yearn for me. I let him because I need to feel him one last time. I need to carry this memory with me forever.

His hands are under my dress, stroking the inside of my thigh. There is nothing gentle or slow about this. It's all feral, all instinct, as if he knows the only thing after this is a wide expanse of nothingness.

I straddle his body as he lifts me off the counter and carries me down the hall into a dimly lit bedroom. My inner voice is screaming no, rebuking me for my selfishness, but another part of me, the part that has fallen so hard for this man is opening her arms to all that he wants to give me.

We fall onto the bed.

With each caress, each kiss, I repeat the same words in my mind, *how could I ever kill this? How could that ever be right?*

Ben is moving against me, and I match his cadence as I touch every part of him that I can manage to reach, exploring his back, his chest, his arms.

I whisper his name over and over and over. Urging him to take all of me. To hell with the magic and the bond. This is real. It has to be. And even if it isn't, would it be so wrong to make love to him just once?

This time Ben doesn't ask me if I'm sure. My every move shouts the answer, and he obliges, running his hand up my bare leg with a dizzying effect. An inch and an inch until his fingers trace the edges of my underwear, until they reach inside. The warmth and ecstasy of him spreads like wildfire and he's whispering something, but I'm so lost, so desperate for more that I don't process whatever it is that he's telling me.

His breaths become shorter and shorter gusts. I'm drowning in want and hunger as I take his mouth again, kissing him deeply. Feeling the weight press against me.

"Are you okay?" he groans and all I can say is, "I want you." I grasp at the button of his jeans, tugging on it.

Ben's mouth drags across my jaw, my neck. "I want you too."

"And I *really* want these damn jeans off," I growl.

He laughs and in an instant the jeans have been peeled away and so have his boxers. Quickly, he tugs my underwear off, lays his body on top of mine.

"You're shaking," he says.

"So are you."

We both laugh, trembling against each other. He's lifting my dress higher, up and around my hips.

My heart is racing; my desire is a wild animal beating against a cage. His groans are louder than mine, swallowing me in their urgency. And, with my legs straddled around his waist, I'm guiding him closer. My mouth is fierce, searching for any inch of him I can kiss, taste.

And then that familiar seductive scent of his washes over me, reminding me of the magic.

No. I don't want it here. I move against him, drawing him closer. And closer. I want this. To succumb to him, to this insatiable desire.

Fuck the magic!

But the tears have begun. Pent-up frustration and a bit of madness maybe. Ben stops and my agony blooms at the loss of his touch.

"Harlow?"

I'm holding him tighter, trying to get back to the moment of intoxicating bliss. "Don't stop," I whimper.

But he's rolled off of me and is looking at me like I'm a madwoman. Maybe I am.

He traces a thumb over my cheek. "Why are you crying?"

I throw my hands over my face. "I'm… I'm sorry, Ben."

"Hey, it's okay. We don't have to do this."

"God, if you only knew how badly I want to." We both sit

up and I take his hands in mine, hating every single moment of this. "I need to know…your feelings. I mean, when did you feel like…" My words come between shuddering breaths.

He huffs out a nervous laugh. "Is that what this is? You think I'm not crazy about you?"

"No, it's not that. I just need to know… I mean…" I gather some composure, tugging my dress down, feeling so incredibly exposed and raw. He takes the cue and tugs on his jeans, never taking his eyes off me.

I swallow a new stream of tears, barely managing to find my voice. "Don't you think it's strange that there is so much between us so soon?"

"Actually," he says, offering only a blank stare, "no."

"How could you not? Like, this isn't normal, Ben."

He exhales, goes silent a moment and then says, "I don't know what's normal, Harlow. All I know is how I feel, and how much I want to be with you, how much I want to talk to you, to see you, to be close to you, to hear your laugh and…"

I shake my head, wiping away another hot tear. And I'm filled with a wishing that burns its way through me.

"I don't get where you're going with this," he says. His eyes are so tender, so achingly beautiful. And then I see it, the flicker of amber light right on the surface this time, and my spirit dissolves.

My shoulders collapse with defeat. "It's not real," I whisper. There. The words I wasn't sure I could say are suspended between us, and all I can do now is wait to see what he does with them.

"Not real?" He recoils. "I'm pretty sure I know how I feel, Har."

"Do you remember when you told me how important honesty is to you? That we should always tell each other the truth? From the beginning?"

A muscle twitches in his jaw as he nods.

"That's why I came tonight. To give you the truth." I wince, knowing there is no going back now. "I didn't know if I could go through with it, but I know…it's not fair to keep you in the dark and—"

"In the dark about what?"

I look into his eyes, staring right at the flicker of magic so alive now I wonder how I ever missed it. Or maybe I just didn't want to see it before.

I don't know what does it, where the strength comes from, but I get to my feet, bringing Ben with me until we're standing face-to-face. With his hands still in mine, I look into his concerned eyes and say, "I'm going to go in the kitchen now to make that drink, and then I'm going to tell you everything."

32

＄＄＄

Alone in the kitchen, I remove the linen bundle from my bag and unroll it on the counter.

There is a note from my mom:

It is no easy thing to break a bond, to extinguish true feelings. I am sending you oceans of love, cariña.

Trembling, I set the note aside, then one by one I drop the chocolate disks into the pot. After adding a bit of water to liquefy the brew, I add the dark root and the dried devil's hair. All the while drowning in a sea of whys and my own self-pity. Reducing the flame, I stir, one rotation and then another.

"You almost done in there?" Ben calls coolly; I instantly feel even more on edge.

Somehow, I manage, "Three minutes."

As I blow a breath across the bubbling chocolate, I can feel the magic warming, growing, expanding. I watch the dried bits of petals vanish into the darkness, and as the mixture thins and begins to bubble, I take the black rose petal, pulsing with warmth, and I place it on my tongue, to infuse it with my essence. The petal has a briny flavor as if it had bloomed in the sea. Instantly, I feel a painful longing; I feel the hand of magic carving out a hollow place in my chest, so painful and tangible that it feels as if I might be swallowed up too.

I lean against the counter to steady myself. Then, as the ache subsides, I let my magic rise—to enchant and strengthen the rose petal's properties.

A moment later, I remove it from my mouth and set it in the pot.

For death and a final goodbye.

There is a spark, a burning scent that emanates from the chocolate. I stare into the dark elixir, marveling at how something so simple can be so complex, something so lovely can be so vile.

A biting chill grips me as I pour the hot chocolate into two short glasses that I find in an overhead cabinet. Then, powered by sheer will, I walk to the living room.

I stop at the edge of the room, watching Ben who clearly hasn't heard me approach. He's standing near the fireplace, looking at a row of photos on the mantel. In that instant, in the glow of the dying flames, I see someone who deserves so much more than this. At least it'll be quick, I think. He'll only feel the pain of the truth until he drinks the chocolate, and then all of this can just fade away; his heart will be his own again.

I clear my throat, and Ben looks up. Our gazes lock. He attempts a smile but it's unsure, a lingering question.

As I set the glasses on the coffee table, he comes over and sits down on the sofa.

"I'm going to tell you something," I say, "and I'm asking that you don't interrupt until I'm finished."

His gaze flicks from the drinks to me. "Okay, but I need to

give you this before I forget." He grabs a leather-bound journal from the table and opens it. The leaf rests between the pages.

I don't remember walking to the sofa or sitting next to him. I don't remember taking the leaf in my hand. But there it is, perfectly preserved in the exact condition it was the day it floated into my lap.

"I'm shocked I didn't crush the thing," he says. There's a hitch in his voice.

Suddenly, I feel unsure, lost, floating somewhere between then and now. I set the leaf on the table. "Thanks."

His arm is resting on the back of the rigid sofa. "So, what's the big secret?" he asks.

A cold fear grips me. I turn to him, bracing myself. "You're magically bonded to me."

Ben barks out a stunned laugh.

"It was an accident," I say, "from the magic in the petals that were meant to stay in your grandparents' bouquet. And that's… that's why you can't stop thinking about me, why you smell traces of my scent, why you want to be near me all the time."

As the last word drops from my mouth, my battering heart goes dark, still, silent. And then I stop. I wait for some kind of blowup, but Ben's face is unreadable. He's silent, his eyes roving back and forth, studying me for any sign of humor. "You're kidding, right?"

"I wish I were," I say. "I didn't know until we were on the river in Canada. I saw the magic, a light in your eyes similar to William's, and that's when I knew. It's why I ran off. I needed to figure things out, decide how to fix it."

"Fix. It." His voice is flat, bordering on anger. "I know how I feel, Harlow."

"Ben, it's the magic. That's what's making you feel…"

"Look, you can call it whatever you want, but you're wrong." He's reaching for me, stroking my hands. I don't stop him. Because his touch feels so warm and good.

"Ben, I'm sure."

He grips my hands tighter, never looking up. And when he does, I see it—the skepticism, the doubt, and the glimmer of belief that splits my chest wide-open.

"Are you seriously trying to tell me that none of this is real?"

I nod, not acknowledging the truth that some of it *could* be real, but there's no way to know that for sure. Bondings blur the lines, the power of the connection itself breeds emotion. So in that sense, the feelings were born from a place that was never authentic.

"And what about you?" He releases my hands. "Are you... bonded to me too? I mean are your feelings—"

"I don't know."

"Jesus, Har—how can you not know?"

"I know how I feel right now," I cry. "I've fallen for you, Ben, and it feels so right. But..."

"But what?"

"But we need to know for sure."

His eyes drift to the glasses and I see the realization dawn. "Is that what this is? Some brew to what...show us the truth?"

I swallow past a hot and painful lump in my throat. "Not exactly."

"Then what exactly."

I freeze. I don't think I can push the words out of my mouth.

"Harlow."

"It's to sever the bond."

His dark eyes narrow. And I want him to say something, anything. But he just keeps staring with stunned silence.

"Ben?"

"Let's just say you're right, and we're bonded," he says, exhaling sharply. "What if I don't want to sever it? What if I just want everything to stay the same?"

My heart is lurching, screaming, *Yes. Yes. Yes.* Before the treacherous thing murmurs, *but it will never be genuine.*

"Don't you want to be certain what we have is real?" I ask, my voice almost a whisper. "And if we don't figure it out now, we'll always wonder."

"I won't wonder," he insists. "I don't even know if I believe in magic."

I hadn't anticipated him making this so much harder. And then I realize. "But you believe enough, or you would have drunk that by now."

He drags his hands down his face, stands and begins to rub the back of his neck fitfully. The fire's flames are mere embers now, glowing their last bit of warmth.

He turns to me. "Why did you tell me?"

"Because I couldn't live with the lie," I say. "Because I didn't want to manipulate you...this. Because I care about you too much."

Ben picks up the glass and my heart skyrockets into a stratosphere of dread and panic.

"So, if I drink this we won't be bonded."

"Right."

He comes to the edge of the sofa and squats before me, his free hand resting on my legs. "There's no way this isn't the real deal. I've kissed you, and touched you, and I know what's inside of me." He seems suddenly restless, lost. "I don't care where the feelings came from, or how—I just, I want to be with you."

I fight the tears threatening to fall as I touch his face, cup his chin, look into his deep dark eyes that hold so much emotion, so much promise. I see a future with him, one I'm terrified I'll never have. "Ben...please."

"Fine," he says abruptly with an overconfidence that twists my nerves. He gets to his feet. "I'm going to prove to you that you're wrong."

His hubris surprises me and yet I cling to it, to his belief that he really can prove me, and the magic bond, wrong.

"And if I'm right?" I ask, rising to my feet.

He looks at me, and for a split second I see the Ben I met at Pasaporte. The one filled with bravado and confidence. The one who's used to getting what he wants. He offers a small hopeful smile. "Then we'll start over," he says. "From the beginning, a real one."

Except that this is probably going to kill any real feelings too.

I nearly say the words, but if Ben is this resistant now, he'll be even more so if he knows the risk.

"Deal?" he says.

I nod. "Okay."

"That doesn't sound very convincing."

"Nothing would make me happier," I manage to say. Then, with a trembling hand I pick up my glass, watching as he lifts his own up into the air.

"Here's to the truth," he says.

"The truth," I echo, feeling ashamed and entirely shattered that I didn't tell him the entire story, that this elixir could change him, his heart. That the magic in my veins is the reason we're in this place right now.

Just when I think he's going to drink, he pulls me into his arms; with his eyes open, he kisses me gently, softly. I meet his gaze, too afraid to blink.

"Nothing," he says, "will ever change how I feel."

"Promise?"

Another kiss, on my lips, "I'm only," on my nose, "doing this," my forehead, "for you."

I nod and as we break apart, I imagine a world where wishes come true, and magic has clean simple lines, a world where Ben and I can be together. Then in a moment of weakness, of sheer desperation, I say, "Maybe you're right. Maybe we can just go on the same way. I mean...who cares where the bond came from, why we feel like this and..." I'm babbling on and on when Ben traces a finger along my jaw. "No, *you're* right,

Har. I see how much this will eat you up, and I'm not willing to watch that happen."

"It won't," I insist.

His hand sweeps through my hair. "You're a liar. A very beautiful liar."

If he only knew. I kiss him once more, deeply, slowly.

"It's going to be okay," he whispers against my mouth.

A moment later, we both drink, swallowing the few ounces of bitter tasting magic until all the chocolate is gone.

I wait to feel something, but nothing happens. Ben sets his glass down. He guides me to the sofa where we both sit. "See?" he says, taking my hand. "You were wrong. I'm still crazy about you."

Is it possible I got it wrong? My heart leaps with the possibility. No! I tasted the magic on my tongue; I enchanted it, made it stronger.

"Now, can we get back to this?" Ben turns my chin toward him. Slowly, he brings his mouth to mine. But before the kiss can take shape, his lips go slack. He rears back, stares into my eyes. The flicker of light...it's gone.

My insides go cold.

Ben blinks, his eyes glaze over. "What the hell was in that? I feel strange..."

"You should probably lie down."

He rests his head on my shoulder, wrapping his arms around my waist. "Don't go anywhere." And then he goes still.

"Ben?" I shake him gently. But he's out cold.

Panic grips me. I know now that my feelings for Ben are real and that I was never bonded. But how will Ben feel about me now?

I slip out from beneath him, easing his long body down onto the sofa. And I wait. I watch him sleep, wondering who he'll be when he wakes. The Ben who can't stop thinking about me? Or the Ben who thinks I need a lucky coin?

With a timid hand, I reach out and touch his dark hair, stroke it gently away from his face, gripped with a knowing. "I think I always knew my feelings were real," I whisper. Deep down, in the furthest recesses of my spirit, I knew that no amount of magic could create this.

The next few minutes are agony. As I wait for this man who I've given my heart to, to wake, to give it back to me in pieces. And in the waiting, my restless spirit begins to hope. What if we really could start over? I mean, he has all these memories of me and so what that no emotions will be connected to them. It's not like I'm a stranger. Maybe he could be attracted to me again, fall for me again. Over time, we could make it good and real.

Feeling flushed, I head into the bathroom down the hall to splash some cold water on my face. The powder room walls are lined with ivy wallpaper and there are expensive soaps and lotions on a gold tray. Helena really does have excellent taste, I think as I wipe a cool cloth over my face, refusing to look in the mirror. Terrified of the reflection that will be staring back at me. A sorceress. A liar.

When I walk back down the hall, I hear sounds coming from the kitchen. Water running. Leaning against the wall, I take a few steadying breaths, knowing that the next few minutes are going to determine my future, with or without Ben.

When I turn the corner, I see Ben standing at the counter. And he has my mother's note, the one I left on the counter in his hands. Hearing my approach, he looks up at me. There is a resentment behind his eyes that scares me, that sends my pulse galloping. "Ben? Are you okay? How do you feel?"

He pulls in a long breath. "What is this, Harlow?" He's holding up the note.

Thudthudthudthud.

He reads the letter to me as if I need reminding. "'It is no easy thing to break a bond, to extinguish true feelings.'"

I'm plummeting, clawing for some purchase, but there is none. "It's a note…from m-my…m-mom," I stammer.

"'Extinguish true feelings'?" He doesn't need to say anything else for me to know what he's asking.

I can't breathe. Can't think.

"You said that drink was to sever a bond," he groans, still gripping the paper.

Hot dread races through my veins. "Ben… I was trying to protect you."

"Protect me," he snorts. His eyes burn with anger. "You told me you didn't want to manipulate me, remember?"

"Exactly!"

"But you just did." He pauses brusquely, but I know the rest of the argument, *like my mother manipulated my dad. Like she deceived him.* Except that this is different, isn't it? I did this to protect Ben. To give back the part of himself that the magic stole.

But he's right. I risked our hearts and didn't tell him the whole truth. "Ben… I didn't want any part of you that you didn't give willingly." The tears are tracking down my face now. "Can you at least understand that?"

He stiffens. "I might have if I'd known everything. If you had just told me the truth. But you never gave me that choice. You decided for both of us."

I'm trembling, grasping at straws. "You would have done the exact same thing," I insist. "It's easy for you to live in your perfect world without consequence, without a magic that—"

"That's where we're different, Harlow," he spits. "I would *never* have stolen your choice."

"How can you say that? How can you know?"

A beat of silence passes between us. And then quietly, he says, "Because for me, it would never have been worth the risk."

"So, you would have let me live a lie?" There is a challenge in the question, but he doesn't respond as I expect.

He studies me with dark, penetrating eyes that cut me to my core. "Were *you* bonded?"

"I…" I give up the lie and fall headfirst into the truth. "No, I wasn't."

"How do you know for sure?"

"Because nothing has changed for me," I say flatly, wondering why he's torturing me with this line of questioning.

"So, I was right."

I stare at him inquisitively through blurred tears.

"If your feelings are real," he says with some kind of affected indifference, "don't you think that maybe mine could have been too?"

Could have been.

A painful heat rises in my chest, burning its way up my throat. "I'm sorry, you're right, but…" I take a shuddering breath. "If I had told you all of it, would you have drunk the elixir, knowing the risk?"

He levels me with a piercing glare. "I honestly don't know."

"And now? How do you feel?" I cling to the tiniest of hopes.

Ben stares at the ground, his shoulders sagging. "All I feel is a strange emptiness, a detachment when I think about us, when I look at you." He swings his gaze back to mine, and his words are a brutal force that nearly knock me off my feet. "I'm just numb. Is that how it's supposed to work?" He's not being cruel; he really wants to know, but I don't have the answer he's looking for so I merely shrug.

The realization emerges slowly, but so brightly I nearly gasp. We could have started over, maybe…if I had only told him the full truth, given him the choice. Now, I've not only destroyed his feelings, but any hope of his trust. And how could we ever build something from that?

"You should go," he says with a finality that tells me this is over.

For a long moment I don't, can't move. And when the silence

between us reaches an agonizing futile point, I grab my purse, turn to leave. He follows behind me and each step I take is like walking over hot coals.

I pass through the living room to the front door when I hear, "Harlow?"

I glance over my shoulder. Ben's expression is soft, filled with a pity that makes me feel suddenly sick. And he's holding that damn leaf out to me. "Do you still want this?" Even after I tricked him, lied to him, he's still showing an ounce of kindness.

I want to say no, to take a last stand of pride, but I can't manage another facade. So, I take the dried bit of gold from him, then turn, and walk out the door.

33

I barrel wildly out of the building, gulping for air, trying to find a steady breath.

Sharp, thornlike pains travel through my body. And all I want is to dissolve, to melt into the concrete. To shed this skin, these bones, this heart.

I wander the city streets aimlessly. Vibrating with both fury and grief as hot tears snake down my face, doing nothing to keep away the early November chill.

The city nightlife is busy, bright with glaring lights, loud with the sounds of honking horns, endless voices, and discordant music.

And there is no expansive sky, just glimpses of darkness.

Because you're always looking at it.

It's in these small, seemingly insignificant moments that Ben has left his mark on my spirit.

A cold wind whips past me, and suddenly I feel unmoored, an outsider who doesn't belong here. To think I lived in this city for so long, discounting my desires, depriving my spirit. I felt it, deep down, didn't I? That vacant space inside of me that grew bigger and bigger, that could never be reconciled by logic or reason.

I take a deep breath, exhaling the cold. I feel so many things at once, ferocious wild painful things, but mostly? I just feel broken.

And then I remember Lil. She's in the city by now. At the hotel, waiting for me. My sister with her memory magic. She alone can pluck Ben from my heart: his dark tender eyes, the way his solid body felt pressed against mine, the whisper of his breath on my skin, that hesitant smile. The total goodness of him.

The idea starts deep inside of me, growing momentum with each breath.

Lil can remove this pain and mend my brokenness.

I come to a sudden halt, blinking against the obtrusive night.

And in that moment, the deep ache of loss decides for me: *I've had my fill of remembering.*

I crunch the leaf in my hand and let its pieces fall to the ground.

Lil left a room key for me at the desk, and by the time I get up to the room, she's there. And my weary body is in her arms. Time speeds up. Everything is a blur, a rapid succession of images one connected to the next with sympathetic words, warmth and understanding, tears and promises. All the truths and lies laid bare before my sister like a dark and heavy cloak.

And when I come back to the rhythm of the real world, when everything has been told, I'm lying on the bed, my sister is lying next to me, her eyes two dark stones.

"Why didn't you tell him the whole truth?" she asks gently and without judgment.

I bite into my bottom lip. "I think deep down, I knew he'd never break the bond, and even if he could live with the not knowing, there's no way I could have."

She offers a small nod of understanding. "I'm so sorry, Bean. This is all so unfair, but at least..." She pauses, studies me like she isn't sure if she should say whatever she's about to. But there is no need. I can fill it in for her.

"At least I have magic?"

"Yeah? I mean isn't that good news?"

"Except that it ruined everything," I growl. "If I wasn't some *enhancer,* Ben would never have been bonded to me, and I'd be safe on the farm with an unbroken heart."

Never taking her eyes off of me, my sister, pushes back a strand of my hair. "But you also wouldn't have had all these wonderful experiences with him."

"I would have been better off."

"You say that now."

My body is one horrific ache. "I'll say it forever."

I may not have given her the nitty-gritty details of mine and Ben's time together, but it was enough to paint a solid picture of him, of why he mattered. "And if you tell me I'll find someone better, or I'll get over it or whatever it is that people say, I'll smother you with a pillow."

Lil sighs, showing the smallest of grins. "I wasn't going to say any of that."

"But you were going to say something. I can see it all over your face."

"I was going to say, want me to order some room service? Pancakes? Hamburger? Tequila?"

I sniffle, wipe my nose. "No, but I *do* need something from you."

Lil sits up, on guard like she's bracing herself for whatever I'm about to ask her. "What is it?"

"I need your magic."

"Harlow."

"I don't want to remember him."

The room goes frighteningly silent. "Bean," she says softly. "You don't know what you're asking."

I bolt upright, grabbing the comforter. "Yes, I do! I can't live like this. I mean a broken heart is bad enough, but this? His feelings, his connection to me, none of it was real. Just some made-up thing, like a nightmare fairy tale. It's all too much!"

"I get it," she says, hands splayed in front of her like she's counseling someone off the ledge. "But you know magic isn't an exact science, and one memory is always tied to another. It's complicated."

Defiant and bruised, I shout, "I don't care!"

"Harlow, I know you aren't willing to risk other memories just to kick him out of your heart."

"Uh, yeah, I am." I know I'm not being rational but it feels good to have a bold plan, to act stronger than I am. "Look, all I'm asking is for you to take the memory of these feelings I have for him. That's what I don't want to remember."

"And what are those feelings?"

I level her with a glare. "Why does it matter?"

"Because the deeper they are, the harder they are to extract."

"Then it's a good thing I'm an enhancer."

Lil gives me a sorrowful pout. "I know how much this hurts."

"Do you?" I feel like I'm one thread away from snapping. "You just play with men. You never *fall* for them."

I expect Lil to launch a grenade at me, to argue some ridiculous point about being too busy, young, career-driven for love, but she glances away like there is more to it. "You're right."

And just like that she disarms me.

"Okay, how about this?" she suggests calmly. "How about you take a long bath? I brought some of Mom's rose vervain oil. It'll take the edge off of everything and then—" she rubs her forehead, and sighs. "If you still want to forget your feelings for him, I'll help you."

It's the only promise I need right now. The promise of extracting Benjamin Brandt from my corazón forever.

My body sags with a twisted sort of relief. "Swear?"

"Te prometo, but only if *you* swear to never tell mom or Tía. They'd kill me. As in feed me to the wolves."

It's true the family doesn't use the magic for our own gains, but this is different. This is for survival. With Lil's gift and my enhancing powers, I'm confident we'd be able to wipe Ben from my memories. I think about Mayahuel, and all she endured, from escape, to love, to being chopped into bits and fed to demons. If anyone will understand this pain, it's her.

A few minutes later, I've shed my clothes and am lying in the steaming oil-infused water. I close my eyes and breathe in the sweet fragrance of roses. Breath by breath, I can feel the tightness in my body loosen. I can see the kaleidoscope of images in my mind retreat then coalesce into something whole. And my heart, broken as it is, finally rests.

I soak up the healing magic, pore by pore.

And it's as if each drop of water fills me with an awareness, a knowing that comes to me in a whisper as I submerge myself beneath the water.

When all has been destroyed, the goddess shall rise.

The path to destruction altered my life more than I understood before now. My mom told me that I awakened a consciousness when I chose a new way, and I don't disagree, but there is more. When I left New York, I chose an unchartered path, a more difficult way that held a mirror up to my life and challenged me to excavate a more authentic version of myself. And it wasn't just the solace of home, or the courage to write, or the manifestation of magic that changed me. It's the daring to embrace it all, to live from a place of utter and wild truth, to accept being human with a flawed and defenseless heart in a messy world.

And now I see. I had to sink before I could rise.

My pulse thrums—impulsive and fierce—and I have an over-whelming desire to write, to purge, to pour this all onto the page. The desire is so urgent, so all-consuming, I jump out of the tub, throw on a robe, and rush out to the desk.

Lil, curled up on a bed, cries out, "What's wrong?"

"I need paper. A pen." I'm rummaging through the draw-ers until I find what I'm looking for. Then, throwing on some slippers, I head for the door. "I'll be back."

"Harlow! Wait!" Lil cries. "You're a sopping mess, in a robe."

But I'm already out the door and in the elevator.

For the first time in several minutes, I consider my choice a bit more methodically. I can't go to the bar or restaurant look-ing like this; plus I need silence. I decide that I'll find a quiet spot whatever floor the spa is on. And extra points for being dressed for the part. A moment later, the elevator deposits me to the second floor, and just as I predicted, the hall is peaceful, still—fragrant with bergamot and chamomile.

I find a gold velvet chair near the spa's closed-off entrance, and collapse into it. With my feet tucked beneath me, and a pad of Ritz paper in hand, I begin to write. I expect a return to Vio-leta's story, but what appears on the page isn't the stuff of fiction. The words surge out of me, emotions, thoughts, deliberations, meditations. Each word punctuated with a sense of grief, loss, anger, and resentment.

As my hand sweeps across the page, I realize that my body is the keeper of secrets, and this pen is its liberator. I don't know how much time passes, or how many tears fall, but I know when my heart has been heard; I know when my spirit is no longer restless. I know when I can breathe again.

I go back, turning the pages to the first line: *I was unknown to myself...*

And then I look at the last: *there is magic in heartbreak.*

In between those two sentiments is an ocean of truth, one that rises inside of me: *every transformation begins here.*

Just then I hear footsteps. I look up and see Lil coming toward me, carrying two paper cups of coffee. "Oh, good," she says with exasperation. "I was worried I might find you dancing on the bar."

"Have I *ever* danced on a bar?" I snort.

"No, but maybe you should try it." She hands me the coffee, which I take happily. "Am I interrupting?"

I sip at the dark brew. "Yes."

"Too bad. I'm lonely upstairs." She sits in the chair next to mine as her eyes flick to the pages, messy with black scribbles. Then out of nowhere she says, "You're lucky, you know."

"Um, lucky? Did you not hear my entire dramatic *woe is me* tale earlier?"

Lil doesn't smile; her dark eyes don't dance. Instead, her gaze stays fixed on the pages. "You're lucky because you found something that makes you tick, that burns a fire in you."

It takes less than point five seconds for me to spit out, "Mmm-hmm, well, so did you, Doc."

She nods but there is something there, a shadow of doubt, a breath of wonder. And I want to probe but I'm way too spent to wander the complicated maze that is my sister.

"You look better," she says. "I mean, you still look like a nearly drowned terrier who just clawed its way out of a whirlpool, but definitely an improvement from an hour ago."

The laugh comes so fast I'm surprised by the force of it. "Well, I think I feel...not better but clearer?"

"Does that mean you've reached a verdict?"

"A verdict?"

She hesitates, then speaks in a low tone as if we're in danger of being overheard. "Are you still going to be needing my *special* services? Because I've come up with a list of all the reasons why you shouldn't do it. First—"

I hold up my hand. "Lil, I don't need the list."

"But you really should know the risks."

"Why do you sound like you're talking to one of your patients?"

"Because tonight you are my patient, sort of." Then with a coy smile, she adds, "But I won't even make you sign a consent form. Now where was I? Oh, right. All the reasons you shouldn't mess with your memories."

"Lil…it's okay."

"I'm going to need more than that," she says. "Okay what? The coffee? My list? Your heart?"

There is magic in heartbreak. Because every transformation begins here.

I get to my feet. Then looking down at my sister, I say, "I won't be needing your brand of magic after all."

34

The farm is an oasis, a refuge for broken hearts and battered spirits.

There is a healing energy here; it's in the sea of color, the sweet aroma of hope; it's in the gentle breeze whispering across the thousands of petals.

When I arrived home, I had expected my mom to hover but after I tell her my story, she gives me my space, showing her patience and care with tiny yellow arrangements of gold dust on my nightstand each evening, a symbol of tranquility. Sometimes she sets a sprig of rosemary under my pillow to ward off nightmares and unwanted dreams. And it's worked, maybe better than expected because I haven't dreamed about Ben.

Like my mom, Rosa doesn't probe, but she dances around me with her usual town gossip. *Did you know Serafino Lopez is having an affair? Diana Palacio's face-lift is stretched tight as a drum. You won't believe who's pregnant. That entromentida Alicia is still pestering our neighbors—why won't that woman give it up.*

I know she's trying to take my mind off of Ben, and sometimes it works. Sometimes I welcome the chisme, delight in it even. But, deep down, I know that only time will heal this gaping wound.

And for the last three weeks, I've felt the seconds ticking like tiny footsteps tapping across my heart. Most days I wake at dawn and stroll the farm, marveling at the morning mist, the silvery sky, the vibrant magical blooms, wondering whose lives they will touch. It's here that I best gather my thoughts and prepare myself for a full day of writing.

I stare at the pages, knowing I'm so close to finishing this book. The petals that bonded Ben and I are still tucked between the pages of Violeta's story. I should burn them or bury them, but I can't bring myself to do it.

I hold one of the petals in my palm, watching as it replenishes its life force at my touch. An idea begins to form, so simple and elegant that it feels impossible.

"Are you close to the end?" Rosa asks as she enters the library.

I tuck the petal back in its hiding space and nod. "So close I can taste it."

She falls onto the leather sofa with a huff. "I spoke to the flowers, asked them if there was anything we could do about this Alicia person."

"And?"

"Silence," she growls. "I hate when they do that."

I stand and go over to my aunt. "I might have an idea."

"Let's hear it."

"I'm an enhancer."

"Yes, we've established that."

"What if...what if we create a protection spell for my book? I mean if it sells."

"It will sell."

"You can't know that."

"If this story came to you from Mayahuel, then it needs to be told and that means it will sell. Well, that and the fact that you are a talented writer," she says.

My entire body feels tight and instantly buzzy at the thought that this story could actually be a book on shelves.

Rosa sits forward. "Even protection spells have cracks. You know that. Otherwise, Alicia would never have entered the farm with her bad intentions."

"But what if there doesn't have to be cracks?" I say, feeling bolder. "What if I can enhance the spell, make it rock-solid?"

Rosa studies me with inquisitive eyes. "How would this hechizo work?"

"Anyone who reads the book will only see it for what it is, fiction. They won't connect the dots. They'll fully accept that I wrote about a legend."

"So, you want to spell your readers?"

I love the idea so much I'm nearly jumping out of my skin.

"What's this about spells?" Mom says, coming in.

I fill her in on my idea, thinking it sounds even better the second time I share it.

"We have to be sure," Mom says, twisting her mouth. "I can use dream magic on you."

"How so?" I ask.

"We'll ask for a vision of the truth, a message of some sort." She folds her arms across her chest. "But, Harlow, you might not like what the dream tells you, so the choice is yours."

It's a risk I'm willing to take.

Rosa says, "But that doesn't take care of that entromentida, Alicia."

"What if we send her a bouquet?" I suggest. "A very precise memory erasing one." I hate doing it without her consent, but too much is at stake.

Mom and Rosa share a glance, then nod simultaneously.

"We can ship something tomorrow," Rosa says.

That night Mom gives me a teaspoon of marigold-infused

honey and sets a canto flower that she's spelled beneath my
pillow. "It's spoken the truth to you before," she says. "It will
again."

It isn't long before I fall into a dream where I'm walking the
aisle of a dimly lit bookstore. I go in search of my book, but the
only one on the shelves is *Beneath the Dark*. Rows and rows of
the black spines with silver lettering. With a trembling hand, I
pull a copy free and flip through the pages.

They're blank.

Until I reach the acknowledgments section.

There I find my name along with a note of gratitude for believing in this story. My heart expands slowly, spreading warmth
across my chest. I expect to read more thank-yous, but I never
get to the next sentence because the pages begin to transform
in my hands—shimmering canto petals that float down to the
floor.

Just as the last page morphs, I look back and see a single sentence: *You have the power. You always have.*

The sound of a rooster crowing pulls me from the dream.
With a strange awareness I roll over and stare at the beamed ceiling, turning the dream over and over in my mind—its imag-
ery, the musty scent of the store, the weight of the book in my
hands, and I know. I can enchant my own book; I can protect
the secrets of our farm.

Today the flower shop is bustling with activity.

It's the first week of December, and people are in a frenzy
trying to complete their orders for Christmas arrangements. I
hurry through the store, past the line of customers, and into
the back where I'm supposed to meet my mom to go over next
year's enchantments, the orders that will be infused with magic.
I feel a tremendous sense of belonging because this is the first
time I can assist in the process, that I can enhance whichever
blooms my mom selects.

A citrusy rose fragrance emanates from every corner, sooth- ing my entire being as I walk over to my mom who is perched on a stool, sitting in front of a long wooden table that was made from a single white oak tree. Orange and pink ranunculuses are sprawled across half of the surface in great heaps, and for a sec- ond, they look as if they are growing straight from the wood.

Mom's studying a sheet of paper in her hands, mouth pursed, frown deepening.

"What's wrong?" I ask as I pull up another stool and sit next to her.

Her smile doesn't mask her concern. "Rosa and I have vetted all of these requests," she says, "and we can only take so many, but I just don't know which story is more compelling, who we should help."

This is the hardest part of what we do. The deciding of fate. It seems unfair that the magic has to be parsed out like this, that some people will be put on a waiting list or worse, denied. But like most things, magic is a finite source.

Fernando pops in looking entirely flustered when he says to my mom, "Someone has a question about the chrysanthemums, and she'll only talk to you."

"I'm coming," Mom says as Fernando disappears back to the shop.

With a sigh, she gets to her feet and hands me the list. "Want to take a look?"

After she leaves, I review next year's requests—wishes laid out before me: *more joy, forgiveness, prosperity, hope, creativity.* There is a short summary with each request, highlighting illnesses, bro- ken hearts, lost dreams, and more. And then my eyes alight on one that sends a shiver up my spine.

When I asked her to leave, it broke me; I was confused and angry and I couldn't bring myself to tell her that I love her. And now I don't know how to win back her heart.

Tears blur the words on the page. I want to tell this person he doesn't need magic. That all he has to do is look her in the eyes and tell her the truth. Put it all out there—tell her he loves her. That's all it would take for her heart to be his again.

For a millisecond, maybe more, I think I can smell Ben's earthy rain-soaked scent, and I feel flushed and light-headed. But even as it fades, my pulse accelerates, and the wondering begins. How did he spend that first night without me? Has he thought about me? Is he still angry? Has he moved on? Forgotten? So many times I've wanted to call him, to reach out in some way but something always stopped me—a voice telling me not to reach back, only forward. Plus I know that if Ben was ready to talk to me—to forgive me—he'd have called by now. And with each day that passes, the likelihood grows smaller and smaller. I try not to think about the choice anymore, but every once in a while, it rears its ugly head, and I wonder how things might have been different. I try to shake the memory away, but his voice rings in my mind with the question that curses me:

If your feelings are real…don't you think that maybe mine could have been too?

"Any progress?" Mom walks back in, tugging her ringing phone from her pocket. "Hello?"

I collect myself, return my eyes to the page I'm not really reading, but I don't want her to see that I'm upset, falling back into a dark ocean of memories that threaten to pull me under.

"Beverly?"

My head snaps up. Mom's eyes flick to mine, and her hand goes to her chest like she's reaching for her heart. "My God, I'm so sorry."

I'm on my feet, suddenly panicked, gesturing for Mom to put Beverly on speakerphone. But she only shoos me away, focused entirely on whatever the woman is telling her.

Too many moments pass without answers.

"How can I help?" Mom says quietly. She's nodding, her eyes

scanning the stem strewn floor. "Okay. Yes. Of course. We'd…" Her voice cracks. "We'd be honored."

Honored? For what?

Everything in me goes cold.

Mom looks up at me and nods again. "I will. I'll tell her."

When she ends the call, I'm springing toward her. "What is it? What's wrong?"

"William died, Corazón. Two days ago."

The world shifts under my feet. He knew, I knew, Beverly knew—we all did in our own ways that he was fading, and yet it doesn't make the goodbye any easier.

And now all I can think about is how shattered Beverly must be. How heartbroken Ben must be. A terrible heat ignites beneath my ribs, spreading across my stomach and chest. "How?" I manage. "What happened?"

"It was peaceful," Mom says. "In his sleep. Beverly wanted me to tell you that she tried to call you so many times but couldn't bring herself to do it, and that she hopes you'll understand."

"Of course," I say, blinking, trying to process the fact that William is gone. "When are the services?" I have to go, to pay my respects, to help Beverly. But then my mind naturally turns to Ben, and I reject the notion. I'm the last person who could offer him comfort right now.

"William didn't want any services," Mom says, "but they're going to spread his ashes in a few places of significance."

I swallow the unshed tears. "Where?"

"I didn't get all the specifics, but Beverly asked if she could place some of his ashes…on the farm."

Before I can ask *where*, I know the answer, even before my mom says the words, "Under the Hylocereus tree."

The Night Queen.

The very tree that I dreamed of the night I was chosen as guardian, and the one that changed William's fate. It's perfect.

I lean against the table, gripped by sadness, thinking about the photos in William's wallet, to help him remember who he loved most. My God, he did everything he could to hold on to every single memory, even the painful ones like losing his son. I feel a sudden shame at how quickly I was ready to abandon mine. But that's what made William who he was, what shaped his life. It was in the people he loved and who loved him.

"Harlow?"

I glance up. "Yeah?"

My mom touches my arm lightly. "Beverly is coming in two days."

"Okay."

"Ben is coming too."

The next night, my hands are busy arranging a bouquet of canto as the night sky consumes the sun. Moths float around the garden lights; some skim the pool's surface as if testing their own daring.

I can't remember a time when I didn't know how to create hand-tied bouquets, using the European spiral technique. When my hands didn't luxuriate in the rhythm of adding blooms and rotating, adding and rotating. And tonight, I'm thankful for this simple task, to create something special for Beverly. A piece of me that symbolizes creativity, cycles, endings, and rebirth. But it's the power of *rebirth* that I focus on as I turn the bouquet one mindful revolution at a time. Slowly, I feel my magic awaken, a warm vibration that courses out through my fingertips.

An alchemical exchange, a union of hearts.

One that holds the promise of renewal.

When the arrangement is complete, I tie it with a purple silk ribbon and lay it gently on the table, hoping it helps Beverly in some small way. I called her earlier, to tell her how deeply sorry I am for her loss, but she never answered so I left a message instead.

Staring at the mysterious blooms, I take a sip of wine and ponder the question that has been plaguing me all day.

Should I call Ben? If I don't, am I an insensitive monster? But if I do, am I being intrusive? Then an unwelcome memory grips me, and I feel as if I'm living that hellish night all over again.

Ben standing there in the dim light of Helena's living room, staring at me, speaking the words that broke me.

All I feel is a strange emptiness, a detachment when I think about us, when I look at you.

Emptiness. Detachment. How could two words cause so much pain?

Lost in the turmoil of indecision, I call Cam, thankful she answered, but when I tell her I'm going to loop Lil in she says, "She's in surgery tonight."

I was hoping to have both of their opinions, a balance of reason and emotion, simplicity and intricacy, meaning and inconsequence.

"You doing okay?" Cam asks. She already knows everything about the Ben debacle; Lil made sure of that. But in typical Cam fashion, instead of asking five million follow-up questions, she planned a virtual girls' night where we (the whole ganga of sisters and cousins) did face masks and watched old movies while sipping reposado and munching on jalapeño popcorn. Lil spent the entire night offering commentary about how unrealistic the movie's love story was while Lantana kept popping off-screen to answer work calls. Dahlia had an allergic reaction to the mask and took some Benadryl only to fall asleep thirty minutes in. It was exactly what I needed that second night home.

After I tell Cam about William, she takes a sharp inhale. She doesn't do well with death or grief or anything that resembles *the end.*

"I don't know if I should call Ben," I say, "to offer my condolences."

"I don't know either, Bean," she says. "I mean, on one hand

you should because it's the proper thing to do, but on the other, everything is still so fresh and he isn't in your life and will it make him feel worse? Because ultimately this is about him not you."

I'm nodding, following her trail of words, but my heart is wanting what it wants. And that's to offer Ben an ounce of compassion during what I know is an excruciating time for him and his family.

"Where's the proper etiquette advice on the hard stuff?" I grumble.

"I think that's called intuition." Cam sighs. Then the dreaded question, "Do you plan to see him…when he comes to the farm?"

"No," I blurt, shaking my head vehemently. "I mean, it's a private moment with his family, and I don't think I can handle his total indifference to me. I plan to make myself scarce. But I did do something for Beverly." I tell her about the enchanted bouquet of heart song.

"See?" she says. "A symbol without words. It's perfect. And Ben will see it, and he'll know how much you care."

"Or he might be reminded of how magic ruined everything between us." I trace my finger across a delicate petal as a soothing breeze sweeps across the courtyard.

"Harlow?"

"Yeah."

"You know what you want to do, so just do the thing."

"And if it blows up in my face?"

"Then you pick up the pieces."

After we get off the phone, I take a deep breath and type out a text to Ben.

I'm so sorry. I know how much William meant to you and how painful this must be. He was a special man and will be greatly missed.

I waver; my finger hovers over the send button. I take the last sip of wine, then delete the message one letter at a time.

Just then my phone rings and when I see who it is, I answer immediately.

"Beverly?"

She's quiet a moment, then in a weak voice she says, "My dear Harlow. I got your lovely message."

"I'm so sorry." I want to say more, but the words won't come.

"You made our last days remarkable, and I want to thank you for that."

I suddenly wonder if Ben has told her anything, or how much she knows.

"It was my family's magic," I tell her, thinking I don't deserve an ounce of credit given that I nearly ruined it all.

"We will have to agree to disagree."

"I'm really glad you're coming to the farm," I tell her, my pulse picking up speed. "It's the perfect place for William."

"I think so too, and Azalea would love it." Her voice cracks. "Don't you think?"

"She would."

I can feel the conversation winding down, coming to a close.

"Harlow, will you do one last thing for me?"

"Anything."

"Will you be there?"

So, she must not know about me and Ben. A slow tremble begins in my legs, traveling up my spine. How can I say no? How can I say yes?

"Harlow?"

"Yes, I'm here," I say, rubbing my forehead, squeezing my eyes closed to the night, the request, all of it. But Beverly is still waiting for an answer. "Wouldn't you rather just have family?"

She sighs, offers a forced chuckle that sounds like it's driven by sheer suffering. "Azalea was family and so are you."

Her words bolster me. I'm stronger than this. This isn't about me or Ben; this is about a woman who has lost the love of her life, who wants to celebrate him in the same place where their story began. "Yes," I manage, "I'll be there."

After we end the call, I sit back, stare up at the dark blanket of night, and wonder how I'll ever be able to face Ben again.

35

※～∂～♨

This is how I will always remember the hours before Ben stepped foot on the farm, before our story came to a close. I lay in bed, staring into the darkness. The hard thumping of my heart filled my ears as I remembered the goddess's ominous whisper that night months ago: *it's time for the beginning.*

I had no idea then that one beginning is actually many, one moment leading to another, each experience shaping me in painful and profound ways.

My thoughts felt too big, too chaotic to contain, so I pulled out my journal and began to write—not Violeta's story but my own.

Life is just a series of beginnings and endings.

It's one long season of learning how to let go. People, dreams, ideas, jobs, love. We hold each close to our bones and spirits, clutching so tightly we risk suffocating that which we profess to love, and then the time to let go comes—it always comes. We can run, or fight, or try to hide, but none of that will change the gathering storm on the horizon.

And maybe it's the storms that change us, that help carve a new path toward who we were always meant to be.

I glance up at the single canto flower in the vase by my bed. Its petals shiver and unfurl before my eyes, each dropping to the floor. A certain calm blooms within me then, a deep and effortless knowing that whatever happens tomorrow, I will be okay.

Ben, Beverly, and Helena are supposed to arrive at five thirty today, a mere two hours away. Beverly made two requests. "This is a celebration. I don't want dark sorrow, so please dress for a fiesta. Dress like the flowers." And she wanted us all to toast with William's favorite liquor, Jameson 18 Whiskey. My aunt and I have already set a small table near the Hylocereus tree, and strung fairy lights across its branches. Then, at the last minute, I created a short path of candles, each ensconced in white marble.

As the seconds tick by, my nervousness increases. Yes, because I'm going to see Ben again, but I also want this to be perfect for Beverly, for William. Her wish is to spread his ashes beneath the Night Queen at sunset, the golden hour, the hour of the goddess.

After I take a long lavender infused bath with a pinch of sweet fennel seeds (for strength), I put on a red maxi dress, a silk A-line with cap sleeves, and tie my hair into a loose chignon.

Rosa has already taken Beverly, Ben, and Helena out to the moon garden. And now, as Mom and I walk down the stony path toward the Hylocereus tree, I grip the canto bouquet I made for Beverly.

"Are you okay?" Mom asks, looping her arm in mine.

What she's really asking is if I'm okay to see Ben again, but I don't want to have that conversation, not now, so I go with, "I just want this to be perfect for them."

"It will be," she says without hesitation, and her voice, and her whole demeanor bolsters my confidence. "It was thoughtful of you to create that bouquet."

I nod and take a deep breath, admiring the watercolor sky, a blend of pinks and oranges with a dash of purple. And the air, as if on cue, is rich with the scent of honeysuckle, lavender, and eucalyptus.

"I've been thinking about the night you were born," she says as we walk. "And I so clearly remember the goddess's whisper, naming you, but it was faint, far away, unlike when your sisters were born. And I think…" She stops now, turning to me. "I think I know why you weren't named for a single bloom."

"Why?"

"Because your magic encompasses all flowers. Your power extends beyond just one."

She's right. I know it the moment her words are in the air between us. "But why a heap of stones?" I ask.

My mom laughs lightly, and we begin walking again. "Stones are gems too, Harlow. And you—you're like a rare diamond."

"You're saying that because you're my mom."

"Ay, Dios," she says, shaking her head with exasperation. "Also, I'm saying it because it's true. You just needed a little polishing."

We both laugh and I feel it lighten my spirit.

But diamond or not, I still have to face Ben. With each step, I feel more light-headed.

The path to the tree, where everyone is gathered, is spellbinding, each candle glowing like a tiny moon. And the Night Queen is radiant, glimmering with strands of lights threaded through her branches.

Beverly sees us first—she's coming over, closing the gap, pulling me into her embrace, and I hold her close, tell her how sorry I am, fight the tears that want to break free. With an unsteady hand, I offer her the canto bouquet. "For rebirth," I whisper for only her to hear.

She smiles, cups my chin in her hand and says, "These are beautiful. I don't think I've ever seen a flower quite like it."

"What are they?" Helena asks. She's wearing a pink halter jumpsuit and a fragrance that is light, evocative, melancholic.

"Heart song," I tell her with a gentle hug.

"Can I please live on this farm?" Helena says with a casual tone that does not match her tear-streaked face.

I'm not sure if it's appropriate to laugh, but I can't help it and Helena laughs too. "My grandparents talked about this place so often and I never—" she sighs looks around "—I could never have imagined how beautiful it is."

"Indescribable," Beverly puts in.

Somewhere behind me, my mother is greeting Ben, speaking words I don't catch while Rosa pours a round of whiskey for everyone.

Ben and I somehow avoid each other, both focusing on other people in the group for the time being, but it's only a matter of seconds until we'll have to acknowledge each other.

Even in the commotion I am acutely aware of his presence. And when I can't bear another moment of denial, I hazard a glance. Our gazes meet.

For a brief second the farm stills, time stops and it's only Ben, his deep-set eyes, his worn face, his sagging shoulders. He looks like a man who's been broken.

I feel myself ache for him.

He doesn't blink, or smile, only holds my gaze with an intensity that overwhelms my senses and feels like too much. In those eyes, I search for the indifference I've been dreading, but all I see is grief.

He moves toward me, reaching out his hand. Is he really offering to shake my hand? I blink, steady myself, and when he is inches from me, I reach up and hug him. Because it's the right thing to do, because he looks like he needs it, because it's who I am.

He doesn't balk, or flinch, or pull away. But the embrace is quick. I never feel the heat of his arms around me, and I feel suddenly cold, longing for the thing I can never have.

"I'm so sorry," I whisper, realizing I've taken his hand in mine. There is no spark of magic, no vibration of warmth. And when my fingers loosen, I swear he holds on a second longer, as if he isn't ready to let go.

"Thank you," he says, and then his hand drops to his side.

Beverly sets the canto bouquet on the table. Then she takes a small silver box from Helena and gestures for us all to gather around. Ben joins his grandmother, saving me the discomfort of having to stand right next to him.

A cool breeze whispers through the bloomless branches.

"I have many happy memories of this place," Beverly says as I inch closer to my mom, "so many bright moments with Azalea and the magic and how much it touched my life and William's, and I want to thank you for that. For this." Her eyes glisten with tears and my own form all too quickly.

"William would want this," she goes on with a trembling smile. "He was a man of many layers, a complicated man who loved his family and his life, and even though he was taken too soon, I know he's with us. I know…" Her voice catches and she averts her gaze, looking suddenly lost. Ben puts his hand on her arm, which seems to strengthen her. A second later, she adds, "I know the magic in this soil will keep him warm."

Rosa passes out the whiskey. "To vida hermosa!" she sings, lifting her glass.

Everyone takes a long pull. The liquor is smoky, malty, complex and it warms me to my bones, but does nothing to alleviate the weight in my chest.

Helena pours herself another glass and holds it up. "To always choosing adventure."

We all cheer, repeating her toast. Ben lifts his glass next. He stares at the amber liquid thoughtfully, raises his brows, then says, "To doing what your heart wants."

I feel a pang between my ribs, and I suddenly imagine the scene from another angle, from William's view—what does he see? A celebration of life? A lovely night garden whose blooms have yet to make an appearance? The woman he loved who alone must now carry their memories?

Ben clears his throat, drawing my attention back. He shifts his stance and takes a breath. "When I was a kid," he begins, "maybe eight, my grandfather told me a story about this tree."

This catches me off guard, and I look up for him to continue.

"He said that he owed his life to this tree," Ben adds, his voice gaining confidence with each word. There's a smile on the edge of his lips; I will it to appear, but Ben holds it in place. "I remember thinking no way could there be a magic tree and I told him so, and you know what he said?" He offers a faint laugh, scanning all of our faces.

Helena is nodding like she's heard this story a million times and Beverly is beaming, looking up at her grandson.

Ben says, "He said that I'd have to see it to believe it."

Are you saying that you believe in magic now?

I'm saying that maybe everyone has their own version of something a little special.

"To believing in the magic," my mom cheers.

After we all drink, Beverly opens the silver box, and together with her grandchildren, they sprinkle William's ashes beneath the tree.

The pang beneath my ribs burns and expands, and I find myself leaning closer to the Night Queen, touching her vines with my fingertips. I allow my magic to rise, warm and vibrant. Slowly, the flowers unfold, awakening in all of their nocturnal beauty.

By the time the ashes have been scattered, the blossoms are in full bloom, and their shimmering appearance is nothing short of exquisite.

My mom touches my waist lightly as Beverly gasps, brings

her hand to her chest while Helena cries through a smile of both grief and awe.

Ben turns to me. I see the surprise in his eyes, the understanding that dawns. He knows that this is a result of my touch. And for a brief moment, I see the eight-year-old boy who wanted to see the magic.

"How befitting," Beverly says, stroking the edge of a petal delicately.

Soon there is a swell of chatter that leads to more storytelling, but it's all so distant because I'm lost in this other place— one where I realize I'm not the same person I was a few minutes ago. I know my full strength. I know I can stumble and get back up. I know I can let go.

Rosa plays an upbeat Spanish ballad from her phone while Helena, maybe on her way to tipsy, throws her arm around my neck, leans closer, and whispers, "My brother needs you."

I attempt a disbelieving laugh, but it comes out fake and hurried. Doesn't she know that the Ben who "needs" me is gone? That he was spellbound? That none of it was real?

At the same moment, Ben appears and tells her, "Maybe you should take it easy."

With a scowl, she shoves him away. "I only had two glasses, Ben. What are you? The damn whiskey patrol?"

A sudden breeze whispers past, extinguishing several of the candles, and bringing an unceremonious hush to the group.

My mom wraps her arm around Beverly and says, "We should head back to the house where it's more comfortable."

Beverly nods, but I can see the anguish in her face; she doesn't want to leave William behind.

"The Hylocereus is the moon garden's guardian," I tell her, trying to offer some reassurance. "She'll take care of him."

Beverly nods with a sort of regal air I admire. "I brought some photos we can look at," she says. "Some of Azalea." And soon everyone is heading back to the house.

Wanting to be alone a moment, I tell them, "I'll be right behind you."

After they leave, I say a silent prayer to Mayahuel, thanking her for a beautiful ceremony, for the magic in my veins. For both the cost *and* the gift.

"Watch over him," I whisper.

Then I look to my own garden. A couple of months ago I would have been restless, impatient to see the harvest, but now? I don't need the earth to tell me what's in my soul. I can decide what grows here, now and forever.

I kneel at the edge of the jardín, set my hands into the cool dry dirt. I can feel the goddess's power vibrating in the earth, pulsating with an energy that seeps into my fingers. My lungs expand as I take the magic in, consume it whole. It's then that I decide to release my own magic back into the soil, imagining the twin Hylocereus tree that will emerge, that will share the burden of guarding the moon garden.

The dirt warms, trembles beneath my touch. There. I can feel the moment the roots take hold, pushing up and up and up.

Just then I'm startled out of my reverie by footsteps.

I jump to my feet, spin.

"I didn't mean to scare you," Ben says.

"What are you doing here?" I feel exposed by his presence.

"I didn't want to leave without telling you thank you."

I'm nodding; my mouth is so dry I can barely get a word out. "Leave? Aren't you staying to look at photos?"

"My grandmother feels tired all of a sudden, so we're going back to the hotel."

"Is she okay?"

"She will be," he says.

"And you?" I hadn't meant to say the words aloud. To put him on the spot like this.

Ben's gaze falls to the ground. "I miss him like crazy."

The urge to hold him is so intense I have to look away, to set my eyes on anything but him.

"I'm glad I got to see the farm," he says, his voice strained. "It's amazing."

I glance up, force a smile; it's polite, tight, uncertain. He's soaking me up with those dark eyes, increasing my pulse, setting my blood on fire.

"That story you told about the tree," I say. "I didn't know."

Ben runs his thumb along his chin. Is he trembling? No. Why would he be? He's indifferent to me. The bond has been broken.

"I didn't remember it—not until my grandfather told me the story again, the night before he died. It was like he knew." He folds his arms across his chest, exhales. "And when he told me, it all came back to me. Weird, right?"

"Memory is always a little weird."

He glances at the Night Queen. "How did you do that? Make her bloom?"

There's no reason to keep him in the dark, to deny the truth about my abilities. So I tell him, the briefest version of what my mom told me.

One side of his mouth turns up like he's not sure if he should smile or smirk. "So, you really do have magic."

I nod.

I see the dawning as it happens in real time, as his mind puts two and two together. "That's how it happened. The bonding. You enhanced..."

"It wasn't intentional," I say. "I didn't know."

"It's not your fault."

I feel the thread of tension between us, neither of us knowing the rules here, what can be said, and what shouldn't be.

But it's Ben who throws the first grenade. "You told me a truth, so I have one for you too. When you left...back in New York."

My entire body freezes, not wanting to think back to that night. "We don't have to talk about that."

"I was mad, hurt," he says, keeping his distance; the garden lights cast shadows across his face. "And it was disturbing to have all those feelings suddenly drained away. It was like losing something you know matters, but there was no longer significance tied to it and you can't—" he pauses, searching for the right words "—reconcile your heart and mind."

I don't want to hear this, but I keep quiet for Ben to continue.

"And then my grandfather died. And I was so messed up inside and I had all these memories of you that were... I don't know... real but they also felt not real, if that makes sense?"

Because I took it all away.

"Ben, I'm really sorry." I had no idea severing the bond would eat him up like this. I honestly believed that after he reclaimed his own heart he would go on with his life, merely remember me as a girl he once knew.

He frowns, swallows. "I just wish that I could match these memories to..." He touches his chest and I long to run to him, to hold him, to tell him everything is going to be okay.

"I'm not telling you all of this to make you feel bad," he says, shaking his head.

"It's okay," I manage. "I'm sure it was confusing and strange and..."

"But do you think..." His expression is so vulnerable, so gentle. "That any of it was real?"

"Ben," I say, swallowing the tears, "don't torture yourself with this." *And don't torture me.*

More than anything, I want to tell him that it was all real. And now I wish that he had never found that note and learned the truth. That he didn't have to carry this weight.

I had never considered how confusing it would be to hold such vibrant memories that *weren't* tied to emotion. How awful it would be to remember something without the feelings attached to it. This…*this* is why breaking a bond is so dangerous I realize. The human heart is complex, intricate, multifaceted… like magic.

"My grandfather must have felt like this," Ben says, "remembering my grandmother but not all of her, not how he *felt* about her." He clears his throat. "Or not at least until the bonding."

The bonding. The magic that healed two hearts and broke two others.

I'm paralyzed with dread, not knowing the right thing to say. Wondering if silence is kinder. "It's going to get better," I lie.

His eyebrows pinch together. He looks so tired. "Enough about me. How are you?"

I see his desperation, a layer of guilt that needs to know I'm okay. And not for any other reason than he's a decent guy. "Being back at the farm has been good for me."

There is a question in his eyes, one he doesn't voice. Maybe it's better that way.

We stand like that in silence as the night garden awakens, as more flowers bloom for the short duration of one night. Ben speaks first. "I better go. We've got an early flight."

Tell him! Tell him it was real. But I don't know if that's true. And he's spiraling. I can see it. Not because of any feelings for me, but because he's so confused. Maybe I rushed the bond breaking. Maybe I should have taken more care, more time.

Ben makes a move to hug me. Every part of me wants to go to him, but then he shrinks back. "All these weeks, packing up my grandfather's things, watching my grandmother fall apart, feeling his absence, it made me think, made me understand," he says.

"Understand what?"

He blinks, inhales, "Why you did it. Why you kept the truth from me, and I want you to know, I'm not mad. Not anymore." He stuffs his hands in his pockets and shrugs. "Death tends to put things in perspective."

I stare at him blankly, lost for words. My mind is a hurricane of thoughts, hopes, fears. If he isn't mad, could we begin again? Or is his indifference, his confusion too great a chasm to bridge? I'm not the one who can answer that question, only Ben can.

He holds my gaze for a breath and then he turns to leave.

"Ben?" I blurt.

He whirls, stares at me in the dim light. "Yeah?"

"It's going to be okay," I say again, fighting the violent tremble moving through my body, battling the tears that so desperately want to fall. "For both of us."

His eyes hold me gently. His mouth curves up, giving me only a hint of a smile, a silent goodbye.

And this time, he's the one to walk away.

36

The next day, I work in the shop until closing, keeping as busy as I can—creating unique Christmas table arrangements with roses, tulips, succulents, winterberry, twigs, and cedar sprigs. The entire shop smells of pine and cinnamon, of burning birch wood and cool, fresh notes of green floral.

It's truly a balm for my soul.

After the last customer leaves, I turn the closed sign in the window and head to the back to sweep up.

My feet are worn and my back is sore after twelve "on" hours. But strangely the aches feel good; they feel earned and remind me that all hurts heal and lessen with time.

As I sweep up the remnant stems and buds, I hear the bell on the front door and curse myself for forgetting to lock it. Setting down the broom, I adjust my apron and make my way to the front.

I stop stone-cold.

Ben.

He's standing near a spray of freesia, just a few feet away, staring at me. His eyes glimmer with an emotion I can't name. "Hi," he says.

I'm struggling to find my breath. To find reason. *Why is he here? Does he want something for Beverly?* "Hi."

His eyes rake over me, taking in my disheveled appearance, the stained apron, wrinkled shirt, and unruly hair poking out of its messy bun. I feel suddenly self-conscious until he smiles, that warm, genuine, showstopping smile.

Damn him.

"I thought that you left this morning," I say, suddenly angry that he's standing five feet in front of me, that every goodbye feels like an invasion, that he won't just let things be. And if he needs to process some more, he's in the wrong shop. As much as I want to help him move on, I don't think I have the fortitude.

"I didn't get on the plane," he says.

Obviously.

"Why not?"

Ben takes a step closer; I can feel the nearness of him—the heat and longing, and I suddenly wish I had something to brace myself against. That's when I notice he's holding something behind his back, but I can't identify what.

"I thought a lot about our conversation last night," he says, "and I realized I was putting the pieces together all wrong."

"Ben," I say wearily, "what are you talking about?"

"I can't stop thinking about you."

Annoyance, confusion, anger—they flare with an intensity that nearly knocks me off my feet. Is he joking? No, Ben wouldn't be so cavalier.

"My feelings *are* real," he declares like it's an irrefutable fact.

"That's not possible," I cry, remembering his cool words of indifference. "You said you felt nothing when you looked at me. *That* was real!" I'm shaking my head, walking about the store straightening things that don't need straightening. "You're revising history because you're emotional right now...you're just in a vulnerable place."

"Then why do I still feel this?" he asks so calmly I want to scream.

My God, this can't be happening. It's bad enough that we ended things the way we did, but now I have to convince him all over again? I keep moving, drawing myself inward, wanting to coil into a tight ball of protection.

"Why do I still see you in my dreams?" he asks softly, trailing me.

My breath catches. I stop, turn to him. "It has to be some leftover piece of magic or..."

"When I saw you yesterday," he says, "I felt something."

"Ben..." I'm trying to stay in control, for him, for me, but there is no way these feelings just reemerged out of nowhere. I search his eyes, looking for any remaining spark of magic, but there isn't enough light to be sure. "Even if that were true," I say, "I don't think it's genuine. I think it's maybe being on the farm or maybe the emotion of the ceremony." *And I just can't take that risk.*

"Harlow—" he inches closer "—you aren't being fair. You aren't even entertaining the possibility of what I am telling you."

"I can't."

My anger surges as his mouth curves up like this is some kind of game.

"Stop. Just stop. Don't look at me. Don't smile. Just—enough."

"I'm just trying to talk to you," he says, "and this is just my face."

"You know what I mean," I growl.

"No, actually, I don't," he says slowly.

Hot painful tears are rising up my throat in a tangled mess of emotion. "My heart broke when I lost you," I say shakily, "and I can't... I can't relive that, Ben. And as much as you want to

believe you felt something last night, this isn't what you think."
It can't be.

"What if I can prove it?" His confidence and bravado are maddening. He produces the thing that was behind his back. The First Impressions journal from Pasaporte, the same one he wrote in that first day we met.

"You stole it?"

"Borrowed," he corrects. Then, "I was trying to match emotions to all these memories of you but then I realized, I had to go back further, to *before* the bond. That's the first memory with real emotion that I could actually still feel. And once that happened, it was like the floodgates opened. Don't you see? It's proof that how I feel about you is genuine." His voice is smooth, deep, confident. "I know you think your magic enhanced the bond and maybe it did, but I think it was a perfect storm because... Harlow, I already felt something that first day. Immediately. I feel it still."

His optimism makes me feel miserable "Ben, you had only just met me. And to be honest, you were..." I search for the right word. Rude? Distant? "You weren't exactly warm and fuzzy."

"Will you just read this?"

I fix my gaze on his, struggling to keep my emotions from spilling over.

"Please?" he says gently. "And if it doesn't mean anything to you then I'll go. For good this time."

What words could possibly change my mind? But I owe him this much.

I take a deep breath and nod, questioning my sanity as he opens the book, hands it to me, then points to a passage floating on the edge of the page, lost in a sea of strangers' words.

My eyes fall to the passage, and as I read it silently, Ben repeats it aloud, "How long will it take to get her out of my mind?"

The simple sentence undoes me, sends my heart soaring and my spirits plummeting because how can I trust it?

"Har," he utters, "I was lost in your world from the beginning. Before the bonding."

My eyes are still glued to his words, and as I reread them, I feel an intensity of magic coursing through my veins, expanding and rising.

I know you think your magic enhanced the bond...but I think it was a perfect storm because... I already felt something.

Is it possible? That his emotions *before* the bonding were the only safe space in his heart, safe from the magic, from the breaking of the bond?

I look up. Ben's dark, mysterious eyes are searching mine, asking...no, begging the question, *will you still risk this with me?*

I swallow the tangle of fear and anxiety. Slowly, cautiously, my hand goes to his cheek. And I know. *I'll risk this and more.*

He must read my answer because his hands are tugging me closer, until our bodies are flush and our breaths are uneven. And the promise of his lips is so close.

But we don't give in.

We stay like this, locked in a moment of eyes searching eyes, of bodies pressed tightly together, chests rising and falling. Ben rests his forehead on mine, closes his eyes.

"Harlow."

"And now?" I ask, needing to be sure. "You remember how you felt in Canada and..."

"All of it." He offers a mere brush of his lips. And it's like a shot of adrenaline to my entire system.

I don't know who is moving first, how we end up in the back of the shop, but if I longed for Ben before, it was nothing in comparison to the ravenous desire I feel now.

No, this dance is different from when we were bonded. Where the bonding felt unexpected, this feels inevitable—a natural union that doesn't need to be questioned. Everything we are and need is right here between us, in this moment.

We finally break apart near the table, and then he's reaching behind me and untying my apron, never taking his gaze from mine as it falls to the floor. I stand perfectly still, savoring the pleasure of his touch. His fingers are unbuttoning my shirt. Slowly, effortlessly, achingly.

My own hands are bunching his T-shirt, trailing his ribs, his chest, bringing the shirt up and over his head. His eyes leave mine for the first time as I open my blouse, peel it off and let it drop to the floor along with my bra. His mouth parts like he might say something, but he merely takes me in.

"You okay?" I tease.

"Better than." He traces a finger over my breast, sending tingles through my body. "So are we going to really do this?" he asks, his voice teetering on the edge of disbelief.

I press my chest to his; the union of our half-naked bodies ignites a new excitement inside of me and all bets are off. Our remaining clothes are stripped off, and in an instant, we're lost in a whirlwind of hands traveling, mouths seeking, tongues exploring.

I take in the entirety of Ben, the cuts and edges of his lean body. "You should never wear clothes again."

He laughs, trails his teeth down my throat, over my breast, down my stomach. I quiver at his touch, grasping his hair in my hands. And then he's lifting me up, carrying me to the oak table.

I sit on the edge, straddling him, feeling his heat so close. Closing my eyes, I inhale the scent of Ben, mixed with freshly cut roses, thinking they might be my new favorite flower. Then I hear the tear of paper.

"Did you think you were going to get lucky?" I toy.

"I hoped." He presses his mouth to mine and I'm wrapping my legs around him tighter, guiding him near and nearer until he has nowhere else to go. With one achingly slow stroke he's inside of me.

The world fades, and this is all there is. Ben, me, moving to the same rhythm of desire over and over, matching each other's cadence beat for beat, breath for breath, moan for moan until it all leads to magnificent gratification.

Afterward, we're both trembling, laughing. He leans against me, holds me like he needs me, like his heart can't manage a single beat without me.

"I thought you didn't like me when we met," I say, kissing his neck.

"Are you kidding?" he says.

"It was the low-cut dress, right?" I laugh.

He's silent a moment, and then he says, "It was some other kind of attraction I can't name, and I know this sounds weird, but it was like some part of me recognized you."

His words are soft, gentle, like the petals of the canto. Is that how it is for some? Does some part of our spirit recognize the other, as if we've lived lifetimes together?

I stroke his back softly, marveling at his solid shoulder blades. "But then you walked away. You might not have ever seen me again."

"I was sort of freaking out," he says, and I can hear his smile. "I thought no way could it be real, so I made a deal with myself that if I saw you again, I'd know it was meant to be."

And he did. At the bookshop.

"So it wasn't the cleavage."

He pulls back, so our eyes meet, and he kisses the tip of my nose. "Well, that was definitely part of it."

We laugh, hold each other tighter.

"Truth?" he says, stroking my hair as he swings me onto the top of the table where I lie on his chest.

"Only if I'm going to like it."

"My imagination was completely wrong."

I laugh, look up at him. "So was mine."

"I definitely think we need to do this again."

"And again."

Ben rises, sitting up on one elbow as he stares down at me.

He doesn't need to say the words, because I feel them like traces of magic floating between us.

"I know," I whisper.

He smiles, and it lights up his whole damn face. A face I want to look at, to wake up to, to fight with over and over and over. "Want to know what I really want?" he asks.

"Other than this?"

He kisses me lightly. "I never want to get you out of my head."

"Promise?"

"Swear. Now, can we get some food?"

Still grinning, I say, "I know the perfect place."

He cups the back of my neck, draws me closer, kisses me deeply. "Or we could stay here," he says.

I laugh. "What good to me are you if you aren't sustained with food?"

"Oh, I don't know. I think I have one more round in me."

I entwine my fingers in his and pull him to his feet. "First some sustenance."

"If you insist."

A minute later, we're dressed and heading out into the cool dark night. Hand in hand, strolling up the cobblestone road. The shop fronts lit with Christmas lights.

"I hear my hotel has a killer old-fashioned," he says, tugging me closer.

"Are you really trying to lure me to your room with liquor?"

Frowning, he looks down at me, squeezes my hand. "Absolutely. Besides, I really want to get you into an actual bed next time."

As we walk, I look up at the night sky, at the landscape of stars so many light-years away that can never be touched, but there they are, burning bright like magic, like love.

And maybe magic and love are one in the same.

Unpredictable. Challenging. Messy. All-consuming. Painful. Beautiful.

But entirely worth the risk.

EPILOGUE

Eighteen Months Later

Ben and I are standing on a wide portal of Leyenda, his new resort that opens in two weeks.

The New Mexico sky is a dusky purple as the sun slips beyond the piñon-dotted horizon. And the air is crisp, cool, with the promise of fall.

When he showed me this storied desert landscape, steeped in red canyons, unforgettable mesas, and endless vistas, I sensed its soul and knew immediately that it was the right place for his first Legend Resort.

He pours me a glass of pinot noir. Taking the glass, we toast and I tell him, "I'm really proud of you."

With an absent nod, he glances at his watch for the seventh time in the last ten minutes.

"What gives?" I ask. "Our dinner reservation isn't for another hour."

Just then his phone buzzes. He scans the screen, then pockets his phone with a wide grin. "I want to show you something."

He takes my hand and pulls me into the resort. The entire place is built on one idea: the feeling of being rooted. The structure is understated yet dramatic, becoming one with the landscape, which continues indoors with minimalist silhouettes.

He leads me down a wide hall with enormous windows that frame the desert vista, and a moment later, we're standing outside the double doors of the library.

Of all the places on this property, this was the room I wanted to feel like pure magic. Everything from the southern facing windows to capture the morning light, to the vaulted hand-painted ceiling illustrating the desert sky.

There is a small brass plate outside the door that reads Corazón lleno, and that's what I hope for anyone who passes into this space, that no matter how they enter they leave with a full heart.

"I've seen the library a million times," I tell him, tugging off my poorly chosen heels that are killing my feet.

"But not like this." He opens the doors with a flourish.

"Surprise!" a crowd of my family and friends hollers.

I startle, fall back, take a breath. "What the…"

Everyone is here. My entire family, as well as Laini, Beverly, Helena, even Abe, and Rosa's novio, Anders.

"What's this all about?" I ask. "It's not my birthday."

And that's when I see the bookshelves to my left, each lined with finished copies of my book: *The Heart of Violet*.

"As you all know, Harlow wrote a book," Ben announces, "An amazing story that comes out next month."

"Damn straight it's amazing." Laini cheers, which earns a ripple a laughter through the crowd.

Ben swings his gaze to mine. "Harlow came tonight, thinking we were checking on some last details of the hotel, but tonight is to celebrate her writing journey with those closest to her before the rest of the world—" he pauses and smiles gently "—discovers her."

Heat spreads across my chest. "How did you ever manage to do all this without me knowing?"

"With my help!" Laini puts in.

"You mean mine," Camilla argues.

"It was a family affair," Lantana says, taking control.

I hate surprises but I could not be more delighted seeing everyone here, and I'm filled with a love I could never have imagined. The kind of love that believes in you, challenges you, walks through fire for you, makes a home for you—the kind of love that transforms you.

When I take in the entirety of the last two years, the pain and suffering, the love and joy, the failures and triumphs, I realize that some paths are made of thorns. But they're also made of flowers, springing up from the earth, leaving gardens in their wake. And if we're going to become our highest selves, we need both.

I raise my glass to my family and friends. "To amazingly kept secrets."

"And to happy endings," Mom says, clutching my book to her chest.

Someone shouts, "Salud!"

I spend the next thirty minutes signing books to those I love most, taking the time and care to write a personal message to each. Lantana is the last one. She stands before me with her auburn hair tucked in a chignon, smiling at me like a Cheshire cat.

She sets her copy of *The Heart of Violet* on the table and leans closer. "I'm also here to collect."

"Collect?"

"Our deal? You wore my dress and..."

Remembering, I lean back and smile. "Okay, prima. What's the payback?"

I expect something light or comical, but her face tightens and she says, "I need you to enhance an elixir."

"What kind of elixir?" I keep my voice low, even though everyone is busy visiting.

"It's no big deal," she says coyly, "just a beauty concoction I made up to get rid of these dark circles."

Except that she has no dark circles, but now isn't the time to ask about it, so I simply smile and nod. "A deal is a deal."

Her entire demeanor relaxes. "Make sure to write that I'm your favorite cousin in there," she says, pointing at the book.

A minute later, I stand and whistle to get everyone's attention. When all eyes are on me, I clear my throat, take a deep breath and say, "This story was a journey of highs and lows, one that began with a single sentence, *The land knew her first.*" I hold up the book proudly. "And I couldn't have done this without my family, without our legacy, and without the love of story instilled in all of us. So, thank you!"

Later, after everyone has left, Ben and I sit by a firepit outside staring up at the distant stars.

"Thank you for tonight, Ben. You don't know what this meant to me," I say, shaking my head that he was able to pull off this big of a surprise.

"You forgot to sign mine," he says, handing me a copy.

I wrap the cashmere blanket tighter around my shoulders and smile. "Oh yeah? What shall I write?"

He gets to his feet, comes over, and kneels in front of me. "Just open the book."

Curious, I do. A single lavender dahlia rests between the pages. I know its meaning, *eternal love.*

Smiling, I set the bloom in my palm and let my magic rise through me and into the flower. Ben's eyes fall to the dahlia just as its tiny petals unfold like a time-lapse video. "I love you too," I say.

Ben blinks, shakes his head. "I'll never get tired of that."

"You better not," I say playfully.

He presses his lips together, takes in a lungful of air. "You know... I'm not great with words."

I'm not sure where he's going with this.

His gaze drops to the flower. "It means forever."

"Right."

Then he looks up. There is a question in his luminous eyes I don't understand until he says, "I want *your* forever."

With trembling hands, he reaches into his pocket. "As you know, I'm a terrible wrapper." He sets whatever he pulled out of his pocket in the palm of my hand. It's a necklace with marquis shaped emeralds and diamonds set in black gold.

"It looks like a vine of stones," I say, my voice barely a whisper.

Ben nods, smiles, helps me put the necklace on. I fall back against his chest, a heap of joy and bliss.

"Does that mean you like it?" he asks.

I touch my neck, tracing my fingers over the stones. My mother's voice echoes in my memory: *you are like a rare diamond.* I nod. "It's beautiful."

Still holding me close, Ben laughs. I can feel his heart beating, soft and steady, and in that moment, it thrums with the sound of forever.

★ ★ ★ ★ ★

ACKNOWLEDGMENTS

Book ideas come to me in first scenes, but this one appeared as a single image of a lush flower farm set among rolling grassy hills, each sunlit bloom swaying in a gentle breeze. I suddenly needed to know who lived here, who tended these blooms, and why they felt so absolutely enchanting to me. And so began my journey to the magical House of Flowers and Light.

Of course, this book would not have been born without my marvelous agent Holly Root. Every time I sit down to write an acknowledgment, I think, this is it. This is the time I am finally going to run out of words to express my gratitude and my absolute astonishment that I get to continue partnering with her on the stories of my heart. Thank you for this incredible journey. And of course, to the entire team at Root Lit: you are all rockstars.

As with all books, there are many behind-the-scenes stars. Laura Brown, my talented, and immensely clever editor is one such estrella. The moment we jumped on the phone I knew that she possessed the passion, creativity, and exuberance to help bring this story to life. And to the entire team at Park Row—thank you all for your enthusiasm and hard work on this book. I am so lucky to be working with you all.

Nicole Luongo, Editorial Assistant

Sophie James, Publicist

Rachel Haller, Marketing Director

Randy Chan, Director of Marketing, Indies and Library

Social Media Team: Lindsey Reeder, Hodan Ismail, Brianna Wodabek

Katie-Lynn Golakovich, Managing Editor

Alexandra Niit, Cover Designer

Erika Imranyi, Editorial Director

To my amazing friends and early readers, Janet, Rosh, and Loretta. Thanks for sharing your lovely minds and hearts with this writer. And Sarah, my assistant—what can I say other than the obvious: you are the rock in every book storm. Thank you thank you thank you.

I am so grateful that I grew up in a house of flowers, where small often unassuming arrangements were tucked here and there. It was my mom who taught me the value of a simple bouquet to not only beautify a space but to nourish the spirit and fill the heart, a tradition I have carried on in my own family. Every book is a gift for my daughters—a gift of life and love and soul. May you always find the goddess within. To my husband—thanks for being my wingman in Quebec, for listening to me talk endlessly about this idea that I wasn't sure would ever be a book, and for believing the trip would be worth it no matter what. You were right.

And finally, a million abrazos to my readers. Without you, the pages would be empty.